Crime Fiction

Number Five in the Best Defence Series
William H.S McIntyre

Also available in the Best Defence Series:

#1 Relatively Guilty
#2 Duty Man
#3 Sharp Practice
#4 Killer Contract
#6 Last Will

CRIME FICTION

This book is a work of fiction. Names and characters are the product of the author's imagination and any resemblance to actual persons, living or dead, is entirely coincidental.

© William H.S. McIntyre
All Rights Reserved 2014

www.bestdefence.biz

There is bad in all good authors: what a pity the converse isn't true!

~ Philip Larkin ~

Chapter 1

'Okay, so you've got seven million pounds. What do you do with it?'

University of Edinburgh Student's Union, November nineteen ninety-four. The eve of the first ever National Lottery draw. Suzie Lake took a sip from a French Martini, set her glass down on a table crowded with pint tumblers and stared around at those others who'd gathered to refresh depleted brain cells after a mind-numbing, two-hour accountancy tutorial.

'It's tax-free, remember,' said Lewis, whose last name I couldn't remember. Tax-free? Unlike me he must have been paying attention at the tutorial. 'I know what I'd do,' he said. 'I'd stick it in the bank and travel the world living off the interest. Either that or I'd donate it to worthy causes, like cocaine dealers and strippers.' Lewis liked a beer and a laugh. Pity that after graduation he'd taken his law degree to the diplomatic corps and now, I imagined, spent a lot of his time drinking spiced-tea with angry Arabs.

Max Hetherington, my best bud, was up next with his wish-list. 'I'd buy my mum a house, myself a three hundred ZX Turbo, no, wait, an Aston Martin, and pay someone to go to mercantile law lectures for me. What about you Robbie?'

Nineteen year-old me pondered the question over a mouthful of Tartan Special. 'Let me see... How much does it cost to buy a distillery?' The general consensus was that even one on the holy isle of Islay could be acquired for a good chunk less than my imaginary winnings. 'Then I'd buy my dad a distillery.'

'It's sweet that the first person you think about is your dad,' Suzie said.

Max laughed. 'Robbie's only saying that because he knows his dad would drink himself to death.'

'After that,' I continued, ignoring Max and happy at having said something to please Suzie, 'I'd buy Linlithgow Rose, build a great team: Malky at centre-half, me at centre-forward, and win promotion to the Premier League.'

'Seriously,' Suzie said. 'What *would* you do, Robbie, Would you stay on at Uni or drop out?'

'Seriously?' Lewis chirped. 'Seriously, I think Robbie would give you the whole seven mill if you'd go out on a date with him.'

I laughed along with everyone else, though I suspected I wasn't the only male present who wouldn't have given anything for one night with Suzie.

'Stay on,' I decided. 'With that kind of money I could set up my own business, take on the most difficult cases.'

'Pro bono?' Suzie asked.

'Of course,' the teenage Robbie Munro replied. Looking back, I wasn't sure if I'd meant the part about working for nothing, but it made Suzie smile when I said it and I used to love it when she smiled. 'Even if I didn't have seven million, even if I wasn't getting paid, if I believed my client was innocent I'd do everything and anything to get him off.'

Lewis rolled his eyes. 'Let's face it, Robbie. If you really *did* win the lottery tomorrow night, you'd probably buy a Ferrari, get rat-arsed and wrap it around the nearest tree.'

Amidst the ensuing laughter, I could see the expression on Max's face change. He pointed a finger in Lewis's face. 'That's enough from you.'

Lewis looked confused.

'It's okay, Max,' I said, 'Lewis didn't know.'

My mum had been killed in a car crash. No Italian supercars involved; just a police vehicle, a wet road and an elm tree. I'd been a baby at the time. You didn't miss what you'd never had.

I told Lewis that there was no apology necessary, which was just as well because he didn't seem inclined to offer one. He turned on Max. 'So it's okay for you to talk about Robbie's dad drinking himself to death, but I can't mention a car crash in case I inadvertently cast-up the memory of his mother?'

'Yeah, well, Robbie's mum is *actually* dead, his dad isn't,' Max said. He pulled apart a bag of Scampi Fries and threw one into his mouth. 'And you've never met his dad,' he added with a crunch.

Suzie entered the fray again, lightening the mood once more. 'Well, I still think it's great that Robbie's first thoughts were about his father. Life is not all about money. When it comes down to it, your family, your parents, your children, that's all that's *really* important. I hope when I have kids they all turn out to be like Robbie.'

'I'm sure that could be arranged,' Lewis muttered into his beer.

'I don't mean it like that,' Suzie said, amidst the laughter, and rather too quickly than was good for my ego. 'But you're probably right, Lewis. Knowing Robbie he'd do something stupid with the money and end up dead or in jail.'

'I would need to be dead, then,' I said, 'because with seven million on my hip, there would be no shades of the prison-house closing on this growing boy, that's for sure.'

'Shades of the prison-house?' Lewis enquired, simultaneously nicking one of Max's Scampi Fries.

'Wordsworth,' Suzie said.

The puzzled expression remained on Lewis's face. 'The daffodil guy?'

Max pulled the bag out of Lewis's reach and looked at me as he thoughtfully munched on a fish snack. 'So what you're saying is that if you win the lottery tonight that'll be like a lifetime get-out-of-jail-free card?'

'Totally,' I replied, overlooking the fact that I hadn't the means to buy a lottery ticket, having already tapped money from Max to buy Suzie's cocktail.

'I don't get it. What good is the money going to do?' Lewis asked. 'This is Scotland. You can't buy your way out of prison here.'

I begged to differ. 'Unless whatever crime I may one day commit is witnessed by the Pope, the Queen and the Dalai Lama, seven million in the right hands will get me out of any scrape. That's all you need to stay out of jail — a lot of money and a little imagination.'

'Then, what you really mean is seven million pounds in the *wrong* hands,' Max said.

'Wrong/right, it depends on how you look at things,' I said.

Suzie disagreed. 'No it doesn't. What's wrong is wrong and two of them don't make a right.'

The discussion quickly became a debate, with Lewis, Suzie and Max on one side and me the other. 'Is it wrong to break the law to ensure that justice is done?' I asked.

'There's no logic to that statement,' Suzie said. 'Justice and the law - they're one and the same thing.'

I was about to explain how wrong she was when Max interrupted. 'Don't get Robbie started on one of his jurisprudential rants. He still hasn't explained why it is that unlimited funds win cases. If that was true, the Crown, with all the resources at its disposal, would win every prosecution.'

If it had been 2004 and not 1994 the snappy answer would have been to refer Max to the Lockerbie trial; the Crown, that is to say the Government, wins the ones it has to, by whatever means.

Lewis stood, stared off into the mid-distance and said, in what I took to be a Churchillian tone: 'in this proud country of ours, we have the finest legal system in the world. A system of justice iron-bound by a code of ethics, practised by an upstanding profession that tries its utmost, whether briefed for defence or prosecution, to ensure that justice is done. One that plays by the rules and will never resort to bribery, corruption, cheating or sharp practice. One that ensures the truth will out.'

I let Lewis finish, raised a glass to toast his fine words, necked my pint and reminded him it was his round.

'He's right, though,' Max said, once we had shoved Lewis in the direction of the bar. 'The Scots legal system...' He lifted the bag of fries and emptied the crumbs into his mouth. 'Best in the world.'

And nineteen-year-old me could only agree, because it *was* the best - then - and I dreamt of the day when, clad in a black gown, I'd be part of it: exposing corruption, using my forensic courtroom skills to secure justice and set the wrongly-accused free.

Fast forward to the present. Livingston Sheriff Court, Friday, June thirteenth. A date regarded by many as unlucky, but for me no worse than any other day when Sheriff Albert Brechin was presiding.

'Mr Munro, would you like to ask the officer any questions?'

I shook off my reveries and rose to my feet in the well of the court. 'So, Inspector Fleming,' I began, 'it's your assertion that so observant are you, you can identify the man in the dock after only a fleeting glance from a motor vehicle heading in the opposite direction, three months ago?' Cross examination of the final Crown witness had commenced after lunch, Friday afternoon. I continued. 'Presumably, then you can tell me...' I turned my back on the witness. 'What colour of tie I am wearing?'

Ninety per cent of all criminal cases in Scotland were dealt with under summary procedure; no jury, only a Sheriff to be judge of the facts and the law. The legal aid fixed-fee was introduced in 1999 and cut by fifteen per cent ten years later. Now some Legal Aid troll had made it a rule that no matter how much time and preparation had gone into investigating a case, if the accused pled guilty before the start of trial, the already sliced and diced fixed-fee was cut in half.

It was justice on the cheap. It was why Munro & Co. clients pled guilty to very little and took their chances at trial.

I could hear D.I. Dougie Fleming sigh almost as loudly as the Sheriff.

When it worked, the old what-colour-of-tie-am-I-wearing routine went down well with the punters, even if Bert Brechin had never been unduly impressed.

'Your tie was red, Mr Munro,' Fleming said. 'But that was before lunch. Now it's blue with white stripes.'

Chapter 2

Late Friday afternoon: other than yours truly, Paul Sharp was the only lawyer left in Livingston Sheriff Court. He was sitting at the table in the centre of the room, wading through a pile of papers. I lobbed my case file onto the table beside him, took off my blue tie, stuffed it into my jacket pocket - next to the red one - and hung up my gown in the Munro & Co. locker.

Paul looked up from his paperwork. 'Seriously? The tie trick?'

'Worth a go.'

'Talk about desperate. I thought you'd reached an all-time low on Monday, when you accused that witness of being in denial.'

'And she denied it. What can I say? Classic cross-examination.'

'For *you*, maybe,' Paul said. 'I don't think there is any record of Cicero coming out with that one in the Forum. So, anyway, the tie-trick - did it work?'

'No, Dougie Fleming practically quoted me the silk to polyester ratio.'

'Guilty?'

'Incredibly. Still, I got the full fixed fee and the client would have been just as guilty if he'd pled.'

'Things really that tough?' Paul asked.

'No,' I said, 'they're much tougher. Anyway, what are you doing still here on a Friday afternoon?'

'Hiding.' Paul returned his gaze to the mound of paper. 'I've got a bundle of stuff to read and if I go back to the office people want to speak to me and the phone keeps ringing.'

I looked at the file. HMA –v– Dominic Quirk; a touchy subject between myself and Paul. Dominic was a former client of Munro & Co., a young man whose father, Aloysius Kenyon Quirk, was well known in West Lothian, having run a string of small bookmaker's shops that had spawned many a rumour of dodgy dealings, match-rigging and loan-sharking. Then one day, when most men would be thinking of retirement, Al the Bookie had woken up and smelt the internet. Quirk senior sold his High Street outlets and spent the proceeds, not on a bungalow and new set of golf clubs, but on a team of IT experts, licensed software developers and a series of TV adverts featuring himself, 'Honest Al', the friendly face of AKQ On-line Betting.

The move from real to virtual was literally a gamble for the Quirk family, but an immensely successful one. Soon Al Quirk could leave the running of the business to others while he devoted himself to good works. In no time at all, he went from small-time bookie to one of Scotland's foremost philanthropists; a man whose modesty would have gone unnoticed were it not for his PR machine's frequent press releases. A man fêted by politicians and local dignitaries seeking endorsement and by charity fund-raisers keen to tap money for worthwhile causes. Few recalled those early, dodgy days. Those who did, dared not mention them; however, it came not as a complete surprise, when, on a like-father-like-son basis, Dominic, aged twenty-one, fell afoul of the law.

'You're not going to start complaining again?' Paul asked. 'You had your chance with Dominic's last case.'

'I had my chance, all right,' I said. 'And I took it. Not proven. What was he expecting? A medal?'

Clients. How soon they forgot. It was only a matter of a few months ago that the Quirk family was practically carrying me shoulder high out of Livingston Sheriff Court.

It was a day for reminiscing, and, whether he wanted them or not, I reminded Paul of the facts of what, in the

Robbie Munro bumper book of famous victories, had to rank in the top ten.

One year before, Dominic Quirk was alleged to have jumped a red light, collided with another vehicle and driven off, leaving Wendy Smith, driver of the other car, bleeding and dying. Range Rover Sport -v- clapped-out Renault hatchback was always going to be something of a mis-match.

He'd been charged with causing death by dangerous driving. The defence maintained that Miss Smith must have pulled out from a side-street before the lights were at green and that Quirk was only to blame for panicking and leaving the scene.

Concerns over the evidence caused the Crown to reduce the allegation to the lesser, but still serious, charge of causing death by careless driving. The trial proceeded before a Sheriff and jury and, when the sole eye-witness did not stick to the script, all the Prosecution had left were some dubious forensics and a series of heart-breaking before-and-after-pictures of the deceased. In its closing address, the prosecution asked the fifteen jurors to infer guilt from the fact that Quirk had failed to stop at the scene. They didn't, at least not eight of them, and Quirk escaped with a twelve month driving ban and a fine of five hundred pounds for failing to stop at the scene of an accident.

Quirk's father paid the fine within the hour and my not inconsiderable legal fee the following day. The newspapers, deliberately misunderstanding matters, as usual, announced that a few hundred pounds was the price the Scottish courts placed on the life of a young woman. If the Lord Advocate was decidedly unhappy, the Justice Minister was furious and all set to amend some laws to make sure more people were convicted and to hell with the evidence and those pesky reasonable doubts.

For Dominic, his acquittal meant that he was free to resume his studies. A former pupil of St Ignatius' College, Scotland's top Catholic School, he had left with the best grades money could buy and the Jesuits beat into him. Even then he'd only managed to scrape his way into something arty at St Andrews University. Not that his academic limitations were a major concern; it was odds-on the Quirk family business would absorb hapless Dominic in due course.

Ten months had passed from the date of the car crash to Dominic's trial and it had been an ordeal for everyone. Afterwards, I hadn't expected any repeat business. I didn't get any. Not even when, only a matter of weeks after the famous acquittal, the young man was again facing criminal charges. This time it was murder, and the Quirk family looked to Paul. When I heard the news, there'd been no confusing me with a ray of sunshine and, without sounding churlish, the fact that I had later been instructed by Quirk's legally-aided co-accused, Mark Starrs, was but slight consolation. Trust me to be stuck with the only poor student at St Andrews.

'I thought I'd avoid interruptions and stay here,' Paul said, after I'd recounted my sorry tale, with which Paul was already very familiar. 'For some peace and quiet.'

In hindsight, he may have emphasised those last words; whatever, I pulled out a chair and sat down at the table across from him. Dominic Quirk's case wasn't only a touchy subject between us because of my ex-client jumping ship. I was in the process of cutting a deal for his co-accused and Paul didn't like it.

The two young men had been charged with the murder of a waitress Doreen Anderson. When my client indicated to me that he had some incriminatory things to say about Quirk, I knew the Crown would be interested. So interested, that I believed, if he cooperated, the murder charge against him would be dropped. If the prosecution proceeded against the two and both refused to testify, actual evidence of who had killed Doreen was pretty thin. The last thing the Lord Advocate wanted was a reasonable doubt creeping into proceedings and Dominic Quirk sailing off into a Monet sunset, leaving yet another dead body in his wake.

'How's the case going?' I asked. 'Found a defence yet?'

'Still working on it,' Paul said, dryly.

'He's definitely taking it to trial, then?' I asked. 'Despite—'

'Despite your client grassing on him? Definitely.' Paul returned to his notes, flicked over a page.

I knew he was annoyed at the deal I was about to cut for Mark Starrs, which made winding him up all the more fun. 'What's the problem? Dominic pleads guilty, there's a discount from the punishment part of the life sentence and he ends up doing fifteen years. He'll be younger than me when he gets out and a lot younger than you.' I gave Paul a light punch to the upper arm. 'Plenty of life in the old dog yet, eh?'

'I'm sure those fifteen prison Christmases would simply fly past,' Paul said, still not looking up from the paperwork.

'Of course they would,' I said, ignoring his sarcasm. 'He was a boarder at St Ignatius' College. After all those years of cold showers, gruel and Hail Marys, he'll probably think Shotts Prison is some kind of spa resort.'

Paul stopped reading and glanced sideways at me. 'Remind me, Robbie. When was the last time you pled someone guilty to murder? Never,' he said, not waiting for my reply. 'You can take it from me that Dominic Quirk is going to trial.'

I couldn't blame Paul for being annoyed at my client doing the dirty on Quirk to save his own skin, but I did get a certain sense of satisfaction from it. I slapped him on the shoulder. 'You win some, you lose some. At least you're not having to lose this one on legal aid. The Quirk family has more money than the Pope. What are you charging it out at?' I asked, trying to keep the envy from my voice. The legal aid hourly rate, like the laws of the Medes and Persians, was cast in stone and set at a level that would bring a tear to a plumber's eye.

'I bet I'm charging a lot less than you charged for his road traffic case,' Paul said, making it sound like it had been a parking offence and not a car crash that had caused the death of a young woman. 'You're just jealous.'

Undoubtedly, but, as people said, though usually didn't mean, *it's no loss what a friend gets*. For Paul, like the rest of us Sheriff Court hacks, the occasional private case was merely an oasis in a legal aid desert. The Scottish Government had put a squeeze on criminal defence lawyers, with a raft of measures to not only cut publicly-funded access to justice, but to erode fundamental principles of Scots law that had for centuries been the envy of judicial systems around the world. The Independence referendum was looming and if your crusade was to run a proper nationalist socialist government, the first people you had to put up against the wall were the defence lawyers.

Whether it was my having disturbed him or if he was finishing off anyway, Paul squared up his papers and tucked them into his briefcase. 'Looking forward to married life? You do know that Jill is way too good for you,' he said, expressing not just his opinion, but my dad's as well. 'How are the wedding arrangements coming along?'

'Expensively.'

'Jill going for the full white elephant is she?'

She wasn't. She'd been married before, in her twenties, a brief affair marred by domestic violence. We hadn't actually fixed a date, but Jill thought it could be organised at fairly short notice. It was to be a low-key affair; the main financial concern being Jill's mum who had emigrated to Canada twenty years earlier, married again and accrued a large number of new brothers and sisters-in-law as well as a battalion of nieces and nephews. Apparently they were all to be invited, and the cost of flying over these hangers-on and putting them up in a hotel was to be done at the expense of the bride and groom, no matter the groom's stated views on the matter. Add to that the cost of a venue and even what appeared on the face of it to be a simple ceremony, was costing in excess of twenty-thousand pounds. Split equally, that was ten grand I didn't have immediately to hand.

'No doubt we'll be scrutinising the fine detail when Jill comes home tonight. We're going to Edinburgh for a meal and then maybe some house-hunting tomorrow.'

I couldn't wait to see Jill. For months now her working week had been spent away from home. Soon, she promised, she'd be transferred permanently to Edinburgh, and I longed for the day when our relationship was no longer just a series of telephone calls, emails and weekends here and there.

'Still too proud to live at her place?' Paul asked.

It wasn't pride… For one thing, Jill was seldom at home, but, mainly, I just wanted to start off married life on an equal footing; to sell Jill's house and my flat and buy a new property in joint names. Except I'd have to find the massive shortfall between Jill's share and mine before we could be equal partners.

'You know what you are?' Paul said, pinching my cheek. 'A good old-fashioned, male-chauvinist pig.'

'Because I want to pay my way?'

'No, because you can't handle the fact that Jill makes more money than you.'

We walked to the door together and down the corridor towards the stairs that led to the courtyard of Livingston's Civic Centre with its throng of humans and civil servants. Imagine a scene from Fritz Lang's Metropolis but without the cheery ambience.

Outside it was a fine Scottish summer's day: cloudy with light drizzle.

'Face it, Robbie. We made the wrong career choice. Scots defence lawyers are a dying breed. If you love Jill and she loves you - be thankful for that. Who cares who makes the most money?'

By this time we had crossed the bridge over the River Almond and reached our cars parked next to Livingston F.C.'s stadium.

Paul was right. My fiancée was lucky enough to have a transferable skill; one that didn't tie her to Scotland and in a business that was bucking the recession. People used to say that doctors and criminal lawyers would never be out of business because there would always be sickness and crime. Those people had been right; ill-health and crime abounded. It was just that while sickness was treated, the Government had decided not to prosecute crime unless extremely serious or it met their politically correct agenda. This policy for the non-prosecution of wrongdoers meant less work for me, so it saved public funds and helped dilute the crime statistics. It was a win-win for the Government and an even bigger win for those escaping court proceedings. It was almost inevitable that in our relationship Jill would be the main breadwinner.

And if Paul was right about another thing: if I truly was a male chauvinist pig – I was one porker ready to do just about anything for money.

Chapter 3

'So, who are you going to kill this time?' I asked.

Until that day, I hadn't thought about Suzie for ages. There had been a time, most of my late teens and early twenties in fact, when I'd thought of little else. She'd been gorgeous then, she was gorgeous now. Knowing Suzie had made an appointment to see me had been the reason for the earlier reminiscences that had helped get me through the Procurator Fiscal's tedious examination-in-chief.

Suzie screwed up her eyes, pursed her lips, wrinkled her nose. Did she know how cute she looked when she did that? I mentally gave myself a slap on the face. *You're meeting Jill in a few hours. Remember? Jill? Your fiancée?*

'I'm not sure,' Suzie said at last. 'My agent says I should set the next book somewhere exciting, exotic, like Hollywood or Shanghai, with actors and triads and stuff. Either that or go more up-market. I was thinking maybe royalty. I can't keep doing politicians, I've bumped-off enough of them already.

Was it possible to bump-off enough politicians? I wondered aloud.

Suzie laughed at what she thought was my joke, and I remembered the girl I'd met when, both eighteen year-olds, we'd stood in the matriculation queue at Edinburgh University, me, jumping around, all spots and hair gel, Suzie, even then, calm, pretty and sophisticated like she'd done it all before. Unfortunately, the calmness had been entirely superficial, for it had disappeared under pressure, her bottle crashing during an important exam.

'I did wonder about making the killer a member of the Royal Family,' Suzie said. 'You know? A prince or something. Public servant by day, out slashing the throats of debutantes by night, kicking-off a huge Government cover-up—'

'Later to be uncovered by the intrepid Detective Inspector Debbie Day?'

'Who else?'

The door to my office opened and Grace-Mary entered. 'Sorry to disturb,' she said. 'It's nearly five and I've the post office to catch. I just wanted to say hello to Miss Lake.' She turned to Suzie and gushed, 'Huge fan. I loved Portcullis. Crime fiction really needs strong female characters like Debbie Day.'

Suzie extended an arm in my direction. 'Well here's the man to thank.'

Grace-Mary glanced around the room as though there might be another male body stashed away somewhere. Satisfied there wasn't, she looked from Suzie to me and back. 'Robbie?'

'Yes, he gave me the idea.'

'Robbie?'

'The inspiration that sparked my literary career.'

'Rob—?'

'Are you deaf as well as late for the post office?' I asked.

Suzie clarified. 'I was through here about three or four years ago, and Robbie took me for a coffee—'

'You didn't take Miss Lake to Sandy's did you?' My secretary asked, horrified at the thought of me dragging a literary genius into the greasy domain of West Lothian's finest exponent of the bacon roll.

I tapped the face of the watch I wasn't wearing.

Grace-Mary ignored me; which was more or less her default setting. 'Sorry, what were you saying, Miss Lake?'

Suzie continued. 'I was working freelance, doing yet another article on Mary Queen of Scots for a history magazine. On my way from the train station up to the Palace, I saw Robbie fixing the Munro & Co. sign at the side of the close and couldn't believe my eyes. We went for coffee and then the pub and spent just about all day catching up and remembering old times.'

'Old times?'

'We were at Uni together,' I told Grace-Mary whose gossip antennae had raised along with her right eye-brow.

'You're a lawyer?'

Suzie shook her head. 'At one time I thought I might be. I've Robbie to thank for that too.'

Grace-Mary looked confused. I saw no need to expand.

'Robbie told me about one of his cases and it inspired me.'

The look of bemusement on my secretary's face was still in situ. 'Which case was that then?'

'One about a gangster who killed two other gangsters. He set up a bogus web-site and sent emails to his victims saying they'd won a competition for an off-road driving experience.'

My client's name had been Joe Finnegan. He'd driven his victims into the countryside, purportedly to collect some quad-bikes that didn't exist, and left them there with less brain matter than that with which they'd arrived.

'Grace-Mary, you remember Joe Finnegan's case don't you?' I said.

'Not really.'

'How could you not? You typed all the precognitions.'

'I try not to pay too much attention to what Robbie dictates,' Grace-Mary confided to Suzie. She turned to me and frowned. 'Anyway, that sounds nothing like the plot for Portcullis.'

'True, I did have to adapt the plot a little,' Suzie said. 'I changed the gangster to a transvestite MP, his victims from a couple of neds to his rivals in the Cabinet, moved the whole thing from Glasgow to London—'

'And,' Grace-Mary finished for her, 'lured the victims to a seedy massage parlour and used medieval torture devices to kill them. Definitely a lot more interesting than just shooting them like Robbie's client did.'

Suzie rounded off her tale. 'After I met Robbie that day, I forgot all about Mary Queen of Scots and her chopped-off head, went straight home and started writing what turned out to be Portcullis. My first bestseller.'

My role in Suzie's literary career fully explained and with the promise of a signed copy of her next book, I eventually managed to dispatch my secretary in the direction of Friday's last post.

After Grace-Mary had left, Suzie and I chatted on for a while. She was single. Those kids she'd once hoped would grow up to be just like me remained unborn. If she noticed the picture of Jill that I kept on my desk, usually obscured by piles of case files, she didn't mention it. For some reason, neither did I.

'How's your dad?' she asked.

'Hasn't quite managed to drink himself to death,' I said.

I'm not sure if my remark jogged Suzie's memory of our student days or not, but she reached down to a voluminous designer handbag and from its depths extracted an object wrapped in a brown paper bag. She placed it on the desk between us. 'Which brings me to the reason for my visit. I never properly thanked you. Sorry about the packaging. I couldn't find anything suitable.'

'What is it?' I asked.

'A thank you,' she said. 'For changing my life.'

'Don't be crazy. I told you about one interesting case. It was you who turned it into an international bestseller.'

'You're right.' She made to put the parcel back into her bag and then laughed and set it down in front of me. 'Honestly, Robbie, I saw this, remembered that you liked whisky and thought it would be a nice gift. I always felt guilty about not even giving you an acknowledgement.'

'We're quits then?' I said.

'The constitutional law exam?'

I nodded.

'It wasn't your fault. Not entirely. I was wound way too tightly back in those days. Debbie Day wouldn't have been the least bit fazed.'

Constitutional law. Probably the most boring topic in all of law and that was saying something. With three hours of essay writing ahead of me, on a subject I knew very little about, I'd needed all the help I could get. It was time to turn up the pressure. Half an hour in, I'd put up my hand and asked for more paper. I'd hardly made a start on the sheets I already had, but, as hoped for, my request caused a ripple of panic amongst my fellow students: Robbie Munro, who'd scarcely attended a lecture, was tearing through first year law's toughest exam like it was The Sun crossword. It was squeaky-bottom time for many and just too much for the tightly-wound Suzie. I'd always felt to blame for her ditching a career in law. Even though her departure in tears from the examination hall turned out to be the best move she'd ever made.

She put the parcel onto the desk. I peeled back the brown paper to reveal a cardboard tube. Highland Heather Dew, allegedly the Co-op's finest blend.

'I remembered you liked whisky. It's supposed to be quite a good one,' she added defensively. 'If you like that sort of thing.'

With some mumbled words of thanks, I put the bottle in the bottom drawer of my desk beside a bundle of legal aid forms and my notary stamp.

'Robbie,' Suzie said. 'There's something I'd like to ask you.'

Here it came. Bestselling authors didn't just happen to pop in on the spur of the moment bearing gifts of whisky, even cheap, blended whisky.

'I'm in trouble,' she said.

'What kind?'

'The worst kind – writer's block.'

'You've not murdered anyone then?'

'No, but I'd like to. I just don't have the plot and I was wondering…'

'If I could give you inspiration? Be your muse?'

Suzie winced. Possibly she was imagining me in something diaphanous. 'Portcullis was such a tremendous hit that I was given a deal for a further three books. The second in the series just about wiped its face, the third has more or less sunk without trace and I haven't written a scintilla of the fourth. My publisher is making noises about a return of some of the advance, which... Well let's just say that might be difficult.'

'I thought the third book was really good,' I said.

'That's because you didn't read it – did you?'

'What can I do to help?' I asked.

'Give me something. Any interesting case you've had that you think I could extrapolate a story line from.'

It was my turn to wince. I had plenty run-of-the-mill assaults, drug-dealings, drink-drivers, housebreakings and one dangerous-dog on the go, but I couldn't see any of them taking the New York Times bestsellers list by storm.

'I don't expect you to come up with something right away.' Suzie picked up her now much lighter handbag and stood. She wrote her telephone number on a pad of yellow-stickies, came around the desk to meet me and gave me a hug and a peck on the cheek. 'Think it over and if you come up with anything, anything at all, be sure and give me a call.'

I walked her to the door. 'Enjoy your whisky,' she said, making a face. 'Personally, I don't know how anyone can drink the stuff.'

Fortunately, I did - and Father's Day was just around the corner.

Chapter 4

The train I was supposed to catch left without me, and so I was half an hour late as I jogged up the Royal Mile and along George IV Bridge at the back of seven that evening. Although the start of the Festival fringe was still several weeks away, Edinburgh was hoaching with tourists and Friday-night revelers getting a head start on the weekend.

Jill was waiting for me in the Barn Door, a well-hidden, basement bistro across the road from the statue of Greyfriars' Bobby. There were two glasses and a bottle of white wine in a cooler on the table. Her sour expression suggested the wine might be corked.

'Why can't you ever be on time?' she asked, as the waitress showed me to the table.

I bent over and gave her a kiss. 'Sorry. I had a late appointment. You'll never guess who—'

She held up her hand. 'Look, Robbie. I've had a really busy week. The flight up from London was terrible, not helped by the security at Gatwick. It's like check-in at a concentration camp. Some of the things they do to you. It's practically sexual assault. I mean do I look like a terrorist?'

I was about to remark that the best terrorists didn't look like terrorists and that, until terrorists started carrying signs saying that they were terrorists, the random security checks would probably continue, when the waitress who hadn't moved from her spot butted in.

'Nightmare isn't it?' she said, thinking she was part of the conversation. 'A couple of weeks ago me and my boyfriend went down to see a show and—'

'I'll give the wine a miss,' I said. 'Just a beer for me. Anything that's not lager.'

It had been my idea to eat at the Barn Door; peaceful surroundings and great steaks, but only after Jill had insisted that we meet up in Edinburgh for a meal rather than at her place.

'So how is it?' she asked, not letting up on the subject of my tardiness, 'that I can travel all the way from London, on a delayed flight, go home, change and be at the restaurant on time, when you can't make a twenty minute train journey without arriving half an hour late?'

'I like your hair,' I blurted. It was a gamble, but I was sure it looked different, shorter. Hopefully she hadn't just washed it or something.

She teased the ends of some strands of hair with her fingertips. 'You don't think they took too much off?'

'No, just the right amount,' I said.

'I was thinking maybe it makes me look old-fashioned.'

'Not old-fashioned. Professional,' I said, and she didn't object. My beer arrived. I drank half of it in one go before asking, 'How's work doing?'

Unlike my own, Jill's career was going places. During a spell in Switzerland, working for their rivals, Jill had been noticed by global pharmaceutical giants, Zanetti Biotechnics Inc. She'd been headhunted, offered a financial package that made my legally-aided eyes water and, once on-board, had somehow managed to make herself indispensable. I didn't have much of a clue about what she did, only that Zanetti was on the verge of something big and extremely important and that my fiancée's opinion was sought at all stages of whatever it was that was so big and extremely important that meant she had to spend most of her time living away from me.

'Work is busy,' she said. 'It always is. Very busy, but very exciting. I wish I could tell you more, but... you know...'

I knew.

The tap of high heels on wooden floor behind me. A tall, harshly-attractive older woman arrived at our table. Late forties? Fifties? It was difficult to tell. Her cheekbones were high, her skin a witness to many years in hotter climes or under sun lamps. My initial impression was Cruella De Ville with a tan and a bleached razor-cut. She placed a mobile phone on the table and sat down. I'd spied her loitering outside the front door when I came in and thought that she'd given me a funny look. It was then that I noticed the third place-setting. 'Robbie,' she said, stretching a perfectly manicured hand across the table to me and gripping the tips of my fingers in what was her idea of a handshake. 'Felicity. We met at Zanetti's New Year's Eve party.'

I smiled back at her. There had been a free bar at Zanetti's Hogmanay bash. That was about all I remembered. That and waking up with a black-eye and a stonker of a hangover.

'Sorry, Jill,' Felicity said, lifting the phone and giving it a little shake. 'That was Hercule from Bern. You know what he's like. The man never takes a break. By the way, he was asking after you.' She set the phone down again and looked from wine bottle to empty glass, her head at a quizzical angle as though uncertain how she could transport the contents of one into the other. I took the hint. As I poured, I gave Jill a quick sidelong look which I hoped relayed the message, *'what's this woman doing here on our first night together in over a fortnight?'*

Felicity's phone flashed and began to vibrate, rattling against a pudding spoon. 'Not again,' she said. Taking a quick sip of wine, she snatched the phone and headed off in the direction of the stairs to the front door.

'Felicity?' I asked.

'Felicity Davenport. Don't you remember her? Of course you don't. She's Zanetti's UK development manager.'

'Your boss?'

'She's a lot of people's boss. We've a meeting with some politicians at Holyrood tomorrow and travelled up on the same flight. I could hardly just ditch her at the airport, could I?' Jill smiled sweetly. 'I knew you wouldn't mind.'

'Wouldn't I?'

Jill poked me in the chest. 'Don't start getting all shirty. Just sit there, eat your dinner and smile. Two beers, no more. After the New Near bash, and I do mean *bash*, everyone in Zanetti UK thinks I'm marrying some kind of wild, whisky-swilling highlander. I don't want you showing me up again. I've told Felicity that your brawl with Desmond was out of character.' She put up a hand to abort my plea in mitigation. 'And I've told her that as far as drink is concerned you can take it or leave it.'

I could take it or leave it. But this was Friday night and Friday night was when I liked to take it.

Jill's pointy finger prodded my breastbone again. 'Two beers max - and no tales from the courts about how you got some crazy client off.'

She really knew how to hurt a guy. Compared to her, when it came to getting all shirty, I was just a big girl's blouse.

'I thought you liked my tales from the court,' I said. She didn't reply. 'You said they were interesting.'

'Some of them could be *quite* interesting,' Jill said. 'But not the way you tell them.'

I was mentally analysing my anecdote delivery, while at the same time conserving rations with a modest swig of beer, when Felicity weaved her way back to the table.

'That's it,' she laughed. 'No more calls. I'm turning this thing off.' She laid the phone on the table again, not, I noticed, turning it off. 'So, Robbie, what's new in the law?' She asked, not looking at me, but at some point over my left shoulder.

'I don't know,' I said. 'They keep changing it without telling me.' Felicity looked confused. To indicate that I'd been joking; very nearly, I laughed. Felicity didn't, just continued to stare right ahead over my shoulder. She was one serious woman.

Jill picked up a menu. 'What are we all having?'

If Felicity was paying I was definitely having the fillet steak. Anyone who was Jill's boss had to be minted, and if there wasn't some unwritten rule about the gooseberry picking up the tab, then there should have been.

'Robbie?' Felicity said. She seemed troubled. 'Who's that man over there?'

'What man?'

'There's a man at a table in the corner who keeps staring over at you. Don't look now, but he doesn't seem terribly friendly.'

I turned and looked over to where I'd been told not to. A middle-aged man, black shirt, fawn chinos, stared back at me. It was true; he didn't look particularly friendly, but, then again, this was Edinburgh.

'Probably a client or someone I've met at court,' I said, recommencing my study of the menu and pondering over choice of sauce to go with my steak. 'I meet a lot of people in my job and I'm not that good with faces. Or names.'

'Well, he definitely seems to know you,' Jill said.

I turned again, this time to see the man remove the white linen napkin, a corner of which had been tucked into the open neck of his shirt. He stood and began to walk towards us. And then I did remember. We'd met a week or so back - he'd been in the witness box and I'd been cross-examining him. He hadn't been very friendly then either.

I rose to my feet just as he arrived at our table.

He pointed a finger straight between my eyes. 'I thought it was you, ya bastard.' His face contorted as he spat the words. He wasn't as tall as me, but much broader. He grabbed a bunch of my shirt in each hand. I didn't know what was going to happen next, though I sensed his forehead was at an optimum head-butting level with my nose and I was now well in range.

My mother died when I was very young. My dad single-handedly raised my brother Malky and me. He didn't teach us how to bake cookies or construct handmade greetings cards; he taught us what he knew, and he hadn't spent thirty years as the only law in Linlithgow without learning how to take care of himself. It was said my dad could clear a pub in less time than the barman could clear away the glasses.

Instinctively, I hooked my index finger in the V between the man's collarbones; the manubrium, that soft gap where sternum meets the clavicle-bones. It's not particularly sore; just hugely uncomfortable. The man recoiled, letting go of my shirt. Before he could step forward and grab me again, I held out my hands, palms outwards. 'Take it easy. I was only doing my job,' I nearly managed to say before he swung an over-arm right at me. He was drunk. I could have ordered a medium-rare fillet with peppercorn sauce before the blow landed. I side-stepped. His weight caused him to lunge forward, right arm hitting nothing but air. He stumbled and fell across the table, upsetting the wine cooler. It toppled. The bottle slid out. White wine glugged across the table and onto Felicity's lap. She shrieked and jumped to her feet, taking a section of table cloth with her. Cutlery, glasses and various other table items clattered onto the floor.

Meanwhile, angry man sprawled across the table, struggling to regain his balance. I kicked his legs away and he fell heavily to his knees, chin striking the table on the way down. A tooth pinged out from between his lips and ricocheted off the little white vase in the centre of the table that held a single pink orchid. I helped the man to the floor with the sole of my foot. By this time the doorman and a couple of waitresses were on the scene. I stood back while they raised Mr Angry from the floor and wrestled him to the door. I could see other diners on their phones, either calling the police or preparing footage for YouTube.

I looked at my grim-faced fiancée.

'Go,' she said, and I went.

Chapter 5

Saturday morning. Jill was escorting Felicity to a conference at the Scottish Parliament building, followed by an afternoon's shopping. The phone rang as I was frying an egg.

The caller had one of those accents that was either Scottish posh or English. Mr Posh wouldn't give his name, just said he was an agent for Victor Devlin, a name I knew vaguely and only by reputation. From what I'd heard, Devlin was scum and, like scum, he'd floated to the top of his profession; if you could call corporate fraud and swindling people out of their life savings a profession.

Why Devlin would want to make contact with me I didn't know. I could only hope he was in trouble and looking for a lawyer. He might be scum, but he was rich scum and rich scum in trouble was my favourite kind of scum.

I emptied the now frazzled egg into the bucket, grabbed a coffee and bacon roll at Sandy's café and made my way down Linlithgow High Street to the offices of Munro & Co. No sooner had I put key in lock than I was joined by a man; late sixties I would have guessed. He was tall and broad, his nose and cheeks a crazed road map of broken capillaries. From bespoke tweed suit, to his highly-polished shoes, to a styled head of wavy, if suspiciously dark, hair and thin strip of a moustache, everything about him oozed money.

'Are you here on behalf of Mr Devlin?' I asked.

The man nodded. I opened the door and he followed me down the close, up the stairs and into my room. Saying nothing, he looked around at the shabby decor, the desiccated umbrella plant and carpet of multifarious stains.

I sat behind my desk and gestured to the chair opposite. 'Be it so humble...'

'Quite.' The posh one flicked imaginary, possibly not, detritus from the chair and sat down. He crossed his legs and leaned back. 'I need your help,' he said, after tugging the sleeves of his shirt in turn, one of them failing to obscure a chunky diamond-studded Rolex.

Music to my defence lawyer's ears.

'Have you heard of Tantalite, Mr Munro?'

I hadn't.

'Perhaps you know it as coltan.' I didn't. 'It's a rare mineral used in the microchips of cell phone batteries. No tantalite, no cell phones. You get the idea. Eighty per cent of the world's reserves are in the Democratic Republic of Congo. It's the new gold-rush. Mr Devlin formed a mining company, Devlin Polymineral Limited, took on board a few wealthy investors—'

'Who all of a sudden aren't quite so wealthy anymore?'

The man stared coldly at me. 'Indeed.'

Perhaps I shouldn't have jumped so quickly to what I thought was the obvious conclusion; however, even based on a hazy knowledge of Devlin's track record, I assumed he hadn't sent Mr Posh to see me because of my in-depth knowledge of company law.

'A complete tragedy,' he said. 'Regime change, civil unrest, miners striking, machinery stolen, friendly government officials threatened or murdered. Happens all the time out there, I'm told. Devlin Polymineral went belly up. The investors lost everything.'

In business there are never losers without winners. I was guessing Devlin fell into the latter category.

'And Mr Devlin?' I asked. 'How did he do out of it?'

Very well, it transpired. When the tantalite dust had settled, a few businesses had made a profit. Quite a healthy one, in fact. Those were the various companies who had supplied goods and services to the failed mining company, all of which corporations were wholly, exclusively and very conveniently owned by Victor Devlin. His posh chum made it sound like good fortune. We both knew differently.

'How can I help?' I asked, hoping he'd come to the point.

He got up, walked to the window and looked out through dusty panes at the bustle on Linlithgow High Street. 'Always background-check your investors, Mr Munro,' he said, as though I might be thinking about setting up my own international mining fraud. 'On this occasion Mr Devlin was lax and as a result has become persona non grata with some very angry men. Men with guns.'

In Devlin's line of work, I felt certain he'd know some men with guns himself.

Mr Posh returned from the window, stood behind his chair and leaned two hands against the back of it. 'The men with guns that Mr Devlin knows are scared of these other men with guns. These men don't start fights, they start wars. He's lost their money, and now they'd like to kill him.'

They might have to join a fairly lengthy queue, I suspected.

'All Mr Devlin wants is to take his profits and disappear somewhere warm before he winds up dead.'

I was also fairly certain that even if Devlin did end up dead, he'd be going somewhere warm all right, but I kept the thought to myself as I sensed we were at last coming to the reason for the posh one's visit.

He took his hands from the back of the chair and began to slowly pace up and down the room. 'Mr Devlin has a problem. His money is mainly invested off-shore: Belize, the Caymans, Switzerland, numbered accounts, of course. It was my job to keep track of them. All the details were stored on a computer. A computer that has now been stolen and, no doubt, thoroughly and professionally hacked. Fortunately, the data is encrypted so it won't do anyone any good, but it means that I don't have the information to hand.'

All highly interesting; however, I was wondering when he'd come to the part requiring my professional assistance.

'As you can imagine, Mr Devlin is not at all happy, though the good news is he has a back-up hidden in one of his little hideaways. All he needs is someone to fetch it. Someone he can trust. I'd go, but there is a possibility the property is being watched. Someone with no connection is required.'

I wondered why he was telling me this. 'You want me to go?' He did. 'Just one question: why does Mr Devlin need a solicitor for this work?'

'Mr Devlin likes to work with professionals. This is a highly confidential matter and he'd like it to remain so. On this occasion he *has* done his research and he believes you can be trusted to carry out this simple task without any risk of breach of confidence.' He stopped pacing and fixed me with a stare, his mouth a grim line. 'A breach of his trust would not, could not, be tolerated.'

'But—'

'However,' he said, all smiles now. 'It is a task for which you would be well remunerated.'

I no longer felt quite the same urge to protest. 'How well?'

'Five thousand pounds.'

Devlin was a master conman. He had to be loaded. 'Twenty,' was my counter-offer.

Mr Posh drew a finger across his moustache. With a bit of luck, he'd offer six and we'd shake on seven.

'Twenty it is.' He reached across the desk and offered me his hand. 'Five in advance, the balance on your successful recovery of the data.

I took his hand. 'If the house is being watched, I can't just go waltzing in or they'll know why I'm there.'

'Not if you have a plan.'

'And what would that be?' I asked.

He stood up and walked to the door. 'For twenty thousand pounds, I'm sure you'll think of something.'

Chapter 6

'What are you doing here?' Saturday afternoon. My dad was in the kitchen, golf bag on the table beside a basin of soapy water and an old towel. 'I thought you were seeing Jill this weekend?'

I'd brought the bottle of whisky Suzie had given to me. The cardboard tube was wrapped in a plastic carrier bag that I had wound around with tape to deter tampering; at least until I had retired to a safe distance. I placed it on a spare, square-foot of worktop near to the bread bin. 'I saw her last night. She's got her boss up from London and they're away shopping or sightseeing or something.'

'Her boss?' He removed a pitching wedge from the bag, took it over to the big Belfast sink and set about the dried-on dirt on the face of the club with a nail brush. 'What's he like?'

'Like a she. A very important she, who Jill's trying to impress.'

'I thought you two would be busy discussing the wedding,' he said, rinsing the club in the basin of water before giving it a dry with the towel. 'I've got to hand it to you Robbie. You and Jill – I never thought it would work out.' He smiled and then was serious all of a sudden. 'Tell me: what thoughts do you have on favours?'

'Favours?'

Aye, you know, the wee gifts you give to the guests at the wedding reception.

I had absolutely no thoughts. The hiring of a kilt and arriving at the altar on time were already pressing at the limits of my logistical capabilities.

'When you see Jill next, tell her I was thinking miniatures.'

'Miniature what?'

'Miniature whiskies of course. For the men that is. She can dish out the white heather and plastic-horse shoes or those sugar almond things to the women, but men should get something too. You can't be too careful these days, not with all those equal rights and Europeans going about. You don't want to go offending anyone.'

'What about tee-total male guests?' I asked. 'Don't you think they might be offended at having a miniature bottle of whisky thrust at them?'

He grunted, dropped the clean pitching-wedge into the bag and removed a seven-iron. 'What's that you've got there?' He plunged the club into the basin, tilting his head in the direction of the not so elegantly wrapped Father's Day gift.

'It's for you. Don't go opening it before Sunday.'

He took a sideways look at the bottle. 'What is it?'

'A surprise.'

He frowned suspiciously.

'It's something you won't have tried before.' That was for sure.

He stopped scraping at the seven-iron with the nail brush. 'Kilchoman,' he said confidently and referring to the latest distillery to open on the sacred isle of Islay. 'I hear the reviews are mixed.'

'Not all whisky comes from Islay,' I said.

'No,' he agreed. 'Just most of the good stuff.'

'I know you'll keep an open mind.' I pulled out a chair from the table and sat down. 'You shouldn't judge a book by its cover. Remember that tomorrow.'

Fathers' Day was something of a well-honoured tradition at the House of Munro. Malky and I would pitch up to my dad's place at the appointed hour and present the old man with gifts, or, to be precise, whisky. There would then follow a breakfast of pancakes before we set off for Linlithgow Golf Club. After a round, which my dad and his highly-versatile handicap usually won, we'd have lunch and a couple of pints at the nineteenth before returning to my dad's to sample the distiller's art.

'Usual plan is it?' I asked.

He didn't answer, just continued to scrub at the seven-iron, though with added vigour, I couldn't help but think.

'I should have won last year. I was driving like a pro.' I stood up and swished the towel, sending a booming drive down an imaginary fairway. 'My putting let me down. I think it was probably the state of the greens. Do you not think they were a wee bit hairy?' No comment from the old man in defence of his local course. I tried again. 'What time's Malky coming? He was late last year and we nearly missed our tee-off.'

Criticism of the golden boy, AKA, my big brother, Malcolm, would surely elicit some sort of response.

It didn't.

'I'd clean my clubs,' I said, 'but it's really only the mud that's keeping them together.'

Nothing. Just extra-hard scrubbing. It was when he started to whistle softly through his moustache that I knew something was definitely amiss. 'Okay, what's up?'

He looked at me and sighed. 'We're not golfing at Linlithgow on Sunday.'

It was a shock, but I'd get over it. 'Where are we going?'

'Turnberry. Malky's got an invite to a pro-am there.'

'Turnberry? You're kidding.' One of the perks of being a has-been, nearly-legend footballer was the occasional invitation to such events. 'Maybe I will clean my clubs after all.'

My dad came over and took the towel from me. He gave the seven-iron a quick rub with it and dropped the club into the bag. 'It's like this, Robbie. When I say *we're* going... The invite is only for two people. Malky's sort of giving it to me as a Fathers' Day gift.

What was he saying? We'd followed the eat-pancakes, play-golf, drink-whisky routine, every Fathers' Day since before I was even old enough to join in the drink-whisky part.

I sat down again. 'But—'

'You don't mind do you?'

I glanced up at the kitchen clock. 'Blast, I've just remembered I told what-his-chops I'd meet him down at the West Port. He's been done with speeding and looking at a totting-up disqualification. I said I'd see what I could do.'

My dad put a hand on my shoulder. 'Things'll be back to normal next year,' he said. 'This is just a one-off.'

'Absolutely no problem, Dad,' I said. 'Enjoy yourself and take plenty of golf balls. Turnberry wasn't built with your slice in mind.'

He took his hand away. 'It's not a slice – it's a fade.'

'Of course it is,' I said, standing up and giving the wrapped up tube of Co-op blended a gentle tap. 'Oh, and enjoy your whisky. You deserve it.'

Chapter 7

Jill had arranged to spend Sunday with Felicity on the assumption that I'd be off golfing and wasn't prepared to alter her plans just because mine had fallen through. I suggested we meet up later, but she had a train to catch early evening and before that a report to read over. So all we managed was a quick phone call late Sunday afternoon.

Afterwards, I settled down with a movie, a jumbo bag of crisps and one or two whiskies. One or two whiskies became three or four, maybe five or six; whatever, Monday morning hadn't broken so much as fractured.

'You look rough.' Joanna Jordan, former assistant of mine, now once more recruited by the dark side of the Force, stared across the well of the court at me. 'I mean *really* rough. Even rougher than usual.'

'Okay, I get it,' I said. 'It wasn't the best weekend of my life, all right?'

Paul Sharp joined me at the defence side of the big table, thumping down a stack of files. 'You couldn't cover these intermediate diets for me could you, Robbie? I'm supposed to be in Saughton for a consultation at eleven.'

'Dominic Quirk?' I asked.

Joanna snorted. 'You're not actually taking it to trial?'

'Innocent until proven guilty,' Paul replied.

'Who've you got as counsel?' she asked. Paul was a solicitor-advocate, but I guessed he was bringing in a big-hitter to lead him.

'Big Jock.'

'Mulholland?' Joanna enquired.

Paul nodded. 'The man, the myth, the legend.'

'That won't be cheap,' Joanna said.

'Money doesn't matter. And my client's family approve: Jock's an F.P. too.'

'Better not reveal your own humble educational background,' I said. 'I don't suppose St Mary's, Bathgate compares too favourably with St Ignatius.'

'But it compares a lot better than Linlithgow Academy,' Paul said, reminding me of my own secular educational origins.

'I didn't hear any complaints when I got him off that death by careless driving charge,' I said.

Paul slapped my shoulder. 'You've obviously been tumbled. When Honest Al Quirk's boy needs a lawyer, no proddies need apply.'

'Robbie a protestant?' Joanna laughed. 'The only thing he ever protests about is the legal aid rate.'

'That and buying a round of drinks,' Paul said.

'Are you wanting me to take care of these IDs for you or not?' I asked.

'Oh, he is touchy this morning.' Paul shoved the files in my direction. 'Don't plead anyone out. Most of these cases came off my duty week and I'll only get half the fixed fee unless they go to trial.'

With a cheery wave he upped and left in the sort of good mood that only lawyers briefed in a privately-funded murder case can fully understand.

'How's your love life?' Joanna asked, as more solicitors wandered into court to occupy the few remaining chairs around the table. 'Fixed a date for the wedding yet? When can we expect to hear the patter of a little Munro's cross-examination?'

'Court!' the bar officer bellowed. Sheriff Brechin came onto the bench looking even less thrilled than usual at the prospect of a morning spent presiding over fifty or so intermediate diets; however, his arrival allowed me to side-step Joanna's questioning.

Half an hour into the court and the bar officer approached and cupped a hand to my ear. 'There's a strange guy outside who wants a word,' she whispered. 'He wouldn't give me his name. Says it's very important. I told him you were busy, but I'd pass on the message.'

Strange guys were my stock in trade. They called intermediate diets in alphabetical order and so I had a ten minute window between my next two cases: surnames Foster and Inglis. From the top of the stairs leading down from the court I could see Mr Posh pacing up and down the courtyard next to the café in a beige summer suit. A lemon silk handkerchief spilled from the breast pocket. What was he doing here? Surely he didn't expect me to have come up with an elaborate and fool-proof plan already? Not when I'd been far too busy moping about and feeling sorry for myself. He saw me coming down the steps from the court and strode over.

'What have you got?' he asked.

'Not a lot.' The more thought I'd given it, the more I'd realised that the sort of people who could scare Victor Devlin would terrify me. They'd also be doing their utmost to track down their money. I made my fears known.

He lowered his head and peered at me over a pair of sunglasses. 'Why do you think you are being paid five—'

'Twenty.'

'Thousand pounds?'

I had only a few minutes until my next case called. 'If you can hang around until court is finished, we can talk,' I said.

'How long is that likely to be?'

'I don't know. Probably another hour or so.'

'Too long.'

'Meet me somewhere later, then. We'll go for lunch.'

Posh's smile was one of exasperation. 'I'm already taking a chance coming here,' he said. 'I can't go swanning off to lunch. Mr Devlin's enemies have eyes everywhere.'

Then why didn't he try being less conspicuous? Waltzing around West Lothian in his summer-finery; would it have been too hard to stick on a shell suit and blend in?

'Well you'll have to wait,' I said. 'I need time to think how I'm going to do this.'

He shoved a hand in his pocket and brought it back out with a brown envelope. 'It'll be done tomorrow or you can forget it.'

With a deftness honed over many years practice, I spirited the brown envelope away and into the inside pocket of my suit jacket. 'Tomorrow it is.'

Chapter 8

My office, Monday, half-past five. Grace-Mary had left for the day. Armed with a cup of coffee, I sat down to think up a way to recover Victor Devlin's memory-stick. Why Captain Posh thought I should be the one to devise a cunning plan when he worked for a man who made fortunes thinking up clever ways to con people, I didn't know; even although I was a little flattered.

The phone on my desk derailed my train of thought. Only two people have my direct dial number. I took it hoping it was Jill. It wasn't.

'What you doing?' my dad wanted to know.

'Working.'

'Too busy to come round and see your old man?'

Great - he'd be wanting me to go over so he could tell me all about his and golden boy's trip to Turnberry. I wasn't interested. 'Snowed under.'

'Well, when you're finished digging your way out, why not come over for your tea?'

He sounded unusually happy and I couldn't say I wasn't intrigued to find out why; however, I was still officially in the huff and my dad's offer of some home cooking wasn't enough enticement to snap me out of it. I well knew my dad's culinary capabilities. When Malky and I were boys, he used to rustle up weird and wonderful meals in which beans featured prominently. We only ate them because there was nothing else and because, apparently, if we didn't we would never make it as cowboys. I was seven when I decided I didn't really mind if I never rode the range and eight before I realised that the smoke alarm wasn't the oven-timer.

I had paused to think up a polite yet cutting way to tell him where to stick his burnt offerings when he announced, 'I'm making pancakes.'

My dad was no chef, but he did retain a small repertoire of recipes at which he excelled and foremost amongst these was the humble pancake. Pancakes were what I should have had yesterday. Was this his way of apologising?

'I've got maple syrup,' he added.

Butter, golden syrup, jam at a push, were the only things my dad would allow anywhere near a pancake. I preferred maple syrup. He knew that. He just refused to buy any. The man wasn't apologising. He was grovelling.

When I arrived at his cottage ten minutes later, there was already a stack of warm pancakes on the kitchen table under a clean tea towel.

He dusted his hands off on his apron and sat down. 'Dig in,' he said.

I joined him at the table and the two of us got stuck in. The man could barely boil water, but his pancake-making skills were second to none. 'You can't go wrong with your granddad's recipe and his old girdle, can you?' he said.

I would have replied if my mouth hadn't been full of light, fluffy pancake, soaked in the juice of Canada's national tree, so I made do with enthusiastic nods of the head.

After we'd consumed our respective body-weights in pancakes, I tried to take the dirty plates to the sink to wash up, but my dad wouldn't hear of it, sending me off to the livingroom with orders to put my feet up.

'I know you've got the car, but one wee dram won't harm you, will it?' he said, and from the cupboard under the sink produced a bottle of Ardbeg Uigeadail. 'Malky got me this for Father's Day.'

Malky hadn't only come up with an invite to an Open Championship golf course, but also a bottle of an Islay single malt, once voted best whisky in the world. What was the old man's game? Was he rubbing it in? Showing me how generous my brother could be while the best I could do was chuck him a bottle of blended whisky that was continually on special offer? If so, he could have done that without the pancakes or lashing out on a bottle of maple syrup. And why did he look so pleased? Any more smiling and he'd pull a muscle in his moustache.

As instructed I went through to the next room and sat down. My dad didn't take his usual chair by the fire, instead, he sat on the couch next to me. He handed me a glass and clinked it with his own. 'Here's tae us, wha's like us?'

He waited, glass poised, for me to finish off the toast in the time-honoured fashion. I didn't.

'Okay,' I said, setting the whisky glass on the arm of the sofa. 'What's this all about?'

'What's what all about?'

'The pancakes, the good whisky, the maple syrup. What's going on?' No way could he be feeling this guilty for having ditched me on Sunday. Unless... 'What happened? Was Turnberry a disaster? Well, don't say I never warned you. Those championship courses are very unforgiving, especially with your slice—'

'Fade.'

'...at this time of year you could hide an elephant in the rough.'

'Could you?' He took a sip of whisky. 'I wouldn't know. I was never off the fairway. Drove for show and putted for the dough. Me, Malky and our pro' tore the course apart. Won second prize: a spa weekend at the Turnberry Hotel and another round of golf.'

Was that why he was so pleased with life? One good round of golf?

'And then, after a lovely day, I come back here and open up your gift to me.' His moustache quivered slightly.

Shit. Here it came. There were few things my dad felt so strongly about as whisky. Not only had I completely ignored the sacred Isle of Islay, I had presented him with a blend. And not just any blend. A supermarket blend.

He went not to the cupboard under the sink where he kept his whisky supply, but to a wooden door set in an alcove next to the fire where I knew he kept those items most dear to him: photographs of my mother, a video of Malky's cup-winning goal. Come to think of it there was a ton of stuff about Malky in there. What was there of mine? My law degree scroll? I didn't remember seeing that again after my graduation, but, if it was there, that was about it. I was mulling over the lack of Robbie artefacts when he returned and sat down next to me again, the offending cream cardboard tube in his hand, a tartan ribbon and stag's head displayed proudly on the front.

'You always were a wee comic,' he said.

The man was taking sarcasm to a whole new dimension and really enjoying himself in the process. His cheeks were rosy, his eyes sparkled. If he'd had a beard to match his moustache there would be kids sending letters up the chimney to him.

'Look, dad—'

He popped the lid off with his thumb and slipped the bottle out of the tube. It was covered in bubble wrap. He removed it carefully and stared down at the bottle in his hands. I thought I saw tears gather in his eyes as he said tenderly, 'the Black Bowmore.'

'I know, Dad, I'm sorry, I never had time to... The what?'

The label on the front of the bottle was black with silver edging and silver script. He gently smoothed it with the flat of his hand. 'Nineteen sixty-four. The year I finished my police probation and became a real cop. Where did you get it? There were only two thousand of the first edition bottled. I know. I had Malky look it up on the internet. They reckon there's only a dozen or so bottles of this left in the wild.'

Carefully, he pulled out a small side table and set the bottle down. 'Never judge a book by its cover.' He gently rapped the empty cardboard tube off my head. 'You really had me going there for a moment.'

I lifted the bottle and had a good look at it. The whisky was dark; testimony, no doubt, to years spent maturing in Olorosso sherry casks. On the reverse was a small white sticker, headed 'McTears Auction House' and 'Lot 234' marked on it.

'I don't know what it must have cost you,' my dad said, thinking I'd held the precious bottle long enough and taking it from me.

'Have a guess,' I said, in a voice an octave higher than normal. I cleared my throat and tried again. 'How much do you think?'

'Malky looked it up on the internet - he's got it on his phone. Did you know they could do that now?'

'How much?'

'According to the whisky web-sites, he says it's got to be worth at least two, three maybe even four...'

How could I have been so stupid? Of course a bestselling author wouldn't come all the way to see me just to give me a bottle of cheap blended whisky. Obviously, the old tube was just there for protection. Why hadn't I at least looked inside before handing over to my dad a four hundred pound bottle of whisky? Well it was gone now. Easier to get your kids back off the social work department than a rare Islay malt from my dad. '...*thousand pounds.*' The splash of single malt that hit the back of my throat was not enough to quell the feeling of nausea gathering in the pit of my wallet.

'Highland Heather Dew,' my dad shook his head, chuckling to himself. 'What a kidder.' He put the prize bottle back into the tube and pressed on the tin lid before ruffling my hair with one of his huge hands. 'I don't care if Malky gets me and him tickets for a fourball with Tiger Woods and Rory McIlroy at Augusta. Next year it's going to be *all* the Munro boys going or nobody.'

Chapter 9

Having just let four grand slip through my fingers faster than a melon seed, I was even more determined to take up Mr Posh's offer. There was no money in the brown envelope he'd given me, just a piece of paper with an address and a phone number on it and a key. It was Tuesday lunch time. I had until close of business to collect Victor Devlin's property or say goodbye to the promised twenty grand.

Plenty of time for what I had in mind.

Initially, I'd wondered about doing a night-time-ninja and visiting the hideaway under cover of darkness. In, out and away before anyone knew. Then I'd wondered; was Mr Posh for real? Yes, I'd been given a key, but did Victor Devlin even own the property? How would it look if I was found sneaking about somebody's house? I might as well wear a stripy, black and white shirt and carry a bag with swag written on it.

So, I'd had Grace-Mary do a search in the Registers of Scotland on the address in the brown envelope and it disclosed the proprietor as Devlin Polymineral Investments Ltd. A free on-line check with Company House showed Victor Edward Devlin as managing director.

That, and the promise of twenty K, was good enough for me, and, so, at two o'clock that Tuesday afternoon, I walked out of a local printer's with a For Sale sign under my arm and, after a one hour drive east, arrived at my destination.

If I'd actually been an estate agent, and not just pretending to be one, I might have described the white-washed cottage, perched on the edge of a cliff, somewhere between North Berwick and Dunbar, as enjoying a quiet and secluded setting. But I wasn't, and if nowhere had a middle I was dead-centre. There wasn't a pub or a shop or any other sign of civilisation for miles around. Not that the location was undesirable. For the holidaymaker, it was close to such renowned golf courses as Muirfield and Gullane, handy for the beaches of East Lothian and the Lammermuir hills were only a hike away. All in all, it was plain to see why it would make the perfect retreat for Victor Devlin. Somewhere he could put his feet up, relax and formulate new and interesting ways to cheat people out of their life-savings.

After a juddering trip, swerving my way up a pot-holed track, dodging protruding boulders that threatened to scrape the exhaust from the undercarriage of my car, I alighted, breathed in the cool, fresh, air and had a good look around the curtilage of Devlin's cottage. If anyone was watching the place they'd have to be hiding in the clumps of straggly silver birch that grew here and there, for there was no other property in line of sight and only fields to the front and the rocky shoreline of the North Sea to the rear.

Still, I had been warned. I opened the boot and removed the For Sale sign and a three foot length of wood. I nailed the sign to the wooden post and then drove it into a patch of soft earth and weeds outside the front door. That done, I proceeded to make a show of walking around the property, gazing up at the roof and scratching my head thoughtfully. I even kicked one of the white-washed walls with the toe of my shoe a couple of times. Every now and then I made a note in my pocket diary. Eventually, satisfied that anyone watching would have got the idea by now, I went up to a front door that was guarded either side by large enamel plant pots, each containing earth and a selection of healthy weeds.

The thought of entering someone else's house when they weren't in was a surprisingly nerve-wracking one, even with their permission. No wonder housebreakers sometimes found it a bowel-loosening experience. A couple of deep breaths and I took the key out of my pocket. It fitted the lock. I turned it, the door opened and I let myself in.

According to Mr Posh, Devlin's memory-stick was in a kitchen drawer, taped to the underside of a plastic cutlery-organiser. I found a drawer right next to the gas hob. I pulled it open. The moulded tray had five compartments holding knives, forks, spoons, teaspoons and a larger one with two wooden-handled carving knives. I glanced about to make sure my actions weren't visible through the kitchen window and then lifted out the cutlery tray and held it up over my head for a look underneath. Nothing. I groped around with my hand. Definitely no memory-stick. There was a tea towel draped over the back of a chair. I spread it on the countertop and, using it to deaden the noise, lifted the cutlery items out of their respective compartments and set them down. I gave the cutlery tray another thorough examination before replacing the various items and closing the drawer. What was I supposed to do now?

Just in case I'd misunderstood my instructions, I searched the bedrooms, checking out wardrobes, bedside cabinets, dressing tables, chests of drawers and any other pieces of furniture that were lying around.

Next was the sitting room. There was not much in the way of furniture, just a coffee table, a wooden stand for the television and a sideboard. The TV stand had a drawer containing a few DVDs. Some crystal-ware was neatly placed on a silver charger on the sideboard and the end cabinets held a wide array of single malts. There was nothing on the coffee table apart from a large hardback book about golf, on which rested a lump of rock the size of a grapefruit. It wasn't what I was looking for and yet I was intrigued. The rock was so silvery-grey that it might have been lead. It certainly felt heavy enough, but its shape was odd, almost crystalline as though it were made of a series of rectangular prisms stuck together at various angles. Was this tantalite? Had Devlin used this impressive sample to lure unwary investors?

The house, even the bathroom having been thoroughly searched, I had no option other than to phone Mr Posh;

something he'd told me not to do unless absolutely necessary. The signal on my phone ranged from weak to dead. I hoped for better reception outside and, still trying to retain an air of estate agency, wandered the grounds of the cottage until I managed to achieve a single bar on my phone display meaning that communication with the outside world was possible.

Posh was annoyed. 'I told you not to phone me.'

'You said I was only to phone if absolutely necessary,' I said. 'Well, it is. The thing I'm looking for isn't where you said it would be.'

'Where have you looked?'

'Everywhere. I can't find it.'

Even with the poor reception I could hear a sigh travel down the line. 'Where exactly have you looked?'

My turn to sigh. 'The kitchen, both bedrooms, the sitting room, even the bathroom.'

'And the utility room?' Either the signal died or he hung up.

Utility room? Where was that? I returned to the cottage and into the kitchen. Sure enough there was a small wooden door which led into a tiny room with a stone floor, home to a washing machine, some gardening implements and, more importantly, a work top with a single drawer. Muttering to myself that this was a utility room and *not* the kitchen, I tugged open the drawer to reveal an identical plastic cutlery tray. This one held a much older range of assorted cutlery and barbecue items. I lifted them out, turned the tray upside-down and found underneath, wedged securely between the compartments for knives and forks, and held in place by sticky-tape, the USB memory-stick that I'd been sent for. I peeled off the tape and prised it out.

A few minutes later I replaced the key under a plant pot as I'd been told and after a few final estate agent type glances under the eaves, returned to my car. Easy. Or so I thought, until half way down the track I met a Jaguar XF coming in the opposite direction.

A man alighted. A very big man. Dark suit, dark hair, dark stubble, dark sunglasses. The black tie around the neck of his white shirt had been tied using a pair of pliers into a knot the size of a walnut. He didn't look like a farmer. I got out to meet him.

'Great property,' I said, attempting a smile. 'Shouldn't be difficult to shift, even in the current climate. These sort of holiday homes are always in demand. Are you interested? I expect it will be snapped-up in no time at all.'

The big man stepped forward. The look on his face suggested that the state of the local housing market was of little interest to him. He took off his jacket, folded it slowly and carefully as though it was as important as anything else he'd do that day and draped it over the bonnet of the Jag.

'I want the data-stick,' he said.

If my smile had at first been half-hearted, it was now on the verge of cardiac arrest. 'I don't know what you—'

'It's simple.' Mr Big turned his solemn attention to the rolling-up of his shirt sleeves. 'We can do this the easy way or we can do it the hard way.'

Chapter 10

I really wished I'd opted for the easy way. But it was the money. I couldn't let it go just like that. Using the door handle of my car, I dragged myself into a standing position. It felt like someone had removed my brain, given it a shake and reinstalled it, upside down.

With an effort I yanked open the car door and let myself fall into the driver's seat. The rear-view mirror showed me what I already suspected: the side of my face was as bruised and swollen as a blind carpenter's thumb.

Whoever Mr Big was, he wasn't some drunk out to take a swing at me for noising him up in the witness box. This guy was quick and strong and knew a lot more about martial arts than Sergeant Alex Munro had ever taught his son. He'd battered through my defence like I'd erected a beach-windbreak in the face of a tornado and the one punch I had managed to throw was still looking for somewhere to land.

I pressed gently against the side of my jaw with the palm of my hand and opened my mouth in a wide yawn. Painful, not broken. I just wanted to go home. First of all I had to call Mr Posh. I remembered the abrupt manner in which my earlier call had ended. I thought he'd just been annoyed. Was there more to it? Those men Victor Devlin had upset; the ones who started wars; it looked like they had their money back. Had that been enough for them? Or had they needed blood as well?

No reply. I tried a few miles further down the road where there was better reception; still there was no answer. He was gone and all I had to show for my efforts was the upfront money I'd insisted on. Unfortunately, Mr Posh didn't deal in cash and had transferred the first tranche of my agreed fee into the Munro & Co. firm's account by electronic transfer. Five thousand pounds for a trip to the seaside on a pleasant summer's day and a sore face. I'd had sore faces for less. The thing was to look at it as five thousand gained and not fifteen thousand lost.

I arrived back home to find someone had entered without my permission. My dad. He'd left a brochure from a company that supplied wedding favours. It was lying open at a page displaying whisky miniatures with custom labels. More importantly, he'd made soup and left some in a pot on the cooker for me. It was a lot easier to suck from a spoon than the day-before pizza I'd originally had on the menu. I pressed an ice-cold can of beer across my jaw, before cracking the tin open. Taking delicate sips, I took it through to the livingroom while I waited for the soup to heat.

The main item on the Scottish evening news was, as usual, to do with the upcoming Scottish independence referendum. As far as I could make out independence meant keeping the Royal Family, Sterling and the submarine bases on the Clyde, while staying in the EU and sharing the British embassies around the world. Given that the SNP's Justice Secretary seemed intent on turning the Scots legal system into a copy of the English legal system, I wondered what we were being asked to vote for and why the politicians found it necessary to waste my TV-viewing time by constantly discussing it on air. I turned to the brochure my dad had left. I thought I'd better at least give it a glance or I'd never hear the end of it. I was disturbed by the buzzing of my mobile phone. It was Suzie. I'd been meaning to call her.

'Listen Suzie,' I said after our opening pleasantries, 'that bottle of whisky, there was no need to go to such expense.'

'Nonsense. If it hadn't been for you I'd still be freelancing historic shorts for the tartan and shortbread magazines. Or, worse still,' she laughed, 'a legal aid lawyer like yourself.'

I tried and failed to find the humour in that last remark.

'Really. You deserve it,' she said. 'Have you tried it yet?'

'Are you joking? How could I bring myself to drink it knowing that every sip was worth hundreds of pounds?'

'I suppose it could be a good investment,' Suzie said. 'Better than drinking it.' She made a choking noise down the line and I could imagine her screwing up her face. 'Whisky, it all tastes like poison to me, especially that peaty stuff, I don't know how you can do it to yourself. Anyway, enjoy.'

The chance would be a fine thing. If, and it was a big if, my dad opened the bottle I would be lucky to get anywhere near it.

'Anyway, the reason I'm calling, Robbie, is because I've made a decision about my next book. I've decided to take a detour from the usual stuff and write something non-fiction like, 'In Cold Blood'. You know? The book by Truman Capote?'

I'd read Truman Capote's non-fiction novel, if that wasn't a contradiction in terms, and seen the films. While Suzie was sufficiently gifted to bash-out a competent pot-boiler, I wasn't quite so sure she would be able to put together something comparable to Capote's masterpiece.

'Won't be easy,' I said, trying to rein in my disbelief.

'It will be a lot easier if I have good material,' she said.

'Like what?'

'Like the low down on the Quirk murder.'

I could see why Dominic Quirk might be good subject matter. His father, once a small-time bookie with a shady past, now Scotland's on-line gambling king. From humble roots the Quirk family had become part of the Scots-Catholic aristocracy and now the heir apparent was facing trial for murder. Throw into the mix a back-stabbing best friend, not to mention his earlier tragic car crash and I could see why there might be the makings of an excellent true-crime story.

'I'm not sure what information I could give you that you won't find from the newspapers and internet,' I said.

Suzie came back quickly. 'You're involved in the case. Can't you slip me some info on his background, past girlfriends, any interesting stuff about his family, his private life, stuff that you might hear about that won't come out during the trial? Don't worry,' she added, reading my mind. 'I'll not name my source and nothing will be printed until the case is over.' She laughed. 'There might even be another bottle of whisky in it for you.'

I thought about the whisky...

'I really need this, Robbie.'

...and about the constitutional law exam. But most of all about Suzie.

'I'll see what I can find out,' I heard myself say. How was I going to find out any private details about Quirk? I wasn't his lawyer. 'No promises.'

'Of course not,' she purred. 'Got to go now, Robbie. Thanks for always being there for me.'

Being there? I had seen her twice in the last fifteen years. I returned to my now cold soup and chewy toast and sat down on the wedding brochure. It was hard to believe. In a short time I'd be married. I tried to imagine our life together. What would the future hold? I closed my eyes and thought about Jill, but the more I did, the more all I could see was Suzie's smile.

Chapter 11

Kings Cross, mid-day Friday. I found Jill among the hordes of people; most of whom were standing next to or sitting on suitcases, staring up at the giant departures/arrivals board.

After we'd hugged, she drew a suspicious hand down the side of my face. I'd thought the swelling had died down completely. Obviously it hadn't, at least not to my fiancée's critical eye.

'Toothache.' I said. 'Murder.'

'What made you come down?' she asked, apparently satisfied at my explanation. 'I could have flown back tonight, or tomorrow morning. What about your work? What's happening to all your court cases?'

'They're being taken care of,' I said, picking up my holdall and following closely behind her until we'd fought our way through the crowd to the front door and onto Euston Road. In actual fact I had so little business that, of the few cases I had, there were no trials, just some intermediate diets and one or two deferred sentences which I'd instructed another firm to cover for me. 'I thought I'd come down and we could make a long weekend of it. Catch a show or something,' I'd blurted before I could stop myself.

'A show?' Jill latched onto my reckless words in an instant. 'You mean like a musical?' Jill knew I hated musicals.

'Not necessarily a musical... A play or something. Or a band. How about a stand-up? There's bound to be plenty of comedy clubs around the—'

'Legally Blonde is not so much a musical as a comedy and you'll like it because it's—'

'About a lawyer?'

'Sort of... Yes...'

'Tell me, do people dance about the stage singing at each other?' I took her silence as confirmation that they did. 'That makes it a musical, in which case I would refer you to my previous answer.'

Jill did an about-turn and marched away. I chased after her, apologising and citing the five hour journey, most of it spent standing, in mitigation.

'Why aren't we taking the Tube?' I asked, when I thought I'd repented sufficiently and was wondering why we were standing by the kerb-side with Jill waving at passing taxis. 'Are they still putting you up in that nice wee hotel in Kensington? That'll cost a fortune by cab and probably be a lot slower.'

'Firstly, no, we're not taking the tube. I'd rather not have to fight my way through a sea of east-European beggars and most likely catch something infectious and, secondly, it doesn't matter how much a taxi costs because I have an expense account.'

Who was being grumpy now?

Eventually, Jill's waving was successful and we climbed into the back of a hackney cab with a custom paint job advertising flavoured mineral water.

'And thirdly,' she said, I hadn't been expecting a thirdly, 'I'm not staying at the Savannah.'

'Where to?' the driver asked.

'The Savannah Kensington,' Jill said.

I was confused. 'I thought you weren't staying at the Savannah?'

'I'm not – you are.'

'Where are you staying?'

'With Felicity. She has an apartment on the Albert Embankment.'

'Where's that?'

'Other side of the River, mate,' said the taxi driver.

'How far is that from the Savannah?'

'Savannah Kensington?' the driver mulled that over for a second while I took the opportunity of reaching forward and sliding shut the panel between front and rear seats, leaving a hand print on the glass.

'How far?' I asked Jill.

'Not all that far,' she said.

'How far is not that far?'

'It doesn't matter. I'll come and see you at the hotel.'

'What's so special about Felicity's place?'

'I've been staying there these last few weeks. Makes sense. And it's lovely. Very modern. Very small, of course, but everything in central London is. It has a glass front looking across the Thames to Westminster. And there's a gym in the basement. A lot of the time she stays at the apartment during the week and goes home on weekends. Just like me, except Buckinghamshire's not so far to go.'

If my geographical knowledge of London wasn't great, the counties of England would definitely not be my choice for specialist subject on Mastermind; however, I did know that Buckinghamshire wasn't London, which meant... 'If Felicity's away this weekend and we're here...'

'No.'

'Why not?'

'For one thing she's staying in London this weekend.'

'And for another?'

'Felicity doesn't like...' Jill didn't finish the sentence.

'Doesn't like what?'

'Doesn't like people staying over.'

'She doesn't seem to mind you staying over.'

'Why should she?'

'I'm just saying that if she doesn't mind you staying over, that doesn't seem to fit in with your comment that she doesn't like—'

'It's you. All right? She doesn't like you.'

Was I hearing correctly? 'Me? What's wrong with me?'

'She thinks you're uncouth.'

'She's met me a sum total of twice!'

'And on each occasion you've been involved in a fight. That time at New Year and last Friday in Edinburgh.'

'I was defending myself last Friday. How is it my fault if I'm attacked by some nutter?'

'That's just it, Robbie. It's never your fault. Everything always happens to you. Did you see a nutter attack any of the other diners? No – just poor old Robbie Munro.'

If I'd wanted an argument I could have stayed in West Lothian and continued my on-going hostilities with Sheriff Brechin. 'All right, all right, I get the picture. I'm an uncouth oaf who's not fit to mix in polite society. I don't want to go to her pokey-wee flat anyway. Probably stinks of sewage from the river. But if you're not staying at the Savannah maybe I should go somewhere less expensive,' I said.

'What do you mean?'

'Well, I thought I'd be staying in your room, but if you're not there anymore...'

Jill sighed. 'Don't worry, I'll pay.'

'I don't mean that.'

'Really, it's fine.'

'Will you put me through on expenses too? How's that going to look? You live with your boss. Don't you think it will be a tad obvious if you start charging for hotel rooms?'

'I don't need to put it through on expenses.'

'I'm not having you pay for my hotel room.'

'Why not? The crime business booming is it?'

'Seeing how you've asked, I did manage to find a good client this week.' Found him and then promptly lost him again. What had happened to Mr Posh? I wondered. Still, I had five thousand of his pounds in my bank account, even though I had been hoping to put it towards a house for Jill and me and not take a chunk out of it with a stay at an overpriced hotel.

'By good client, I take it you mean a bad client? Like the rest of your clientele.'

'Actually, he wasn't a criminal client, some of whom are innocent by the way. He was instructing me in a civil matter, sort of, and didn't mind paying for the privilege.'

'I don't care. I'm still going to pay for your hotel,' Jill said.

We continued to argue about who was going to pay my hotel bill until the taxi stopped next to the sandstone columns either side of the front doors of the Savannah. Jill handed the taxi-driver the fare and waited for a receipt.

I was standing, holdall in hand, expecting her to alight, when she closed the door and sat back in her seat.

I saw the driver turn his head and say something and Jill say something back. She rolled down the window. 'I've got to go.'

'I thought you might have been coming up to my room,' I said, poking my head through the window at her. 'You know, for a drink or something. Preferably something.'

Another cab arrived and pulled up behind ours. 'I'll need to get a move on, love,' the taxi driver said.

'Look, Robbie. You can't phone me at six in the morning to announce that you're coming down here and expect me to drop everything. I've got a job to do. I had to take an extended lunch hour to collect you from the station—'

'Well, can't you extend it a little more?'

'No, and the longer you keep me talking here, the longer I'll have to stay at the office to catch up.'

I pulled my head out and stood there, doing my best to appear aloof, looking over the top of the taxi at a London sightseeing tour bus collecting passengers in a bay on the opposite side of Holland Avenue.

Jill came to the window. 'It's Saturday tomorrow, we can do something nice.' The other cab honked its horn. 'You got your mobile with you?' She didn't wait for an answer. 'I'll call you when I've finished work and we can meet up for dinner. I'll make the arrangements.' The taxi began to drive off. Through the rear window I saw Jill mouth, 'I'll call you,' while raising a hand to her face, pinky to lips, thumb to ear, in the universal gesture.

Right at that moment it felt like she was making another universal gesture, involving two different fingers.

Chapter 12

Jill didn't call. Her PA did, to say that she'd booked a table for eight o'clock at Orgoglio di Napoli, an Italian restaurant in Knightsbridge.

I pitched up right on time and had been chomping on giant green table olives and fresh, crusty bread for a quarter of an hour before Jill arrived, still in her work clothes and looking flustered.

'Sorry I'm late,' she said. 'You've no idea what that place is like. It was going like a funfair all day and of course it didn't help that I had to—'

She was interrupted by a waiter who gave us each a menu and heartily recommended the Linguine con Vongole e Gamberoni, which he translated as pasta with clams and tiger prawns. According to the waiter, the chef's signature sauce, with garlic, cream and tomato, would take my breath away. If it didn't, the price would. I ordered it anyway and Jill opted for Ravioli Tino.

'I always go for the ravioli when I come here,' she said. 'Either that or the Zitoni Toscanini.'

'And there was me going to ask you if you came here often.' I said.

She smiled. 'Sorry to ruin your only chat-up line.'

We clinked wine glasses. I liked red, but Jill much preferred white so in a spirit of conciliation I'd ordered a bottle of her favourite Blanc de Rossis without any discussion.

'And I'm sorry if I was short with you earlier,' she said.

'That's okay,' I lied. 'I realise my surprise visit must have caught you on the hop.'

'Doesn't matter, I shouldn't have just dumped you at the hotel and run off. And I wouldn't have if things weren't so busy just now with the amalgamation.'

'Amalgamation? Is that the important thing you're not supposed to tell anyone about?'

'That was last week. They made the official announcement two days ago. This time last year no one had heard of Lyon Laboratories.'

I still hadn't.

Jill swirled the wine in her inordinately-large wine glass. 'Then they had that break-through in gene therapy and now it makes perfect sense for Zanetti to take them over.'

I took a sip of wine. It was good. Not forty-two quid a bottle good, but definitely good. 'I thought you said it was an amalgamation?'

'That's what the big company calls it to keep the smaller company happy, but really, in business, there are no mergers, only acquisitions.'

I couldn't believe what was happening. Was this really Jill? Sitting here, a few Rolls Royce lengths from the world's most famous department store, dining beyond my means and lecturing on corporate take-overs?

'It's all timed perfectly to coincide with the opening of Zanetti UK's new technology park near Lasswade.'

I had a feeling Jill had told me about this exciting development previously. I think it may have been during a football match on the telly. She reminded me. Zanetti was about to complete the construction of a centre for pharmaceutical research and development, manufacture and distribution. The site was to the east of Edinburgh, on land that was formerly part of the green-belt. The company had promised, in exchange for the relaxation of certain planning restrictions, to create nearly two thousand new jobs. The Scottish Government was very excited. So was Jill. So was I. It meant Jill would return to Scotland to work and we wouldn't have to continue our long distance relationship.

A buzzing sound. By the time I'd laid down my glass and reached for the phone in my pocket, Jill had hers pressed to the side of her head, the palm of her other hand clamped over the opposite ear.

'Felicity,' she said, after a brief conversation in which Jill's involvement was limited to a hello and cheerio.

'Not joining us?' I asked, unable to blunt the edge off my voice.

'Apart from by the magic of telecommunications, no,' Jill replied and took a slug of white wine. 'She was phoning to tell me we have a breakfast meeting tomorrow.'

'Tomorrow? I thought we were going to do something?'

'Like what?'

'I don't know. You said we would do something nice together.'

'We will. I'll not be busy the whole day.'

Our starters arrived. I'd ordered the Bresaola Della Valtellina, thin slices of beef fillet, marinated in olive oil and lemon juice and topped with rocket and parmesan shavings.

'What time is your meeting?' I asked.

'Seven-thirty. Which means I'll have to be up early to look my best.'

'Where is it?'

'Westminster.'

'The Houses of Parliament?'

'We usually meet in the dining room on the ground floor.'

Oh, she did, did she?

'Anything to do with genetics is terribly sensitive. The sort of cutting-edge research that Zanetti will be taking on once Lyon Laboratories is on-board means we must have the Government on our side. That involves a lot of lobbying, which is what Felicity excels at. She has those M.P.s eating out of her hand.'

More buzzing. This time it was my phone. I glanced at the display and returned the phone to my pocket. 'And where do you fit in?'

'I help explain the scientific side of things in layman's terms - so that even politicians can understand.'

'You?'

Jill stared at me through narrowed eyes. 'Yes me. I happen to be good at it.'

'I didn't mean it like that—'

'Well what did you mean it like?' Jill set down her knife and fork, reached over and took my hand. 'I'm sorry, Robbie. I don't know what's wrong with me.'

'You're under a lot of stress,' I said. From years of painful experience I knew to make no mention of, *that time of the month*, even when all the evidence pointed to *that time of the month*. 'Let's eat up and I'll take you back to Felicity's.'

'We could go back to the hotel if you like.'

'No, you've got an early start,' I said.

She didn't quibble. We started making inroads into our antipasti.

'If the meeting goes well I'm sure Felicity will let me have the rest of the day off and I'll come see you,' Jill said.

'That would be great,' I replied, my mouth full of starter, the next wafer-thin slice of cured beef, dangling from a prong of my fork.

'I've always wondered how they manage to cut the meat so thinly,' she said.

I'd always wondered that too, but right then I was wondering more why I had a missed call from Suzie Lake on my phone.

Chapter 13

'This is a coincidence,' Suzie said.

The small bar, just off the lobby of the Savannah Hotel, was all whirring ceiling fans, palm trees and cane furniture. We sat on high stools: Suzie sipping a French Martini and attracting admiring glances from every red-blooded male in the W11 postcode area, me enjoying a reassuringly-large tumbler of Glendronach and the envious stares.

'Fancy us being in London at the same time,' she said. 'What brings you here?'

'Oh, business,' I said. 'You?'

'The same. I'm here to tell my agent the good news. About my new book,' she added. 'I really think it's going to put my name back on the map. A non-fiction novel, it's the sort of thing they dish out literary prizes for. My credibility rating will soar. It will—'

'What have you written so far?' I asked.

'Don't worry,' she cocked an exquisite eyebrow. 'Once I have the material I need, the words will simply fly onto the paper.'

I finished my whisky. The Glendronach 15 year-old Revival was a masterpiece of distilling art. Dark and sherry sweet, a drop of water brought out a flood of flavours and made it far too drinkable. Ignoring my, admittedly feeble, protests, Suzie ordered me another and when it arrived she lowered herself from the stool. 'Come on,' she said, lifting her own drink from the bar. Let's find somewhere more comfortable and you can tell me everything you know about young master Quirk. She led me over to a small couch in the corner. Barely large enough for the two of us, it was a tight squeeze. I thought it rude to complain.

'Tell me the story,' Suzie said. 'Right from the start. Pretend I don't know anything. I don't want to go into this with any preconceived ideas.'

I didn't normally discuss my cases with anyone, but this was different. This was Suzie Lake in the flesh, and that flesh was sitting so close to me that our legs touched. Anyway, was what she wanted to know really all *that* confidential? The trial would start in a few weeks and everything would become public knowledge then, or, at any rate, most of it. The woman only wanted a head start. Guilty feelings thus assuaged, larynx lubricated by the fine fifteen year-old single malt, I commenced what I expected to be the opening chapter to Suzie's soon-to-be bestseller.

* * * * *

In every criminal case there are at least two accounts of what happened: the prosecution version and the defence version.

In the case against Dominic Quirk and Mark Starrs, I suspected there might be three accounts, Quirk's, Starr's and the Crown's. There might even be a fourth: the truth; something that could easily get in the way of what each side wanted most: not justice: victory.

The Crown's view was simple and straightforward and had been disclosed to the defence in a flurry of witness statements, recorded interviews, scene of crime photographs, pathology reports and forensic analyses. Quirk and Starrs had abducted Doreen Anderson, taken her to Quirk's house, plied her with drink and drugs, murdered her and dumped her body in the woods.

As for the defence, what Paul was preparing for Quirk was still shrouded in mystery. All I could relay to Suzie was my client's version of events, and she seemed happy enough with that. Sitting beside me, staring up and absorbing every word of mine through those beautiful big brown eyes.

To replace the Range Rover, wrecked in the recent, and fatal for some, accident, Santa Claus had brought Dominic

Quirk something sporty in estoril blue that could shift from zero to sixty in less time than it took to say jingle bells. The only problem was that he couldn't drive until his ban was up and so his friend and fellow student, Mark Starrs, was acting as chauffeur for the remaining few months. Easter Saturday night they'd been cruising the streets of St Andrews and spied Doreen walking the narrow, cobbled surface of North Castle Street. She'd accepted their offer of a lift home, but instead they'd driven to Quirk's student accommodation in the nearby village of Dunino, one of those blink-and-you'll-miss-it places, that are scattered about the East Neuk of Fife.

Quirk's property had two public rooms and three bedrooms and had been purchased especially to see him through his University years. It was described in the Estate Agents' schedule of particulars as *a charming detached property within a breath-taking woodland setting*. Mark Starrs couldn't afford to stay there during term-time, though he was a frequent visitor and often stayed overnight. He described Quirk's pad as a party house and assured me there had been no abduction. Doreen had been happy to go along with them. They'd had a few laughs, a lot to drink and sometime well after midnight Dominic had gone to his bed, Doreen to a spare room, while Starrs crashed out on the living room sofa, something he'd done many times previously. My client recalled being awakened, sometime in the early hours, by noises coming from Doreen's room. He heard shouting and the sounds of a struggle and had been rousing himself to go through and see what was going on, when, just as suddenly, the commotion stopped. Still half-drunk and not sure if he'd imagined it all, he went back to sleep. The next thing he knew, Dominic was charging about screaming that Doreen was dead.

It wasn't hard to imagine the conversation between the two, quickly sobering-up students. There was a lot of explaining needing done, careers hung in the balance. Eventually, it was decided that the easiest course of action would be to ditch the body and act as though nothing had happened. It was a plan that might have worked had it not been for a passing lorry driver who had noticed a brand new BMW convertible abandoned on a roadside verge. He took the registration number, called it in, but when they police arrived they didn't find a car, they found the body of a dead girl in the undergrowth. The mystery of Doreen's disappearance was solved before she'd even been reported missing.

Professor Edward Bradley carried out the Crown autopsy and pronounced death by asphyxiation. He ruled out accidental death on the basis of petechial haemorrhaging in the eyes of the dead girl. There was no fracture of the hyoid bone to suggest strangulation, and so the Professor opined that while Doreen could have been suffocated in various ways, the most likely cause was a pillow placed over the face. Although there was little sign of blunt trauma to suggest any degree of violence, this did not surprise the Crown expert as the toxicology report revealed such high levels of alcohol in Doreen's bloodstream that her respiration would have been impaired and any resistance negligible.

'So that's your client's defence - it's was all down to Quirk?'

'It's all we have. When Starrs was arrested he declined a lawyer and what I've told you is more or less what he told the cops.'

'And Dominic Quirk? What did he tell them?'

'He did the right thing. He asked to see a lawyer. Paul Sharp was there in no time at all and Quirk told the police nothing.'

'That's good, right?'

'His powder is well and truly dry,' I said.

'So he could blame Starrs?'

'He could - but say what? He's got absolutely nothing to back up an incrimination of my client. No motive. No nothing. Why should anyone believe him when Starrs has got his knife in first? And, of course, there's Quirk's DNA.'

'What about it?'

'It's all over Doreen.'

'In what way?'

In intimate ways, was the answer. Forensics disclosed that shortly before death there had been sexual intercourse. A used condom was found on the floor by the bed and a DNA analysis concluded that the chances of the semen tested not having come from Dominic Quirk was a one billion to one shot.

'So what do you think actually happened?' Suzie asked.

I hadn't thought too hard about what actually happened, only about how to convince a jury my client wasn't there when it did.

'Come on,' Suzie said. 'You must have at least a notion of how Doreen ended up smothered. You've seen all the evidence. Give me the Robbie Munro theory. Off the record.'

Off the record didn't exist, not with cops, not with journalists, not with anyone. I knew that, but one single malt top-up later and I had it all worked out and was happy to opine. 'Okay, here goes... You've seen Quirk's photo. His mother doesn't have a display cabinet full of beautiful baby rosettes. My client on the other hand is a good looking lad. It's obvious who Doreen must have—'

'Not to me it's not,' Suzie butted in. 'Starrs is not rich like his pal. Dominic Quirk is the man with the country property and new beamer...'

'That's very shallow of you,' I joked.

'What's shallow? Is fancying someone for their money any more shallow than fancying them because they've got a nice face?'

Touché. 'Whatever, I'm not sure what Doreen knew. Remember, it was Starrs who was driving the car when they picked her up.'

'I suppose,' Suzie said, allowing me to continue with my version.

'They all go back to Quirk's place, have a few drinks and in the middle of the night he goes to her room and tries his luck. Clearly, they have sex, whether it was consensual or not is another question.'

'What do you mean?'

'According to Starrs, everyone was very drunk. Maybe Doreen was too drunk to know what she was doing.'

'You mean she could have been raped? I thought there were no injuries. What makes you think she could have been forced?' Suzie asked.

That wasn't the legal test any more. A woman could be too drunk to consent to sex, even though a man was deemed never too drunk not to know what he was doing.

'So, you think she woke up later, found Quirk in her bed, realised what had happened...'

'Started shouting, there was a bit of a struggle, Quirk tried to quieten her down...'

'With a pillow over the face?'

'He'd been drinking and wasn't thinking clearly.'

'She suffocates? Just like that?'

I drained the last drop of Glendronach. By this stage it could have been Glen Paraffin and I wouldn't have known the difference. 'Easily done. Especially if all concerned have had too much to drink.'

'You make it sound like a tragic accident,' Suzie said, as the waiter arrived bearing the same again for me and another French Martini for Suzie; a round of drinks I had no recollection of ordering.

'Probably was.'

'It would explain why Starrs allowed himself to be persuaded into assisting Quirk to get rid of the body - if, as you say, it was all a mistake.' Suzie was forgetting that I was only guessing at what happened.

'I'm only interested in seeing that my client isn't convicted of a murder he probably didn't commit.'

'Probably?'

'Good enough for me.' I was conscious of slurring my words, just not sufficiently to care about it. 'The evidence against him is so thin it's practically non-existent.'

'Then why has he been indicted for murder?'

Even in my tipsy state I could answer that one. 'Don't get the idea that the evidence and what the Crown puts onto an indictment are directly related.'

'I don't get it,' Suzie said.

'You would if you were charged with a murder you didn't commit and the Crown sidled up to you and offered to make it all go away, just so long as you grass-up your best mate.'

'But surely Starrs could be called as witness anyway?'

'Not by the Crown. Not while he's still on the indictment for disposing of the body.'

'But he'd have to give evidence in his own defence,' Suzie said. 'His version would come out then.'

Suzie had departed law school before we studied evidence and criminal procedure. I explained. 'Starrs can just sit there and say nothing. The Crown has to prove the case against him and they have nothing, no evidence at all to say that he had any reason to harm Doreen or that he assisted Quirk in any way prior to getting rid of the body.'

'Then why doesn't the Crown use his statement to the police against Quirk?'

'Because at trial what an accused has said to the police about his co-accused is inadmissible. He would actually need to testify.'

'Sounds complicated,' Suzie said.

'Not really. The Crown just has to figure a way to make him go into the witness box.'

'And so they charge him with a murder they don't think they can prove?' Suzie dipped into her handbag. It was different from the last one, just as huge, but black patent leather with gold fixtures. She took out a very small notebook and started to jot things down.

'The Crown is trying to help Starrs to concentrate on what is important,' I said. 'And what the Crown thinks important is that Quirk is convicted. Starrs was prepared to help Quirk bury a dead body, that's what I call friendship. The prosecution can't assume that he'll say anything remotely incriminatory without a little persuasion.'

'Sounds like blackmail.'

Suzie was getting the idea.

'And is Starrs taking the deal?' she asked.

'With both hands.'

'What if he does and then they drop the murder charge and he refuses to speak up at the trial?'

'That won't happen. He'll agree with the Crown in advance what his evidence is going to be and he'll sign an affidavit to that effect. If his evidence diverges from what is set out in the affidavit he'll go to prison.'

Suzie sipped her martini. She had a slightly puzzled expression so I explained. 'If he changes his story it means that he's either lying in the witness box or he lied in his sworn affidavit – it's perjury whichever way you slice it.'

'Sweet.'

'Standard Crown practice.'

'So Starrs turns stool pigeon and what? He walks?'

'No. The AD wants him to plead guilty to attempting to defeat the ends of justice by helping Quirk dispose of the body.'

'Why should he?' Because he did it and was found doing it by half of the local constabulary, was the obvious answer, but before I could slur it, Suzie was off again. 'Doesn't seem like a very good deal to me. He gives the Crown Quirk's head on a platter and he still has to go to jail?'

'Not for very long,' I said.

'How long?'

'With remission, about two or three years, maybe more.'

'That's the best you can do?'

Up until then I'd thought it was an excellent deal. Okay there wasn't much evidence against Starrs, but you can't bury a dead body without some mud sticking to you. Jurors were strange creatures. If he went to trial on the murder charge and only eight out of the fifteen took a no-smoke-without-fire view of things, then my client would end up doing life and he needn't expect the Appeal Court to ride to the rescue. These days its sole purpose was to justify convictions, not set them aside.

Suzie didn't see it that way. 'It just means he's getting off with something he didn't do. I thought you'd be able to do better than that, Robbie.' She laid her glass down on the low table in front of us and looked up at me. 'I'd heard you could do miracles when it came to court work.'

I finished my whisky and aimed to put my tumbler down beside Suzie's martini glass. The surface of the table was a mosaic and the glass slid across the tiny ceramic tiles and almost toppled over the other side. I didn't know what time it was or how long we'd been talking. I did know I'd consumed way too many drams of fine Highland malt in the process.

'So what's the plan?' Suzie asked.

'That's more or less it,' I yawned.

'No, I meant what's Dominic Quirk's plan? If he's pleading not guilty, how is he going to counter Starrs' evidence?'

I'd no idea. That was between Quirk and his lawyer.

Suzie pouted. 'Don't you have any inside information? I thought you were friends with Quirk's lawyer?' Somehow she managed to wriggle even closer.

'I..,' I cleared my throat and tried again. 'I am but Quirk said nothing to the cops. I won't know his defence until the trial, like everyone else.'

'What would you do if he was your client?'

'You're asking me to...' I took a couple of goes at speculate and settled for guess. 'How can I when I don't know Quirk's position? I only know what Starrs has told me.'

Suzie sipped her martini, so close to me I could smell the sharp tang of the raspberry liqueur. 'What if you really wanted to get Quirk off? Imagine he's your client and all you are interested in is seeing that he isn't convicted of a murder—'

'That he probably didn't commit?'

'Or even that he probably did. Imagine you had absolutely no scruples.'

That I could do.

'It's so hot and stuffy in here.' Suzie wafted herself with the tiny notebook two or three times. She straightened up the two empty glasses on the tiled table. 'Why don't we talk about this somewhere cooler?'

Chapter 14

It was the sound of running water that woke me next morning. I was slouched in the armchair in my hotel room, a blanket draped over me. The sheets on the empty bed were drawn back and rumpled.

The sound of running water ceased and shortly afterwards Suzie appeared wrapped in a white dressing gown, rubbing her wet hair with a towel.

'Sleep well?' she asked.

Tongue like the candlewick bed spread, I could only grunt. Single malt made for a terrific sleeping draught, but every joint in my body had seized. With an effort, I threw off the blanket, straightened my spine and flexed a few essential but recalcitrant muscles. Apart from a lack of shoes, I was fully clothed.

'Looks like we're going to miss breakfast,' Suzie said. 'Why don't you jump into the shower and I'll call room service?'

I reached over to the bedside and grabbed the clock radio. The red digits pronounced 09:35. Having worked out the time, I was trying to remember what day it was. Saturday, I finally decided. What were my plans? Oh, yeah, I was meeting Jill. When? After her meeting finished. What time would that be? Well, if it was a breakfast meeting, probably no later than ten o'clock. How long by taxi from Westminster to Kensington? Time enough for a quick shower? I couldn't risk it. I had to lose Suzie. I shook my head, felt my brain rattle. 'No, no room service.'

I prised my aching bones from the armchair and found my shoes.

'What's wrong?' Suzie asked.

'Last night,' I said. 'When you asked me why I was in London and I said I was here on business...'

'Yes?'

'I'm not... here on business. I'm visiting my girlfriend.'

'Oh.'

I sat down on the edge of the bed to take off my shoes. 'My fiancée, in fact.'

'Even more, oh.'

'And she'll be here any minute. So...'

'You'd like me to go?' Suzie floated across the room towards me, untying the belt of her dressing gown en route. 'Then I'd better hurry and get dressed.' She let the garment fall the length of her perfect body to the floor. I'd wanted to see Suzie with her togs off since I was eighteen years old and here she was at the foot of my bed. 'If that is really what you want.'

It was, wasn't it? I closed my eyes tight, ran a hand through my hair and realised that panic, or, more probably, lust had seen off my headache.

'Is it?' Suzie asked.

I didn't answer, couldn't answer. I flopped backwards onto the bed. The glorious pressure of Suzie's body, started at my feet, then slowly padded its way on all fours up the mattress towards me. I shouldn't be doing this, but—

A knock at the door. Jill's voice. 'Robbie?'

As hangover cures go, the sudden fear of your wife-to-be strolling into your hotel room to find you on the bed, straddled by a very attractive, very naked woman, is an incredibly effective one. I leapt up, knocking Suzie to the side and jumped into my shoes. In ten seconds, I was at the door. In two more I was in the corridor giving Jill a peck on the cheek.

She pushed me away. 'You smell like an old jakey. Have you even brushed your teeth this morning?'

'After breakfast,' I said, taking hold of her arm and dragging her along. 'If I hurry, I can still make it.'

Chapter 15

Having pretended how much I wanted breakfast, I had to force some down. Scrambled eggs and lightly buttered toast was about all I felt I could safely manage.

'You really are in a bad way,' Jill said. 'First time ever in the history of the world that Robbie Munro didn't go for the five-star fry-up.'

I smiled humourlessly over a cup of tea and awaited a lecture on over-indulgence. It never arrived. Did Jill feel partly to blame for my binge, having abandoned me the night before?

When we returned to my room so I could shower and change my clothes, Suzie was gone. Thankfully, the bed showed signs of only one occupant and no traces of make-up on the pillow.

Jill suggested a trip to the shops, and I didn't have the physical or mental strength to object. Physically I was tired and aching all over. Mentally, I was... what? Guilty? Why? Nothing had actually happened between Suzie and me. Was my guilt to do with a degree of regret about that?

Self-psychoanalysis over, my penance was to let myself be dragged off in the direction of Oxford Street, where our morning's shopping excursion lasted until around four in the afternoon. Just when I thought things couldn't get any worse they did and, after a pre-theatre dinner off Covent Garden, I found myself in the circle watching a blonde, ex-soap-actress bend and snatch while a lot of other people danced around her singing.

Later we returned to the hotel and stopped off at the bar. I ordered a shandy for me and a glass of pinot grigio for Jill.

'You sure?' asked the barman, with a look of overt innocence. He turned to Jill. 'I do a lovely French Martini.'

'No, white wine will do,' I said, and asked him to bring the drinks over to the very same sofa where Suzie and I had canoodled the night before.

'What was that about French Martinis?' Jill asked, once our drinks had arrived.

'He's probably on commission and trying to punt fancy cocktails,' I said.

'I don't even know what's in a French Martini. Do you?' Jill was looking straight at me. I was a firm believer in feminine intuition; my secretary being one of the world's greatest exponents; but there was no way Jill could be suspicious. Was there?

'I think it's vodka-based with pineapple juice or something.' I swigged some shandy. 'I know it's a big favourite at the Red Corner Bar. A lot of the jakeys will drink nothing else.'

Jill smiled unconvincingly and took a sip of wine.

'But you were right,' I said, in a less than seamless segue. 'That was a great show.'

Jill brightened. 'I told you you'd like it. What was the best part for you?'

'Oh, it was all good,' I said. 'You know all the dancing...' I drank some more shandy, 'and the singing... and stuff.'

My theatre review was interrupted by a distant buzzing. By the time Jill had raked around in her handbag and come out with her phone, the buzzing had stopped. 'Felicity,' she said, reading the screen.

'Ignore her.'

Jill's phone buzzed again.

'Here, give it to me.' I reached out for the phone, but Jill pulled it away and put it to her ear.

'Hi Felicity... No, we're back at the Savannah... Yes, we're in the bar.... Just a shandy... No, no immediate signs of a struggle, but it's still early.' There followed a lot more of Jill listening before she finished with an, 'okay, see you soon.'

'How soon?' I asked.

'Very. She's with Rupert.'

'She would be.'

Jill dropped the phone into her bag. 'You don't even know who Rupert is.'

That he was called Rupert was all I needed to know. I asked anyway. 'Okay, who is he?'

'Haven't a clue. She's just met him. Apparently he's very rich and with loads of contacts. Lots of fingers in lots of corporate pies. You never know, he might be able to find you a proper job.'

'A proper job?' I asked in a country-yokel accent. 'You mean like being a proper lawyer doing proper legal work?'

'Yes, I do. And you can stop the Long John Silver impersonation now.'

I took a gulp of shandy. Far too much lemonade. 'What I do *is* a proper job. It's just not properly paid. What's more proper than joining the fight for truth and justice?'

'And hoping they lose? I've really no idea.' Jill checked her lippy in a compact mirror. 'Anyway, Felicity and Rupert are dropping by for a nightcap. So I want you on your best behaviour.' Jill snapped the mirror shut. 'That means no courtroom stories about war-torn West Lothian.'

A loud coo-ee from the doorway and Felicity arrived in a swirl of Gucci and a waft of Coco Chanel. The perfect end to a perfect day. We both stood.

'Rupert?' Jill asked with a mischievous smile.

'We met this morning, just after I'd left you. I was stepping out of a cab and his car practically ran me over.'

Better luck next time, I thought a millisecond or two before Jill nipped my leg. Hard.

Felicity was at full gush. 'He was out of the car in a flash to see how I was and he gave his chauffeur a terribly hard time. It turns out we have a lot in common. Rupert has a wide range of business interests and tells me a generous donation to Zanetti's favourite charity at the upcoming gala ball might not be entirely out of the question. Isn't that right, Rup...?' She turned the palms of her hands upwards. 'Where'd he go?' She looked around her, as though somehow her rich new friend had become detached. She took a couple of backward steps and glanced into the lobby. 'There he is. I think he's met someone. What a man. He knows simply everyone.'

While Jill accepted Felicity's perfunctory hug, I looked around for some seats; there was barely room for two on the sofa that Jill and I had been sharing, and the place was busy now. Some football pundits were holding court at a table in a corner and their presence had attracted a number of admirers, which meant that there were a few vacant stools around the bar.

'Why don't you and Felicity sit here,' I said. 'I'll send over some drinks and save a seat for Rupert at the bar?'

Felicity seemed happy enough at that suggestion. Apparently, it was only a flying visit and Rupert could slum it on a stool for five minutes.

Jill had a worried look. 'Don't worry,' I told her. 'I'll keep Rupert amused with some of my courtroom tales. You know how interesting they can be.' My fiancée fixed a smile like she was fixing a bayonet. I downed the rest of my shandy and turned to Felicity. 'It's the way I tell them.'

Felicity looked from me to Jill as though something was lost in translation. I left Jill to explain and was trying to attract the barman's attention when a hand clamped down on my left shoulder.

'Well, well. Robbie Munro. Fancy meeting you here.'

I recognised the voice even before I spun around to stare into the smiling, florid face of Mr Posh. My head was spinning, an effect not brought on by a pint of weak shandy.

'Don't say anything you might regret later,' Posh said. An order I obeyed easily because I was totally gob-smacked. After a moment or two I noticed that there was a man at his side, white shirt, black bow-tie, a towel draped over a forearm. He smiled and, white-gloved hand extended, gestured gracefully in the direction of a table that had mysteriously appeared and at which, beneath the drooping fronds of a potted palm, Jill and Felicity were already seated. Posh and I had no sooner joined them than another waiter arrived with four flute glasses and a bottle of champagne.

After the waiter had poured and made himself scarce, Mr Posh, or Rupert, raised a glass to Jill and Felicity. 'To the two most beautiful women in pharmaceuticals,' he said. The women giggled politely and we all sipped from our glasses. Champagne was not my drink of choice, and, yet, I was familiar enough with the sparkling wine to realise that whatever it was I'd been imbibing previously, under the guise of champagne, had in fact been some inferior fizzy drink that bore little resemblance to the splendid liquid that now sashayed its way across my tastebuds.

'Two thousand and two, a great vintage, don't you think?' Rupert held his glass aloft, tilting and swirling it so that the light caught shoals of tiny golden bubbles swimming to the foaming surface. He took another drink then stopped, almost choking, smiling. 'Got a good one for you,' he said. 'Julius Caesar walks into a bar and orders a French Martinus. The barman says, don't you mean a French Martini?' By now Rupert was grinning so much he seemed unable to deliver the punchline. 'No, says the bold Julius,' Rupert emitted an involuntary snigger. 'If I'd wanted a double I'd have asked for it.'

The sound of Rupert's laughter was matched in volume only by Felicity's shrieks of merriment. I smiled politely. Jill hid her confusion behind a sip of champagne. Amidst the hilarity, Rupert excused himself. I wasn't sure where he'd gone. Maybe he'd found his joke so funny there had been an under-pant accident and he'd gone to the toilet.

Felicity gave Jill a nudge with her elbow. '*Martinus*. Told you. Rich and funny and with a classical education.'

The two women chatted and I drank more champagne until Rupert returned. When he did, Felicity said, 'forgive me, Robbie, you and Rupert haven't been properly introduced. Robbie Munro meet—'

'Robbie Munro?' Rupert exclaimed. He extended a hand and took one of mine in a firm grip. 'I've heard that name before. In fact I met someone only today who knows *you*. Suzie Lake. The author,' he said to Felicity, who seemed to be the only one in need of clarification.

'You know Suzie Lake?' Jill asked me.

I could feel the colour drain from my face. 'We were at Uni together.'

'You never said.'

'Didn't I? It was a long time ago. She left after the first year. Went on to great things.'

'Do you two keep in touch?' Rupert asked, way too innocently.

'As a matter of fact I met her quite recently,' I said. There was no good trying to conceal the meeting at my office. It could easily come up during one of the frequent sessions Grace-Mary and Jill had to discuss my numerous professional and personal deficiencies. 'She dropped into the office a week or so ago.'

'Suzie Lake was in your office?' Jill asked incredulously.

'Would I have read anything of hers?' Clearly, Felicity was feeling out of things.

Jill ignored her. 'Why would Suzie Lake come to see you?'

'Just looking for a spot of legal advice.' I tapped my nose. 'Confidential. You know how it is.' I took the champagne bottle by the scruff of its neck and studied the label. 'Good stuff this.' I took another swig of vintage champagne, frantically thinking of something I could say to change the subject. Fortunately, I didn't have to. Felicity removed a mobile phone from her sparkly clutch and studied the little glowing screen. 'It's a text from Hercule. Something's cropped up. He's flying in from Bern tonight and wants to meet us first thing. Which means we'll need to go over a few pointers tonight.'

Jill shrugged and pushed her glass away. 'Then, let's go.'

Rupert knocked back his champagne and stood up. 'I'll have my car brought around.' He put an arm around my fiancée's shoulder, while looking at me. 'Anyone ever tell you how lucky you are, Robbie?' He gave Jill a little squeeze, his eyes flashing me a warning. When he spoke, his previously smooth tone had an edge to it, like sand in the gearbox of his limo. 'Whatever you do, don't let her get away.'

Chapter 16

Jill left with the others, leaving behind one puzzled fiancé and a barely touched glass of champagne. The former drank the latter while simultaneously trying to phone Suzie Lake. No answer. I left a voicemail message.

Should I be worried? My wife-to-be off in a limo with the right hand man of a notorious fraudster. A man who seemed to know far too much about me and a certain best-selling author.

When I checked out of the Savannah first thing next morning, my bill had already been settled. I called Jill from Kings Cross. No reply. What was the point of mobile phones? No-one ever seemed to answer them. I left a message thanking her or her Zanetti expense account for covering my stay and saying that I was returning to Scotland and would give her a call later.

I arrived home around noon to find my dad in the kitchen, stirring something in a big pot.

'Oh, it's yourself,' he said, measuring some salt out into his hand, tipping it in and stirring some more. 'Back early are you not?'

'What are you doing here?'

'Thought I'd come round and make you something nice for your tea.'

'Thanks, but you didn't have to do that.'

'No problem. I knew you'd be tired and hungry after your long journey.'

I went over and took a look in the pot. Mince.

'I was going to make some of that spaghetti Bolognese, but they'd run out of spaghetti and I didn't know what else to use. How many kinds of pasta do the Wops need? Got to over-complicate everything. It's just flour and water, what difference does it make if it's long and thin or short with holes in it?'

He went on at some length about Italians, touching momentarily on the war, but what I took from his rant was that he'd decided not to encourage Italian frippery and so we were having plain mince and tatties.

'I've put some peas in it. I know you like it that way,' he said, before shooing me off. 'Away and put your feet up. I'll put some spuds on to boil and we can have an early tea.'

I dipped a teaspoon into the pot and tasted it. Not bad. There were really only two possibilities. Either I had stumbled through some kind of rip in the time/space continuum into a parallel universe or it was all to do with a certain expensive whisky gift. That and the fact my dad was still feeling guilty about having bumped me on Fathers' Day. Might as well milk it. 'Nice mince. Pity, though. It's never the same is it?'

'What isn't?'

'Mince. Without doughballs.'

I thought I saw an eyebrow twitch and the ends of his moustaches lower.

'I don't suppose you've got suet?' he said.

He might as well have asked if I had a half dozen fresh Dodo eggs in the fridge.

'Never mind,' he said. 'I'll nip down to the shop. Keep your eye on the pot and give it a wee stir now and again.'

While he was gone Suzie returned my call.

'We need to talk,' I said.

'About the book?'

'About Rupert.'

'Rupert who?'

'Rupert who knows you and who I met in London?'

Someone at the front door.

'When can we meet,' I asked. My dad came in holding a carrier bag. 'Call you tomorrow.' I hung up and put the phone back in my pocket.

'Call who tomorrow?' my dad asked.

'Just a client.'

'Phoning you on a Sunday afternoon?' He walked past me, through the livingroom and into the kitchen.

'Criminal defence,' I said. 'It's twenty-four, seven. Not like you cops and all your days-off-in-lieu if you have to work five minutes over the end of a shift.'

He had his back to me. It stiffened, but he said nothing, just dug into the carrier bag and produced a box of suet. First mince and doughballs, now I could slag off the cops without any come-back. The loss of a four thousand pound bottle of whisky was almost worth it.

I left him to it while I went for a shower and changed from one shirt and a pair of jeans into another, cleaner shirt and a different pair of jeans. By the time I had returned to the kitchen he was pounding a pot of spuds like he hated Walter Raleigh.

'Ever heard of a Victor Devlin?' I asked.

My dad's mental database of Scotland's known felons whirred into action. 'Big time fraudster.' He gave the pot of potatoes a final pummelling. 'Carried out a scam all to do with mobile phones and one of you lot got him off.'

'What about an associate of his, Rupert someone?'

He wiped his brow with a sleeve and set down the masher after piling heaps of potato onto two plates. 'Rupert who?' he said, turning his attention to the pot of mince.

'I don't know his second name. I think—'

'Och, never mind all that. Take a break from your work for five seconds, I have some important news.' He eased out big dollops of mince and fluffy-white doughballs with a wooden spoon and carried the heaped plates over to the table, where he set them down beside a bottle of HP sauce.

He took a seat and patted the chair next to him. 'I've made a decision.'

I joined him at the table.

'The Black Bowmore. I'm going to open it. No point dying and letting you and Malky inherit. You'd probably sell it.'

No probably about it. I had just one question. 'When?' If I was going to lose out financially, I wasn't going to lose out gourmetically.

'I don't know the exact date. Yet.'

'Come on. What's the big occasion? Wait a minute - are you taking about my wedding day?'

My dad poked a gravy-soaked doughball into his face and shook his head. He chewed for a moment. 'No, there will be plenty enough whisky around that day, once you hurry up and speak to Jill about the miniatures.'

'Then when?' I asked. 'I know you. You'll have your golfing buddies round one night, and I'll not get so much as a sniff at the cork.'

'Not at all.' He mashed some mince and potatoes together, added a splodge of HP sauce and balanced the lot on the end of his fork. 'You'll get a taste, but there's only one occasion special enough to merit a dram of the Black Bowmore.' He pushed the whole lot in and spoke with his mouthful. 'You, me and Malky will wet the head of your first born with it.'

Chapter 17

I woke Monday morning after another bad night's sleep. Rupert: who was he and what did he want? If ex-police sergeant Alex Munro hadn't heard of him, Mr Posh couldn't have much in the way of form, that was for sure; however, if my dad had been of no help, other than by dishing up a fine plate of mince and tatties, he had given me a line of investigation with his remark about Victor Devlin: *'one of you lot got him off.'*

While I was at court that morning I asked around and discovered that in connection with his VAT difficulties, Victor Devlin had been represented by Gail Paton, a lawyer and ever present at Glasgow Sheriff Court who I'd come to know well from my time working in the wild west. Gail had been a defence agent so long that she could probably remember the last time the legal aid fee went up. I made a point of accidentally bumping into her early the next morning in the agents' room of Europe's busiest court building. She was standing in the queue at the snack bar when I sidled up to her.

'Not seen or heard from Devlin in yonks,' she said in reply to my casual question and after we'd shared the usual moans about the lack of prosecutions, legal aid and a Scottish justice secretary intent on creating an English justice system north of the border.

'What was the last case you had for him? VAT fraud or something?' I asked, pretending I hadn't spent the night before checking up everything I could find about Devlin on the internet.

Gail confirmed that Devlin had been shipping mobile phones to the continent and claiming back VAT. 'Been at it for years. Must have made millions. Nothing wrong with doing it, of course, providing the phones actually leave the warehouse. Not always that easy if they've never existed in the first place.'

According to Gail, there had been a lengthy and thorough Customs & Excise investigation and a report submitted to the prosecuting authorities. That's where matters had ended. The case gathered dust on the floor of an over-worked, Crown-depute's floor for a few years until someone had decided it was all just too old, too complicated and too expensive to see the light of a courtroom day.

'Three years of my life I gave that case,' Gail said. 'Trawled through oceans of paperwork and never got anywhere near a court. That's the trouble with those type of cases. The Crown just doesn't have the time, the money or the inclination to see them through to trial.'

I knew what she meant. Most prosecutors knew as much on the intricacies of carousel fraud as they did about how to fill in a legal aid form. And who wanted to run a trial for several months and at great expense, only to lose on the verdict of a bored and confused jury?

We sat down facing the big window looking out over the bleak, greyness of the Clyde and the city beyond. 'What do you know about Tantalite?' I took a sip of coffee from a foam cup, aware that my questioning was straying too far from the casual.

Gail didn't answer, just snapped a chocolate biscuit in half and dunked it.

I tried again. 'Ever come across a friend of Devlin's? Rupert? Big, red-faced guy. Dead posh?'

'I didn't think Devlin had any friends. Lots of enemies mind you.' Gail expertly popped the soggy, yet structurally intact, piece of chocolate biscuit into her mouth and chewed for a moment. 'All right, Robbie. what's up?'

'This Rupert guy came to see me the other day and said he was Devlin's representative.'

'A lawyer?'

'Don't think so.'

'What did he want?'

I couldn't say too much. 'He said Devlin had made a fortune out of mining for some kind of some rare in Africa.'

'Tantalite?'

'That's what he said. Ever heard of the stuff?'

Gail disposed of the second half of the biscuit in like manner to the first. 'I know you either love it or you hate it. No, wait, that's Marmite,' she laughed, displaying a set of chocolaty front teeth. 'Sounds to me like you've been a victim of a prank, Robbie old son.' Finishing her coffee, she reached for her court gown. 'Seriously, Robbie. No offence, but if Victor Devlin was looking for legal advice, I think he'd come to see me - personally - not send a rep to see you. Me and Victor go way back. I can remember when he was making fortunes on dodgy endowments in the eighties. I know —'

'Where the bodies are buried?'

'Not exactly, but I do have directions to the cemetery.' She licked the chocolate off her teeth, dabbed gently at her lipstick with a paper tissue and smiled. 'No, what I was going to say was that I know there are angry people out there who'd love to get a piece of Victor Devlin. He's ruined a lot of lives. Right now I'd be surprised if he was even in the country. You need to watch you don't get suckered into doing something crazy.'

I took her advice with a shrug and we chatted some more. Shortly before ten the room cleared in a flurry of black gowns heading for the various courts throughout the building and I left for Queen Street station to catch the Edinburgh bound train.

I arrived at Waverley Station about half eleven and as I climbed the New Steps to the Lawnmarket, I wondered why Rupert, whoever he was, would pose as Victor Devlin's representative? What was on the memory-stick? What had happened to it? He'd been so keen to recover the thing and then when he had the chance to talk to me in London, he didn't even raise the subject.

The more I thought about my trip to Devlin's coastal hideaway, the more I thought it strange that, if Rupert really believed the cottage to be under surveillance, he'd chosen me. Why not someone who might actually get away with it? I had umpteen clients who would have done a better break-and-entry job and for a lot less money than I'd been offered. I mean twenty grand? What was it Gail had said? *You need to watch you don't get suckered into something crazy.*

Sound advice. But possibly too late.

Chapter 18

Mobile phone reception was poor in the High Court, so I stood on the pavement outside and phoned Suzie. She sounded pleased to hear from me. I couldn't help remembering the hotel room, her naked body and what might have happened, but for Jill's unexpected early arrival. I had a lot to ask her and no time to do it in, so we arranged to meet the following day after the preliminary hearing.

In the advocates library on the second floor, Fiona Faye, my perennial first choice QC, was sitting at the highly-polished mahogany table in the centre of the room. She was reading the only Hello magazine amidst a forest of Scotsman and Herald newspapers.

'About time,' she said, when she saw me homing-in on the coffee-making facilities.

'You having one?' I asked, pouring coffee into one of the white porcelain cups on the sideboard.

'There's no time for coffee, Robbie, we were supposed to be meeting the Advocate Depute at eleven-thirty. It's quarter to twelve.' Where's your client?'

Prosecuting counsel was Cameron Crowe, my second favourite prosecutor in the world; my first favourite being all the others. Meetings with Crowe were never happy affairs and for the moment my client was best kept out of his reach.

'Not coming,' I said, sipping with unnecessary caution on a lukewarm brew.

'How can he sign an affidavit if he's not here?'

'He can't,' I said. 'But he can be brow-beaten into agreeing a deal by Cameron Crowe, which I don't think will be in his best interests. So I've told him to stay away and leave the bargaining to the experts. There will be plenty of time to sign before the preliminary hearing tomorrow, *if* we can get a reasonable deal out of the Crown.'

A not so merry member of the band of junior counsel trudged into the room and tossed his wig onto the table. He had the face of a man who'd literally lost his appeal. Fiona called over to him. 'Jamie, be a doll, nip along to the AD's room and let him know I'll be there in five minutes. Something unexpected has cropped up.'

The junior rolled his eyes, about turned and left the room. Fiona came over and poured herself a coffee. She looked at my cup. 'Did you pay for that?' Without waiting for a reply and assuming, correctly, that my answer would have been to the negative, she dropped some coins onto a saucer that was heaped with loose change.

'So, tell me,' she said. 'What, in the eyes of Robbie Munro, would be a reasonable deal?'

I finished my coffee in one swig and set down the cup and saucer. 'If Starrs gives evidence he should walk.' Suzie was right. I was Robbie Munro. What kind of deal was it for one of my clients to plead guilty to one charge just because the Crown agreed to drop another they hadn't a snowball's chance of proving?

'Seriously? The Crown is offering to drop the murder charge and you want them to drop the attempt to defeat charge as well?'

'Why not? There's no way they can prove the murder against Starrs,' I said.

'Robbie,' Fiona slipped effortlessly into the tone that had softened the granite heart of many a High Court Judge. 'You've done a great job so far, but we both know that the only reason this deal is on is because Cameron Crowe wants to be a judge and the road to a red jersey is paved with high profile convictions. Somehow you've managed to persuade him that the Crown's best chance for a conviction is to go against Dominic Quirk alone and use Starrs as a witness. That's what I call a result for your client. Don't force Crowe's hand. If the Prince of Darkness runs the pair of them to trial he might just win. It's a thin case, and you can never tell with a jury. Never mind the evidence, a girl has been killed and there's a couple of rich boys in the dock.'

'Starrs isn't rich. He's on legal aid, remember?'

'He's at St Andrews Uni and a pal of Dominic Quirk. So far as the jury will be concerned he's a stuck-up kid.'

I thought it over. I knew what juries were like, but Crowe also knew what Fiona Faye's and Big Jock Mulholland's jury-speeches were like. With that pair acting for the two accused, anything was possible. 'If my client is going to grass on his pal, he deserves something for it and several years on the protection wing at Shotts isn't what I had in mind.'

'Helping to dispose of a body is a serious crime. This isn't the JP Court and a charge of fly-tipping.' One sip of cool coffee was enough for Fiona. She put her cup down beside mine on the sideboard.

The depressed junior counsel arrived at her side, back from passing the message of our delay. 'Any more little jobs for me?' he asked. 'Spot of lion-taming? Crocodile-wrestling?'

'AD growing a tad impatient?' Fiona asked.

'You could say.'

'Sorry, about that, Jamie,' Fiona said. 'Have a coffee on me.' She gestured to her discarded cup. 'I've only just poured that.' She turned to me. 'I'm not happy about this, Robbie. I've more or less told Crowe the whole thing is a done deal. Have you bothered to ask your client for his views? These aren't your dice to roll.'

When I wanted my client's opinion I'd give it to him. This was high stakes poker and I didn't want my client throwing his hand in while he was holding all aces. 'Why should he plead guilty to the only thing the Crown can actually prove? I don't call that reasonable.'

'It's reasonable because otherwise there is a risk, slight though you think it may be, of his being convicted of murder.'

I disagreed. 'No, there's got to be give and take. The Crown give Starrs a walk and they get to take Dominic Quirk off on a life sentence.'

'Got it all worked out, haven't you?'

I liked to think so.

Fiona sighed. 'Come on then. Better not keep his Lordship-to-be waiting.'

Chapter 19

To my mind, wanting to be a judge should have been a bar to judicial appointment, but, scarily, there was a real danger that one day Cameron Crowe Q.C. would be granted his most fervent wish. You could count on the fingers of a leper's hand the number of Scotland's top defence Q.C.'s who had been elevated to the Bench and, yet, for a Lord Advocate, the offer of a red silk robe and horsehair wig were as guaranteed as the copper-bottomed, publicly-funded pension.

Yes, there was nothing the Judicial Appointments Board looked for more in a candidate than a keenness to prosecute and so, after the briefest of stints at the defence bar, Crowe had returned to Crown Office as a depute to the Lord Advocate, Scotland's top prosecutor, a man kept busy clamping-down on crime, providing his definition of crime coincided with that of the redtop newspapers and a posse of politically correct pressure groups.

When Fiona and I walked into his room, Crowe was sitting spider-like in a large leather armchair. He successfully fought off the urge to give us a welcoming smile and with a wave of a bony hand, gestured towards some chairs in a corner.

'Your client not here?' Crowe asked, after Fiona and I had dragged over and sat down on two chairs that were considerably smaller and a lot less well upholstered than the AD's own.

Fiona said nothing, just tilted her head at me.

'I've read over the draft affidavit. Seems fine,' I said. 'Starrs will sign once we're all quite clear on what's to happen to him.'

'I am clear,' Crowe said. 'Crystal in fact.'

'Robbie thinks the lad should walk,' Fiona said, before I had the chance.

Crowe's brows met. 'Walk? Walk where? Walk free?'

'He talks the talk, you let him walk,' I confirmed.

'I don't think setting it to a rap track is going to help,' Fiona said to me out of the corner of her mouth.

Crowe screwed up his face as though having difficulty picturing my client without steel bars in the foreground. 'But he's guilty. He helped dump the murder victim. When they caught him his hands were still dirty. He's admitted it.' Crowe banged the top of his desk with a fist, making a row of pens jump about. 'I know I'm only Queen's Counsel, but in what way does that make him *not* guilty?'

I had to concede that there were certain unhelpful adminicles of evidence; however, Crowe was missing the point. I put it as simply as I could. 'In return for you dropping both charges, he gives you Dominic Quirk on a plate. He's happy, you're happy, the dead girl's family is happy, most of all the Lord Advocate and the Daily Record are happy. In fact only Dominic Quirk is unhappy and that's really what you want isn't it?'

Crowe leaned across at me, teeth like daggers, hands clasped on the desk top, knuckles whitening. 'But I've already agreed to drop the murder,' he said through clenched teeth.

'I know. Because you can't prove it. Not exactly deal of the century is it? You might as well chuck in a charge of treason and say you'll drop that too.'

Crowe sat back in his chair. He unclasped his hands, donned a pair of reading glasses, picked some sheets of paper from the desk and began to read. After a short time he lowered the sheets of paper, raised his spectacles and stared at us as though surprised we were still there. He stretched his lips, revealing no ivory.

'So, is that agreed then?' I asked.

Crowe returned his gaze to the sheets of paper and flicked one over. 'Thanks for coming,' he said, eyes not leaving the page. 'See you in court.'

Fiona put a hand on my arm and squeezed. When she stood up, I did too. I crossed the room with her expecting we'd be called back the moment we reached the doorway, like a couple of tourists given a Moroccan market-seller the old walk-away routine. The call never came.

'I hope you know what you're doing,' Fiona said, as we parted company at the top of the stairs.

'He's just playing hard to get.'

Fiona wasn't so sure. 'I think we better consult with the client first thing, before the preliminary hearing. I'll let you explain to him what just happened.'

'Don't worry,' I said. 'Mark Starrs has every faith in me. He'll understand.'

Chapter 20

'You did what!'

Mark Starrs was not cut out for a life of crime. For a start there was his hair. Red is never a good colour for a criminal; the ginger is always ID'd. Then there was his fondness for the sound of his own voice. Maybe that was why he had decided to study drama, but there was a time and a place for monologuing; Macbeth act two, scene one? Fine. St Andrews police station when detained on a murder charge? Not so fine. Is this a confession I see before me? You bet it is.

Leaving aside his propensity for talking to police officers, Starrs was a polite young man, respectful and happy to take my advice. I liked him. His parents were a different matter. They'd split-up many years before. Mr Starrs senior now lived in Glasgow, Mrs Starrs in Perth with their only child. There had been two or three procedural diets so far along the way. One or other of my client's parents always came along for those appearances, usually Mr Starrs, who, though easier to deal with, was generally very angry about something. The polar-opposite was my client's mother. With Mrs Starrs around, understandably worried though she was, it was difficult to fit a word in sideways and, when I did, it was only because she was having one of her panic attacks and I'd have to repeat myself over and over again before she could understand what was happening.

For that reason, when the whole constellation of Starrs arrived in Edinburgh that Wednesday morning, for the preliminary hearing in Her Majesty's Advocate against Dominic Quirk and Mark Starrs, I left both anxious parents in the Lower Aisle café below St Giles Cathedral, while I escorted my client across the road to the High Court. The hearing wouldn't take long. Better for Mr and Mrs Starrs to stay where they were and have a coffee and one of Edinburgh's finest fruit scones rather than run the gauntlet of press photographers and TV cameras. It also allowed me to speak to their son alone and explain why he wouldn't be pleading guilty to an attempt to defeat the ends of justice that morning and why he still faced a murder charge.

'But you said it was a done deal. Last time we met you said I'd plead guilty to helping Dominic dispose... get rid...you know... and they'd drop the murder charge. What went wrong?'

Fiona in full battlefield regalia: crisp silk gown, high necked white blouse with pearl buttons, cleared her throat, but didn't speak. We were standing on the first floor landing, solicitors and advocates, punters and clerks crisscrossing this way and that around us. In another corner, the Quirks: father and son, Paul Sharp and the towering figure of Jock Mulholland Q.C. stood discussing their defence. If they'd managed to find one.

'It's like this, Mark,' I said. 'The Crown needs you to prove the case against Dominic. If you keep schtum, they've got nothing.'

Fiona gave another little cough.

'Well... Not very much.'

'But it could be enough?' Starrs said.

'Possibly against Dominic. I just can't see a sufficiency of evidence against you.'

'But if it goes to trial, even if I'm found not guilty of murder, I'm still going to be found guilty on the other charge, so what's the point?'

Fiona studied the pristine white paintwork of the high ceiling.

'It won't come to that,' I said. 'Once the AD has applied his very small but vindictive brain to the issues, he'll realise he needs you and do what we ask. After all, it's only reasonable. What kind of deal would it be if you gave the

Crown what they wanted but they didn't give you what you wanted?'

Starrs remained unconvinced. 'I was happy with the deal we had. I told you that. I'm twenty-two next month. I can do a couple of years in jail. I can't do life.'

I shook my head. 'If the AD wants to play hardball, so can we. If things work out, you won't be going to jail at all.'

'You mean that?'

The look of hope in his eyes made me feel suddenly nauseous. 'Yes. If all goes to plan.'

He turned to Fiona who at that moment was finding something fascinating about the three vertical abstract tapestries, hanging on the exterior wall of courtroom three. 'Really? No prison?'

A loudspeaker announced the calling of the case. We went into court. The two accused entered the dock and took up position between a couple of security officers. Jock Mulholland was first up to bat. He intimated a plea of not guilty and requested a continued diet in two weeks' time to enable those instructing him to finalise certain enquiries with regards to the instruction of an expert witness. He didn't expand further. If he'd been junior counsel, the judge would have been firing questions at him and jumping him through all sorts of procedural hoops, but if Jock Mulholland Q.C. said he needed more time to prepare then that was good enough for the man on the bench.

Fiona was next up. She confirmed a plea of not guilty, advised the court that, though her client's case was fully prepared, she would have no objection to a continuation.

So far so good.

Cameron Crowe rose to his feet, a glint in his eye. I had expected him to oppose any further delay in proceedings. He didn't. 'I am content that a further and final hearing be set down two weeks hence, M'Lord.' He handed some typed sheets of paper to his Crown junior who handed one to the Clerk and then came around the table and presented first

Paul and then myself with copies. A section 67 notice. A criminal indictment must be served twenty-nine days before the trial starts. It includes details of the charges as well as all the witnesses to be called by the Crown. Additional witness can be added by giving notice to the defence seven days prior to a preliminary hearing. Surprise witnesses only happened in the movies. By seeking a continuation of the preliminary hearing, the defence had opened the door to a new prosecution witness.

The clerk announced the date of the continued diet and the hearing was over. The macer pulled back the judge's chair, the man in the wig and red silk gown stood up and everyone else followed suit.

Dominic Quirk was led away downstairs. Since the adoption of the European Convention on Human Rights in 1999, murder-accused had been eligible for bail in Scotland. It was a principle, like many others set down in European law, which the Scottish courts tried their hardest not to follow whenever possible.

Dominic's previous road traffic conviction for leaving the scene of a fatal accident, had been enough to convince the Sheriff at Cupar, before whom the two accused had first appeared on petition, that he might be a flight risk and as such not a suitable candidate for bail, and, though that decision had been appealed, the High Court had not seen fit to interfere with the Sheriff's view on the matter.

I met my client as he emerged from the dock and we stood to one side to allow the prosecution team to file past. I held out the section 67 notice to him and pointed to the name.
'Who's he?'

Starrs stared down at the piece of paper and then looked up at me. I'd seen pints of milk with healthier complexions. Beads of cold sweat studded the roots of his fringe. He shook his head, and then returned his gaze to the sheet of paper. 'I've never heard of him.'

Cameron Crowe at the rear of the Crown party reached us and stopped, looming over my client like the angel of death. He had a lot of white teeth and they were all on display. 'Well, Mr Starrs,' he said. 'He sure as hell knows you.'

Chapter 21

After an uncomfortable after-court chat with my client, and a promise that we would consult again soon, I set off for my rendezvous with Suzie. She was waiting for me beneath the Scott Monument on Princes Street, clinging to a small wicker picnic basket.

'It's such a nice day, I thought we could lunch al fresco,' she said, and we strolled together along the walkway to Princes Street gardens and down the grassy slopes to the lawns. Clear blue sky, a warm breeze, flower beds in full bloom and the castle rock a magnificent backdrop. It was the sort of beautiful day that Edinburgh could muster only occasionally, but, when it did, there was nowhere quite like it. We found a relatively secluded spot on the grassy parkland that was host to a number of open air diners and as Suzie threw a tartan travel rug across the closely mown surface, the one o'clock gun sounded from the nearby castle battlements. The noise made me jump and scattered a passel of pigeons. A few passers-by paused to check their watches.

'What do you think of this as an idea for a murder?' Suzie asked. 'Picture the scene. The victim is found dead at Edinburgh Castle or somewhere nearby. He's been shot in broad daylight, but no-one heard a thing. Why?' Before I could suggest that a silencer might have been used, Suzie answered her own question. 'Because the murderer timed the fatal shot to coincide with the one o'clock gun.'

She looked pleased. I felt worried. Was it a scene from one of her books? The ones I'd told her I enjoyed so much, but hadn't actually read? I really should say something. 'Difficult to time the two shots exactly. Synchronicity is everything.' I smiled and gave a little involuntary laugh.

Suzie flushed' What's so funny?'

'Nothing.'

'It must be something or you wouldn't be laughing. What's wrong. My plot-lines not up to scratch?'

Touchy. Lesson one when talking to authors: anything other than unalloyed praise of their work is considered criticism. I'd have to explain. 'I was cross-examining a witness once. She was a former school teacher, literally old-school, like something out of the Prime of Miss Jean Brodie. It was all to do with historic acts of violence towards pupils in the sixties and seventies. The sort of acts seen as horrific these days, but, back then, a dunt across the earhole was all in a day's work and helped concentrate a pupil's mind.'

Suzie's pretty face was now wearing a wry expression, not buying any of what I was saying. 'My plot. *Synchronicity is everything*?' She reminded me.

'Well she needed to fart, but in the witness box there's nowhere to hide.'

'And?'

'She coughed to camouflage the sound except she coughed too early. The coughing finished and...' I provided the necessary sound effects to finish the story. 'Without the required synchronicity, the cough only highlighted the fart and what she'd been trying to do which, of course, made the whole thing much funnier. Some of the jury corpsed and the Sheriff had to adjourn the court for ten minutes. The same would happen with a gunshot and the one o'clock cannon. Unless they both happened simultaneously, one would draw more attention to the other. Witnesses would remember the day they heard two one o'clock guns. That would be worse for the murderer than letting off one random—'

'Okay, I get it,' Suzie said. She coughed, blew a raspberry and started to laugh. 'You should write a book of these stories.'

I didn't remember Jill being so enamoured by that particular tale when I'd recounted it to her and, yet, who didn't love a fart gag?

'Seriously, I'll put my agent on to you.' Suzie looked over her shoulder and jerked a thumb westwards. 'I should have asked him to come down and have lunch with us, his offices are just the other end of Princes Street .' She opened the picnic hamper and set down a plastic box of sandwiches, a brown paper bag, two glasses and finally a bottle of red wine which she cracked open while I dived into the tub of sandwiches. Suzie was a vegetarian. She'd either made up a couple of tuna pieces especially for me or else, like a lot of veggies, she thought that fish was a fruit.

Suzie passed me a glass of wine.

'About London...' I said.

'You snore a lot, did you know that?'

It had been remarked on previously, so I let that topic of conversation drift away with dandelion seeds. 'You didn't just bump into me did you? I mean what were the chances?'

Suzie bit the corner off a water cress and egg sandwich. Chickens or, at least their unfertilised ovum, weren't meat either. 'I've made a good start on the new book,' she said, after a few chews. 'More or less drafted a rough outline for part one. The rest—'

'I met a man called Rupert in London, the night after I met you. He said he knew you.'

'A lot of people do. I'm a famous author, remember?'

'A famous author with two agents?'

Suzie didn't say anything, just chewed chopped-egg and cress.

'You told me when we met in London that you were down seeing your agent,' I said as unaccusingly as I could. 'Now you've just told me your agent is based right here in Edinburgh.'

Suzie set the uneaten half of her sandwich down on the travel rug and wiped her mouth with one of the red paper napkins that were held in a little pouch on the inside of the hamper lid. 'Is this why you wanted to see me? To practice your cross-examination techniques?'

'I'm just wondering why you lied to me, that's all,' I said, prepared on this occasion to overlook the suggestion that my cross-examination techniques weren't sufficiently honed already. Defence lawyers could be sensitive to criticism too.

Suzie held my gaze for a long moment and then lost our staring competition by reaching for her glass of wine. 'I didn't lie to you. Not completely. I went to London to see Rupert, but he's not my agent, he's a financial adviser. He wanted to talk to me about a new publishing deal I have in the offing. My present agent doesn't know about it and I don't want it leaking out that I might be jumping ship, so I'm terribly sorry that I didn't tell you the truth, the whole truth and nothing but the truth.' She smiled mirthlessly, then cheered up and gave me a friendly shove. 'A girl's got to have some secrets you know.'

Posh Rupert an investment adviser. Why didn't that surprise me? I remembered what Jill had said about him. A man with digits in a portfolio of corporate pies. 'Is Rupert's surname top secret too?' I asked.

Suzie drank some wine, dabbed her lips again. 'Smith.'

I gave her an is-that-the-best-you-can-come-up-with look.

'That's his name. Smith. Oh, and, while I'm confessing my sins, no, I didn't just happen to bump into you. I called your office and your secretary said you'd gone to London for a few days. I asked where you were staying and she told me. It wasn't exactly a job for the intrepid D.I. Debbie Day.'

I could only apologise. 'I don't mean to pry into your affairs, I was just worried about you.'

Suzie looked puzzled. 'Why on earth—'
'Have you ever heard of Victor Devlin?'
She hadn't.
'Well I have. He's a world class conman.'
'So?'

'This Rupert Smith is an associate of his. He came to see me recently—'

'Who did?'

'Rupert. He was asking for some... legal advice in relation to his boss.'

'What sort of legal advice did he want?' she asked.

I didn't answer.

'Oh, I see. Confidential is it?' Point made, Suzie took another bite of sandwich. On such a warm summer's day I could detect a distinct touch of frost. 'So is that the only reason you wanted to see me? To check up on me?'

Though the answer to that question was yes, I decided to phrase it another way. 'No, of course not.'

'Then why?'

'I thought you'd want to know what happened in court today.' Come to think of it, if Suzie was so keen on writing a book about the Dominic Quirk case why hadn't she been there? The hearing hadn't been in private.

Suzie relaxed. She finished the sandwich, lightly dusted crumbs from her fingers and ripped the side of the brown paper bag to reveal a couple of sticky-glazed, cinnamon pastries. She took one delicately between thumb and forefinger and with her other hand gently nudged the bag in my direction.

'So it looks like you're all set for trial,' Suzie said, after I'd given her an update on the court proceedings and she had packed everything bar our wineglasses back into the hamper.

'One more preliminary hearing first to make sure everything's ready,' I said. 'And then it's the real thing.'

'What would you do, if it was you?' Suzie asked. 'Would you stay around for trial or head for Brazil or somewhere?'

'Brazil's no good now,' I said. 'You'd need to head for somewhere like Iran or North Korea, somewhere without an extradition treaty.'

'You know what I mean. Would you stay or would you go?'

'Depends.'
'On how guilty you were?'
'On how good my defence was.'
'And if you were Mark Starrs?'
'I'd stick around.'
'Dominic Quirk?'
'He's got no option. He's on remand so he has to stick around.'

'Doesn't seem very fair to me,' Suzie said. 'Both charged with the same crimes and one is out and about, the other banged up.'

'One has a previous conviction, one doesn't,' I said. 'It's still possible that Quirk could get out before trial, if there was some substantial change in his personal circumstances that allowed the High Court to reconsider and grant him bail.'

'Like what?'

I couldn't think of anything obvious offhand. The most common reason for accused persons being released on bail was because the Crown couldn't start the trial within the one hundred and forty day time limit.

'How long has he been in so far?' Suzie asked.

'Let me see. Got to be well over a hundred days by now. Anyway, it's academic. The Crown seem to be ready. They've cited a new witness, but apart from that it's all systems go.'

'If I were your client I'd disappear,' Suzie said. 'Not to Iran. I'd just move to the Highlands or slip over the channel, go to Bulgaria or somewhere, change my name and work as a grape-picker.'

I laughed. 'Maybe in one of your books. In real life, people don't just move to the Highlands or slip across international borders. We live on an island. An island with the most CCTV in the world. Mark Starrs would be traced and arrested in a matter of weeks.'

'And if money was no object?'

'For Mark Starrs money is very much an object and, in any event, if he doesn't turn up the only person benefitting would be Dominic Quirk.'

'How come?'

'Firstly, running away would make Starrs look guilty, which would help any incrimination attempt by Quirk. Secondly, I can't see the Crown running the trial without him. They need Starrs as a witness to incriminate Quirk.'

'So if Starrs didn't show, they'd let Quirk go free?'

'Not exactly. They'd put him on trial by himself if they had to, but they wouldn't be keen. First of all there would be a manhunt for Starrs, during which, Quirk would enjoy some time out on bail. After all, if Starrs did a runner and the trial had to be put off, it wouldn't be Dominic's fault and they couldn't keep him on remand beyond the time limit.'

I was sitting cross-legged. Suzie had been sitting on a hip, propped up on one arm. Without warning, she uncoiled, reclined and rested her head on my thigh. She closed her eyes. The light breeze blew a strand of hair across her forehead and I only just managed to resist the urge to brush it back.

Suzie sighed contentedly. 'And this new witness. Do you know what he is going to say?'

I had absolutely no idea and right at that moment I could not have cared less.

Chapter 22

Thursday. Remand court day at Falkirk Sheriff Court and, compared to the usual stagnant flow of business at Livingston, things were moving along like an express train. Why couldn't all my clients commit crimes in this jurisdiction? My case called, my client was made the subject of a community pay-back order and I was sitting in the court café drinking coffee, or something very like it, by half past.

Paul Sharp came up the stairs after a visit to the cells. These days my friend's attire was not quite the show-stopping material it had once been. Gone was the sixties gear, the safari suits, cravats, skinny trousers, skinny lapels and even skinnier ties. Paul wanted to be a Sheriff. I knew he'd applied once and been knocked back. Although he'd never mentioned it to me, I did wonder if someone had had a word in his ear about his dress sense. It was all very well having a personality disorder, it was more or less expected in the average Sheriff, but wearing funny clothes? Not on, old boy.

Paul came over to the table where I was sitting and threw his gown and case file onto the marble bench that ran around the circumference of the semi-circular café. He went to the counter and pumped a large silver vacuum flask.

'Another satisfied client,' he said upon his return, carrying a foam cup filled with a murky brew. Paul had been acting for my client's less fortunate co-accused. A man who, with three pages of previous and a couple of bail contraventions to boot, was now on vacation courtesy of the Queen. 'Four months was about right. He was always going to get at least one month consec for the bail act. He'll be out before your client has finished his two hundred hours, Robbie.'

We were joined by a local lawyer, Simon Kendall. Everyone called him Minty, after the cakes, I assumed. He brought with him tea, not in a polystyrene cup like the rest of us, but in his own mug. A moment or so later one of the counter girls came across with a cheese toastie on a paper plate. Minty ripped open a small sachet of salt and, like a farmer sowing seed on a tiny ploughed field, sprinkled grains of salt into the ridges of the top slice; presumably the combination of cheese and fried bread wasn't sufficiently unhealthy already. 'Good to see you two on speaking terms,' he said.

'Why wouldn't we be?' I asked.

Carefully balancing the toastie so as not to let any of the salt run off, Minty took a bite, recoiled and dropped it onto the plate. For a moment or two he juggled a blob of molten cheese in his mouth, before spitting it out on to the plate. 'Ow, ya bastard! That's f—'

'Hot?' Paul enquired.

Minty looked round accusingly at the girl who'd brought him the dangerous food item. 'These things should come with a health and safety warning,' he yelled in the direction of her two fingers. There then followed a passionate, if unedifying, rant from Minty on the subject of delictual liability for the non-risk assessment of toasted-bread products, which Paul and I endured while we drank our coffee and the offending toastie cooled down to a safer temperature.

As Minty risked another bite, Paul drained the last of his coffee. He either had an asbestos-coated mouth or took his extra-milky because I'd hardly started mine. He looked at his watch. 'Got to go,' he said, grabbing his gown and file. 'See you, Minty, catch you later, Robbie.'

'Busy man,' Minty said. 'Glad someone is.'

'What did you mean about being pleased to see me and Paul still on speaking terms?' I asked.

'I was kidding. I know you two are pals. You've got to do what you've got to do.' He put a straight index finger across his top lip and sat up straight. 'I voss only following orders,' he said in a high-pitched voice.

'You've really got that Welsh accent off pat,' I said. 'But, really. What are you talking about?'

'The big case.' By this time Minty was crunching through the toastie like the Third Reich through northern France circa 1940. 'I was talking to Jock Mulholland yesterday afternoon, trying to instruct him in a murder. Dead straight forward, just an assault that went a bit wrong, but he wouldn't touch it. He's taking no new instructions until you and Paul's case is over.'

I already knew that Quirk's father had insisted the Q.C. took on no other work.

'Nearly broke his heart turning me down. You know what Big Jock's like,' Minty said. 'Usually charging all over the place, running two trials at a time, leaving his juniors to do all the work and if you're lucky he might actually turn up to do the jury speech. Makes it up as he goes along half the time.'

'Seems to work for him,' I said.

Minty nodded on agreement, pulling a piece of toastie away from his mouth, trying to sever stretchy strings of cheese at the same time. 'Jock told me you've lodged a section seventy-eight and are going to incriminate Quirk.'

'So?'

'So, I was just kidding about you and Paul not being on speaking terms.'

'Big Jock tell you anything else about the case – or did he put an advert in the paper?'

'It wasn't like that, Robbie. Just chat between lawyers. You know how it is, but if you'd rather not talk—'

'What was he saying?'

'Nothing much. Just that the trial was going ahead. I was hoping there might have been a plea and I could have instructed him in my case.' Minty washed down the last morsel of toastie with a long drink of tea and placed the mug on his head.

The girl from behind the counter came over, took it from him and patted his hair. 'You all right Minty, pet? Want me to phone your mum next time and get her to come and blow on your din-dins?'

'Did Jock say anything else?' I asked, after Minty had waved her away.

'Not really. I'd describe him as quietly confident.'

'Doubt it,' I said. 'Dominic Quirk's defence team has nothing to be confident about, quietly or loudly.'

Minty shrugged. 'All I wanted to know was if Jock would be available. He's not available until after your trial is out of the way. He said he thought at one point there might have been some kind of deal organised, his client pleading to a culpable homicide or something, but that because of a recent development the case was a definite runner. You and Paul will know better than me if that's right.'

New developments? Paul might know what they were, but I didn't. Come to think of it, where was Paul rushing off to in such a hurry? He'd knocked back that cup of coffee like he was dousing a fire in his stomach.

One of Minty's junkie clients came into the café, wanting to speak to him about a warrant for an unpaid fine - like there was any other kind of fine.

I stood up and collected my things. Maybe I could catch Paul in the agents' room before he left. As I made my way to the door, I looked out of the window and saw him leaving the court building at a trot. Whatever it was that made Big Jock Mulholland quietly confident, I wasn't about to find out from his instructing solicitor anytime soon.

Chapter 23

The electronic age had dawned slowly on the average criminal defence lawyer, who, while forced to do certain administrative tasks on-line, still depended largely on dead trees for the day-to-day practice of law. iPads, laptops and USB sticks were all very well, but sometimes you needed a piece of paper to wave at somebody and that's why I kept case files.

When the doors to Munro & Co. first opened, I had a fairly orthodox filing system: every new case was given its very own plain, buff-coloured folder with the client's name on the front. It was simple, but, I thought, effective. Grace-Mary saw room for improvement. Soon, summary cases were put into pale blue folders, solemn into red and the old buff folders were reserved for miscellaneous bumph. The problem was that sometimes we ran out of certain colours.

Friday morning, my secretary stomped into my room. 'I wish you'd stop doing this.'

At the time I didn't know what she was going on about, and too busy filling-in yet another legal aid form to bother looking up at her.

'Robbie, you know this is a pet hate of mine,' she said, not really narrowing things down. My secretary had so many pet hates she could have started her own zoo. I kept on completing the form until a blue folder was shoved on top of it and under my nose.

'Writing 'This is a Red Folder' on a light blue file doesn't actually change its colour,' Grace-Mary said. 'How am I supposed to carry out a proper file check if the colours are all wrong?'

She dropped the file on my desk. It was the new correspondence folder I'd opened for Mark Starrs because the first was bursting at the seams. The most recent addition was the recently-served section 67 notice, intimating the Crown's latest witness: Clyve Cree. I wondered - was he the new development Big Jock had been talking to Minty about? Who was he, apart, that is, from someone whose parents couldn't spell? His address was given as c/o St Andrews police station, to where the initial report concerning dead Doreen had been made. I checked with Grace-Mary. The new witness's police statement had not yet arrived via the Crown's secure email system. I had to find out what he was saying.

For those who couldn't afford a defence the Scottish Legal Aid Board existed. It was supposed to place an accused on the same footing as the prosecution, to ensure an equality of arms and uphold the right to a fair trial to which every accused was entitled under the European Convention of Human Rights. In actual fact SLAB was a government quango, established with the best of intentions no doubt, but now staffed with hordes of civil servants who never darkened the door of a courtroom, but liked to tell those who did how to run a trial - though not how to do it on a rate of pay that hadn't increased in two decades.

In any legally-aided High Court case, the defence, if it was to be properly prepared, had to be subsidised by the defence solicitor, for the fees payable would be funny if the issues not so serious. Take for example Clyve Cree. I knew the Crown would be disclosing the witness's police statement in due course, but those were notoriously inaccurate, full of witnesses egressing from public houses and ambulating in north-westerly directions. I needed to sound this guy out for myself, hear what he had to say in his own words, not in police speak. The trouble was I simply couldn't afford a round trip of one hundred and twenty miles to the East Neuk of Fife; not when I had other business in court that day and not for a legal aid fee of twelve pounds per hour and a mileage rate fixed by someone who didn't know the price of running a car or who did, but didn't like lawyers.

There were two calls I had to make. The first was to the PF's High Court unit. It went surprisingly well. The second, I was sure, would be more difficult.

'But, Robbie, it's half-eleven on a Friday morning...'

My dad had correctly identified the time and date. It was that kind of factual accuracy, developed through years of policing, that made him the ideal man for the job. That and the fact that he wasn't getting paid. 'All you have to do is—'

'And you know very well that I have a two o'clock fourball on a Friday afternoon.'

'So what? Put it back a couple of hours. All you do is drive to St Andrews, take the statement and home again. I've tee'd up the appointment,' bad turn of phrase, 'for the start of the shift at one forty-five. You know where the cop shop is don't you?'

'Robbie—'

'While you're there you might even have time to look around the new whisky shop on South Street. Bound to have some interesting stuff in stock.'

'The answer is—'

'Of course, I'm not sure if they'll stock the Black Bowmore...' I'd played my ace. I waited. And waited.

'I want petrol money.'

'Legal aid rates, forty pence a mile,' I said. 'It's got to be nearly eighty miles there and back.'

'More like a hundred.'

'Done. Now get here as soon as you can so I can fill you in.'

Chapter 24

Never mind the one o'clock gun; no cannon shot was required to tell me when it was 5 pm each day. At one minute to, Grace-Mary's coat was on, at one minute past you'd have needed a bloodhound to find any lingering traces of my secretary in the offices of Munro & Co.

At twenty to five that Friday afternoon, I was in reception with Grace-Mary who was trying to talk me through the new on-line banking system, when my dad marched in.

'All you have to remember is your customer ID and password and you can authorise payments from anywhere,' she said.

I wasn't really that big on sending money to people. Why, if I ever had the notion, I'd want to do it from somewhere other than the comfort of my own office, I didn't know. I let it slide and turned my gaze from the computer monitor to my dad. 'I thought you'd be on the golf course giving your handicap its weekly work out.'

'Golf? Are you kidding? It was roadworks all the way from Auchtermuchty. This is me just back.' My dad rubbed his lumbar region and grimaced. 'There's no chance of me swinging a club this weekend.'

'I'll have Grace-Mary notify the PGA straight away,' I said. 'Now where's the statement?'

'Never fear...' My dad tapped his forehead. 'It's all in here.'

'Well get it all out of there and slap it onto a piece of paper. Do you think SLAB's going to pay me for an imaginary precognition?'

'Don't worry, I'll write something out for you later. First things first.' He approached the reception desk, hand held out. 'Forty quid, please. I should be charging you more considering the amount of time I spent in traffic jams and nothing on the radio except for teuchtar music or Gardeners' Question Time.'

Before I could say anything, Grace-Mary had mined the petty cash box and was counting out four tenners into my dad's enormous outstretched mitt. 'There you are, Mr Munro. Now why don't you come back nice and early Monday morning, tell me all about it and I'll type something up for Robbie?'

'No thanks. I've wasted enough time on this without traipsing in here again next week.' My dad folded the cash into his wallet and returned it to his back pocket. 'Right,' he said, 'there's good news and there's bad news.' He looked around for a seat.

Grace-Mary came from behind the reception desk and pulled a chair over.

My dad nodded his thanks, sat down and made a painful show of crossing one leg over the other. 'The good news is that they abolished the death sentence back in the sixties. The bad news is that this guy Clyve Cree is going to sink your client faster than Armitage Shanks. Okay...' he said, clearly warming to his task, 'the details. Cree seems a nice enough bloke, widower, late-thirties, tall and built like a brick sh...' He smiled at Grace-Mary who was looking up at a clock that showed fifteen minutes to the weekend. 'Like a brick chicken house. He's ex-Army, got no previous and now works in security, nightclubs, personal protection. Not a guy you'd want to mess with. In fact—'

'Did you get a note of his shoe size?' I asked.

'Funny.'

'Then get a move on, Dad. It's Friday. I have a life and Jill will be—'

'In Switzerland this weekend,' Grace-Mary said. 'Do you read any of the notes that I leave on your desk?'

What was she going to Switzerland for, again? I reached into my pocket for my mobile phone. A few months back, Sheriff Brechin hadn't taken kindly to a brief rendition of The Clash's 'I fought the Law' during the PF's speech in a domestic breach, and even though I'd never thought Crown submissions strictly necessary to secure a conviction from Bert Brechin, there had been talk of a finding of contempt if a ring-tone of mine was heard again. I knew nothing would give him greater pleasure than to convict both accused and defence lawyer at the one sitting, and, so, since then my phone had been constantly on silent for fear of further musical interludes.

I checked the phone display: two missed calls. One was from Jill. A small cassette icon on the display indicated a live voice mail message. Great. Another weekend with Jill working.

'Next time you speak to her, remember and tell her about my idea for the favours. I know a guy who knows a guy whose brother used to work for Diageo and can get his hands on a staff discount card. He can get some decent miniatures for—'

I let the phone drop with a clatter onto the desk. 'Would you stop banging on about whisky for five minutes, Dad?'

'It's your wedding I'm talking about. Someone's got to show an interest.'

Grace-Mary clapped her hands together. 'That's enough, the pair of you.' She turned to my dad. 'Mr Munro, if you'll just tell me what the witness said, I'll jot it down in shorthand and type it up later.'

My dad acceded to her suggestion with a grunt.

Grace-Mary turned to me. 'And Robbie...'

'Yes.'

'Put a sock in it.' My secretary took a clean sheet of paper from the desk drawer and poised a sharp-pointed pencil over it.

My dad began his narrative. With a little prompting from Grace-Mary he had Cree's statement summed-up in under five minutes.

Easter Saturday, Cree was on a night out with friends in St Andrews. He wasn't drinking because he was working the following day and had brought the car. The pub had been full of noisy students playing drinking games and he'd left early, using his early start the next morning as an excuse. His car was parked outside the Byre Theatre, and walking back to it around about eleven o'clock he took a short-cut. He couldn't remember the name of the side street; however, he did recall coming across an argument between what he described as a couple of teenagers: a male and a female. He'd thought about intervening but it was over before he could do anything. After the argument the couple had driven off in a blue BMW M3 convertible. Strange enough, but what really stuck in his mind was that he heard the ginger-headed boy say to the girl: 'I'm warning you. If you go near Dominic again, I'll kill you.'

Apparently, Clive with a Y had thought Dominic an unusual name. The incident had stuck in his mind and then he'd read about the case in the newspaper. Two days before the preliminary hearing, he had dropped into St Andrews' police station and provided a statement.

Dropped in and dropped a bomb on Mark Starr's defence.

The phone rang. My secretary answered and listened for a moment. 'It's Zoë,' she said.

'Who?' It took a moment or two for that information to sink in. 'You mean Zoë, Zoë?'

Grace-Mary nodded.

Zoë, Munro & Co.'s former receptionist and one time love of my life, had emigrated to Australia three years before, taking a piece of my heart with her.

'What's she wanting?' My dad growled. He knew exactly who she was.

'What does she want?' I whispered to my secretary.

'To speak to you.'

'Well he's not going to speak to her,' my dad said in a voice that scarcely needed telecommunications to be heard in Australia.

'Ask her to call back,' I said

'Tell her not to bother,' my dad said.

If Grace-Mary looked up at the clock again, she'd wear the face off it. I wondered - what time was it in Australia? Five in the morning or thereabouts I guessed. Had to be important if Zoë was calling so early, but I couldn't speak to her; not with my dad there. Even the most polite chat with my ex-girlfriend would be tantamount to adultery in his eyes.

'Say I'm not here,' I instructed my secretary. 'Take a number and I'll call her later.'

My dad's aching back seemed to have loosened off. He stood up and pushed his face, moustaches all a bristle, into mine. 'No you will not!'

Grace-Mary removed her hand. 'Hang on a sec, Zoë.' She jabbed a finger at me and then at the door and mouthed, 'get out.'

'Sorry Zoë, Robbie must have left.' I heard Grace-Mary say from my position standing outside in the corridor. 'I can't see him.'

I returned to reception once the good-byes had been said and the handset replaced. 'Did I really have to step outside so you couldn't see me?'

'Yes, you did.' Grace-Mary stood. 'And don't bother giving me that look. You don't pay me enough for what I do, far less to tell lies for you as well.' She lifted her handbag and slung it over her shoulder. 'Zoë is looking for a new job.' My dad's face reddened, his eyes began to bulge. 'She wonders if you'll give her a reference and so I told her of course you would. She'll call back next week sometime.' From under her desk, my secretary collected a few carrier bags full of groceries. I was pleased to see that she'd found time, during all the work she wasn't being paid enough to do, for a spot of shopping.

My phone illuminated and began to judder on the desk.

Grace-Mary smiled reassuringly at my dad. 'Don't worry, Mr Munro, Zoë and Robbie—'

'Ancient history,' I said, snatching up my mobile in case it was Jill. It wasn't. It was Suzie. I stuffed the phone into my pocket.

'There's only one woman in Robbie's life,' my secretary said, and, lifting her carrier bags, walked out of the door as the town clock struck five.

Chapter 25

I called Suzie from the safety of my home phone. She wanted to meet and talk about the Quirk case. There wasn't much I could tell her that she didn't know already and, in any case, when she suggested we get together that Friday evening, I had to tell her I was committed elsewhere.

That other commitment had been added to my schedule by my brother, Malky, who, having been tipped-off by my Dad that I was a free agent for the weekend, had called me into the squad for his weekly five-a-side game. There was a group of around fifteen, some of them, like Malky, ex-professional players, others, like me, most certainly not, and because of the inevitable call-offs there was often a problem finding ten willing men last-minute on a Friday night. Things must have been really desperate for him to ask me to come and bring along a pal.

So, instead of a quiet evening in the company of the woman of my dreams, I found myself in a breeze-block changing room, struggling into a Boca Juniors strip that had shrunk since its last outing. From bitter experience, I found it always best to wear some kind of neutral playing-kit when five-a-siding with people you didn't know that well. Unless Malky had invited along a supporter of River Plate, I wouldn't be singled out for special treatment. My jaw had more or less recovered, but I didn't fancy it getting another dunt anytime soon.

Paul Sharp, who had also been pressed into action, had decided to come along in a replica of the Celtic strip circa 1967.

'Did you forget that Malky used to play for Rangers?' I asked him as he drove me home after the game.

Paul didn't answer, just grunted in pain as he pressed down on the clutch to change gear.

'A lot of the people who play on a Friday are Rangers supporters. Not everyone has Malky's ecumenical outlook on Scottish football and—'

'I was asking for it, is that what you're saying?'

'No. Just that if you are playing against a bunch of has-been or wanna-be blue-noses, probably best not to cross yourself when you score a goal.'

The traffic lights ahead changed to amber and Paul let out another involuntary groan as he clutched and braked. 'Point taken, though, actually, I'm not so sure sectarian influences were at work,' he said. 'Some of the Huns had a nibble at me, but it was the fat guy in the Hibs' top that crocked me.'

I remembered the incident. Paul had been racing down the right and about to cut in on goal when he'd been scythed down by a tackle that wasn't so much late as early for next week's game.

We came to a halt at the red light. 'I thought you were going to do a Dominic Quirk and jump it,' I said, using the moment to rather clumsily raise the issue of the upcoming trial.

'I wondered how long it would take you to bring that up.'

'How long have you known?' I asked.

'About what?'

'Not what - who - Clyve Cree.'

Paul kept looking straight ahead as the amber light came on and he readied to move off again. 'Look, Robbie, it's half-nine on a Friday night. I can't go for a pint because I'm driving, the wife's got a weekend of DIY lined up for me and my left ankle is throbbing like buggery. I'm not in the mood for guessing games. What... who are you talking about?'

Was he serious? Did he not know about Cree's evidence? Then again, why should he? The Crown hadn't disclosed the witness's statement yet and Paul didn't have a ready-made precognition agent on hand like I had.

'Forget it,' I said. Paul had kindly agreed to take a slightly roundabout route on his way home to Bathgate so I could be dropped off at my dad's house, where I'd arranged to meet up with Malky. 'I shouldn't be talking shop on a Friday night.' We were approaching the Low Port end of town and I directed him towards the old Edinburgh Road, past the newly rebuilt Star & Garter Hotel.

'No, I'm happy to talk about it,' Paul said, striking it lucky with a green light and driving under the railway tunnel.

I watched a couple of raindrops compete for first place to the bottom of the passenger window. What a climate. The amount of rain that had fallen, it was all set to be Scotland's wettest summer since the last wettest summer.

Up ahead another tunnel and another set of traffic lights at which Paul was less fortunate. 'Let's have it,' he said, bringing the car to another painful halt. 'Who is this witness... what's his name?'

'Cree. Clyve Cree.'

'And why is he so important?'

'Who said he was important?' I asked. But my air of innocence was ignored.

'Robbie...'

There was no real reason why not to tell Paul what I'd learned. He'd have Cree's police statement on his desk in the next day or so anyway and he had the funding available to pay a team of precognition agents, or better still himself, to go and precognosce the Crown's latest witness.

I relented, turned myself away from the raindrop Olympics and told Paul what I'd learned. We were outside my dad's cottage when I'd finished. I thought he'd be pleased and ready to declare war on Mark Starr's defence.

But happy he was not. 'Bugger!' Paul slammed the heels of his hands against the steering wheel.

I didn't understand. Paul wasn't stupid. He was a terrific defence lawyer, so terrific, in fact, that he'd probably never make Sheriff. He had to see the new picture. A paint-by-numbers job that Quirk's defence could simply colour in. If Cree was to be believed, Starrs and dead Doreen knew each other. My client was a jealous young man and by all accounts had good reason to be. Quirk and Doreen had slept together, the forensic evidence was clear. The question was: how had Starrs felt when he discovered that? Drunk and angry enough to put a pillow over sleeping Doreen's face? I could see Dominic Quirk's defence counsel, Big Jock Mulholland, sell that scenario to a jury inside the average time it took Sheriff Brechin to return a guilty verdict.

Paul battered the steering wheel again. 'Bugger, bugger, bugger—'

'What's wrong?' I asked. 'Looks like you haven't so much found a defence as have a defence find you. There was never any motive attached to Starrs before - well there is now.'

Paul turned to me. 'Yes it's a defence, it's a great defence. But it's not *the* defence that Quirk has given me or senior counsel.'

I was intrigued, as much by the idea that, pre-Cree, Quirk had any defence at all, as by the idea that a change of client's instructions would cause Paul such an ethical dilemma.

'So you're just going to ignore it?' I asked.

Paul shook his head, the fringe of his still damp hair falling across his forehead. 'Obviously, I'll have to tell my client about this development and let him know that an alternative line of defence may have opened up for him, a better one, but not one that I or counsel can present, standing our earlier instructions.'

'And you think he'll go for it?' I asked, clinging to the hope that, like his solicitor, Quirk would do the honourable thing and stick to his original defence, whatever that was.

Paul emitted a little sarcastic laugh. 'His dad is a bookie. Once he learns that there has been a shift on the odds, he'll be all over this new defence like a Liverpool housewife on the Grand National.'

'So what was the old defence?'

Paul wasn't keen to divulge.

'Come on, Paul. You can trust me...'

Paul glanced unnecessarily, I thought, askew at me. He sighed. 'I suppose it's a line of defence that will be history come Monday morning, anyway.' He switched off the engine. 'We have an expert coming over from the States. The preliminary hearing was postponed so we could finalise a few matters with him.'

'An expert in what?'

'Neurology. He's going to say that Doreen's death may very well have been down to vagal inhibition.'

'You were going for culpable homicide?'

Paul switched off the engine. 'Quirk's position to me was that he and Starrs gave Doreen a lift. They went back to his place, everything was fine and a lot of drink was taken. Starrs fell asleep on the couch. Doreen went to a spare bedroom and later on Quirk joined her. They had sex, fell asleep and a couple of hours later Doreen woke up crying. Quirk tried to console her, but she started shouting and screaming that she'd been raped. Quirk was in a flap. He didn't know what to do, and, not wanting Starrs to wake up hearing cries of rape, he put a pillow over Doreen's face—'

'And smothered her?' As I vaguely recalled it, Paul was more or less setting out the drunken opinion I'd provided to Suzie after a few too many Highland malts; a version that suited my client's defence perfectly.

'No, not smothered her,' Paul said. 'Accidentally applied pressure to the carotid sinus, on the neck, just at the angle of the jaw. The vagus nerve was stimulated, cardiac arrest followed and Doreen was dead in seconds. The expert says that vagal inhibition is more common in women than in men and exacerbated by alcohol.'

'And Professor Bradley's post mortem report?'

Paul shrugged.

'Petechiae in the eyes?' I reminded him.

'Not necessarily down to asphyxia. Our expert says that haemorrhaging can occur during bouts of vomiting or even crying during periods of high emotion. Add to that the fact that the lack of trauma to Doreen's body doesn't suggest the kind of prolonged struggle you'd expect from someone being suffocated and fighting back and —'

'What do you think Prof Bradley is going to make of this theory of yours?'

'Our expert is coming from the John Hopkins in Baltimore. He's the head of teaching in the hospital voted number one in America for neurology and neurosurgery, number two in cardiology. Prof Bradley will probably ask for his autograph.'

I had to admit it sounded good: for Quirk as well as my client. Mark Starrs' evidence was to the effect that he had only heard Doreen shouting. Were they the cries of an hysterical girl who'd had too much to drink and woken up to find herself in a situation her sober self would never have allowed? Quirk's impulsive action with the pillow was rash and clumsy, but understandable and without murderous intent. It was a reasonable defence for Quirk; more importantly it vindicated my client completely.

'But it's not a complete defence,' Paul said. 'It's culpable homicide. Along with disposing of the body, it would still add up to a fair amount of jail time. I'll need to give Jock Mulholland a call.'

'Paul,' I said. 'I think Jock already knows.' I told him about my discussion with Minty the day before.

'If he knows and hasn't mentioned it to me...'

'It's because he thinks you'll do the decent thing, and if you cease acting for ethical reasons, then Jock will feel obliged to bale out too.'

Paul could see where this was going. 'But if he gets Quirk to ditch me before I do, Jock can just keep on going and have a different solicitor prepare the new defence for him. This new evidence... think where it could lead in the right hands.'

Maybe he should have said, *in the wrong hands*.

Chapter 26

After Paul had finished his story, I went inside to find my dad in his usual armchair by the fire. Malky, who had raced away early from the game to watch the final part of a US cop drama he had been following all week, was slouched on the couch. I flopped down beside him. It looked good. Plenty of shooting, running around and screeching of tyres.

'Never saw that coming,' Malky said, eyes fixed on the action. 'Looks like the District Attorney was the murderer all the time. Used his position to cover up the crimes – clever. I did think it was an inside job, mind you, but my money would have been on the Captain.'

'Not that clever,' said my dad, the TV critic, from behind his newspaper. 'And it was never going to be the Captain.'

'You say that now, but I was sure it was either going to be him or that other detective, you know, Johnny?'

My dad lowered the newspaper, shaking his head at his elder son's naiveté. 'The Captain is black. The senior cop is *always* black and always dead grumpy, but he's never bad. He's the one who's forced to takes the hero's badge and gun off him in the first episode and then gives it back to him at the end so he can go solve the crime. Rich white Americans make these TV programmes. If they start making a black cop the baddy, everyone will know they're racist. They have to make the arrogant, posh, white guy the baddy. Then everyone is happy when he gets killed at the end. Common sense really.' He raised the newspaper and then lowered it again. 'Oh and if Johnny is the hero's buddy, you'll find he's blotted his copy-book in the past, but will redeem himself in the end.' He turned a page. 'Shortly before he gets bumped off.'

My father was a man of many opinions and few doubts.

'Have you seen this before, Dad?' I'd seen some of the trailers and thought they'd been promoting a brand new series.

'No, but Yank telly is all the same, they just shuffle the actors about.'

Malky's snort of disdain was drowned by an on-screen shot ringing-out and loud cries of, 'officer down!'

A bullet-holed cop made a few last remarks and with a final gasp died, head cradled in the arms of the hero, whom I recognised as a bit actor from other US shows and who'd obviously been promoted to a lead role.

'Johnny?' I asked.

Malky made a growling sound in his throat, pointed the remote at the TV and pulled the trigger. 'I need a drink.'

My dad folded his newspaper and stuffed it down the side of his chair. 'I'll make you a cup of tea - you're driving. And remember you've to drop Robbie off on the way.' He levered himself up into a standing position. 'Fancy a beer, Robbie? I've got a couple of bottles of your favourite in the back fridge.' And upon my confirmation that I'd love a beer, he sauntered through to the kitchen.

Malky tossed the TV Remote onto the now empty armchair. 'Got him wrapped right around your pinky, haven't you?' That was rich coming from Golden Boy. 'Where did you get the money to buy a four grand bottle of whisky? I thought I was going crazy buying him a bottle of Ardbeg unpronounceable. Do you how much that stuff costs? North of fifty quid. It's a lot of money to pay for some water and barley. And then you stroll in with a, *'here Dad, have a bottle of some whisky so rare Indiana Jones couldn't find it with a map'*. You must really—'

'It was an accident.' I immediately regretted my words. I'd just wanted to halt Malky's rant, not let slip such sensitive information.

Malky perked up. 'Accident? What do you mean?'

I'd done it now. I'd have to tell him. Malky had a mouth the size of Grangemouth and my only hope was to swear him to secrecy, a vow he took rather too easily I thought.

'Someone gave me the bottle as a present. I didn't know the value of it and, well, Fathers' Day was coming up so—'

'You idiot. Sorry, I'm not laughing.' Malky was still laughing when my dad returned with my bottle of Innes & Gunn and a chilled glass.

'What's all the hilarity?' my dad asked, before disappearing once more into the kitchen.

'Robbie just told me a great joke,' Malky said, when, moments later, my dad re-appeared, this time with Malky's mug of tea and a whisky for himself.

My dad looked at me enquiringly, as yet no hint of suspicion on his face.

From somewhere I dredged up a one-liner from a past Edinburgh Fringe stand-up. 'I was telling Malky I'd phoned to book tickets for Deep Sea World.'

'So?'

'They said my call might be recorded for training porpoises.'

In the comedy world eons passed, tectonic plates shifted. It was probably five seconds in all before my dad let loose an almighty guffaw. 'Porpoises. Brilliant, Robbie.' He raised his whisky glass. 'Here's to you.' The tumbler was almost at his lips, before he stopped and raised it again. 'Oh, and to you too, Malky.'

'Is that the whisky I bought you for Fathers' Day?' Malky asked.

My dad looked at the glass. 'Aye, the Uigeadail. Not a bad drop,' he said of the single malt that he'd once declared his favourite.

'I thought it might be the one Robbie got you.'

I sensed a note of mischief in my brother's voice and felt sure he was all set to break his earlier promise. Time to derail this particular topic of conversation.

'Thanks again for taking that precognition for me today,' I said.

My dad closed his eyes and waved a hand across his face. 'If you can't depend on your old man, who can you?'

'Robbie dragging you out of retirement, then?' Malky asked. 'How did he manage that?'

'It's an important case. I needed someone who knew what they were doing and they don't come more experienced at taking statements than a cop with thirty-five years' service,' I said.

My dad smiled modestly.

'What did you do, Dad? Take him into a wee room and punch a confession out of him?' Malky sipped his tea and made a face. 'Did you not put sugar in this?'

'Sugar in your tea? What are you - a big wean?'

I couldn't believe it. A front row seat to the desanctification of St Malky of Munro.

Unused to criticism from his father and not sure what to do, Malky took his mug through to the kitchen. 'What important case have you got?' he asked me, upon his return. 'One of your junkie clients in bother again?'

My dad was immediately there in my defence. 'Robbie's involved in a big murder case with the laddie Quirk. You know, the boy who killed that woman last year? Well, he's murdered someone else now.'

The upcoming trial had been mentioned in all the papers, but, if it wasn't on the sports' pages, it wasn't news so far as Malky was concerned. 'Any relation to Al Quirk, the bookie?' he asked.

'His son,' I confirmed.

Malky scowled. 'He'll be a crook, then. Just like his old man.'

My dad's disregard for the presumption of innocence was well documented, but what had Quirk senior ever done to Malky for him to make such a sweeping statement?

He enlightened us. 'Remember my first year with The Rose when we got to the cup final? We were unbeaten that year, best defence in the league by a mile. Training night before the semi-final, Al Quirk meets me in the car park. He's driving a Merc, I'm seventeen, just passed my test and driving shoe leather. He asks if I'd like some money to buy myself a car.'

My dad spluttered over his next mouthful of Islay's finest.

Malky continued. 'All I had to do was give away a penalty.'

I was about to mention that there was nothing hugely unusual about Malky fouling the opposition in the penalty box or anywhere else, when my dad was on his feet, almost, but not quite, spilling his drink.

'Why did you not tell me?' he roared. 'I'd have been down on him like a ton of bricks.'

'I didn't want to involve the law.' Malky sipped his sweetened tea. 'Anyway, I turned him down flat, except he wasn't happy, started threatening me, telling me to watch my back etcetera.'

My dad's knuckles whitened around the whisky glass.

'Take it easy, Dad,' I said. 'Malky didn't cheat and nothing happened to him.'

My dad relaxed a little. 'What did happen?'

'I told the team captain.'

'Back then that would have been Geordie Rafferty,' my dad said, after a moment's recollection. 'Geordie was a hard man, but he was fair.'

Hard but clinically insane was my boyhood recollection; whatever, my dad was certain the battle-hardened midfielder wouldn't have taken any snash off the likes of Al Quirk.

'What did Geordie do when you told him?' I asked.

Malky took a sip of hot sweet tea. 'Clattered their striker inside the first five minutes. They scored from the spot-kick, we went on to win four-one and Geordie was on the bell all night.'

'Did you know about this?' my dad asked me.

I'd have been about fourteen at the time. Even then I wasn't in the habit of listening much to what my big brother had to say; a habit I'd never quite managed to shake; however, I did vaguely recall him saying something once about a bookie asking him to cheat. I think it was years later when we were watching On The Waterfront and Marlon Brando was giving the big, *I coulda been a contender* speech. Until now I hadn't realised Malky had been talking about Dominic Quirk's dad.

Malky clapped his hands together. 'So, Robbie's been telling me all about this rare bottle of whisky he gave you.'

My dad beamed. He laid his glass down on the arm of the chair, went over to the wee cupboard stashed full of Malky memorabilia, and took out the Co-op blend cardboard tube. Face flushed with pride, he sat down and, holding it on his knee, popped the lid off the tube.

'Must have cost you a fortune, Robbie,' Malky said, the obvious note of irony in his voice evading my dad.

The old man pulled the bubble-wrapped bottle from the tube and stopped, looked up at me. 'Well? *Did* you know about this thing between Malky and Quirk?' he asked.

I shrugged.

'And you never told me?'

'Sorry, Dad, I promised Malky I wouldn't say anything.' I fixed my brother with a hard stare. 'And you know us Munro boys always keep our promises.'

Chapter 27

The following day, Saturday, I met Suzie at the Peel, as the grounds of Linlithgow Palace are better known. It was early evening and a grey-suited, jailer of a sky showed signs of permitting an early-evening release to a sun it had held prisoner all day. Suzie had been in Dundee at a literary festival and returned worn-out from book-signing. I took that as good news. She didn't see it that way.

'The book they all want signed is Portcullis,' she said. 'Don't get me wrong, it's my main bread-winner, but every book becomes dated. I've tried to freshen things up and yet the next two in the series are nowhere near as successful, no matter how hard I try to plug them.'

I had yet to read the latest books and didn't want to stray too far in that direction in case I was asked for my views. So, as we walked across the lush, undulating landscape, down the hill from the ancient ruin itself and along the path adjacent to the loch, I explained to Suzie why the denizens of the Royal Burgh were referred to as Black Bitches; recounting the legend of the black greyhound whose master had been sentenced to starve to death on one of the two tiny islands in Linlithgow Loch.

'The people of the town couldn't understand why he wouldn't die,' I said, pointing to the clumps of earth breaking the surface of the loch, each populated by a few scrawny trees. 'Some thought it witchcraft, then it was discovered that his faithful greyhound was swimming to the island every night with food.'

'It's a better story than Greyfriars Bobby,' Suzie said. 'Is there a happy ending?'

'Only if Disney remakes it. When the town folk found out, they chained the bitch to a tree on the other island and master and hound both died.'

'That was a bit rough.'

'You mean *ruff-ruff*?' I barked. Even I didn't find me funny.

'She was only being loyal, after all.'

'True, but there was no SSPCA back then and you couldn't have people, not even dogs, or, rather, bitches, attempting to defeat the ends of justice,' I said.

Which remark brought us neatly around to the reason why Suzie had asked to see me.

'I thought I should let you know that I'm not going to write the book: the one about Dominic Quirk,' she said. 'I think I'll stick to what I know and what I know is how to make stuff up, not how to make real murder sound interesting.'

That was the trouble with real life killings: lots of head-stamping, stabbing, strangling and shooting: not much in the way of transvestite, serial-killing Parliamentarians abducting rivals and wreaking revenge with mediaeval instruments of torture.

Suzie grinned apologetically. 'Sorry if I've wasted your time.'

'You haven't,' I said. 'And if in the future I have an interesting case I think you can adapt, I'll let you know. We can meet up.'

We walked side by side, down from the Palace to the small marina.

'How is Mark Starrs' case coming along?' Suzie asked, stopping to watch blue-hulled rowing boats bobbing on the choppy surface of the loch. 'Did you manage to secure him a better deal?'

I explained that all deals were off the table. 'It looks as though we could be in for a real cut-throat trial; each accused blaming the other.'

'Why would Quirk want to blame your client all of a sudden?'

'Let's just say that up until now he may have been exploring a different line of defence, playing the odds.' Without mentioning my conversation with Paul Sharp the night before, I explained how the arrival on the scene of Clyve-with-a-Y had shifted the balance of power between Quirk and Starrs. 'It's not essential in a murder case to prove motive; however, it's what the jury will be looking for. Why was Doreen Anderson killed? It's now open to Dominic Quirk's defence to say it was all down to his friend's jealousy. Every man and woman on the jury will be able to identify with that emotion.'

'You think Quirk might change his story and lie?'

'Don't go confusing me with someone who knows what the truth is. And don't confuse the truth with guilt or innocence,' I said. 'The truth is what the jury say it is. Ask yourself - would you believe that story?'

Suzie pondered aloud. 'Rich boy steals poor boy's girl. Poor boy is so overcome by jealous rage that he does something stupid? A crime of passion. Not exactly a ground-breaking plot-line, but all the more believable for that. Yes, I could sell a plot like that to my readers.'

We had reached the east-most edge of the Peel. Before its boundary with the bird sanctuary there was a small play park. Suzie went over to the swings and sat down on one of them. 'Come on. What are you waiting for?'

I went behind and gave her a push.

'Well?' she said. 'What have you come up with? How is the famous Robbie Munro going to get his client out of this mess?'

I wished I knew. I gave Suzie another push and stepped back. Soon she was on her way, higher and higher, leaning back, legs outstretched, feet pointed at the dark water and the hills beyond.

'All I have is the fact that Starrs got in first with his explanation,' I called to her.

Suzie put her feet down and skidded to a halt. 'I'm getting dizzy. It's a long time since I beamed-up on a swing.' She stood, tottered and grabbed hold of me for support. For a moment I thought we were going to kiss. Suzie drew her face away, stepped back. She took my left hand, gripped the fourth finger and shook it. 'Are you forgetting something? Or someone?' She let go and walked on. I followed feeling foolish, disloyal and not a little disappointed.

'What were you saying?' she said, once I'd caught up with her.

'I'm saying I can't think of another case where more depended on the accused's own evidence. In a way it's good that he didn't exercise his right to silence. Quirk's decision to say nothing to the police might go against him, because we can accentuate the fact that Mark Starrs cooperated fully with the police and that his statement, given a very short time after the alleged offence, bears the hallmark of truth.'

'Ooh,' Suzie fluttered her eyelashes, 'the hallmark of truth. I bet you say that to all your juries.'

'If things go the way I think they will, it's all we have left. We put Starrs in the witness box and let him have his say. Why would he admit to helping dispose of a body if the rest of his story wasn't true? His defence paints the picture of a young man with nothing to hide, a man who told the police the truth right from the outset and his version hasn't changed one iota since.'

The sun's sentence had been recalled and it was once more firmly incarcerated behind clouds of steel. The wind had picked up and carried with it a smir of rain and spray from the loch. We turned our back to the stiffening breeze, following the path to the Burgh Hall's rose garden and the shelter of its walls.

'And when will it all happen?'

'There is final preliminary hearing in just over a week. I can't see the judge put off fixing a trial any longer. With Dominic Quirk on remand it has to start within a hundred and forty days of his full committal, and the time-bar is fast approaching.'

I waited for the question that every remanded accused client always asked me. Suzie didn't disappoint. 'What happens if they can't?'

'If the Crown isn't ready and needs to extend the time-bar, it can hardly object to Quirk's release on bail if he's not to blame for the delay,' I said.

The shower of rain remained a threat. We strolled through the rose garden, now in full bloom and a cascade of bright rose petals. Past The Green Man, a statue of John Hope, former Marquess of Linlithgow and first Governor General of Australia, we went, through the small archway outside the Masonic Hall and onto the cobble stones of Linlithgow Cross.

'You mean he'd get out? What would happen then?' Suzie asked.

'He'd be in the same position as Mark Starrs. The Crown have a year to start a trial against an accused who's on bail.'

To complete the circuit and end up back at Suzie's car we commenced the ascent of the Kirkgate, a steep, narrow brae leading back to the Palace, where along the wall to our right, blue enamel plaques set out the royal line of succession from James V to Elizabeth, first of Scotland, second of England.

Suzie took my arm. 'Do you think your client can do it? He's so young to have to go into a witness box and testify on a matter so important to him.'

I didn't know. All I could say was that Mark Starrs was a drama student and, if he was lying, he'd have to put on the best performance of his life or end up doing life.

We stopped beneath the stone archway leading to the Palace grounds. Dating from the fifteen hundreds, the gateway featured four carved and painted panels representing the orders of knighthood borne by James V, who like his more famous daughter, Mary of the head-chopped-off, was born in the Palace. Suzie looked up at me with those eyes of hers. I knew we only had a few more minutes together.

'And if he's telling the truth - what then?' she asked.

'If he's telling the truth, he won't need to act. Sometimes you find the truth can take care of itself.'

We had reached Suzie's car. She took a set of keys from her handbag. 'What about justice? Can it take care of itself? Or don't you think it sometimes needs a helping hand?'

'You mean bend the law a little?'

'Or even break it, in the name of justice.'

'Didn't you used to believe that the law and justice were the same thing?' I asked.

Chuck in a pint of heavy, a French Martini and a packet of scampi fries and we could have been finishing a pub discussion we'd started nearly twenty years before.

Suzie leaned forward and kissed my cheek. 'I used to believe a lot of things.'

Chapter 28

Mark Starrs was worried. 'I knew we should have taken the deal,' he said, politely enough to suggest that he had been in some way responsible for my rash decision to reject the Crown's earlier offer.

'Don't blame yourself,' I said. 'The Crown only put the deal out there as a carrot when they thought the case unlikely to prove.'

'And now?'

And now, with the arrival of Clyve Cree, it was a lot easier to prove; especially against the young man sitting across the desk from me that overcast Wednesday afternoon, one week before his next court appearance.

Cree was the worst kind of prosecution witness: one with no axe to grind. There was a clear inference to be drawn from his statement that my client had known the murder victim, that she'd cheated on him with Quirk before, and that Starrs had warned her what would happen if she did it again. Well, according to the forensic evidence, it was a billion-to-one certainty that she had. The question for the jury was: had Starrs followed through with his threat? Had he murdered Doreen out of jealousy? Suzie called it a believable plot-line; one she could sell her readers. I'd bet Jock Mulholland Q.C. could sell it to a jury.

No need to send my client into a fit of depression, though. There would be plenty of time for that later. 'This is a criminal trial, Mark. A murder trial. There are always new developments as the big day approaches. The ground is constantly shifting. The trick is to keep calm, keep your balance and have a game plan.'

He looked over at me. The clouds of despair in his eyes threatened to clear and reveal outbreaks of hope. 'Do we have one?'

I laughed at the absurdity of his question.

'Do we?' Apparently Starrs hadn't intended his question to be rhetorical and wanted more than just my laughter in response. I rummaged around in a desk drawer, while I rummaged around in my brain for an answer.

'Okay,' I said, producing a legal notepad and setting it down on the desk in front of me. 'What do we have? Well we're stuck with what you told the police.' I'd seen the DVD of the interview. The police had repeatedly asked Starrs if he wanted to consult with a lawyer and provided him with cups of tea throughout. That more or less took care of any suggestion of unfair police tactics; unless we took exception to the absence of chocolate digestives.

'Good,' he said, 'because I told the police the truth.'

Why did clients think that the truth was going to help in a criminal trial?

'Then we have truth on our side,' I said, wishing I believed what I was saying, 'and in the fight for justice that's half the battle.'

Starrs seemed to take heart. I continued. 'We know what our position is with regard to Dominic. What we need to do now is decide how we deal with the new witness.'

'Easy,' said my client. 'This guy, Cree, must be mistaken.' I had never set eyes on Doreen before that night. Me and Dominic were out for a drive—'

'Looking for girls?'

'Yes, but not how the police make it sound. We were taking a shortcut up one of the side streets and saw this girl crossing the road. Dominic said he recognised her from a café he went to sometimes. We pulled up alongside and asked if she wanted a lift. I never even left the car. It was Dominic who spoke to her through the passenger window. She got in and as we were driving her home she agreed to come back to

Dom's for a drink. He said he'd pay for a taxi to take her home again.'

'So why is Cree saying otherwise?' I asked.

'Like I've already told you, he's got to be confused.'

'I had an ex-cop precognosce him on Friday.' I looked again at the statement hot off Grace-Mary's printer. 'He doesn't sound confused to me. He says he heard a person threaten the girl by saying he'd kill her if she went near Dominic again.'

'So?'

'So, he says that person had ginger hair.'

'I'm not the only person in St Andrews with auburn hair.' Starrs slouched lower in his chair. The clouds of despair that had temporarily cleared, rolled in again. 'Can I ask my dad to come in?'

I told him I'd rather he didn't. What was said between us was confidential. Theoretically, anything he said in the presence of his father could be used in evidence. Not that it was at all likely that Mr Starrs would go running to the Crown, but it was a good enough reason to stop his perpetually angry dad sticking his oar in. There was enough confusion already.

'We need to stop and look at this logically,' I said.

He stared blankly at me.

'You know like Mr Spock on Star—'

'I'm twenty-one, not twelve. I know what logically means.'

'Then let's look at your suggestion that Cree is mistaken. Logically, if you are telling the truth, he must be talking about another ginge... auburn-headed young man who's driving a different brand new M3 convertible with a custom paint-job and talking to a different girl about some other person called Dominic.'

'It's possible,' he sulked.

And he was right. In an infinite number of parallel universes there was an infinite number of possibilities. I kind of hoped I was living in the universe where our meeting was interrupted by a bikini clad model bursting into the room with a case of champagne and news of my lottery win. I waited. It wasn't.

'Possible but extremely unlikely,' I said. 'Which takes us, logically, onto the only other possibility – Cree's lying.'

'Why would he do that? What possible motive would he have? He doesn't even know me. Why—'

'Let's take this step by step,' I said, talking as much to myself as my client. 'Unless Cree is a mad attention-seeker, the only reason for lying would be to have you convicted.'

'Why would he want to do that?' Starrs asked, predicting step two.

'Either because he thinks you are guilty and wants to make sure of the verdict. In which case he could be some kind of vigilante—'

'You mean, maybe he knew Doreen and wants someone done for it?'

'Or someone else has put him up to it.'

'One of Doreen's friends or relatives, do you think? She's got brothers. They've threatened me before.'

'People wanting revenge for Doreen's death would want you both convicted. If Cree is fabricating his evidence—'

'He is.'

'Then he would do it so as to stitch-up both you and Dominic. Easily done. He would just have to change what he says he over-heard. Don't you see? If Cree is lying, the logical outcome is he wants you convicted.'

'I get that.'

'Well don't you get it that if Cree's evidence is bad news for you, it's extremely good news for Dominic?'

'But the forensic evidence? Doreen's body? His car? How can he say he didn't...'

I let himself work out the answer to his own question. It didn't take long.

'No way! Dominic is my friend. He would never do anything to get me in trouble.' So said the young man who minutes earlier had wished we had sealed the deal for him to testify against his friend.

'But all I was going to do was tell the truth,' he said when I pointed this out to him.

'It would be nice to think that a criminal trial was a search for the truth,' I said, 'but, in actual fact, it's all about winning, and it seems to me that your friend is intent on not losing.'

'But how would he do it? If Dom was going to get someone to be a false witness it would have to be somebody he knew and really trusted.'

'Or who's been bribed.'

'What does Clyve Cree look like?' Starrs asked.

'What difference does that make?'

'You said he can identify me. Maybe I can identify *him*. I know all of Dominic's friends. If it's one of them it would give us something to go on.'

I had to admit that I had not set eyes on the new witness. I referred again to the precognition my dad had taken. 'Thirty-eight years old. Do you know any of Dominic's pals that are that old? According to my... to my precognition officer, he's a great big bloke. Ring any bells?'

Starrs shook his head. 'It's a stupid idea. How could Dominic set something like that up? Firstly, he's in prison and, secondly, even if he wasn't, he wouldn't have the first idea how to go about bribing somebody.'

A good enough point to make, I thought - were it not for the fact that, firstly, Dominic's dad wasn't in prison, and, secondly, Al Quirk would know precisely how to go about fixing the odds.

Chapter 29

Next day, I had Grace-Mary dig out the old file for Dominic Quirk's RTA case. She brought it through to my room before she left for the evening. It was three inches thick, tied up neatly with red tape. The book of photos which had been a Crown production was in an A5 envelope, sealed with sticky-tape and stapled to the inside cover. My secretary didn't want anyone accidentally stumbling across graphic reminders of the accident in which a young woman had died.

I turned to the back of the file and recovered the brief, sewn with pink thread. It contained all the statements and documentary productions. What I was looking for was the actual indictment. I found it and turned to the attached list of witnesses. There she was; witness number 5: Sophie Pratt. I remembered her statement to the police. It had been a horribly wet night. While she'd been standing at the crossroads at Linlithgow Bridge, waiting for the green man, she'd noticed what she'd described as a big white jeep bombing along Main Street. The traffic lights changed to amber then red. The oncoming vehicle showed no sign of stopping. It was at this point that Sophie had noticed the family hatchback pulling out of Mill Road, indicating right. Realising the inevitable, unable to do anything but scream, Sophie watched as over two and a half metric tonnes of SUV slammed into the six year old Renault Clio side-on.

Before Sophie was called to the witness box at Dominic's trial, the Crown had set the scene with some forensic evidence. Because of the rain and the wet road, there had been a lack of skid marks making it difficult to calculate the speed of the Range Rover. Expert witnesses were instructed by each side and there was much talk of impact zones, velocity vectors and friction coefficients. A lot of what was said must have sailed over the heads of the jurors, who just wanted to know how fast Quirk had been travelling. The prosecution expert was a police sergeant from the Traffic Headquarters who had been sent on some courses. By his calculations, the Range Rover had been travelling at over fifty miles per hour in the prevailing thirty mile per hour speed limit. The expert Al Quirk had stumped-up for entered the witness box in a sharp suit and sharper hair-do. She had run several computer reconstructions and confidently assessed that there was simply insufficient data to arrive at any assessment of speed on which to accurately rely. When cross-examined why there could possibly be such a disparity in opinion, she suggested that the Crown's expert might want to take a refresher course with reference to a new Department of Transport sponsored report containing all the latest scientific findings on the subject. She'd be happy to provide the Crown expert with a copy; she'd written it.

And then into the witness box came Sophie Pratt, chief witness for the Crown, an extremely nervous twenty-four year-old woman, whose child was being looked after by the court's witness support team. She held up her right hand, took the oath and rambled her way through a version of events that did not remotely compare with either the statement she'd given to the police or the precognition she'd provided to me. Try as he might, the Procurator Fiscal could not get Sophie back on message. She said she'd been distracted at the time of the accident. The baby was in a right mood, chucking toys around. Yes, she'd told the police the lights were at red, but she couldn't say for definite. Maybe the wee car had pulled out too early, and, as for the speed of the big white jeep, well... it was difficult to say.

I hadn't even cross-examined for fear her evidence might start swinging back the other way. I'd seen that happen too often and, besides, it made for an excellent jury point that the defence had not even required to question the evidence of the Crown's only eye witness.

Why had she changed her story? Did the spotlight of the witness box concentrate her mind? Or was there another reason for her change of tack? I jotted down Sophie Pratt's address on a yellow-sticky and decided to visit her later that evening. A single mum she was bound to be in, feeding the kid, bathing the kid, reading it bedtimes stories or having it defragment her computer hard-drive.

She was doing none of these things.

'Gone to Thursday bingo, mate,' said the man who answered the door, shorts, sweat-stained T-shirt, can of lager in hand. I recognised him from court. Not one of my clients, but a regular.

'When will she be back?' I asked.

He slurped some lager out of the top of the tin and laughed. 'Soon, knowing her luck.' He peered closer at me, as though having difficulty recognising me dressed in jeans and shirt as opposed to my usual working garb: suit, tie and black gown. It was the sort of stare I was sure Clark Kent got a lot. 'You're that lawyer, eh? Soph in trouble?' he slurred, before I could confirm his previous question.

'Not at all. I just wanted to speak to her about a case she was a witness in. I'll come back tomorrow.'

'So what case is that then?' The man was joined at the door, first by a wicked smell and then by a toddler dressed in a grubby white vest and a disposable nappy that had turned an ugly yellow colour and was practically dragging along the floor.

'I'll go. You've got your hands full,' I said.

'S'all right. You can tell me. What are you wanting her for?'

'I need to speak to her in private. I'll come back later.' I waggled my fingers at the child's sticky wee face and made to turn and leave.

'Is that bitch trying to get rid of me? She trying to get an injunction or something?'

'That's not why I'm here,' I said. 'And it's not called an injunction in Scotland, it would be an interdict she'd be looking for. But she isn't. At least not through me.' I stuck solely to crime; civil law, and family work in particular, being far too murky a world.

He took a slurp from the can. 'I hardly touched her. It was just a shove. It was her who hit me first. My lawyer said the case would get booted out.'

It had been a long day in court followed by appointments at the office. Afterwards, I'd gone home to find my fridge had gone Old Mother Hubbard on me and the joys of a supermarket trip awaited me once I'd met with the bingo kid. There were happier bunnies. 'Listen to me,' I said. 'I'm not here about you. I'm here to see Sophie about something that has absolutely nothing to do with you. Tell her...'

I noticed that Mr Sweaty-T-shirt had managed to shake off the child and was now coming down the two steps from the front door, with a less than welcoming look on his face. I backed away. He tossed the half-full can of lager into a pile of weeds that festooned the dilapidated wooden fence running alongside the gable end of the property. Not a good sign; he didn't seem to me the sort of person who threw alcohol anywhere other than down his throat.

'What you really here for, ya bastard?' he shouted.

I'd already explained the purpose of my visit as best I could and didn't see the merit in further discussion. I showed him my back, started down the path of broken concrete slabs and was almost on the pavement when I heard rapid footsteps and heavy-breathing. A hand clawed at my face, a finger dug into my left eye. Diplomatic ties now severed, I dipped a shoulder, spun around and landed a punch to the angle of my attacker's jaw. The blow really hurt my hand. It didn't do the babysitter's face much good either. He staggered sideways off the path and tripped over an upturned yellow tricycle that was rusting on a patch of unkempt grass, a single stabiliser reaching for the sky. He didn't get up.

Smelly-child sat down on the top step and started to pick at one of the tabs securing its nappy. The kid was an ecological disaster waiting to happen. I went over to Sweaty-T-shirt and gave him a nudge with the toe of my shoe. He groaned, but other than that showed no signs of immediate recovery. I went down the row of terraced houses, knocking on doors as I went until I found an elderly woman who looked like she might know her way around a nappy. I pointed her in the right direction and then did the only thing I could. I found the discarded can of lager, wrapped Sweaty-T-shirt's hand around it and called the emergency social work team. I had a feeling Sophie Pratt would be getting her interdict, whether she wanted it or not.

Chapter 30

The phone was ringing when I got home after work on Friday evening.

It was Jill. The good news was that she was back in Scotland. The bad news was that she had brought Felicity with her. The amalgamation of Zanetti Biotechnics and the other mob, whose name I'd forgotten, was proceeding apace and the company's development on the outskirts of Edinburgh was set to open with a ceremony in a week or so's time followed by a grand charity ball in the evening. Jill and Felicity had been sent north to make the final arrangements.

'You're always working. I never seem to get to see you these days,' I complained.

'Why don't you come through and we'll go for a drink?'

It was nearly eight o'clock, I hadn't eaten, my left eye was sore from my brief encounter with Sophie Pratt's childminder the night before and I had some papers to look at for court on Monday, not to mention preparations for Mark Starrs' continued preliminary hearing on Tuesday. I didn't care. I hadn't seen Jill for the best part of a fortnight. I caught the next train and was there before nine. Felicity had booked into a hotel on the Royal Mile and I met them in the basement bar.

'We're having French Martinis,' Jill announced as I approached. Usually, Jill could never make up her mind what to drink and almost always plumped for a glass of white wine. 'This is my third. They kind of grow on you don't they? I don't know what put the idea into my head.'

If Jill saw any change in my facial expression she didn't mention it, because Felicity had noticed something else.

'Robbie, whatever happened to your eye?'

Jill looked at me over the top of her martini glass.

'Accident in the garden,' I said. 'Same again?' I went over to the bar and when I returned with another round of cocktails, a bottle of Czech beer and a wooden bowl of nibbles, the conversation had moved onto the guest list for the upcoming junket.

'Your invite is in the post, of course, Robbie,' Felicity said. 'These sort of shin-digs needs a little livening-up. Some bare-knuckle boxing might be just the thing.' She raised her martini glass to me in a toast and I reciprocated with my bottle. Maybe she wasn't so bad. At least after a few cocktails.

Meanwhile, my fiancée was failing to see the funny side.

Felicity noticed. 'Seriously, Robbie, you're most welcome,' she said. 'Jill's been a real brick. We could never have got this far so soon without your better half. She's quite the little taskmaster when she gets started. Not one to let an obstacle get in her way.'

'How's Rupert doing?' I asked, a fraction of a second before Jill's heel crunched the top of my foot.

Felicity frowned, tanned wrinkles deepening. 'Seen neither hide nor hair. One minute his Merc is mowing me down and it's the theatre and champers all round, the next he won't return my calls.' She tutted. 'Men.'

'That's a shame. I've been trying to track him down myself,' I said, dragging my injured foot away to safety. 'We had a business deal and—'

'You did not,' Jill said.

'How do you know we didn't?' I asked.

'Why would someone like Rupert want to do business—'

'With someone like me?'

Jill backed off and took a sip of her cocktail. 'What I mean is—'

'I know what you mean and—'

'If you don't mind...' Felicity stood. 'It's been a long day and we've an early start.' She came around the table, gave Jill an arm's length hug and patted me gingerly on the shoulder, as though I might be contagious. 'Night all.'

'That was your fault,' Jill said, after her boss had drifted away.

I didn't want to start an argument and, anyway, if I had been responsible for Felicity's early departure, I was glad.

Jill was only getting started. 'Oh, and the fresh black-eye was a nice touch.'

'It's not a black-eye. It's a graze. Quite sore, though.'

Jill feigned a sympathetic face. 'Gardening - it's a dangerous business.' Her expression swiftly changed. 'Especially when you don't have a garden.'

I took a slug of beer and smacked my lips. 'Miniatures,' I said, trying to lead us onto the well-worn path of wedding arrangements. 'My dad said I was to ask you about miniatures.'

'Miniature whats?'

I explained about my dad's idea in relation to wedding favours.

Jill sighed, took a gulp of her cocktail.

'What's wrong?' I asked.

'The wedding,' she said. 'I've had so much on my mind with the Zanetti/Lyon amalgamation and now I've been put in charge of organising this opening ceremony. After that, goodness knows what else will come up. When am I supposed to have time to arrange a wedding? And then there will have to be a honeymoon and—'

'Let's not have one,' I said. 'Let's save ourselves twenty grand, nip along to the registrar's and we can go off on a holiday when things are less busy for you.'

'Oh, I see. So what do I tell my mum? Don't bother buying a hat, me and Robbie are jumping the broomstick?' Jill wasn't letting up, face flushed, eyes flashing. 'And at the same time I'll tell my Canadian relatives: you know that trip to Scotland? Well it's off, but, hey, never mind we'll send you a postcard from somewhere hot. Is that it?'

That did more or less sum up the Robbie Munro ideal wedding. 'You're the one who's too busy to plan a wedding,' I said. 'Why not tell your Canadian cousins, who have never bothered to visit you ever, that if they'd like an all-expenses-paid trip to Scotland, they should enter a competition?'

'Everything's always about money with you isn't it?' Jill said.

It was the sort of thing people who had money said to those who hadn't.

The waiter came over to our table, putting hostilities on hold. He asked if we wanted anything else to drink. According to Jill, we didn't. She knocked back her pink cocktail and set the glass down on the waiter's tray. The waiter handed me the bill. Jill snatched it away, took out a pen, wrote a room number and signed.

'Staying here tonight?' I said, once the waiter had wandered away. 'Zanetti paying?'

Jill had calmed down. She smiled at me, her lips not troubling her eyes. I'd seen the signs before. I was in deep doo-doo. I'd fallen into some kind of trap. To paraphrase a line from the movies: I was dead - I just didn't know it yet.

'Yes, the accounts department will be wondering why there are so many French Martinis on my expenses sheet this month.'

I still had half a bottle of beer left. I drank it. I had a horrible feeling where this conversation was headed, but it would have been unwise to give away anything at that stage.

'French Martinis in Edinburgh, French Martinis in London. No, wait, I didn't have any French Martinis in London and yet...' Jill delved into her bag and produced a hotel receipt that seemed very readily to hand. She spread it out on the table. 'Why did the Savannah charge me for all of these? I mean, the single malt whiskies and white wines are easily explainable, but, somehow, Robbie, I've never seen you as a vodka, raspberry and pineapple cocktail kind-of-a-guy,' she said in a get-out-of-that-one kind-of-a-way.

I decided to go with the truth. 'I met a friend: Suzie Lake. Remember Rupert said he'd bumped into her? She was in London to meet with—'

'And she bumped into you too, did she? The woman is a human dodgem car, all the bumping she does.'

'We had a few drinks, talked about old times and I gave her some advice on a new book she was thinking of writing.'

'Of course,' said Jill, mistress of irony, 'it makes perfect sense. Why wouldn't Suzie, the famous bestselling author, seek literary advice from a man who spends his time filling out legal aid forms and never reads anything but the sports pages?'

'Not literary advice, legal advice.' I drank the last of my beer. 'She was thinking about writing a true crime novel—'

'That still doesn't explain why she just happened to stumble across you in the teeming metropolis.'

'In all the gin joints, in all the towns, in all the...' Humphrey Bogart didn't help. Time to turn the tables. 'If you'll remember, it was the night we were out for dinner at that Italian next to Harrods. It was you who had to leave early. If you hadn't, I wouldn't have gone back to the hotel alone and I'd never have bumped into anyone. As it was, Suzie just appeared. What was I supposed to do?'

Jill's frozen face showed no signs of thawing. The truth was not all it was cracked up to be. Why hadn't I gone with a line about having developed a sudden craving for girly drinks?

Jill's voice was now practically a whisper. 'When I came to the hotel that Saturday morning was she in your room?'

The trouble with the truth is that it can become a habit if you're not careful. I shrugged the smallest shrug that could be shrugged. 'Yes, but it's not what you think. Nothing happened. We had a lot to drink, it was late and Suzie—'

'Had a sleep-over? Bring her jim-jams did she?'

'She slept on the bed. I slept in a chair. You saw the state of me when you came to the door. I was fully clothed, I'd just woken—'

'Then why didn't you tell me?'

I wasn't used to being cross-examined. That was my job. 'If I had told you, would you have believed me?'

'Let me put it this way,' Jill said. 'Because you *didn't* tell me, I *don't* believe you. And if I can't trust you...' She put both hands on the table between us, removed the engagement ring from the fourth finger of her left hand. 'I can't marry you.' She placed the ring on the fourth finger of her right hand, got up from the table and walked out of the bar and out of my life.

Chapter 31

Saturday morning. My dad was in the garden mixing cement on an enormous sheet of plywood. I didn't ask why.

'Not seeing Jill this weekend?' he asked.

Just the mention of my ex-fiancée tore at my insides.

'I saw her last night,' I said. I might be son-of-the-moment, but the procession of special treatment I'd received ever since my accidental gift of a bottle of rare single malt would come screeching to a halt the moment my dad learned that I'd screwed things up with Jill. He had always predicted our relationship would founder on the rocky shore-line of my stupidity. True, on past form, the smart money had always been with him, but of late he had started to come to grips with the idea that I might actually have done something romantically right for once. I had to sort things out with Jill, pronto.

My dad looked up from the pile of sandy mixture he was attacking with a shovel. 'Is Jill home, then?'

'She and her boss are in Edinburgh arranging a big do for when her company's new centre opens.'

He grunted and returned to his mixing. 'Did you talk about the wedding?'

'We went over a few things. We still haven't settled on a firm date yet. Jill's very—'

'Do you ever talk about... afterwards?'

'After what? The wedding? The honeymoon?'

'Kids.'

We had talked about children. In summary, Jill wasn't keen.

My dad made a well in the centre of the mixture, wiped his brow with the arm of his sleeve and looked at me expectantly. 'Well?' He stood the shovel upright and then let it fall towards me.

I caught it. 'We discussed the miniatures,' I said, pouring some water from a watering can into the well and starting in at the mixture, glad to be avoiding eye contact. 'Jill says just to go ahead.'

My dad splashed on some more water as I churned the mess, over and over. 'Does she have anything particular in mind?'

Whisky was the one subject on which I could safely say Jill had nothing particular in mind and, besides, I was ready to tell him just about anything to keep him sweet so long as he didn't get a sniff of what had happened the night before. I desperately needed to stall for time while I put mission Win Back Jill into operation. I lifted a dollop of wet mortar, slapped it down again onto the plywood board and chopped at it with the blade of the shovel. 'She says to leave all that up to you, you'll know best.'

I kept lifting, slapping and chopping for the next minute or so. When I stopped my dad was standing there, staring into the cloudy sky and muttering to himself.

I pointed the business end of the shovel at the pile of cement. 'What do you think?'

He rubbed his jaw and stroked his moustache, still gazing heavenwards. 'Well, a blend is obviously out of the question, which leaves a choice of—'

'Not about the miniatures.' I tilted my head at the fresh mortar. 'How's that?'

He took the shovel from me, used it to flip the mortar over a couple of times and then propped it against a wall. 'It'll do, I suppose. You see, if you go for a Lowland malt, well, some folk think it's a wee-bit girly.'

'No they don't, Dad, only you do. Why don't you stop mucking around? You know you're going to choose an Islay malt.'

'Not necessarily,' he said, trying and failing to sound open-minded. 'Although, I suppose it might help if we narrowed things down to the one region, right enough.'

'Dad, you know it's going to be a toss-up between Ardbeg and Caol Ila.'

'The bloke I know, his discount card is for Diageo.' He clapped his hands together. 'So, Caol Ila it is then.' He went off and came back carrying a tin pail. A pointing trowel rattled around inside it. 'So long as we stick to the twelve year-old we shouldn't start getting into silly money.' He set the pail down, removed the trowel and stuck it, point first into his back pocket. 'How many? Four dozen?'

'Better make it six, just to be on the safe side,' I said. 'If there's any leftover I'm sure they'll not go to waste.'

My dad wasn't arguing. He filled the pail with mortar, lifted it and, whistling as he went, lugged it down the garden a distance and then stopped. He turned. 'Why are you here?'

'Do I have to have a reason for visiting my dad ?'

'No, but you usually do. What do you want? This bucket's not getting any lighter and my new barbecue's not going to build itself.'

'Remember that witness you precognosced?'

'What about him?'

'I want you to follow him.'

My dad set the pail down on the ground. 'You're asking me to put a tail on him?'

'It's not the movies, Dad. All I want is for you to keep an eye on him for a day or two, see what he does, where he goes, who he talks to.'

'No.'

'Go on.'

'No. You're right. It's not the movies and I'm not Sam Spade.'

'Then at least ask some of your old cop pals about him. See what you can find out.'

'I've already met the guy.' My dad took the trowel from his back pocket and began to clean his nails with the point. 'He seemed okay to me and if he had a record the PF would have sent you a copy. I don't understand what the big deal is.'

'The big deal is that I don't trust him. He appears from nowhere, two weeks before the trial, and presents Dominic Quirk with a twenty-four carat defence.'

'So what? I thought you liked it when criminals got away with murder?'

'Not all criminals.'

'Just your criminals?'

'My clients.'

'I think the real reason you don't want to see the laddie Quirk get off is because he bumped you and went to a different lawyer.'

'That's rubbish, Dad. I'm not happy because Cree, from out of nowhere, gives my client a motive for killing Doreen Anderson.'

My dad put the trowel back in his pocket and hoisted the pail again. 'Ever thought that might be because he did kill her?' he said, making his way down the garden again.

'Or because someone wants it to look like he did, so that Dominic Quirk gets a walk.' I called after him. 'Someone who'd happily bribe a person to lie for him.'

He turned. 'You think Al Quirk is behind it?'

I didn't know what to think, but I intended to find out.

Chapter 32

'A meeting with my client's father is completely out of the question.'

Paul Sharp had been one hundred per cent correct. The arrival on the scene of Clyve Cree and, with him, the opening up of a new avenue of defence, had seen the Quirk family dispense with Paul's services and the instruction of someone who wouldn't ask too many questions why.

Nic Hart was smarmy, a know-it-all and president of his own fan club, and those weren't the only reasons I didn't like Quirk's new lawyer. He had a pony tail. Seriously. The man was fifty-five. He didn't even have that much hair. By my way of thinking pony tails were for schoolgirls and, maybe, female roller-skaters in sawn-off denims and halter-neck tops. Them and ponies. Hart was, however, a very quick walker because I was having some trouble keeping up with him as we climbed the steep flight of steps leading from the reception area of Edinburgh High Court. At the top I had to break into an unseemly trot as he marched across the mezzanine and only managed to catch up with him at a set of doors. I resisted the temptation to yank him back by his daft, greying ponytail and instead darted around the side and stood in front of the double doors.

'I'm not asking you for a favour,' I said. 'I am going to speak to your client's father. I'm just letting you know that, out of professional courtesy. You can either set up the meeting or I'll slap him on a witness list and seek an order for a precognition on oath and Al Quirk can talk to me in front of the Sheriff with his right hand up to God.' Hart tried to push past, but I stood firm.

'Al Quirk has no role in this case other than as an anxious father,' he said.

'You tell him I want to see him.' I stepped to the side and pulled one of the doors open for him. 'I'll decide what his role is.'

I let Hart go on his way and had only made it out of the building and the few hundred yards to where my car was parked when my mobile went off.

'What you wanting?'

I'd met Al Quirk several times during the prosecution of his son on the road traffic matter and would have recognised his gruff voice anywhere.

'I'd like to ask you a few questions,' I said.

'About what?'

'About your son's trial, and I don't want to do it over the phone.'

'And if I say no?'

I explained what would happen. If I was forced to cite him to attend court it was bound to attract a lot of publicity and the questions I had to ask were ones I didn't think he'd like publicised.

Al wasn't happy. He was even less happy when I pitched up thirty minutes later at St Mary's on Broughton Street. It was raining. Monday's twelve forty-five mass had finished and celebrants were leaving, coming down the stone steps, hoisting umbrellas and pulling up the collars of their raincoats.

'You've got five minutes,' Al said, walking down from the cathedral, dismissing his chauffeur with a wave of the hand.

'Nice to see you again, Mr Quirk?' I said. 'My brother, Malky, was asking after you.'

He stared at me for a moment as though wondering where I was going with that remark. I went no further. Did he even remember his attempt at bribing Malky?

'Good player,' he said at last. 'He just played for the wrong team. Shame what happened to him.'

I didn't have a coat. I looked skywards. 'Any chance we could talk inside? Your car maybe? I'm getting soaked.'

Al Quirk looked to where his apple-green Bentley Flying Spur was parked between two orange traffic cones and decided that the calfskin leather interior could do without the unwelcome attentions of a slightly-damp lawyer. He crooked a finger. 'Come with me.'

I followed him up the wide stone steps to the Cathedral. 'It's the Cathedral's bi-centennial this year,' he said, when we reached the top. 'They're arranging a celebration, building a special display for the relics of St Andrew.'

'What? The actual St Andrew?'

'Brother of Peter, patron saint of Scotland. The cathedral is home to a large part of one of his shoulders and a piece of his skull.'

'Why—?'

'I don't know why or what they intend to do. They've just asked for my input and when organisations ask someone like me for their *input* they mean one thing: money. Anyway, I'm happy enough to assist.'

'And the Church isn't fussy where the money comes from?'

'What do you mean by that?'

'Gambling.'

'There's nothing in the Bible about not gambling,' Al said. 'If you ever read it you'll find even the Apostles drew lots. What's that but a raffle?'

We stepped through the arched portico.

'Hail, Mary full of grace, be a doll and deal us an ace?' I laughed. He didn't.

'I know why you want to see me,' he said. 'You want to know why I didn't instruct you in Dominic's case after the fine job you did the last time.'

'That's not why I want to speak to you. I assumed that you'd chosen Paul Sharp because of his... religious leanings.'

'Paul's a Catholic. So what?'

'I thought maybe you'd realised who my brother is.'

'I've always known who your brother is. Don't tell me you think that because he played for Rangers, I ditched you for a nice Celtic-supporting lawyer?' There was a long table, draped with a cloth of burgundy velvet and gold trim and upon which sat a wooden plate for donations and a scattering of various religious leaflets. Al leaned his back against it. 'I'm from Linlithgow and so are you. We're too far east to get bogged-down in all that West of Scotland bigoted shite. Yes my father was Irish, but my wife's from Malta. Ever been there?' I hadn't. 'The place is full of magnificent Roman Catholic cathedrals.' He waved a hand about. 'Some twice the size of this place. More silver and old bones than you could shake a stick at. It's also littered with Union Flags and pictures of the Queen. The Maltese are devout Catholics who love Britain and the Royal Family. Send your average Glaswegian, Roman Catholic of Irish descent over there and his head will explode. No, Mr Munro, I'm a businessman. I choose the right person for the job no matter their religious beliefs. Believe me, choosing a different solicitor was nothing personal - happy?'

Not really. 'So what made me wrong on this occasion if I was the right man last time?' I asked, conscious of being diverted from the real purpose of my visit, but curious.

'I'm a businessman and my business is gambling. You're a lawyer, I am too, except the only law I deal in is the law of averages. You got Dominic out of a tight jam once. I didn't fancy the odds of you doing the double.'

Did that even make sense? I'd been given five minutes. I was lucky if there was thirty seconds left. Time to move on. 'That's what I want to talk to you about. The odds on Dominic's road traffic case, the one I acted in. You didn't happen to do anything to shorten them, did you?'

Al looked from his feet, to his watch, to me.

'Sophie Pratt,' I said.

'Who?'

'The eye witness. She changed her story. I was wondering why.'

Al squinted. 'Sorry, are you accusing me of something?'

There were more subtle ways of answering his question, I just couldn't think of any. 'Yes, I'm accusing you of bribing Sophie Pratt, like you tried to bribe my brother to throw a match twenty years ago and like I think you've done with Clyve Cree in Dominic's murder trial.'

Al Quirk stared at me expressionless. Suddenly he reached out and took the collar of my jacket. 'Come with me.' Maintaining his grip, he tugged me along like a naughty schoolboy being dragged by an ear to the headmaster's office. Through the West Door we went, past a font of holy water and into the nave, where amongst the rows of seats, one or two of the congregation were sitting or kneeling in prayer. He let go of my collar. 'I'm not a devoutly religious man, Mr Munro, but I'm not going to lie to you here of all places.' He shrugged. 'Okay, what can I say? Many years ago I asked your brother to give away a penalty in a nothing game that his team were always going to win by a distance. So what?' Some of those praying looked across at us. Al was oblivious. 'When Dominic was in trouble last year I had a visit from a young woman. She was carrying a child. It couldn't have been more than a few months old. Caused quite a stir in the household at the time. A woman turfing up at my door with a kid. I can tell you Mrs Quirk wasn't best pleased.'

A priest had noticed the disturbance and walked up the aisle towards us.

Al took no notice and continued. 'The young woman's name was Sophie Pratt. At the time I didn't realise that she was a witness in Dominic's case. Of course, I knew there was a female eye-witness - you'd told Dominic and he'd told me - I just didn't make the connection.' The priest homed in on us.

When he was only a few steps away he must have recognised Al, because he smiled and turned his attention to those few women who, still kneeling, were now looking over at us, not best pleased themselves. 'Looking back on it, she must have thought I'd twig. She told me that she was in debt. She'd gambled everything on AKQ on-line fruit machines and bingo. She wanted the best for her child and asked if I could do something for her.'

'And could you?' I asked.

'I gave her the best betting tip ever. I told her gambling was for mugs and that if she didn't believe me I could show her around my big house and give her a hurl in my Bentley. The girl started to cry. So did the baby. I was about to close the door in their faces when my wife took pity. She told the girl that if she promised never to gamble again, I'd refund her losses. The girl agreed and my wife made sure I kept to the promise she'd made for me. It was only a couple of grand. I never saw her again until the trial.'

The priest had led those praying off to a more peaceful area and we now had the nave to ourselves.

'You don't think what you did influenced her evidence in any way?' I asked.

He shrugged. 'What was I supposed to do? And what about you?'

'What about me?'

Al Quirk glanced again at his ingot of a wristwatch. My audience was almost over. 'You thought you knew what Sophie Pratt was going to say, you told my son on a number of occasions that she was the biggest problem for the defence and yet when she changed her story you didn't bother to ask why. No. She took the stand, she took the oath, my son was acquitted, you never objected, just took a large fee.' He curled an arm around my shoulder in a friendly, but very firm, grip. 'And it was money well spent, Mr Munro. You see, I'm an investor in people. My on-line gambling business is run by people who know what they are doing.' He spread the fingers of his other hand and pressed it against his chest. 'What do I know about the internet? I'm nearly seventy. I can't write software or design a web-site. When I was at school computers were science fiction and email came on long strips of paper that were only good for chucking out of New York skyscrapers at returning astronauts. Whether it's business, justice or old bones, I keep my input purely financial. Everything else I leave to the experts.'

The priest reappeared, hovering all-smiles in the background. Al released me, gave the man in black a regal wave and led me back out into a dreich Edinburgh afternoon. At the sight of us leaving the building, the Bentley eased out of from between the traffic cones and rolled to a halt. By the time we'd reached the foot of the steps, the chauffeur, big and fat, grey uniform, peaked cap, mirrored sunglasses, had come around and opened the back door. 'If you fear someone is going to bear false witness, Mr Munro, that's terrible, but you're going to have to point your finger at someone else.' Al Quirk pushed his face close to mine. 'Either that or tell your client to do the decent thing and admit he's the murderer.'

Chapter 33

Thankfully, it seemed like word of my break-up was not yet public knowledge. If anyone would have known about it, it would have been Jill's friend, Kaye Mitchell, editor of the local newspaper, and, yet, when I met her at Sandy's she never mentioned it. While we were waiting for our respective bacon rolls, I discovered by way of some discreet questioning, that Kaye was hoping to persuade Jill to give the Linlithgow Gazette an exclusive interview on the opening of the Zanetti technology park at Lasswade. They would be meeting up soon for an interview, probably when Jill next came up from London. I decided that was when I would strike and knew I'd have to make the most of the opportunity. No point in me hammering Jill with more reassurances that what had happened in the London hotel room had been a lot of talking and even more snoring. She needed to hear it from Suzie too.

Sadly, the latter had gone completely off radar. I tried Suzie's number for the umpteenth time as I wandered up the Royal Mile and before I entered the mobile-phone dead-zone that was the High Court. Still no answer. My messages already had to be into double figures, so I left it at that and was shoving my phone back into my pocket when I saw Mark Starr's father standing outside the front door of the Lawnmarket building, looking worried and staring down the High Street at me.

'Mark not here yet?' I asked.

He shook his head. 'When is this all going to end?' He tossed his head at the posse of journalists and cameras that had taken up position outside the big bronze door of the

High Court building. 'I'm not sure how much more I can take of this circus.'

I didn't like to tell him that this was nothing compared to the media spotlight that would shine down on his boy once the trial eventually kicked-off for real.

'The lads at work are being all right about it,' he said. 'Most of them. But I know what they're all thinking and maybe they're right. Maybe I should have stayed with Mark's mum, for his sake. A boy needs a role model, someone to look up to. I never thought I'd see the day when a son of mine—'

'Mark didn't killed that girl,' I said. 'He was stupid and took his friendship with Dominic Quirk too far, that's all. We both know he's not a murderer. There's nothing you could have done to change what happened. Remember that.'

He looked at me, his chin jutting out a little further than before. 'Thanks,' he said.

'Don't thank me yet. There's a lot of work to be done. First of all we have to find Mark. Then we'll walk him past those cameras like the innocent man he is. No skulking about or hiding. Where is he anyway?'

Mr Starrs checked his watch. 'I told him to meet me here at half-nine. It's quarter to ten. I better give his mum a phone and see if there's a problem.'

Mr Starrs found his phone. The battery was dead. I gave him mine. 'I hope he hasn't done something stupid,' he said, pressing the numbers. 'I thought he was going to cut some kind of a deal, do a few years, come out and make a fresh start. But when he came back from seeing you the other day, I sensed he'd lost hope and... Hello?' Mr Starrs pressed the mobile phone to his ear. 'Where am I? I'm outside the court with the lawyer. Where's Mark?'

After some listening Mr Starrs handed my phone back to me. 'He's in his bed.'

'What?'

'His mum says he was out for a few drinks last night, came home late and when she tried to wake him this morning he said it was all right and that he didn't have to come to court today.'

'How long will it take him to get here?'

Mr Starrs thought for a while as though I'd asked him to calculate a return trip to Mars.

'He'll need to get up and dressed, take a bus to the train. I suppose he could take a taxi and then... What times are the trains from Perth?'

'I pushed the phone at him. Call him and tell him to be here as soon as possible, if not sooner. I'll go and let counsel know that Mark's having transport difficulties or something, and see if we can have the hearing put off until later today or even continued another week.'

Defence counsel was less than receptive to my suggestion.

'The case is calling at ten. It's a peremptory diet,' Fiona said, adjusting her wig, putting just the right amount of tilt on it, 'and your client is on bail. The best I can do is get word to the clerk and see if he'll hold the case back.' She pushed past me. 'They won't give him more than half an hour. There only is one other preliminary hearing today and it's a knock-on that will take about five minutes.'

Half an hour wasn't going to be enough time. While Fiona went off to speak to the Clerk, I went downstairs to the lobby and found Mr Starrs. Taking my phone from him, I took it outside so that I could receive a signal and pressed the last number called. No answer.

'What happens now?' Mr Starrs asked when another attempt to call his son went equally unanswered.

I told him the best outcome would be a continuation, the worst, and most likely, being a straight to jail warrant. With that, I returned to the advocates' room. Fiona wasn't there, so, while I waited, I drank a cup of coffee and caught up with the back pages. The football season was well over, but there was plenty of transfer speculation. In Scotland the football didn't stop just because there was no-one playing.

Fiona returned in ten minutes, wig in hand, face like thunder. 'Did you know about this, Robbie?'

'About what?'

'About your client doing a runner?'

'A runner?'

'I spoke to Cameron Crowe and told him we had problems. He sent the cops round to his house. He wasn't there. His mum said he'd slept in and that after you'd phoned he got up and ran out of the house. She doesn't know if he's coming to court or not.'

'Of course he's coming to court,' I said.

'You know that do you? For certain? Or is that another Robbie Munro assumption?' Fiona launched her wig onto the middle of the big central table. 'Traffic difficulties.' She went over to the sideboard, poured herself a coffee and took a sip. 'Do you know how it would have looked if I'd stood up in court and told the judge that and later it was found out your client couldn't be bothered to drag himself out of bed to get to court on time?'

The speaker in the ceiling announced the calling in Court Three of Her Majesty's Advocate against Dominic Quirk and Mark Starrs. Fiona collected her wig from the table and gave it a light dusting with the back of her hand. 'Let's go and get this over with.' She took another mouthful of coffee, positioned her wig and, duly chastised, I followed her out of the door, down a flight of steps and into court. It took the judge less than a minute to grant the Crown an apprehension warrant for my client. As soon as Fiona sat down, Jock Mulholland was on his feet as though the two counsel were on either end of the same see-saw. As predicted, unlike Paul, Dominic Quirk's senior counsel had not felt any ethical urge to withdraw from proceedings merely because of his client's change of defence. It was funny how ethics varied from person to person and, usually, inversely with the hourly rate of pay.

Big Jock confirmed Quirk's plea of not guilty. 'There anent...'

'Here it comes,' Fiona whispered.

'I lodge a section seventy-eight notice.' Quirk's Q.C. passed a sheet of paper to the clerk and asked the macer to distribute a copy of the incrimination notice to the Advocate Depute and myself.

It was not unexpected. Quirk's defence had done an about-turn and was going to use Clyve Cree's evidence to impeach my client.

With the announcement that Quirk's defence was ready for trial, his senior counsel sat down again and, across the well of the court, Cameron Crowe rose slowly to his feet. One accused nowhere to be seen, the other with a new and excellent line of defence, Crowe looked like a vampire out for blood and dished-up a back pudding.

'I think your Lordship will appreciate the difficult situation in which the Crown finds itself,' he said. 'Until such time as the first accused is apprehended, I don't think it would be prudent to fix a diet of trial.' He suggested another preliminary hearing in a fortnight's time by which time, hopefully, my client would be collared.

Jock Mulholland murmured his disagreement. His instructing solicitor's pony-tail swished this way and that as he looked from the Advocate depute across the table, to his client in the dock and up to the bench.

'I hear what you say, Mr Crowe, but there are obvious time-bar issues here,' the judge said. One of the problems with successfully opposing bail was that the Crown had to be ready to start the trial within one hundred and forty days. Dominic Quirk was already well into triple figures, and the further delay occasioned by yet another preliminary hearing before fixing a trial would stretch the time limit to the maximum.

The judge looked down to his left. 'Any thoughts, Mr Mulholland?'

Defence counsel turned to Pony-tail, who got up and went over to the dock. After a brief conversation with his client, he returned and passed on instructions.

'I sympathise with the situation the Crown finds itself in,' Big Jock said unsympathetically. 'However, it was Mr Crowe who insisted that this hearing be marked as final, and a further two week delay means another fourteen days in prison for my client, with no guarantee that his co-accused will be apprehended or that we will be any nearer to fixing a trial date.'

Cameron Crowe stared across the table at me as though I were somehow to blame for the whole predicament. What would he do? Fix a trial and hope for the best? The judge wouldn't take kindly to a motion to adjourn made on the morning of the trial on the grounds that Mark Starrs was still on the run, and, yet, without my client, Crowe knew it would no longer be a cut-throat defence. Only one accused would be left holding a knife, and Jock Mulholland Q.C. would know how to wield it. The chances were that Dominic Quirk would be acquitted.

I was positive my client would be caught in a matter of days if not hours. Would Crowe risk it?

'M'Lord, I'm moving to desert this case pro loco et tempore,' he said, eventually. The courtroom buzzed while spectators tried to work out what the AD meant by that.

'Mr Mulholland?' the judge enquired.

Quirk's counsel could hardly object. A desertion, literally at this place and at this time, meant the case was dropped temporarily, but could be resurrected by the Crown in due course. It meant that instead of the balance of one hundred and forty days, they had one year, minus Quirk's time on remand, to try him. The downside was the accused's immediate release on bail.

The court rose, the judge was led off, Dominic Quirk punched the air and his parents, like most of the other onlookers, watched in stunned silence wondering what had just happened.

Fiona went off to change. I left the building and stood at the front door. Like a lawn spewing forth earthworms after a rain shower, news reporters emerged from the court, wriggling and jostling their way up the Royal Mile to where Dominic Quirk hugged his father and weeping mother.

Soon, Nic Hart, pony-tail blowing freely in the wind, oozed onto the scene to face the TV cameras and magnanimously accept full credit for his client's release.

Fiona materialised at my side. 'What do you want me to do with the bundle?' she asked. With the grant of a non-appearance warrant, counsel and solicitor could render their fees. I suggested that she hold off and hang onto the papers meantime. I had no idea what Mark Starrs was playing at, but I still suspected it wouldn't be a case of if, but, rather, when we saw our mutual client again. And the next time he'd be behind prison bars.

'Hard to believe,' isn't it?' she said, watching the Quirk family reunion. 'Just a few weeks ago he was in jail, without a defence. Now look at him. A free man. And I'll bet even his dad wouldn't give you odds against an acquittal.'

Chapter 34

'You're back early,' Grace-Mary said, when I returned from the High Court and trudged into the office around midday. 'Everything go okay?'

I explained that everything had gone very not okay, on account of our client failing to trap.

From my desk phone I tried Mark Starrs' home number.

'Don't get too comfortable, you've got a custody at Stirling,' Grace-Mary shouted through to me.

No answer yet again from my client. There wasn't much I could do except wait for his arrest. 'Any other calls?' I yelled, sifting through the mail on my desk. I didn't bother to sit down, I'd be off again in a couple of minutes.

'Your brother was looking for you and Zoë phoned again.'

Zoë. Blast. I'd meant to get in touch about her reference.

'You didn't actually believe all that did you?' Grace-Mary asked.

I left the morning mail and went through to reception. 'What do you mean?'

'The other day when Zoë called, it was personal. I couldn't very well say that in front of your dad, he was bad enough when he thought it was business.'

'Personal. How personal?'

Grace-Mary put in her earphones and started to bash out a letter. 'Personal enough for me to know not to ask.'

'Really?'

Grace-Mary stopped typing. 'All right. Personal enough for her not to tell me.'

'Have you still got her number?'

Grace-Mary had written it down on a yellow-sticky and stuck it to the frame of my computer screen in time-honoured fashion. I went through, peeled it off and, having decided to phone when I got back from court, and after Grace-Mary had left for the day, headed out of the office and proceeded in a northerly direction.

Court security systems in Scottish courts are by-passable only by those in the know or by students of history. I punched in the requisite four digit memorable date at the door to the cells, wandered through to the interview rooms adjacent to courtroom two and having announced my arrival via a squawky intercom, waited for my latest client to be brought from his cage. He was sixteen years of age and charged with a breach of the peace. It was an exceedingly minor matter, but, unfortunately for him, in the course of the disturbance he was alleged to have called someone 'a poof'. That made it a homophobically aggravated. offence. That made it zero-tolerance. That made it a prosecution. In a bizarre reversal of *'sticks and stones may break my bones, but names will never harm me'* the Scottish Government let violent offenders roam the streets with impunity, but call someone a bad name and you could expect the full weight of the law to come down on you – even if you were a school boy overheard slagging-off one of your mates.

It being mid-week, my client was one of only a handful of custodies. Having taken instructions and tendered a plea of not guilty, I was leaving court when I came across Gail Paton in the lobby, leaning against an ancient, ornate, cast-iron radiator, chatting to another female lawyer and one of the clerks. When she saw me walk by she detached herself from the conversation and came over. 'Robbie, I've been meaning to give you a call,' she said, looking around shiftily as though she was about to try and sell me a dodgy wristwatch. 'Can we go somewhere private?'

The same four numbers got us into the agents' room. There was no-one else there. 'It's about Victor Devlin,' she said. 'Have you seen him recently?'

What was she talking about? The whole reason I'd gone through to Glasgow two weeks before was to ask if Gail knew her client's whereabouts.

'Are you sure?' she asked, once I'd told her I hadn't met her client recently or at any other time in the past.

'Of course I'm sure. Why?'

'When we spoke, you were asking about Devlin and a mining operation. What was the stuff called?'

'Tantalite.'

'That's it. You wanted to know if I'd seen him. Well, you're not the only one. The cops have asked me the same question.'

'Did they say why?'

They had. As I'd learned in my initial discussions with Rupert, Devlin had invested a lot of other people's money very unwisely. Unwisely for them, not so much for him. The police as well as some officers from Her Majesty's Revenue and Customs wanted to ask him a few questions.

'They can't find him, but they know he's still active. They put a trace on his company's bank account to monitor it and see where it led them. By the time they decided they needed to put a freeze on it, the account had been cleared out by electronic transfers.'

It sounded like Victor Devlin, or, possibly, some men with guns had got hold of a certain memory-stick.

'You seem to be well up with the police investigation,' I said.

'I have a contact. Well he's more than a contact actually, or he would like to be.'

'Aren't you the right wee Mata Hari?'

'It's not like that. Brian's a forensic accountant. I met him during Devlin's first case that never went to trial. He was helping the Crown crunch the numbers. After the case was binned he called me, well, actually, I made him call me, he just didn't realise it, and we've been going out ever since. He's working on the new case now and our relationship has made some of the proceeds of crime team a trifle jumpy, so we've had to promise never to talk shop. Jim insists we keep to that promise. Which is why I have to take the occasional shufty into his briefcase, otherwise I wouldn't even know I was on the Crown's list of possible money-launderers.'

'What are you going to do? Is there any way I can help?'

Gail laughed. 'Don't worry about me. It's no big deal. Of course I had money in my account from Victor Devlin. He was my client. I'm not a charity and payments in lieu of legal fees are exempt from the anti-moneylaundering regulations, so long as the fee can be justified. Not a problem for me. I have a stack of files to show the work done. What about you?'

'What about me?'

'Robbie,' she said. 'You're on the list too.'

Chapter 35

I was outside Stirling Sheriff Court, hunting for my car keys when I felt my phone buzz. Over lunch-time, I'd borrowed a phone from another lawyer and called Jill hoping the unrecognised number would fool her. I'd met with some limited success by way of a promise from her P.A. that she'd have Jill call me back.

I drew the phone from my pocket like a gunslinger. It wasn't Jill. It was Malky.

'Do you never answer your phone? I've been trying to phone you all day,' he said.

'What is it, Malky?' My brother only called when he wanted something or was in trouble. So fairly often.

'I've got a wee problem,' he said, sheepishly. 'Well, actually, it's you who's got the problem - and it's not really all that wee.'

'Malky, just tell me what it is, will you?' I might as well add it to my other problems like being a cancelled bridegroom and a suspected money-launderer.

I climbed into my car. One good thing about the recession was that a lot of traffic wardens had been paid off. Either that or I'd just been lucky and the out of date ticket that I kept lying along the top of the dashboard for all occasions had been enough to keep those still in a job at bay.

'That whisky you got Dad for Father's Day,' Malky said. 'I was round at his house and he was showing it off to me - again.'

'Tell me you haven't dropped it.'

He hadn't. It was much worse than that.

* * * * *

The first pleasant evening in a while and my dad was making the most of it, dressed in T-shirt and baggy shorts, sitting in a deckchair at the bottom of his garden doing a newspaper crossword. His feet were resting on a pile of bricks and next to them, on top of a partially constructed barbecue, was perched a familiar cardboard tube, complete with printed tartan and an embossed stag's head.

'Okay, what did Malky tell you?' I asked.

My dad didn't acknowledge my presence. 'Three across, four letters, first letter 'L', last letter 'R', one who tells lies.' He tapped his pen against his front teeth. 'I'm sure I should know this.'

'I didn't actually lie to you,' I said.

'Didn't you?' He cast the newspaper aside. The crossword was already filled in. He'd been sitting waiting for me. There was no way this was going to end well. 'You gave me that...' he pointed the careless toe of his sandal at the whisky tube, 'and let me believe you meant it as a gift. When...' he stifled my attempt at a protest, 'you didn't even know what was in it. Although you thought you did. You thought you were giving me a bottle of, of...' He could hardly bring himself to say the words. 'Co-op blended. A gift from one of your junkie clients. It's probably nicked.'

Malky had left nothing out and added some more to the story by the sounds of it.

'It's not stolen, Dad. It was a present, but not from a junkie client, from a friend of mine.'

I could have pretended that I'd only told Malky the story so he wouldn't feel bad about his gift, but the truth was out now and I couldn't get the genie back in the whisky bottle. I told him about Suzie, my role in her breakthrough novel and her thank-you present.

'Then the whisky is yours,' he said.

I hesitated. There was four thousand pounds worth of whisky in that tacky cardboard tube after all.

'Will you drink it?' he asked.

'I don't think so. I'd see it as more of an investment.'

He grunted. 'I saw the laddie Quirk on the news tonight. What happened to your boy?'

'Wish I knew.'

'How's business otherwise?'

Seeing as how I was in truth mode, I told him. 'Shocking.'

'Then take the whisky. You know me - Islay malts - I can take them or leave them.'

Even he found it hard to keep a straight face at that. 'What I mean is that if you're not going to drink it, sell it. Put it towards that new house for you and Jill.'

I'd never experienced a panic attack, never really understood the concept until that moment. My chest felt tight, my breathing came sharp and short. Sweat broke out on my brow. If my dad found out that I'd mucked up my relationship with the daughter of his deceased best friend, that there was to be no wedding, no grand-children, no Caol Ila miniatures...

My phone buzzed. I checked the number and didn't recognise it. I used it as an excuse. 'Got to go, Dad.'

My dad heaved himself out of his deckchair. 'Wait there a minute,' he said, and set off down the garden returning minutes later with a paperback edition of Portcullis, first in the Debbie Day series. I didn't recognise the cover picture. It had obviously been revamped since the first edition came out a few years previously. 'This her?' He opened the book to reveal a full page photograph of Suzie on the inside of the cover, looking prettier than ever, but in a serious, authorly sort of a way. 'Di Prentice up at St Michael's gave me a loan of it. She's a big fan.'

I never quite knew the set-up between my dad and Dr Diane Prentice other than they collaborated a lot over charity events for the local hospice. Whether there was any more to the relationship was something I didn't care to dwell on.

'If I'd known the hero was going to be a woman, I wouldn't have bothered.' My dad had obviously judged the book by its gory cover and not by the blurb on the back. 'Pretty good, though.' He flicked through the pages and then held out the book to me. 'I've read the other two as well. Got them from the library. She's not too bad a writer for a woman. Keeps the usual boyfriend trouble and shoe-shopping to a minimum.'

I took the paperback from my dad the literary critic. In the unlikely event that I ever managed to find Suzie, I could give her the good news that I had a promo for the cover of her next book. I could see it now. *Praise for Suzie Lake. 'She's not too bad a writer - for a woman', Alex Munro.* 'Thanks, but I've read it,' I said.

'I don't want you to read it. I want you to get Suzie Lake to sign it. It'll be a nice present for Diane - and it's the least you can do.'

Chapter 36

Mark Starrs was in custody. So Grace-Mary informed me when I arrived at my office next morning, coffee and bacon roll in hand. She put that day's court files on a chair in my room and the mail requiring my attention in a wire basket on my desk. 'He was caught last night at his house.'

The only entry in my diary that Friday was a trial that had been postponed at an earlier intermediate diet due to problems with Crown witnesses, and so I had the morning to myself. It was a chance to catch up with some paperwork, which usually meant bureaucratic gymnastics with the Scottish Legal Aid Board.

'Where is he?' I asked.

'Barlinnie for the moment. They're not sure if they're going to shift him to Saughton or Lowmoss. It depends on the bail situation.'

I couldn't see there being a bail situation for Mark Starrs. How was I supposed to persuade a Sheriff to release once more an accused who couldn't be bothered to get out of his scratcher for something as important as a preliminary hearing in a murder trial?

'Are you going to visit him?' Grace-Mary asked.

'Maybe later in the week. I'm too busy today.' There was also the fact that even though this was a high-profile murder case, the Scottish Legal Aid Board would only sanction two prison consultations and I'd rather use them up when I had something worthwhile to talk to my client about and not merely his non-existent bail prospects.

Fortified by another bite of bacon roll, I logged into SLAB's on-line system. Grace-Mary was about to leave the room when I called her back. 'I have a wee job for you, involving your favourite author,' I said.

'Oh, yes. And what would that be?'

'Find her for me. I need to speak to her urgently.'

I could tell my secretary was dying to ask why, but she didn't. 'I bet you haven't phoned Zoë yet, have you?' she asked on her way out of the room.

'I'll do it straight after this,' I called to her, through a mouthful of bread and Ayrshire's finest.

The phone rang. It was Fiona Faye.

'I take it you've heard?' I said.

She had. 'The Crown is not going to waste any more time. A fresh indictment is ready to be served, expect a final preliminary hearing to follow and the trial up and running inside two or three weeks. It doesn't give us a lot of time to deal with the damaging new evidence from this guy Cree. Any more info on him?'

I told her what I knew, which wasn't a lot.

'I think Mr Starrs should have stayed better hidden,' Fiona said, and I knew what she meant. There was nothing worse than a Crown witness with no axe to grind. Cree's evidence was good ammunition for the Crown and even better for Dominic Quirk's defence. With it, all guns would be aimed at Mark Starrs. We agreed to consult with our client sometime soon in order to finalise the line of defence and decide how best to tackle the Crown's new witness.

Half an hour later, Grace-Mary came through with a spiral notepad. 'Right. The only definite lead I had was the Hay-on-Wye book festival, she was doing a talk there, but that's passed now.' She must have sensed my impatience, because she scowled at me and flicked over to the next page. 'Her next engagement is Bloody Scotland in Stirling and that's months away. I can't find word of her appearing at anything in between.'

I didn't see how you could lose an internationally acclaimed crime writer during a summer when just about every city, town and village in the UK was hosting a book fair. 'Have you tried her agent?' I asked.

'You mean to say you know who her agent is and you never thought to tell me?'

'No. I thought you might have found that out.'

'How?'

'Have you tried typing: *Suzie Lake's literary agent*, into Google to see what it comes up with?'

'No,' Grace-Mary answered. 'Have you?'

I hadn't, but I did. The search engine came up with someone called Sam Travers of The Travers, Cowgill + Thomson Agency. They had an office in Edinburgh.

I phoned, gave the receptionist some old chat about a highly confidential, but extremely urgent matter concerning Suzie and was offered an appointment in a fortnight. Nothing I could say would change her mind. Mr Travers was out to lunch and wouldn't be back until later in the day. I could try calling then. I didn't. Instead, I caught the next train to Haymarket, walked down Shandwick Place and located the offices of Travers, Cowgill + Thomson in Rutland Square at the foot of Lothian Road.

By the time I arrived, Sam Travers had only just returned from lunch and would have great difficulty cramming me into his afternoon's busy schedule. I said I was prepared to wait and was grudgingly shown to a room with some uncomfortable hard-backed chairs and an ancient teak coffee table that was host to a thousand mug-rings. High in one of the corners of the room a tiny flat screen played CNN, volume off, subtitles on. After I'd read the rolling news a few times I lost interest and, before I felt compelled to read one of the mags, I glanced around the wall at the framed photographs of those I reasonably inferred to be clients of the firm. Some I guessed would be authors and thus readily unidentifiable. One, a former soap star, I recognised from TV; any more of a ham and he'd have been honey-glazed. Nowadays he spent a lot of time extolling the cuisine at a particular fast-food restaurant chain, the doors of which I doubted very much he had ever darkened without a fat endorsement cheque on his hip. In the main they were just people with lots of tooth enamel.

Eventually I was forced to flick through one of the magazines, before turning my attention to the Independent: a newspaper with little enough Scottish football in it at the best of times, far less the close season. I had been waiting at least forty-five minutes when the receptionist came through.

'Mr Travers wonders if you'd like anything while you're waiting,' she said.

'A coffee would be nice,' I ventured, before realising that I had interrupted her.

She gave me a tight little smile. 'There is a water cooler outside this door and, if you like, I can fetch some more mints.' She gestured to a small smoked-glass ashtray on the edge of the coffee table that contained a few sweeties and then left.

I was on my fifth pan-drop when she returned to say that Mr Travers would see me now. I followed her through.

For some reason I had imagined Mr Travers as an elderly gentleman in a tweed suit with a reasonable amount of facial hair, who'd managed to struggle back to the office after a liquid lunch and planned spending the rest of the afternoon dashing off a batch of rejection letters. He was in fact very young in T-shirt and jeans, with a mass of dark hair that was arranged in a fairly haphazard fashion on the top of his head. He sat reclined, ankles crossed, heels resting on a chrome and glass desk, the tyre-track soles of his boots on display. He didn't get up when I was shown in, just swirled a finger around in the air and then pointed grimly at the plastic bucket chair in front of me.

'You've got five. Pitch it,' he said, leaning back, hands clasped behind his head.

'I'm not—'

Mop-head unlocked his hands and snapped fingers at me. 'Synopsis?'

'No, you don't—'

'What are we talking? I don't do kids, Y A, poetry, short stories and no porn unless it's Fifty Shades—'

'I'm not here about a book,' I said. Fifty shades of grey best described my underwear drawer. 'I'm here about Suzie Lake. We're friends. I've something very important to ask her, but I can't seem to track her down and she's not answering her phone.'

He looked at me suspiciously. 'Friends? Who are you again?'

'Robbie Munro. We were at Uni together. I gave Suzie the idea for her first book, you know, featuring what's-her-name, the policewoman.'

'Debbie Day?' Travers jerked a thumb at a framed promotional poster on the wall displaying the three covers of Suzie's crime series fanned out and the author's signature boldly scrawled across the bottom in black marker-pen.

'Yeah, that's it, the first one, Portcullis, that was me.'

The young man removed his feet from the desk and sat up straight, a worried look on his face. 'Can I see some ID?'

It wasn't a problem. I took out my Law Society photo identity card and handed it over to him. He studied both sides of it and handed it back. 'Are you a lawyer?'

I stifled the surge of sarcastic comebacks and settled for, 'yes.'

'Then I know exactly why you want to speak to Suzie and...' He rose from his seat, walked over and opened the door. 'I think you should leave.'

He couldn't possibly know what I wanted to speak to Suzie about. I told him so. 'It's a personal matter. All I need is a means of contacting her. Maybe she has a new phone. How about an email address?'

'I'm going to count to three,' he said.

After the 'are you a lawyer' remark, I had my doubts he'd manage. I stood. 'I think you've got hold of the wrong end of the stick, Mr Travers. I'm Suzie's friend.'

He held the door open even wider. 'You're either a stalker, in which case I'm going to call the police, or you're here to serve a writ or something. Either way, you're leaving. Understand?'

No, I didn't understand. Not yet. But I would.

Chapter 37

'Women!' Ever since I'd arrived at his place that Friday night my dad had been pacing the kitchen, muttering to himself while Malky and I discussed the size of the five-a-side blister I'd acquired that evening and wondered whether to alert the Guinness Book of Records.

'Can't live with them...,' Malky said to him. 'Murder them and you end up with someone like Robbie getting you the jail.' It was the standard of humour I'd come to expect from my brother.

'Ha, bloody, ha.' The old man turned on me. 'Have you got that book signed for Diane, yet?'

'You gave it to me yesterday.'

'It was the day before.'

'Well, you never said it was urgent.'

'Well it is now.' He waited to be asked why. I knew better than to start him off on another rant.

'Get what signed?' Malky asked.

'Robbie knows this famous author; she's Diane Prentice's favourite. Things between Diane and me are a wee bit... you know, and I thought that if I, well...'

'Fallen out with the foxy doctor and looking for a peace offering, is that it?' For once, Malky was quicker than me on the uptake.

My dad shoved my blistered foot from the kitchen chair on which it was delicately propped and sat down. 'I was up at the Hospice this afternoon, telling her about my idea for a quiz-night. All I did was ask her out for dinner and she got all bolshy with me.'

I'd met Diane Prentice on a number of occasions. Bolshy I couldn't imagine.

Malky winced. 'Knock-back? Happened to me once. Actually it never, I'm just saying that to make you feel better, but, Dad, I don't know how to say this. Dr Prentice...' My brother rubbed the brow that had headed a million footballs. 'If for argument's sake we say that she's playing in the Champions League. You're probably more—'

'The East of Scotland Shield?' I suggested.

Malky was more charitable. 'I'd say Europa League.'

'Are you two quite finished? I wasn't knocked back.' My dad folded his arms. 'It was bad enough when she told me I didn't have to keep opening doors for her. Now Diane's insisting on paying the next time we go out for a meal,' he said, to his sons' looks of bemusement.

'And?' we asked in unison.

'And, she's a woman. I'm a man,' he added, as though we might have somehow failed to spot the gender difference.

'Come off it Dad, you're a man, not a caveman,' I said. 'It's not like she can't afford picking up the occasional tab. She'll be earning a lot more than you, even on your police pension.'

But it appeared I hadn't quite grasped his point. 'Do you expect me to go out for dinner, maybe a nice bottle of wine, perhaps a wee whisky afterwards...' Who was he kidding? There would be no perhaps about it. 'And then sit there when the waiter comes with the bill and let my date dig into her purse? Why don't I let her open the door for me on the way out, walk me home and send me flowers in the morning?'

'Wouldn't bother me,' Malky said.

'A lot of things don't bother you, Malky. But I have certain standards. And taste. If Diane is Champions League, your mother was World Cup material.' He snorted. 'I mean, look at that thing I saw you with the other night.'

'Janie?' Malky said, after giving it some thought.

'That her name? What a sight. Earrings everywhere and more tattoos than the Edinburgh Festival.'

'I think he means, Babs,' I said.

Malky rummaged around in his memory some more. 'Babs. Shit. I was supposed to phone her and I don't even know what I did with her number.'

'Don't worry, you should find her quite easily with a magnet,' my dad muttered.

'What are you getting on at me for?' Malky asked. 'Have a go at Robbie, for a change. You've seen some of the hing-oots he's had over the years.'

'Well, he's getting married and settling down. What's wrong with you?'

Malky snorted. 'I've already got one of those new TESCO carriers. That's the only bag-for-life I want.'

My dad wasn't having my fiancée spoken about in that way. 'Jill's not like the slappers you dodge about with. She's a proper lady. You'll not see her paying for dinner any time soon. Am I right Robbie?'

I mustered a sickly grin. How right he was.

'So you're saying Diane Prentice isn't a proper lady?' Malky said. 'Just because she wants to be treated like an equal and allowed to pay her own way?'

My dad had to think about that one. 'Diane's definitely a lady, she's just... a little misguided and confused. That's why I want to patch things up with her. As for being equal, that's nonsense of course.'

'Don't you think women are as intelligent as men, then?' Malky sneered.

Clearly pre-Dr Diane, the women in my dad's past had been intelligent enough to let him shell-out for dinner, but, instead of saying so, I thought it best to try and wrap things up by suggesting a drink. I was parched after football and mention of beer was pretty much guaranteed to end most of my brother's conversations. That and the introduction of logic. 'I'm gasping for a—'

Malky cut me off. 'Diane Prentice is a doctor, what were you, Dad? Oh, yeah. Thirty-five years in the Force and you ended up a uniform-sergeant.'

I was getting worried for my brother; he had the mouth for an argument, just not the brains.

My dad's face flushed, his moustache trembled. 'I'll tell you what I am, sonny. I'm homo sapien, that's a human being to you Malky. And what is homo sapien? It's a species of animal. Evolution has made male and female animals different, physically and mentally. The male is *supposed* to be dominant. The male elephant-seal goes bashing other elephant-seals about the place, there's tusks and blubber flying everywhere. What does the female elephant seal do? She sits on an ice-berg and watches or maybe goes for a dip in the Arctic Ocean. I mean, you don't see a stag taking off his antlers and saying to his doe, how about you go rutting for a change, dear? I'm knackered, I think I'll stay home and watch the fawns today.'

It would be giving the old man too much credit to think he'd intended the 'dear' pun.

'So you're saying that women are the weaker sex?' Malky said.

'Physically, it's obvious. You've seen women's sports. Has there ever been a woman centre-half who was your equal? There's nothing to stop a woman playing football for the Scotland team if she's good enough.'

'Okay,' Malky said, 'what about intelligence?'

'They'd need to be pretty stupid to be less intelligent than you, Malky,' I said.

Malky ignored the jibe, intent on continuing the debate with his father. 'Are you going to start spouting off about how all the famous scientists have been men? Do I have to mention *doctor* Diane again?' He was really going for it. I could only assume he felt aggrieved at his recent, if temporary, demotion from favoured-son status and in that brain of his, softened as it was by a thousand penalty box clearances, had formed the idea that he could wreak some kind of revenge by mocking my dad's views on sexual equality. I sat back to watch the mis-match of the year.

My dad glowered at him. 'If you'd keep your trap shut for two seconds you might learn something. Men and women are different. We're not equal physically and, intelligence-wise, we're wired differently. Women were blessed with a different intelligence to men,' my dad explained. 'They're smarter. It more than makes up for muscles and inventing rocket-surgery. You don't think it's called Mother Nature by mistake do you? It's a rigged game. Women live longer than men, for one thing, and look at Wimbledon. The female tennis players get the same money for playing worse tennis and only three sets instead of five. How did that happen? Can you see a man coming along to the All England Club and saying, I'm not as good at tennis as those other chaps, and I like to finish work early, but is it all right if I get paid the same money?'

'So what are women better at?' Malky asked.

'Lots of things. Looking after kids is the big one, raising the next generation of homo sapien, securing the survival of the species despite all those clever men with the biceps trying to blow everyone up. If more women were in places of power there wouldn't be so many wars.'

'Just a lot of jealous countries not talking to each other,' I said, but my dad was not to put off.

'And then there's lap-dancing,' he said. Where was he going with this? It was descending more into a stream of consciousness than a reasoned argument; however, if I told him that it would only get worse. 'Two women were debating lap-dancing on telly last night. One woman says that men who try to stop independent women working as sex professionals are prudish and domineering, the other says, no, those same independent sex-professionals are being exploited by men. Face it, boys, we live in a man bad, woman good world. What's the opposite of feminism? There isn't one. Your either a feminist or you're a male chauvinist pig. Woman are either right or men are wrong.'

'I take it you've never been to Afghanistan?' I said. 'I think you'll find there are some women there who might want to argue the toss on that.'

My dad grunted. 'Well, I don't live in Afghanistan. I live in Scotland, and if there ever was a war of the sexes in this country, then we lost it a while back, it's just that the women thought it best not to break the news to us.' My dad turned to my brother again. 'Malky, I'm not so stupid that I don't know Diane is a lot more intelligent than me. I know it, she knows it, but that doesn't stop me being a man.'

'I still don't see the big problem in letting a woman pick up the bill now and again,' Malky said. 'A night out with foxy Dr Di and your dinner for free? If you ask me it would be a smart move on your part to accept.'

'Well, no-one is asking you. Like, I've already told you, I'm a man...' He paused, I thought for a moment it might be to beat his chest, but it was only to catch his breath. 'And if the only self-respect I can cling onto is exercising good manners when a woman is leaving or entering a building and forking out for the occasional steak and ale pie then that's how it's going to be. Got it?' He thumped the table, climbed to his feet and trod on my sore foot in the process. 'And you. Put some socks on, this is a kitchen you're in.'

'I'm sorry I asked now,' Malky said, after the old man had stomped out of the room and we heard the front door slam. 'Where's he gone, do you think?'

'Probably off to find another elephant-seal to bash into,' I said, rubbing my sore foot.

Malky got up and went to the cupboard under the sink. After a rummage around he came out with the bottle of Ardbeg, nearly empty, or if you were an optimist, not nearly full.

'You're driving,' I reminded him.

Malky put the whisky back under the sink and settled for what he called a soft drink, and other people called beer. He took a couple of bottles out of the fridge and popped them.

He handed one to me. 'So, Dad's okay about the mix-up over that rare malt you accidentally got him for Fathers' Day?'

'Yeah, you breaking your promise not to say anything worked out quite well as it happened.' I took a drink of beer. 'Dad's happy that I sell it and put it towards a new house for me and...' No way could I go down this avenue of conversation. If my brother caught onto the fact that my relationship with Jill had stalled, my dad would hear about it shortly afterwards and it would make the whole whisky-gate affair seem like nothing. I took another swig of beer.

'How's Jill doing?' Malky asked, polishing off his bottle of beer in two long pulls and one loud burp. 'Dad was talking about grand-kids the other day. I think I should tell you there was mention of biological clocks.'

I took another rapid swig of beer. I had to find Suzie. Only she could sort this out. 'You ever thought of writing a book, Malky?' I asked.

'Me? What about?'

'About yourself.'

'You mean a biography?'

'Yeah, well, an autobiography. A lot of ex-footballers do it. You don't have to write it yourself, though, you pay a ghost-writer to do it.'

'If I don't write it myself, how's it an autobiography, smarty?'

'It's like you are writing it, but really you just tell someone your life story, they write it and you wait for the royalties to roll in.'

At that point my dad arrived back carrying a stack of kindling wood. He dropped it on the hearth and came through to the kitchen again, perfectly calm now. He was like his old coal fire, heating up in no time and cooling down just as quickly. 'What are you two talking about?'

'I was saying to Malky how he should write a book about his football career,' I said, stepping onto safe ground. Football and the Golden Boy's career were two of my dad's favourite topics.

He grunted his interest. 'I've just read Billy Bremner's biography.' He went over to the fridge and helped himself to a beer. 'Keep Fighting, it's called. A fitting title. Billy was a right wee battler. Did I ever tell you that I met him once?'

He had. My dad's story about meeting the Leeds United and Scotland legend in a London pub after a Wembley encounter with the Auld Enemy was dragged out and given an airing on a regular basis.

He raised his bottle in salute. 'Billy Bremner: one of the immortals.' He drank some beer and licked the foam from his moustache. 'Of course, he's dead now.'

'So what do you think, Malky?' I asked.

Malky was definitely up for it.

'Good, then I'll need to find you an agent. Now let me see...'

'Someone will need to write the book first,' my dad said.

I put him right on that score. 'That's only for real writers, Dad. If you're a celebrity, even a clapped-out centre-half like Malky, there are agents and publishers fighting over you before pen's hit paper.'

'What about your friend the author?' my dad said. 'Has she not got an agent?'

But I was way ahead of him.

Chapter 38

'You want me to pretend to be your brother's private secretary?'

I gathered my Monday morning case files and stuffed them into my briefcase. 'If you don't mind,' I said, jotting down the name and number of Suzie's literary agent on a Post-it and handing it to Grace-Mary. 'Say you'd like an appointment with Mr—'

'Travers?'

'No, better make it one of the others. Tell them *the* Malky Munro is looking for a publisher and seeking representation for his forthcoming autobiography entitled... Just make something up.' I grabbed my briefcase and headed for the door. 'My phone will be on silent, so leave a message.'

The message came through around noon, after I'd finished the cited court and was waiting with baited breath to see if any of my client's who'd been lifted and held in custody over the weekend would be prosecuted.

I dialled my answering service. I had two new messages; both from Grace-Mary.

'I phoned the agency. Mr Thomson died fighting for his country in World War two,' she intoned in message one. 'Mr Cowgill is Miss Cowgill and she's never heard of your brother. Bye.'

The Grace-Mary of message two was more upbeat. 'Miss Cowgill phoned back. She's heard of Malky now and is free at four today. I said you'd be there. You've no appointments this afternoon and I can sign your mail for you. Bye.'

More good news: two of my custody clients were the lucky recipients of summary complaints. Well, maybe it wasn't such good news for them, but I had a business to run.

The custody court was late in starting, as Sheriffs vied for the privilege not to do it, and Malky, who I'd phoned at lunch-time, was pacing up and down on Rutland Square when I parked my car outside the offices of Travers, Cowgill + Thomson at the back of four that afternoon.

'What's the plan?' he asked.

The plan was to blag my way in again and find out how I could contact Suzie.

'Leave it to me,' I said. I led him across the road, up the three large stone steps and in through the big front door. If the receptionist remembered me, she didn't say. There was no waiting room and no pan-drops. We were shown straight through to an office twice the size of mop-head Travers's, where I was not so much met as engulfed by a large, plump woman with a shaggy perm, dangly-earrings and dressed in an enormous floral frock that billowed about her. Somewhere there was a set of curtains with a very big hole in them.

'The famous Malky Munro, great to see you,' she enthused, releasing me from her hug.

'I'm Robbie, Malky's brother,' I said. With a thumb over my shoulder I gestured to Malky who was standing behind me in the doorway. 'This is Malky.'

Unfazed, the big woman put her hands on my shoulders, studied me at arm's length and pushed me aside. 'Of course it is.' Arms out wide, she closed in on my brother. 'Malky, how the hell are you? I'm Eleanor. Big fan.'

Malky, who'd always been quick on his feet, side-stepped, putting me between himself and the oncoming swathes of floral material, and there was an awkward moment or two before the agent invited us to park ourselves on a brutally soft settee, while she sat cross-legged on a multi-coloured rug on the floor and looked up at us.

'Not sure I like the title,' she said, 'but we can change that.'

'I was thinking,' Malky said. Never a good idea. 'Robbie says I should hire someone to write the book, but wouldn't I make more money if I wrote it myself? Everyone's got a book in them, haven't they?'

Eleanor gave him a patronising pat on the knee. 'They have, love, and I usually find it's best left right where it is. Don't worry,' as I'd suspected, she was sanguine about such trivialities as there being no actual book, 'ghost-writers are ten-a-penny. I'll set up a meet. All you need do, Malky, is regurgitate your life story - all the good stuff about rising through the amateur ranks, your time with Rangers, Scotland, the brilliant cup final goal...' Someone had been doing their homework. 'The booze, the birds...' The agent frowned and lowered her voice. 'The tragic death of your partner, mirroring the death of your mother when you were just a...' She noticed the concerned look on my brother's face. 'I'm sorry to have to bring up these events, Malky, but—'

'It was the Juniors,' Malky corrected her. 'I was never an amateur. Unless you count the school team. I went straight into Junior football with The Rose and then Senior with Rangers.'

It was Eleanor's turn to look concerned. I explained that despite the title, Junior football was played by adults. It was a rung lower than the Senior game, but a step up from Amateur.

'Unless, it's Queens Park,' Malky corrected me, only helping to confuse matters further. 'They're amateurs, but better than Juniors and play in the Senior league.'

Eleanor let that wave of information wash over her for a moment or two. 'You tell the story, the spook will get it all down on paper. I'll make a few calls and see whose available; someone who knows a bit about football; seniors and juniors and all that stuff.'

'I was wondering about Suzie Lake,' I said. 'I believe your firm represents her.'

Eleanor let rip a loud laugh. 'Suzie? Firstly, I doubt if she knows any more about football than I do, and, secondly, she's an internationally acclaimed author and, even if she is skint, do you know how much she'd charge?'

Suzie skint? I laughed at my own stupidity. 'You're right. We'll leave the choice of writer to you.'

Eleanor seemed happy at that. Somehow she raised herself from a cross-legged position on the floor without using her hands and, lifting a wooden box from her desk, opened it to reveal neat rows of cigarettes. She offered the box around. Malky and I declined.

'I've cut down to five a day,' she said, sticking a cigarette between her lips and lighting it up in one smooth, yet frenzied, motion.

'How is Suzie, these days?' I asked.

Eyes closed, the literary agent inhaled deeply then let out a steady stream of smoke. After a moment or two's bliss she opened her eyes again and wafted a hand in front of her face as though trying to get a better look at me through the fog. 'You know Suzie?'

'We're old friends.'

'Must be a while since you saw her last, if you don't know the state she's got herself in, the poor lamb.'

'Last time I saw her she was complaining of writer's block,' I said.

'Well she'd better unblock it fast. If she doesn't bash out another bestseller soon, the publishers will be looking for their advance back and there's nothing that idiot next door will be able to do about it. The boy's not a fraction of the agent his father was. Mike Travers always protected his clients and could have sold white heather to a gypsy. It was Mike who spotted Suzie. He encouraged her, edited that terrible first book of hers, proof-read it, did everything bar paint the cover.' Eleanor flicked a length of ash into an empty coffee mug. 'What was it called again...?'

'Portcullis? I gave Suzie the—'

'No, no, way before that. It was some romantic drivel. Bombed like a B forty-two, but Mike stuck with her. When

Portcullis came along, he secured a three book deal and the biggest advance in this agency's history. Then he went and died. Heart attack.' She took a few rapid draws, stubbed out the remains of the cigarette and pointed to the mug from which a few stray wisps of smoke were rising. 'By the way, I'm only counting that as half.' The mug seemed pretty full of half cigarettes. 'You didn't mind did you?'

Malky was bored now and had started to wander around the room, looking at framed photographs similar to the type I'd seen in the waiting room on my previous visit. 'Is that not her off the telly who used to be married to that guy who was in... What was the name of the band?'

Eleanor swished over to where Malky loitered. 'The Pink Pineapples,' she said. 'Strange isn't it, how many bands are named after fruit? Pink Pineapples - got to be something Freudian going on there. Anyway, Natalie Jack, one of my clients, married the lead singer, discovered he was one, a fruit I mean, and divorced him - but not most of his money. After that she wrote a book about what a bastard he was. It's what publishers call a divorce made in heaven.'

'What are these?' Malky asked, pointing to what were patently hardback books stacked neatly on a nearby sideboard.

'Signed copies from one of our debut novelists. Go on, take one. Could be right up your street.'

Malky's literary street was something of a cul-de-sac of football and car magazines; nonetheless, he picked up one of the hardbound volumes and studied with more than polite interest a bright front cover on which I glimpsed a submarine and some helicopters featuring prominently.

Before Malky could ask any more inane questions, I joined the pair of them and tried to steer the good ship Eleanor in the direction of why I'd really come. 'So what's Suzie's problem?' I asked. 'I'd like to be able to help if I could.'

Eleanor smiled. 'I'm sure you would, dear, but it's all about money. She's being sued right left and centre. What Suzie needs right now is either a lottery win or a sugar daddy, and, sadly, it's all this guy's fault.' She picked up one of the hardbacks from the pile. I thought she was going to give it to me, instead, she turned it over to show a photograph of the author on the back cover. The mug-shot was in black and white in soft focus, a strong, serious face, beneath a harshly-cropped head of hair.

'Then again,' Eleanor said, 'that big pussycat hasn't had his own troubles to seek. Tragic really. Two such terribly good people with such terribly bad luck. I wouldn't be surprised if one day they got together, despite everything.' She flipped the book around again and placed it back with the others.

By this time Malky had finished reading the blurb on the inside cover and was examining the signature on the fly-leaf. 'Is that his real name? How come all those famous writers have weird names?' I really hoped he wasn't going to suggest he change his own name, not for his autobiography. He closed the book and studied the cover, where the author's name was writ large in bold crimson lettering. 'Weird,' he said. 'I've never seen Clive spelt with a Y before.'

Chapter 39

I dropped Malky off at Haymarket Station, did a quick about turn and drove east to North Berwick.
Fiona Faye had recently remarried. I'd only met her latest husband, Tim, once; at their wedding. I liked him. He was a good ten years older than Fiona and an expert in clocks and barometers with a major auction-house. A quiet man, with a dry sense of humour, he'd somehow managed to, first of all, talk Fiona into marrying him and then, even more surprisingly, to sell her beloved New Town property and move to his sandstone villa on the outskirts of North Berwick. A property only six or seven miles from Victor Devlin's hideaway, but not in nearly so remote a setting.

Fiona's clerk had given me the address and rough directions. None of the properties on the street seemed to have numbers, only names, mostly on a nautical theme: Sea Breeze, Windward, The Crow's Nest, and even though I drove slowly down the quiet country road, houses to my right, fields and the North Sea to my left, I would have driven past had I not spied a tall, lanky frame at the garden gate, wearing a Bill and Ben hat and attacking an innocent rosebush with a pair of secateurs.

I parked opposite the house, half on the roadway, half on the raised stretch of dirt that served as a pavement, and climbed out of my car.

'Fiona!' Tim yelled, as he saw me approach. 'You've a visitor.' He snipped of a stalk that so far I could see was meaning nobody any harm.

'Tell them to go away!' I could hear Fiona, but couldn't see her.

Tim pricked himself on a thorn, sucked at the bead of blood that had formed on the tip of his finger and then wiped his hand on a trouser leg. He stepped aside to let me past. 'Enter at your own risk. Her ladyship watched a cookery programme on TV last night. Believe me it's a bloody sight safer out here.'

As he renewed his assault on the vegetation, I walked down the path, through the open front door and followed the smoke trail to the kitchen where Fiona was standing at an open oven door, looking in. With a degree of hesitation, she reached a set of pink oven gloves inside and they came out with a loaf tin, the contents of which were gently smouldering.

'Oh, it's you,' she said, when she saw me come into the room.. She carried the loaf tin to the sink, placed it in the basin and ran the tap across it. 'What is gas mark five, anyway? I don't have gas mark five, mine starts at a hundred and goes right up to two-twenty.'

'What was it supposed to be before you burned it at the stake?' I asked.

'Banana chocolate chip loaf.'[1]

'Ambitious.'

'It's supposed to be *easy-peasy* banana chocolate-chip loaf.' Fiona pulled off the oven gloves and pitched them onto a big oak table that was strewn with mixing bowls, spoons, bags of sugar, cartons of milk, boxes of eggs, all covered in a layer of flour. 'To what do I owe?' She pulled out a chair and sat down. 'Make it quick, I'll have to try again, I promised Tim I'd bake him something. He's been pruning things all afternoon. Problem is, I know as much about baking as he does about gardening.'

'Okay, don't think I'm crazy.'

'Too late for that love.'

'Clyve Cree?'

'Who?'

'The new Crown witness in Mark Starr's case. Turns out he's a former Royal Marine, now an author writing lad's fiction, full of explosions and helicopters. My brother's a big fan of his.'

Using the side of her hand, Fiona gathered a small pile of sugar and flour and pulled it off the table into her other hand. She leaned back in her chair and dropped the mixture into the sink. 'Very interesting but it's not baking me any buns.'

'I have an old friend, Suzie Lake—'

'The writer? I loved Portcullis. Great book. Keep meaning to buy her next—'

'Do you remember Joe Finnegan?'

'The guy from Shettleston who shot those two—'

'I told Suzie about the case and she wrote a book about it.'

'What's it called?'

'Portcullis.'

Fiona looked as confused as I imagined she did when reading a cake recipe. 'What's Portcullis got to do with your gangster client blowing holes in the heads of his drug-dealing rivals?'

'It doesn't matter.'

'Then why are you telling me? Listen, Robbie. I so enjoy our little chats, but can this not wait? Why don't you swing by Parliament house one afternoon when we're both not so busy?'

'I'm not busy now.'

'Well I am. Tim will be finished maiming the plant life in a moment or two and all I'll have to show for my afternoon's efforts is a charcoal log.'

'So what you can't cook? Are you telling me Tim thought he was marrying a Michelin star chef and not a Q.C.?'

Touchy subject. It turned out that Chris's first wife was a domestic goddess who could whisk-up a sponge cake so light that on baking days air traffic control had to be notified.

'Surprised he let her get away,' I said. 'What happened? Did they make an Eton Mess of the marriage?'

Fiona didn't find that nearly as funny as I did. While I was laughing at my own joke, she leaned to her left and looked down the hallway. Coast clear, she whispered. 'Let's just say he no longer employs a gardener and that these days he refers to his ex as 'the Tartlet'.' She stood up again and dusted her apron. Clouds of flour rose about her. 'I know it shouldn't bother me that I'm so hopeless in the kitchen, it just does.'

I winked at her. 'I'm sure you make up for it in another room of the house.'

'The bedroom? Trust me, Robbie. When men of a certain age are given the choice between sex and a really good Eve's Pudding, there's only one thing getting covered in whipped cream and it ain't the wife.'

I took off my jacket and hung it on a hook on the back door. 'Leave this to me.' I strode across the kitchen, placed my hands on Fiona's shoulders and gently pushed her down onto the chair again. There was already sugar, flour, milk and eggs on the table. 'Right, I'm going to need a drop of oil and one really big frying pan.'

Inside twenty minutes I'd knocked out a dozen pancakes that my dad and his dad before him would have been proud of. I let them cool, wrapped in a clean dish towel, while I told Fiona about Clyve Cree and his potentially damaging evidence.

Fiona couldn't resist taking a peak below the dish towel. 'And you think this has got something to do with Suzie Lake in some way?' she asked, nipping a chunk from the side of a pancake.

I explained how Al Quirk had past form for trying to influence the outcome of certain events and the chats I'd had with Suzie on the problems with Dominic Quirk's defence. 'Then out of the woodwork pops Clyve Cree. Ready-made witness all set to give our client a motive for murder and

Quirk an incrimination defence that didn't exist a fortnight ago.'

'Mmm. These are really good pancakes,' Fiona said, stealing a second piece. 'Who taught you to bake?'

'My dad.'

Fiona couldn't stop nibbling. 'Then the man's a culinary genius.'

'Trust me,' I said. 'He's not. But he does have a fool-proof recipe. Do you have maple syrup?'

She didn't.

'Don't worry. Golden syrup is just as good,' I said.

'I probably should, but I don't even know what that is.'

'Then we'll just melt some sugar and butter in a wee pot and...'

Fiona went off, presumably in search of a sauce pan.

'Not now,' I said. 'The deal was I made pancakes, you listened to what I had to say.'

'I thought you'd finished. Very interesting it was too. And imaginative. Have you ever thought of writing a book? I'm sure Miss Lake could help you - once she gets out of jail, that is. After all, if what you're suggesting is true, and I doubt that very much, she's guilty of attempting to pervert the course of justice.'

The front door opened. Tim clumped into the porch and began to divest himself of gardening clobber.

'Let me take care of Suzie,' I said. 'You've just finished a stint in Crown Office. All I'm asking is that you put out a few feelers. Find out if there is a link between Cree and Al Quirk. I'd do it, but there is no way the Legal Aid Board would cover the costs of a private detective. I might as well ask them to sanction funds to send Philip Marlowe off in search of the Maltese Falcon.'

'Sorry. No can do. And the Maltese Falcon was written by Hammett, not Chandler, so it would be Sam Spade, not Philip Marlowe.' Fiona made a move towards the pancakes. I stepped in front of them. She sighed. 'It's like this, Robbie. Al

Quirk's a philanthropist who sits on some of the same charitable committees as the Lord Justice Clerk. Hard to believe, I know, but I wasn't universally loved at Crown Office; too fond of antiquated notions like sufficiency of evidence and the presumption of innocence. There's some of them in there who'd be more than happy to go running to the LJC if I started casting aspersions about his chum.'

Tim stuck his head into the kitchen and inhaled deeply. 'Smells great.' He clapped his dirty hands together. 'I'll just nip off and have a quick shower. Staying for supper, Robbie?'

'Sadly, not,' Fiona answered for me. 'The work of a defence solicitor is never done.'

I said my farewells to Tim before he went off in search of soap and water. 'There's got to be somebody you trust who can make a few discreet enquiries,' I said to Fiona.

'I'm sorry, Robbie.'

'But I made the pancakes...'

Fiona smiled. 'And I listened. That was the deal, wasn't it?' She lifted the tea towel and nicked another morsel from the already savaged top pancake. 'Tim is going to love these.'

'And he'll love you all the more for having made them. In fact he'll probably want you to make them again and again. It's going to be a huge disappointment next time when I'm not here and you dish him up a stack of rubber frisbees.' There was a notepad on one of the kitchen counters. I picked up a nearby pen and tapped my chin with it thoughtfully. 'If only you had some kind of... I don't know... fool-proof recipe.'

Chapter 40

Tuesday mid-July. Grace-Mary was looking for a pay-rise. It was a regular, though, thankfully, not too frequent, occurrence, which, like my secretary's request for air-conditioning, delivered annually during Scotland's one week of sunny weather, I generally played with a straight bat.

'You do know you've got twenty thousand pounds sitting on deposit?' she said, and deploying some arcane rites and a computer keyboard, brought up a screen full of figures in an instant. She pointed to some of them. Devlin Polymineral Incorporated had paid me another three instalments of five thousand pounds over the past three weeks, to go with the first five grand Mr Posh had paid me up front. It didn't make sense. The deal I'd struck was to recover and make over a memory-stick full of important data, and in that task I had singularly failed. I told Grace-Mary that I'd take her request into consideration and asked her to try and get me Gail Paton on the phone. Gail wasn't available. Her office said that she'd gone to Barlinnie Prison and wasn't expected back until the afternoon.

The drive west took me around half an hour. Most Scottish prisons had been refurbished in recent years. Not so long ago, the greasy, cramped surroundings of the average prison visit room would have appalled a sardine. Now they were clean and spacious. The other difference was that they were empty of lawyers. Legal aid rates for prison visits were outrageously low and often non-existent. For a legal aid lawyer, a client in jail was a drain on resources, so if you were having to drag yourself all the way out to prison, it made sense to see as many clients as possible in order to make it pay. I had only one client in Barlinnie in need of a visit. I liked to think that having so few clients behind bars was down to my success rate, but it was probably more to do with lack of business. At any rate it was a good chance for me to kill two birds with the one stone.

I spied Gail as I was walking down the centre aisle between the two rows of glass-fronted interview rooms. She was sitting with her back to me, a client in red prison-issue polo shirt and jeans sitting across the table from her, between them a stack of case files. I opened the door and poked my head in. Gail said she would be another half-hour, which was enough time for me to have a word with Mark Starrs and to discuss his negligible bail prospects.

There were twenty of those thirty minutes remaining when my client appeared with his prison escort through the door at the top of the hall.

'Starrs!' the screw shouted down the length of the hall.

'Room five!' his colleague, who was sitting at a computer screen at the other end, called back and the prisoner was pointed in the direction of my booth. He wasn't happy.

'What's going on, exactly?' he asked, taking a seat across the table from me.

It seemed simple enough to me. What was going on, exactly, was that he had got blootered and been too hung-over to crawl out of his bed in time for his preliminary hearing.

'When you failed to appear they granted a warrant,' I replied, not bothering to add the part about how he had since been arrested and taken to jail, thinking that much was obvious.

'But I got a phone from the cops telling me I didn't need to go to court,' Starrs said. 'I was going to phone you and then I got your email saying the case had been put back a week.'

It wasn't unusual for preliminary hearings to be postponed. It could be done by a judge in chambers, if sufficient grounds were set out in a section 75 minute and both Crown and defence agreed. In the case against Starrs and Quirk the first two preliminary hearings had been knocked-on in that way, while the defence awaited disclosure of evidence, but if that was the best excuse my client could come up with, it wasn't good enough.

'I didn't send you an email,' I said.

Starrs looked at me as though I were mad. 'But I emailed you back. You wanted to meet me and wondered when would be best. I emailed back to say any time was okay.'

'Think Mark. When have I ever sent you an email? I don't even know your email address. I hardly know my own.'

'It's easy enough to remember,' he said. 'mail at bestdefence.biz.'

I liked it. Pity it wasn't mine. If he was telling the truth then it was clear someone had played a trick on him. If his mum could provide me with a print out of the bogus email from his home PC, I could see his prospects for bail increasing from nil to slim.

The door of the cubicle next to mine opened and first her client and then Gail Paton exited. Her estimation of time had been spot on.

I told Starrs that there was no time to waste and that I would contact his mother straightaway to obtain a copy of the email. All going well I could have a bail petition lodged before close of business. With a bit of luck we could have a bail hearing arranged for the following week. My client groaned. If he thought another few days in custody was bad, how would he handle a life sentence?

After a brief farewell, Mark Starrs and I went in opposite directions down the hall; the young man to his cell, me to the waiting room just outside the interview room complex, where Gail Paton was sitting on one of the ridiculously low chairs. I never understood how such a soft seat could be so uncomfortable.

'What's up, Robbie?' she asked.

I didn't mention the twenty thousand pounds in my bank account from Devlin Polyminerals, only that I was wondering if there was any more word on the conman.

'The Crown's Confiscation Unit is all over Devlin because of that tantalite mining thing you were telling me about,' Gail said. 'It's been decided to raise a civil action to recover what they see as the proceeds of crime. A lot of important people have been scammed and they are more interested in getting the money back, rather than waiting five years in the hope that Devlin might be convicted of something. For one thing, they'd have to catch him first.'

That had been the problem with the old procedure; before you could recover the proceeds of crime there was the not so small matter of having someone convicted of committing a crime. In a complicated case that could take years with no guarantee that a bored and confused jury would see things the prosecution's way after months' of trial. Raising civil proceedings was evidentially a lot simpler. The standard of proof was lowered to the balance of probabilities, rather than beyond a reasonable doubt, and civil actions were decided by judges not juries, who were paid to be bored and less prone to confusion when asked to make a finding in favour of the Crown.

'I had been hoping for a criminal trial for obvious reasons,' Gail said. 'It may still happen and so I'm trying to keep in the loop, but I've already had Messengers-at-Arms at my door trying to serve an Initial Writ. I had to tell them to get lost. I don't know where Victor Devlin is, far less have instructions to accept service of a civil writ craving twenty million.' Gail pulled herself out of the seat. 'Which, from my memory of civil procedure, means they'll have to serve it edictally, pin the writ up on the walls of court and advertise it in the newspaper, all that stuff. If Devlin doesn't put in a notice of intention to defend, they'll be granted a decree by default which will enable them to go against his assets.'

'So where do I fit in?'

'The Crown has two lists. The first is a list of some companies in which they think Devlin has an interest. It's watching the bank accounts of those companies and making a second list of where the money is going. Your firm's name appears on that second list. How much have you got? I wouldn't touch it if I were you. You're probably going to have to pay it back at some stage, if it's deemed to be proceeds of crime. Wait and see what happens.'

'How long is that likely to be?'

'Ages,' Gail said. 'One of the Messengers-at-Arms was quite chatty while trying to squeeze Devlin's whereabouts out of me. He was saying that Devlin has literally scores of companies, mostly registered off-shore and in countries with some very unhelpful governments. The Crown is suing Devlin personally at the moment and also the Polymineral Company, but word is that the bulk of the assets are out of reach, a lot has simply disappeared and much investigation will need to be carried out. Meantime, some people who were caught in the fraud are raising their own actions because it's not clear what will happen to any proceeds of crime the Crown does recover. Most likely the Scottish Government will just take it and splurge it on important things like Gaelic lessons for Polish immigrants.

'I've been thinking about what you told me earlier and putting the money through as a fee,' I said. 'If I just leave it where it is it's going to look suspicious.'

Gail shrugged. 'Might work. If you can show that you were properly instructed by Devlin or one of his companies.'

'How about if I was instructed by his representative?'

'I take it you carried out a proper client identification, completed an anti-money-laundering matrix?' she said in a tone that suggested she knew very well I wouldn't have bothered.

'You've had a lot of dealings with Devlin and his business associates over the years. Rupert Smith? Recognise the name.'

Gail creased her face, mouth turned down at the corners. 'Nope. I think I'd have remembered a name like Rupert.' We walked along the corridor and through the security door and I waited in the reception area while Gail collected her handbag from one of the plastic cubicles. For some people, prison is a revolving door; Barlinnie actually has one, and after we'd walked through it to the outside world, Gail stopped.

'Hang on a moment, Robbie. She took her cellphone from her bag, prodded the screen and put it under her hair. 'Jim, it's me,' she said. 'About the Devlin case. Yes, again. He's my client, remember? Away you go. How can the case be confidential if they're about to pin a writ to the walls of court and advertise it in the Scotsman? Never mind how I know. Any more snash and I'll not be letting you buy me dinner tonight.' She winked at me. 'So, are you sitting comfortably? Good. I've a name for you. Rupert Smith. Is he involved in anyway? Maybe an associate of Devlin, a director or a secretary of one of his companies or something like that?' She listened for a while, tapping her foot on the tiled floor. 'Right. Thanks. See that wasn't so difficult was it? No, not Italian again: Thai, that new place in the west end. No, the other new place down the west end. Well, find out. I don't know - ask one of those policemen you're so pally with. See you at eight. No jeans. And not that old pair of cords either.' She pressed the screen to end the call.

'What did he say?' I asked, feeling slightly sorry for Jim whoever he was. An accountant and Gail's boyfriend. Some people had no luck.

'I was wrong,' Gail said. 'I know, I know, doesn't happen a lot, but apparently there aren't two lists: there are three. The third being a list of Victor Devlin's victims in order of those who've lost the most money. And...' She stuffed the mobile phone into her handbag again. 'It would seem that your Rupert Smith is right at the very top.'

Chapter 41

'There's someone here to see you,' Sandy, proprietor of Bistro Alessandro, master of all things fried and percolated, whispered to me as I ordered my Wednesday morning coffee and bacon roll. Without looking up from the counter, he jerked his head at a corner table, where even a broad-brimmed summer hat and dark glasses couldn't disguise the elusive Suzie. 'Bella, bella.'

I told Sandy I'd be sitting in for breakfast. He had already anticipated my instructions and set down on the counter a bacon roll on a saucer and a mug of black coffee. I carried them over to where Suzie was sitting in front of an untouched cup of tea, a thin slice of lemon drifted across the surface. From her expression it looked like she'd been sucking on it.

According to ex-Police Sergeant Alexander Munro, there was no such thing as a coincidence; that was the first thing new recruits to the Force were told. That and how not to leave bruises. Suzie had served me up a whole bunch of coincidences, right from her re-entering my life after an interval of almost twenty years, to accidentally bumping into me in London and coaxing out of me the entire background to the Dominic Quirk case, to her sharing the same literary agency as surprise witness Clyve Cree. I had so many questions to ask I hardly knew where to start.

Suzie kicked things off. 'We can't see each other anymore, Robbie. You have to stay away, for both our sakes.'

'I don't think that's such a good idea,' I said.

She stirred the tea with a teaspoon, chasing the lemon slice around the rim of the cup. 'It is. Trust me.'

'But I don't trust you, Suzie. I know you're involved with Al Quirk. You used me to find out how to get his son off with murder and it looks like you're now part of a plan to falsify evidence to secure the boy's acquittal by using Clyve Cree as a witness.'

Suzie didn't reply. She took the slice of lemon for a few more spins around the cup before hooking it out with the teaspoon and laying it on the side of the saucer, where it drooped over the edge like a dead anaemic goldfish, dripping onto the table.

'It's not too late,' I said. 'Tell Al Quirk and this guy Cree to back off. Cree just needs to go to the cops, tell them he was mistaken and it must have been some other conversation he overheard on a different night between different people. Things will go back to how they were. Without Cree's evidence, the Crown will offer the old deal; the one you thought wasn't good enough. Mark Starrs will do a couple of years and Dominic Quirk can take his chances at trial with his original defence.'

Slowly, Suzie lifted the cup from its saucer and wet her lips. Eventually she looked up at me. Even through the sunglasses her eyes looked tired, sad. 'Robbie, you think you know what you're talking about, but you don't.'

I took her hand across the table. 'Listen to me, Suzie. You're my friend, but Mark Starrs is my client. It's my job to secure him the best possible result. I'm not going to sit back and watch him go off to prison, just so that Dominic Quirk can walk away from yet another dead body.'

'You don't say.' Suzie pulled her hand away. 'And here was I thinking you had more than a little to do with him walking away from the first one.' She drank some more tea. 'But, of course, last time his father was paying you. Who are you to judge? It's about money with you, Robbie. At the end of the day, everything in this world is all about money.' She pulled a napkin from the wooden holder in the centre of the table, dabbed her mouth and looked at it as though she expected to see something interesting.

Sandy came over, wiping his hands on a blue and white chequered tea towel. 'Everything all right?' he asked, staring suspiciously at my untouched Americano and intact bacon roll.

I assured him everything was fine. He took a step or two away from the table so that he stood directly behind Suzie. He jabbed a finger down at the top of her sunhat and silently, but dramatically, mouthed, 'who's she?' He let his hand go limp, waved it from side to side, narrowed his eyes and blew out through his rounded lips. I lifted Suzie's cup and saucer, handed it to him and asked him to go freshen it up.

'What if you believed that a certain person was guilty,' Suzie asked, after Sandy had retreated back behind his counter. 'Would it change your mind if you knew that, at the end of the day, justice was going to be done, no matter how it was achieved?'

'It depends very much on whose idea of justice we're talking about. Do you remember I told you the story of the Black Bitch? Her master was left to die of starvation. Theft was a capital offence back then. Nowadays he'd probably have been given a community payback order. Was death by starvation a just sentence because it happened to be the law back then?'

'If you can't do the time, don't do the crime,' Suzie said.

Suzie's tea arrived, with what looked suspiciously like the same slice of lemon taking another dip. I gave Sandy what he eventually recognised as a step-away-from-the-lady stare.

'Eternity is a long sentence,' I said, after the cafe-owner had grudgingly obeyed.

'What about for murder?'

'That takes us back to who you're asking.'

'The people with power decide what justice is,' Suzie said.

'And the people with money are the people with power, is that right? Suzie I know you're in a financial mess. Don't try to justify your actions with pseudo-jurisprudential waffle. Leave that sort of thing to me. How much were you paid? Enough to clear your debts?'

Suzie took a final sip of tea, collected the shoulder-bag that hung from the back of her chair and stood up. 'It's been nice chatting, Robbie; however, I only came to warn you to stay away. You think I'm in trouble? You should think of yourself.'

I had been looking for Suzie so long I couldn't just let her go. I got to my feet and stood in the way, blocking her path. 'If Cree goes into the witness box and lies, I'll have no option other than to take you down with him. Think about it. Attempting to pervert the course of justice, perjury, these all carry long prison sentences.'

Suzie draped the strap of her bag over her shoulder. 'You would do that?' she said. 'You'd see me sent to prison to save someone who for all you know killed an innocent teenage girl?'

'That's right because for all I know, he didn't. And even if I did know, it wouldn't change my duty to do my best for my client.'

Suzie put her hands out and took me by the wrists. 'There is a bigger picture here that you can't see, Robbie,' she said. 'With you on his side I'm sure Mark Starrs will do just fine.'

'I meant what I said, Suzie.'

She ran the flat of a hand down the side of my face. Please don't do anything stupid, something you might regret.' I'd never been threatened in such a pleasant way before, it took a second or two before I realised what she'd said. She took her hand away, unbuckled the front flap of her bag and removed an A5 sized package. 'How's Jill?' she asked, a smile tacked on. 'Wedding plans moving along at apace?'

And that was another thing, never mind getting her to sign a book for my dad: how could I ask Suzie to plead my case to my ex-fiancée now?

She stuffed the package into my hand, dipped a shoulder and pushed past me. 'I really do hope everything goes well.'

With a tinkle of the bell over the café door she was gone.

Sandy came over. 'Give me her phone number and Jill need never know any of this ever happened,' he laughed, flicking my legs with his tea-towel.

I stared down at the envelope in my hand. It was brown and fat, just the way I liked them - except I had a funny feeling I wasn't going to like this one.

Chapter 42

From Sandy's, post bacon roll and coffee, I made the short trip to my office and began to sift through my in-tray of non-urgent mail.

'Why not start with the urgent stuff first?' Grace-Mary asked.

When I told her what I was looking for, she disappeared through to reception and returned with an A5 size gold-coloured card in her hand.

'Invitations belong on the mantelpiece,' she said.

I took it from her. My invite to Zanetti's opening ceremony, with charity ball to follow. I was supposed to RSVP.

'Have I?' I asked.

'Have you what?'

'RSVP'd.'

'You mean have I RSVP'd for you?'

'You are my secretary.'

'True, but I'm not your psychic secretary.'

'Why didn't you tell me it had come?'

'Why do you think it was on the mantelpiece?'

It doesn't matter how good you are at tennis, at the end of the day, the wall wins. There was an email address at the foot of the card. I bashed off a message of acceptance. My finger had no sooner departed the send button than another email bounced back at me advising, with regret, that my name was no longer on the list of official invitees and wishing me good health and a nice day.

I screwed up the invitation, threw it across the room and very nearly into the bin. With any chance of assistance from Suzie out of the question, the idea of catching Jill at the

Zanetti charity ball had seemed a brilliant one. On the walk back from Sandy's, my brain cells electric with caffeine, I had imagined it all: music, dancing, champagne, I approach Jill with my truthful explanation, she's resilient at first, but my charms prevail, then come the tears, forgiveness, re-engagement, perhaps some more champagne.... What was I left with now? Camping outside Jill's house, hoping to catch her on one of her rare trips home and probably being lifted for stalking?

No. Desperate times called for desperate measures.

Kaye Mitchell opened the brown envelope and pulled out a photograph. She studied it for a moment or two. It was a picture of Suzie and me sitting at the Savannah Hotel bar. 'You know Suzie Lake?' She laid the photograph down on the desk and dealt the next face up on top: Suzie and me cuddled up on a very small sofa. 'Yup, you know Suzie, all right.' She turned over the next: Suzie and me, arms around each other, stumbling along a hotel corridor. By the time she'd flicked through a picnic scene in Princes Street Gardens and come to the last photograph: the two subjects standing next to a playground swing, lips inches apart, Kaye had made her diagnosis. 'You're stuffed.'

Normally, I wouldn't have dreamt of disclosing to Kaye anything that I didn't want widely publicised. A life in newspapers had left the editor of the Linlithgow Gazette with a tendency to spread news, some of which was best unspread.

'What's the plan?' she asked, stuffing the photos back into the brown envelope. She looked out of the window and the thirty or so feet down to the High Street. 'I can open the window for you to jump just now or would you rather wait here and I'll get Jill to push you out?'

I sat down across from her and pushed a stack of past editions to one side so that I could see her across a Himalaya of paperwork. It was how my desk would have looked, but for Grace-Mary. 'Jill's already pushed me,' I said.

'As in...?'

'As in, these photographs will only confirm what she already believes. She broke off the engagement a couple of weeks ago.'

Kaye stood and leaned over the desk at me. 'And no-one told me?' she said, as though she'd missed a UFO landing on Linlithgow Cross while she'd been out to lunch.

'I was trying to keep it quiet, until I had a chance to explain.'

'Two weeks?'

'Two weeks last Friday.'

'Jill's never mentioned it.'

If Jill hadn't yet confided in her pal, then maybe she wasn't fully committed to the break-up. Maybe she was just trying to teach me a lesson.

Kaye thought about it. 'Right enough, it's over a fortnight since I saw her last. You would have thought she could have given me a call, though.'

'When's the interview?' I asked. 'Your exclusive look around Zanetti's new research facility?'

'I told you about that did I?'

'You mentioned you were trying to arrange one. We were in Sandy's. Has it happened yet?'

'Oh, yes, Sandy's. I remember. You never had enough money for your rolls and I had to—'

'I've been trying to speak to Jill, but she won't meet with me, won't even answer the phone, and so—'

'You thought you could tag along with me to the interview and tender the most important plea in mitigation of your life, is that it?' Kaye had grasped the point and summed it up perfectly in twenty-five words or less. Those early years in small ads hadn't been wasted. She hauled open a desk drawer, then another and another until, at last, she surfaced with an ivory card embossed with gold lettering. 'No, that's not it.' She threw the card back into the drawer and came out with another. The invitation was printed on white card, not gold like mine had been, but it had the unmistakable yellow and blue Zanetti Biological's logo at the top. 'My hopes of exclusivity were unfounded,' Kaye said. 'I'll be there, but along with the rest of the press pack. There's a free bar - things could get messy.'

I couldn't help notice that the invitation was addressed to Ms Kaye Mitchell and partner.

Kaye sighed when I pointed this out to her. 'Have you even got a dinner suit?' she asked. 'One that fits?'

I did. Somewhere. That probably fitted. Once.

'Okay,' Kaye said. 'But you owe me one.' She handed me back the brown envelope 'And, by the way, you're our designated driver.'

Chapter 43

Like me, Al Quirk did a lot for charity. I called mine legal aid work. He called his the Quirk Foundation, an organisation that promoted the arts and medical research, but mainly Al Quirk. His well-publicised philanthropy and resulting popularity made him easy to locate, but incredibly difficult to get close enough to talk to, especially for me. Since our encounter at St Mary's Cathedral, I knew he wouldn't be thrilled to meet again. And yet, I needed to pass a message to him. Fortunately, I had another avenue to go down.

The Quirks had not been resident in Linlithgow for many years and the family now resided in an immense sandstone property on a quiet street in the Grange area of Edinburgh. It was the kind of neighbourhood where you got funny looks if you were so poor you had to drive your own car. The property was surrounded by a high wall, topped with black arrow railings, broken only by formidable entrance gates that I was surprised to find wide open when I drove up to them that Thursday night. From the early evening Scottish news, I knew Al Quirk was in Glasgow, addressing officials from Creative Scotland on the importance of funding a national youth arts strategy. No doubt they were happy to put up with Al rabbiting on at them for a while so long as he shoved his hand in his pocket at the end.

I had expected to be received by a maid, but there was no immediate answer to my tug on the brass bell-pull that protruded from the wall next to the front door, and I was about to try again when I heard a sound from within.

'Is that you, Al?' The muffled voice of Mrs Quirk, who I'd met on several occasions during her son's earlier difficulties.

'It's Robbie Munro, Mrs Quirk,' I shouted through four inches of solid oak.

There was the sound of a key turning and the door swung slowly open. Christobel Quirk squinted at me through a pair of ornate spectacles. *'Who* is it?'

'Robbie Munro. I acted for Dominic in his... In his last case.'

She smiled. 'Of course you did. I knew your mother, did you know that?'

I did. On every occasion we'd ever met, Mrs Quirk had told me that.

'She was a lovely girl. We met on our first day at school, sat side by side at the same desk at West Port Primary. They knocked it down. It's a roundabout now. How's your dad?'

Before I could answer she was off again, telling me how she could remember when a young police cadet had asked to take her friend out on a first date to see the new James Bond movie at The Ritz Cinema; a baronial building, its facade all battlements, machicolations and rope mouldings, now a derelict and crumbling edifice on Linlithgow High Street, just an uncoiled reel of film from my office.

'Mrs Quirk—'

'Don't be silly. It's Chrissie. Have you come to see Aloysius? If you have, I'm afraid he's out - as usual. Away speaking to some art students in Glasgow. Dominic has gone too. I'm glad. It's the first time he's left the house since he got out on bail. We've tried to encourage him to go visit friends, after all, even although he's not allowed to drive yet, we've got chauffeur on tap.' She shook her head sadly. 'To think I used to complain about him treating this place like a hotel. Now he just wants to sit in his room and mope. He might as well still be in prison.'

'Actually, Chrissie, it's you I came to speak to.'

Her smile dropped. 'Nothing bad has happened has it? Is it about Dominic's case? You know he's got a new lawyer don't you? I told Aloysius we should have stuck with you, but he was adamant...' She stepped back. 'Sorry, I'm being rude. Come in. Sorry about the state of me.' She looked down at herself as though she were wearing filthy rags and not a cerise trouser-suit straight off the Milan cat-walk, albeit after some serious letting-out.

'I was through the back watering my plants,' she said, setting off down the wide hallway, me following, my feet sinking ankle deep into the thick pile of a ruby-red carpet. We passed several rooms and continued right to the end, where there was a set of French doors and, beyond them, a wide sweep of floodlit lawn. We took a right turn and entered what Mrs Quirk called the conservatory, which it was: in the same way the London Eye was a fairground Ferris wheel. It was the sort of structure I'd have expected to find in the tropical section of a botanical garden, housing exotic plant species and perhaps the occasional rare butterfly or hummingbird. The incredibly humid atmosphere was disturbed only by the gentle background hum of an irrigation system. Jill would have loved the place. Her own house had once been full of plants, nothing like on this scale, yet it had broken her heart to give them away to friends when she realised she'd be spending most of her time in London or further abroad. The only alternative had been to leave them in my charge; might as well entrust the Scottish justice system to the Scottish National Party.

Mrs Quirk offered me a seat. I preferred to stand. She waved a hand at the sea of pot plants, heavy with sweet smelling blossoms. 'Dominic calls them my surrogate children.' She picked up a plastic spray bottle and gently blasted the foliage. 'Evening is the time to water. Do it during the day and you'll only end up scorching the leaves.' Some spray landed on her glasses. She put down the bottle and from somewhere secreted about her person produced a small white square of cloth which she used to clean the lenses. 'Micro-fibres. They don't smear like a hanky,' she said.

I didn't know when Al Quirk was due to return. I only knew that I didn't want to be found bending the ear of his wife when he did, and that debating the benefits of microfibres over the clumsy, big-old fibres of a cotton handkerchief was only wasting time. 'Mrs Quirk—'

'Chrissie,' she reminded me, giving her glasses a final polish. 'No need to be so formal. I think we know each other well enough to be on first name terms, don't you?'

'That depends,' I said. 'I'm here to talk to you about Dominic's case. I've already spoken to your husband and he won't be very pleased if he finds out I've been here saying the same things to you.'

She fired off another rapid burst from the spray bottle, then put it down and perched herself on the edge of a wooden rocking chair. 'You were very good to Dominic in his first case. Do you know it's almost a year to the day since the crash? There's not a day goes by without me thinking about poor Wendy. When I was in court and saw those photographs the police had taken...' She conjured up once more the little white square and blew her nose on its microfibres. 'I send flowers to the grave every month. I told Aloysius you should be acting for Dominic in this one too. Now he's saying you're trying to put the blame on Dominic for killing that girl in St Andrews. Is that true?'

'Yes... that's sort of why I'm here. I'm worried that your husband is trying to fabricate evidence to have Dominic found not guilty.'

'What do you mean fabricate?'

'Making it up. Bribing a witness to say he heard something that he didn't, to put the blame on my client.'

'Dominic says—'

'I'm not interested in what Dominic says.' I apologised for my abruptness. 'Chrissie, I can't talk about Dominic. What he has to say he needs to keep for his own lawyer.'

'His new lawyer's an idiot. And I'm not just talking about his stupid hair. Mr Sharp was a lot better.'

'Mr Sharp had to pull out of the case because he was going to lead a particular defence for Dominic, one that even if successful would have sent him to jail, though only for a relatively short time. Not life.'

'I don't want him to go to jail at all,' she said.

'And that's why your husband has taken him to another lawyer, because this new lawyer is going to proceed with a different defence.'

'A better one? One that doesn't get Dominic the jail?'

'Yes...'

'What's wrong with that?'

'What's wrong is that the defence is based on the evidence of a witness who I think your husband is paying to lie in court.'

Mrs Quirk didn't say anything.

'I know how difficult this must be for you, but I think you, and especially your husband, should know that if he goes ahead with the plan, I aim to reveal it to the court and Aloysius and everybody else involved can expect lengthy prison sentences.'

'Is that a threat, Mr Munro?'

I turned. I hadn't heard Al Quirk come into the room. He was standing there in a sports jacket and flannels, Dominic behind him, his chauffeur, minus hat and sunglasses by his side.

'Not a threat. Advance notice,' I said. 'This isn't a football match. I'm not going to sit back and let my client go off to prison because you've decided to put the fix in. Does your wife know what you're doing? Does Dominic?'

Quirk's step forward was matched by that of his chauffeur: his chauffeur with the cropped hair, square jaw and strong, serious face. A face no longer in soft focus on the back of a book, but in the flesh and staring right at me. It was shameless. Quirk sending one of his employees to perjure himself in order to save his son. In fact it wasn't only shameless, it was downright arrogant and extremely stupid. 'That's enough,' Quirk said. 'You were warned.'

'Yes, I was warned. And you can stick your blackmail photographs—'

'Blackmail? Are you insane?'

'No, and I'm not stupid either. You think you're in control, but I'm warning you. If you—'

'Get him out of here,' Quirk said, and instantly the chauffeur was on me, gripping my wrist and upper arm. 'We can do this the hard way or the easy way,' he snarled, and it was then I realised that I had not only met him on the back of a book. I'd met him on a dusty track leading to Victor Devlin's house.

This time I plumped for the easy option.

Chapter 44

Friday dawned and I'd hardly slept a wink.

Suzie, Al Quirk and Clyve-with-a-Y all acting together. I had to admit, it was quite clever to have Suzie extract from me my views on the problems with Dominic's defence and to remedy those defects by introducing a witness who's evidence was subtle and yet potentially highly-effective. And yet, had I been Al Quirk, I'd never have chosen someone connected to me. How could he be so brazen as to set up his own employee to testify for his son at trial? Had he really expected it not to be found out? Had the Crown not made any background checks? When my dad went to take a statement from him, Clyve Cree had never mentioned anything to him about his job as Al Quirk's chauffeur, presumably he didn't mention it to the police. It was flattering, in a way, that Al had thought I might discover the plot, otherwise why go to all the bother of his back-up blackmail plan with photographs of me and Suzie?

I was still thinking things over when I arrived at work that morning. I was late but intended to make up for it by leaving early.

'You do know that you're supposed to be in Cupar Sheriff Court for ten don't you?' Grace-Mary asked, as I struggled into the office.

If I had ever known I'd totally forgotten.

'Remember how you asked me to type up that bail petition for Mark Starrs on Wednesday afternoon, like the world was about to end? How you made me phone the clerk's office to sweet-talk them into fixing an early date? Well I did and it's today.' She dropped the case file on the desk in front of me. 'There are problems on the Forth Road Bridge as usual. You'd better get going.'

There are no particularly quick routes to Cupar in Fife, but one of the good things about setting off late was that all the early starters who clogged the Forth crossing at morning rush hour, had gone ahead leaving the road relatively clear. It was dead on ten o'clock when I parked in the town centre car park which Fife and Kinross Council kindly provided for free. From there it was but a short walk across the road to the pink-fronted Sheriff Court house, one of ten to close in a few months' time under the Scottish government's scorched earth justice policy.

Two young men: dead Doreen's brothers, tracksuits and trainers, stood leaning against the public waste bin to the left of the big white entrance doors. They'd never missed a step in the procedure to date. I'd seen them hanging around the High Court on a number of occasions, sullen-faced and mouthing threats. They watched me cross the road towards them, eyes never leaving me as I walked past and up the three stone steps to the court.

Inside the building, on the ground floor, Mark Starrs' father was sitting in the café. He saw me and waved me over. He had brought with him a copy of the bogus email Mark had received, purportedly from me, and telling him he wasn't required to attend the preliminary hearing. Fortunately, the Sheriff presiding that morning was about as reasonable a Sheriff as I could have hoped for; however, it still wasn't going to be easy persuading him to grant bail again for a man who had failed to show for a High Court preliminary hearing.

By the time I made it upstairs and into court, the Sheriff was already on the bench and my client in the dock. The original indictment having been deserted due to Mark's non-appearance, proceedings had reverted to the original Petition which had first called in court over three months before. The case had to call in private and the clerk had thought it best to deal with it first, before the courtroom opened to the public.

'The Sheriff's been waiting,' the clerk said.

I apologised to the bench and, after the case called and my client had identified himself, launched straight into the bail application, presenting the bogus email and laying on thick the fact that had someone not played a trick, Starrs would have attended court just as he had when required on all previous occasions.

The PF depute, a bored looking young woman with a lot of hair, sat across the table from me, fighting sleep. When her turn came, her most effective point in opposition would be to say that Starrs' failure to appear had followed immediately upon the Crown disclosing the potentially damaging evidence of Clyve Cree, thus making him a flight-risk.

I was ready for that. A flight-risk didn't stay at home waiting to be arrested; he jumped on a ferry and headed for the continent. I sat down, keeping that comeback up my sleeve.

The woman across the well of the court checked her papers, presumably instructions from Crown office, and barely raised her bottom off the chair. 'The Crown is not opposing the bail application,' she said.

The Sheriff had the final say, but faced with only one side of an argument and no prospect of an appeal, granted the application. Mark Starrs was led away again until his bail papers were ready for signing. If the application had been unsuccessful, I would have taken the time to follow him to the cells to speak to him. Legal aid rates being what they were and with a lot of travel on one-half rates ahead of me, I made do with nipping into the café on the way out of court and telling his dad the good news.

My other reason for not waiting to speak with my client was that he'd want to know what was going to happen next. How could I fail to mention my discovery that the witness the Crown was relying on to convict him was employed by his co-accused's father? Before I revealed that, I wanted to speak to Fiona Faye and discuss how best to use the information. At the very least it would make for some pretty interesting cross-examination. The two brothers were still waiting outside the court building. The younger was standing, smoking. The older sat atop the big black waste bin, white trainers dangling. 'What happened? Is Starrs getting out?' he shouted at me.

He wouldn't want to hear that my client was about to hit the street, unless it was face first. I gave the pair of them a thin, non-committal smile on my way to the kerbside, where I waited for a break in the busy traffic.

'Aye, you'd better fucking move,' one of them called to me. He dropped down from the bin. 'When he steps out of that door, ahm gonnae—'

'You're going to do nothing.' Mark Starrs' father exited the building. He closed in on the young men. 'I've told you two before. I'm sorry about your sister, but my son had nothing to do with it - okay?'

Nothing was perhaps taking it too far. It was generally agreed that at the very least his son had helped remove their sister's dead body from Dominic Quirk's accommodation and dump it in some bushes. That wasn't nothing.

The older and taller of the two brothers stood face to face with Starrs senior. 'Your son is a dead man,' he sneered. 'Him *and* Quirk. I know people. That pair will not last a week in the jail. If I need to, I'll get put inside and do the job myself.'

'That right?' Starrs' tone was way too casual.

I sensed what was coming. Unfortunately, the young track-suited man didn't, not until it was too late and his nose was meeting the older man's forehead with a squelch. He staggered back, hands clutched to his face, blood dripping between his fingers. Starrs strode after him, jabbed a finger in his bleeding face. 'You touch him and you'll be joining your sister in a ditch.'

The younger boy stepped forward, angry, uncertain, scared to join in, too scared not to.

I put a hand on his chest, keeping the boy at arm's length. 'Far enough,' I said. I grabbed Starrs by the sleeve of his jacket. 'Go to your car. I'll bring Mark to you.' I gave him a gentle push in the direction of the car park. The older boy was recovering from the initial shock of the blow, screaming revenge after Starrs and spitting blood but not, I noticed, going after Starrs senior. I gave him a hanky. He took it without a word of thanks and clamped it against his nose. It wasn't hard to feel sorry for him. Would I have felt any different? His sister had been killed, her body dumped and over three months after the tragic event, no-one had been convicted and the two men, one of whom, at least, was guilty were both at liberty. Why shouldn't he be seeking justice or, even better, revenge?

Mark Starrs appeared in the doorway clutching a carrier bag of belongings and his bail papers. He looked from me to the bleeding youth. 'Where's my dad?' he asked.

By the time I'd dragged him off and we'd made it to the car park, my phone was buzzing. I sent my client off with promises of a meeting in the near future and took the call. It was Fiona.

'Where are you?' she asked.

'Cupar. Mark Starrs is out on bail again.'

'Good, 'cos the deal is back on and Crowe wants to meet again. Your client cops a plea to attempting to defeat the ends of justice for helping to dispose of Doreen and gives evidence at trial against Dominic Quirk. It's the deal he should have taken weeks ago when he had the chance. Is he there now? Why don't you have a quick word, take instructions and we can strike while the iron is hot? Crowe wants to get the show back on the road as soon as possible. Take instructions and get back to me. I'm free Monday afternoon.'

I had all the instructions I needed. 'What's wrong with today?' I asked.

Chapter 45

As it happened, there was nothing wrong with today.

I met Fiona on the corner of Chambers Street and George IV Bridge, not far from Edinburgh Sheriff Court and opposite the National Museum of Scotland. She declined an invitation to buy me lunch and soon we were shoogling our way upwards in a ludicrously ancient, wooden-lined elevator.

Scotland's senior law officer, the Lord Advocate resided on the first floor of the Crown Office building, it was about as down to earth as he ever came. His deputes, those who did his bidding, were situated on the floor above. That was where we alighted to find the door to the main open-plan office thrown wide and Cameron Crowe standing at a tall window, looking out at the rain in a room that smelled of despair. He turned when he heard us enter. 'Come.' He crooked a finger and we followed it to a glass-walled interview room, known colloquially as the 'squash court'.

'Here!' He lifted a document from the desk and tossed it to me. It was folded in half vertically. I opened it. An indictment. Two accused: Dominic Quirk and Mark Starrs. Two charges: murder and an attempt to defeat the ends of justice. My client's name was only on the latter.

'I see you've changed your mind,' I said.

'Not yet,' Crowe replied. 'That's a draft. When your client signs an affidavit blaming his co-accused, I'll sign that indictment, keeping his name off the murder charge.'

I lobbed the document onto the desk. 'I'd prefer if you'd do a re-draft and put Mark Starrs on the murder charge too. I want the Crown to formally accept his plea of not guilty. I don't want you finding some way to prosecute him for it later.'

'Trusting aren't you?' Crowe said. 'Okay, If my word isn't good enough...'

It wasn't. 'And I also want you to accept a plea of not guilty to the second charge.'

'Not this again, Robbie,' Fiona said. There were two chairs on our side of the desk that separated us from the AD. She pointed to one. 'Sit.' I sat. She joined me. Crowe remained standing, leaning against the edge of his desk. 'Now let's not go down this same old line again. Robbie, Cameron is offering to accept your client's plea of not guilty to murder—'

'Because he can't prove it,' I said.

Fiona sighed.

'If you like I'll give it a try,' Crowe said. 'I'm only making this offer because the Lord Advocate wants Dominic Quirk behind bars. He's made the Crown look stupid once, it's not to happen again. Me? I'm not so pessimistic as some in this building that I can't have both Quirk and your client convicted.'

'That's not going to be easy without your star witness,' I said, not asking him to excuse the pun. 'I take it that's what's really brought about your change of heart?'

The normally ice cool features of the AD were showing signs of thawing. He wiped a bead of sweat from his forehead under guise of sweeping back his hair.

'That's right, isn't it?' I said. 'Clyve Cree has flip-flopped on his original statement?'

'What are you talking about, Robbie?' Fiona asked, at last showing some interest.

Before I could speak, Crowe explained. 'Cree doesn't think it could have been Easter Saturday that he heard the conversation between Starrs and the deceased. Turns out he wasn't in St Andrews that weekend after all.'

'When did he hear it then?' she asked.

'Later,' Crowe said.

'How much later?'

'It doesn't matter,' I said, 'because the next day Dominic Quirk and Marks Starrs were both in custody. Whatever conversation Cree says he heard, it couldn't have been between Doreen and anyone else because she was already dead.'

'When was I going to be let in on this little development?' Fiona asked.

Crowe shifted slightly, crossed his feet at the ankles. 'The new statement is in the secure email system somewhere. It was going to be disclosed in advance of the next preliminary hearing.'

Fiona was puzzled. 'So if it hasn't been disclosed, how do you know about it?' she asked me.

I could tell Crowe wanted to know the answer to that as well. I was going to enjoy telling him. 'Because I discovered last night that Clyve Cree works for Dominic's dad.'

Fiona was on her feet now. She was listening to me while staring straight ahead into the eyes of Cameron Crowe. 'Am I hearing this correctly? Al Quirk provided a bought and paid for witness so he could save his son, and the Crown didn't even bother to check him out?' Crowe tried to speak, but Fiona wasn't finished. 'Think carefully before you answer, Cameron. You either did check Cree out, in which case you knew the potential for a miscarriage and did nothing about it, or else you just presumed he was a neutral witness in which case you're incompetent. Which is it? Crooked or incompetent?'

Some people go red with rage. Crowe was ashen. He pointed a talon at me. 'I have absolutely no idea what this man is talking about,' he said.

'Incompetence, then,' I said. 'I thought Quirk was behind the surprise witness right from the start. He's always had a reputation for match-fixing. I put it to him a while ago and he denied it, swore an oath. And then last night I was at his house and—'

'You went to the home of your client's co-accused? Was his lawyer present?' Crowe asked.

'No, and I didn't go to see Dominic Quirk. I went to see his mother to try and have her talk sense into her husband before he got himself and others into a lot of trouble. While I was there, I happened to discover that Clyve Cree worked for the Quirk family as some kind of chauffeur/bodyguard. That's when Al must have realised he'd better pull the plug on the whole idea. And that's why Clyve-with-a-Y has suddenly remembered he was somewhere else on the night in question.' Everyone else was standing so I stood too. 'If this case goes to trial, you haven't a hope in hell of convicting Mark Starrs of murder. Not after we've revealed how Quirk's father tried to pervert the course of justice and the Crown were ready to stand back and let him. Why was that do you think? Anything to do with the fact that Honest Al and the Lord Justice Clerk are bosom buddies? How's that going to look across the front page of the Daily Record.' Point made, I resumed my seat.

Crowe thought about it. 'That's quite a speech. You seem to be suggesting some kind of cover-up, all revealed by your little visit to the Quirk's house last night.'

'Look,' I said. 'I don't care how incompetent you've been or if Clyve disappears over the horizon in Al Quirk's Bentley Flying Spur, my lips will be sealed. What's more, you can have an affidavit from my client as discussed. All I ask is a formal finding of not guilty to both charges.'

Crowe shook his head. 'I don't think so.' From the green leather inlay of his desk top, Crowe lifted a bundle of papers and thumbed through them. After a while, he produced a police notebook, bent back the turquoise cover and turned to a page marked by a paper clip. He handed the notebook open to Fiona. 'Clyve Cree's new statement,' he said.

She read the first few lines and then looked at me over the top of it. 'Robbie, this statement was given to the police ten days ago. She scanned the rest of the statement and handed it to me. 'Though I don't know why it's taken this long to be disclosed.'

'It might have been quicker if proceedings hadn't been delayed because your client can't get up for court in the morning. The fact is,' Crowe said, looking at me, 'that you had nothing to do with the witness's change of statement. He obviously just gave it a lot of thought and realised he'd made a mistake. What is more, I don't believe what you say about him working for Mr Quirk, but if your conspiracy theory is correct, why would he change his mind ten days before you say you uncovered the plot?' He picked up the draft indictment. 'I'll meet you halfway,' he said. 'I'll re-draft the indictment and put Starrs on both charges. If on or before the next hearing he presents me with an affidavit incriminating Dominic Quirk, I'll accept his not guilty plea to the murder charge. After that, he can either plead to disposing of the body or go to trial and be convicted. That's my final offer.'

'You didn't think of letting me in on your discovery?' Fiona asked, as we juddered our way to the ground floor.

'We had an agreement. You were going to try and find a link between Clyve Cree and Al Quirk. If I could make the connection in five minutes, what was stopping you?'

We walked through the foyer onto Chambers Street, where traffic wardens scurried about trying to make their daily quota.

'Pity Quirk and Starrs hadn't murdered one of *them*,' Fiona said, eyes on a warden who was standing by a bright red Audi soft-top, ready to pounce. 'No jury would convict.'

'Did you make any enquiries at all?' I asked.

'Look, if you're wanting your pancake recipe back... actually, you're not getting it back - it's too bloody good.' She looked at her watch. 'I've still five minutes left on that ticket. I think I'll wait here for a couple more before I go over. It's more fun if you let them build up hope before breaking their spirit.'

'Even if Cree did withdraw his statement before I went round to Al Quirk's house last night, it only happened because he knew I was onto him,' I said.

'Give it a break, Robbie. Whatever you did or didn't do, Cree is out of the picture. We're back to square one and this time we have to take Crowe's offer. We can't risk a murder trial. After all Starrs did admit to dumping the body and if you fly with the crows you get shot with them. I can easily see a jury convicting both men just to be sure they get the right one. And by the way, I did make some enquiries about Quirk and what's-his-name and haven't heard back from the person I delegated to the task. That person is taking a risk. I'm just pleased I can call them off now before Crowe discovers they're nosing about in his case.'

The traffic warden dragged his eyes from the digital face of the clock on his portable ticket-machine and started to punch some buttons on it.

'He's keen,' Fiona said. She took a black and chrome key from her handbag. 'Got to go. Tell Starrs to take the deal.'

'Crowe will change his mind nearer to the trial date,' I said.

'Please don't start all that again.' Fiona squeezed the key and the indicator lights on the convertible blinked on and off. The traffic warden looked about. Fiona waved to him cheerily as she walked over to her car. 'Crowe isn't bluffing,' she called over her shoulder to me. 'He'll take it all the way if you push him. Think what's best for your client, and remember what they say – the Crown was sent to try us.'

Chapter 46

Friday night was now officially football night. Following a spell of reasonable weather, Malky's five-a-side squad had grown into a seven-a-side squad and no longer played indoors. Instead the game had moved west to the LK Galaxy astro-turf pitches at Little Kerse on the outskirts of Falkirk, a bright swathe of emerald against the silver and smoke of Grangemouth oil refinery.

Malky arrived late, which meant that the teams were already picked by the time the soles of his Adidas Sambas hit artificial turf.

'I've got you have I?' he said, managing to conceal his enthusiasm, and, having appointed himself captain, allocated us other six with our positions in a two, three, one, formation; Malky being the one up front. I was told to stay in the middle, break up the play and not to 'try any fancy stuff'.

When talking football tactics with my brother it was better just to smile and nod, but there was no way I was donning shorts and dragging my excess calories down the M9 on a Friday night just to 'break up play'; by which Malky really meant, you're hopeless, so see if you can run around and bump into a few of the opposing team and maybe they'll lose possession. Trying fancy stuff was precisely why I was there and at six a piece, with seconds remaining, a mazy run by me with an attempt at a Diego Maradona spin, nearly paid off. Actually, it did pay off, but, not for my team. Mid-spin, heading sort of goal-wards, I lost control, and the opposing full-back sent a long ball forward that was collected by his striker and steered into the net for the winner. According to Malky, the loss was all my fault, even though our keeper had been busy lighting up a premature post-match cigarette when ball had hit net. My brother was still in the huff and not talking to me after, showered and dressed, we made our way to the car park.

'Takes it seriously,' Paul Sharp, scorer of the winning goal, said to me as we threw our holdalls into his car and climbed in after them. 'Wouldn't like to have seen him back in the day after an Old Firm loss. If I'd known I was going to cause such acrimony in the Munro household, I would have blasted my shot wide.'

'Yeah,' I said. 'Like you usually do.'

Paul laughed. He was in a good mood and not just because he'd scored the winner. The change of statement by Clyve Cree had set in motion a chain of events. Pony-tailed Nic Hart had been reined in and Paul instructed again given that Dominic Quirk had little option than to revert to his original defence, one that Paul had already meticulously prepared.

'It's good news for everyone,' he said. 'The AD will accept your plea of not guilty to murder and if your client testifies against him, so what? Starrs' evidence will more or less tie in with what Quirk will have to say: that he had a bit of a tussle with Doreen, put a pillow over her face momentarily to keep the noise down and she died of vagal inhibition. The Crown can't prove that isn't how it happened. They can't show an intention to kill nor any wicked recklessness, because there is absolutely no motive for murder and no other injuries to suggest excessive force—'

'Except Prof Bradley and his finding of petechiae in the eyes,' I said.

'Which our expert can easily explain away.' Paul started the engine and we followed Malky's BMW out of the car park. 'Dominic will be convicted of culpable homicide. Big Jock Mulholland will do a tragedy, tragedy, plea in mitigation and the judge will sentence accordingly. I'm thinking somewhere around seven years, even taking into account the botched dumping of the body, which was just the panicked reaction of a young man who'd made a terrible mistake.'

I remembered Dominic Quirk's other victim; the one he left dying by the roadside. The young man seemed prone to panicked reactions, especially after he'd killed people.

Paul took a left at each of the next two roundabouts and we were back onto the M9 heading east. It was nine at night, the summer sky clear and not nearly dark enough for headlights. 'I bet Nic Hart is furious that he's been ditched,' he said. 'Al Quirk was on the phone to me as soon as he heard that Clyve Cree had changed his mind. He told me to get straight on to the expert witness from the States. He knows that we should have always gone with the truth.'

Yeah, I thought, but only if there were no other options open.

'And you really do think it is the truth?' I asked.

'It's as near to it as we're going to get, no thanks to you,' Paul said.

'What do you mean no thanks to me?'

'Jock Mulholland tells me the Crown is practically biting your arm off to have Starrs testify against Quirk. You must really have told your client to lay it on thick about what he heard that night.'

'I've told my client nothing,' I said. 'And before you go any further, just remember it's me you have to thank for being back in the case. Who do you think got Clyve Cree to change his statement?'

Paul laughed. 'What? You did that? Don't be ridiculous.'

'Why do you think he changed his mind? It was because I found out he was working for Al Quirk and was about to blow the case wide open.'

Paul squinted sideways at me. 'Robbie, what are you talking about?'

'Clyve Cree. He's Al Quirk's chauffeur-come-bodyguard. He was obviously—'

'Al Quirk's chauffeur is Thomas Bain. He's a great big fat guy. I've met him a few times. He's worked for the Quirks for quite a while. He drives Al about, takes his missus shopping, he's practically one of the family.'

'Well he's not working for them now.'

'Am I dropping you off at your dad's?' Paul asked, changing the subject. He obviously thought I was talking rubbish or didn't really care. Why should he? He was back on the gravy train.

Malky, who'd refused to give me a lift, was already at my dad's house. I found him and my dad waiting for me when I entered; a strangely subdued reception party, their smiles, unusual in themselves, strained and as fake as a Turkish Rolex.

'You having a beer?' Malky asked, his huff having lifted in a new personal best time. 'I'm having one. How about you, Dad?' My dad was having one. We all had one; sitting gathered in the livingroom, a cold TV in the corner, a cold beer in our hands, looking at each other, the clock on the mantelpiece and the occasional creaking timber providing the only sound in the room.

I took a slug of beer. Malky and my dad, fixed smiles, looked from me to each other and back to me again. No-one spoke. This was serious. There hadn't been this long a silence in the Munro household since... There had never been this long a silence. It could only mean one thing: my dad had learned of my break-up with Jill. Typical; I'd managed to keep a lid on things for weeks, and, now, a mere forty-eight hours before I was due to put operation reconciliation into motion, he finds out.

Eventually, my dad cleared his throat. 'So, Robbie,' he said. 'Malky said you had a good game tonight.'

I doubted very much that my brother had said anything of the sort.

'It's good to get a bit of exercise,' my dad said. He sounded friendly. Way too friendly. If he had heard about me and Jill, why wasn't I pinned up against a wall with his hands around my neck?

'Never mind the game,' I said.

My dad looked aggrieved.

'Out with it. What's going on?'

'You left your mobile when you went to play football.'

'So?'

'You had a call and... I need to talk to you about Zoë,' he said.

Sudden relief. 'Not this again, Dad. I've told you there's nothing going on between me and Zoë. It's got to be at least three years since I last spoke to her. She lives—'

'She's dead, Robbie,' Malky said.

Did he say dead? What did he mean dead?

'Her sister phoned. Dad took the call.'

My dad took over. 'It was some kind of sudden illness. She went to the doctor with a pain, a month or so ago, and was told she'd not long to live. Just like that. I'm sorry, Robbie. She'd been trying to speak to you. That day when she called the office and I stopped you...'

I told him it was all right. It was exactly three weeks since she'd first called; the day my dad had come back from taking a statement from Clyve Cree. I'd had plenty of opportunity to call her back since and kept forgetting. 'Is there a funeral?'

'Monday,' my dad said. 'Last Monday. In Australia.'

My phone buzzed. I went outside to take it. The cool air washed across me. I looked at the indigo sky, closed my eyes and thought about my time with Zoë. So beautiful, such great fun to be with. I'd been devastated when she'd decided to go through with the emigration plans that had been in the pipeline long before she'd started work as a temp with Munro & Co. Now she was dead. What kind of jinx were the Munro men? First my mother dies before I even get to know her. Then Cathleen Doyle runs off with my brother and dies in a car crash. Now Zoë. Maybe Jill was well rid of me.

The phone stopped buzzing. I checked the screen. Fiona. I waited. It buzzed again and a little icon appeared to say she'd left a message. 'It's me. Fiona. Tim asked if he could have Saturday morning pancakes and I felt guilty. I've made a couple of calls. There is no link between Al Quirk and Clyve Cree. You must be mistaken. Cree has never worked for Quirk, his chauffeur is someone called Thomas Bain, has been for a few months now. I've got his address in case you want to check it out, but I don't think there's any point. Let it go. Tell your client to plead and we'll speak Monday afternoon. Ciao.'

When I went back inside there was another, more pleasant surprise awaiting me; a carrier bag with a cardboard whisky tube inside. I pulled it half out of the bag, just enough to read the label: Highland Heather Dew.

'Thanks, Dad,' I said. It was a nice gesture, but it would take more than an expensive bottle of whisky to make me feel better.

Chapter 47

I rolled over in bed, unable to sleep for the second night in a row. When I'd returned home from my dad's with a bottle of beer and a couple of whiskies under my belt, I'd crashed out more or less immediately, dreamt of Jill, weddings, Zoë and death, before waking from my troubled sleep. I checked the bedside alarm clock. Four o'clock. I spent the next hour lying awake, thinking about the Mark Starrs' case. Maybe Fiona was right and I should just let it go. After all, my client was getting away with murder. That was a result in anyone's book. More to the point, he wanted to take the deal the Crown had offered. He'd resigned himself to spend some time in prison, so why was I rocking the boat? If he didn't take the deal, Al Quirk might come up with some other dodgy plan to have his son acquitted and that could only be bad news for my client. No, Mark Starrs would take the deal, do his time and choose his friends more carefully in future.

Even with that decided, I still couldn't sleep. Al Quirk's role I could perfectly understand. But why would Suzie fall in tow with him? I remembered her words at our last meeting in Sandy's. *At the end of the day, everything is all about money, and* Eleanor the agent had told me Suzie had money problems, that what she really needed was a sugar daddy. How come? She was a best-selling author. She could afford to give away four grand bottles of whisky as presents. Could she really be so financially desperate as to hook up with Al Quirk in order to fix his son's trial? If Suzie's involvement was all down to money, it certainly made things seem a lot simpler.

I got up, showered and dressed. Clyve Cree had to be the link. I didn't care what Paul and Fiona said. I'd seen Cree with my own eyes in the Quirk family home, wearing a chauffeur's uniform and, according to Eleanor, he knew Suzie. What remained a mystery was why it had been necessary for Cree to have met me outside Victor Devlin's hideaway home and forcefully relieved me of a memory-stick. A memory stick containing information apparently so important to Rupert Smith, so urgently needing to be acquired, that the posh one had never bothered to mention it to me again. Where did the florid-faced one fit in to it all?

And then there was Victor Devlin. Were we all flies caught up in one of the arch-conman's intricate webs of deceit?

I phoned the number Fiona had given me for Thomas Bain, Quirk's usual chauffeur. It only rang once before a female's voice answered. 'Falcon Security, Liz speaking, how may I help?'

'I'm looking for Thomas Bain,' I said, taken aback that the call would be answered so quickly.

'Who's calling please?'

'It's Al Quirk,' I said, in my gruffest voice.

'Sorry, Mr Quirk, I didn't recognise your voice. What can I do for you?'

'I've got to be at the airport by seven. Where's Thomas?'

She laughed. 'Thomas?'

I laughed too, as I imagined Al Quirk might: a short rasp. 'Tommy—'

'Tommy?' she laughed again.

'I mean... Tam.'

'Tam?' There was a rustling of paper. 'Tam is with you, Mr... Hold on,' Liz's highly-polished telephone-voice had faded somewhat, 'you're not Mr Quirk. Who is this? Is that you, Davie?' she laughed. She laughed a lot for someone who had to work at half-five in the morning. 'Got a new mobile number?' My number must have come up on her display.

Since the fake Al Quirk voice seemed to be a dead-ringer for Davie-whoever-he was, I stayed with it. 'Yeah, I had some trouble with the bill,' I said. 'They wanted me to pay it.'

'If I'd known it was you, I'd not have answered.' More laughter. 'What are you wanting Tam for now? Is this about the stag-night again? If it is, he can't go, he's working.'

'No, it's not the stag-night, it's something else really important. Will you get him to phone me? I tried to phone him at Al Quirk's Thursday night and got told he wasn't working. Now I've lost my mobile with his number on it.'

'He must be dodging you, Davie. Tam has been working all week for Quirk. He's on again today and tomorrow and not off until Monday. I'll try him for you. If I can't get him I'll leave a message.' We said our good-byes, I made myself a coffee, took it through to the livingroom and waited. And waited. The next thing I remembered was being awakened by a giant bee that turned out to be my cellphone buzzing. I was lying on the sofa, with an empty mug in my lap. I put the phone to my ear.

'All right, Davie? Liz says it's urgent. Make it quick.'

'It's not Davie,' I said.

'Who is it?'

'I want to talk to you about Al Quirk.'

'Who is this?'

'When did Clyve Cree start working for him?'

A pause; too long to support the denial that followed. 'I don't know what you're talking about.'

The line went dead. The number was now on my call log. I pressed redial. Someone answered but kept silent.

'I think you do know what I'm talking about,' I said. 'Why did Clyve Cree take your place on Thursday night?' Still no response. I spoke quickly in case he hung up again. 'Maybe I'll phone Falcon Security again and ask them. I found Liz very helpful, I'm sure she could put me onto your boss.' If he had nothing to hide Bain wouldn't take that as a threat.

'What's the big problem?' Tam's voice was less aggressive now. 'I wasn't feeling well. I gave someone else my shift. So what?'

'Not over the phone,' I said. 'Meet me.'

'Who are you?'

'Meet me.'

'Where?'

'The Red Corner Bar.'

'Where's that?'

'Linlithgow. Right on the High Street. You can't miss it.'

'Lithgae?'

'How long will it take you to get there?'

'When does it open?'

'Be there at ten.'

Tam grunted. 'Not a word to nobody in the meantime.'

As soon as he'd gone, I called Falcon Security again. 'Liz? Hi it's Davie. I spoke to Tam and he says I've to phone Clyve.'

Liz's laugh was less spontaneous. 'Davie, I've no time for this. Away and prank call someone else.'

'No, really. I need the number for Clyve . It's about the stag-night. You must have it somewhere.'

'Clyve? Clyve who?'

'Clyve Cree?'

No laughter, just a disdainful snort. 'Is that supposed to be some kind of joke name like Hugh Jarse? If it is, I don't get it. Sorry, Davie, I've got to go.'

Laughing Liz hung up. When she next spoke to the real Davie, whoever he was, it would make for an interesting conversation.

Meantime, I had an even more interesting conversation awaiting me at the Red Corner Bar.

Chapter 48

Ten to ten on a Saturday morning and Brendan Patterson, Linlithgow's very own Commonwealth-gold-winning flyweight turned publican, was washing the wooden floor of the Royal Burgh's dingiest pub.

'What are you wanting?' he asked.

I tip-toed my way over damp sections of wood until I found a dry patch at the far end of the bar.

'I'm meeting someone here at ten o'clock,' I said.

'Too bad, I'm not open until half past.' Brendan dipped the head of his mop into a tin pail on wheels and sloshed it around, striking bar stools and table legs that had too many dents already to care.

'That's why I'm meeting him at ten o'clock,' I said.

'Here?' Brendan shot the mop head across the floor, dragging it along the foot of the counter, making me step back to avoid having my shoes covered in white foam. 'Why don't you see him at your office, it's two minutes up the road?'

'Because you're not there.' I put an arm around his shoulders, rubbed the top of his head. 'You're here. And I feel safer when you're around.'

'Get away.' He shrugged me off. 'Away and fight your own battles.'

'It's not necessarily going to be a battle. It's just that I'm meeting someone. Someone big, who...'

'Doesn't want to meet you?'

The wee man was perceptive for someone with a head that had been punched so many times as his.

'Just watch my back,' I said. 'Remember all those times I stuck up for you in primary school.'

Brendan had started boxing early. He'd been small for his age. He still was and he was lateish thirties now. Back then his hobby had made him a target for bullies and I'd had to help out a few times. I normally did this by telling Malky, who was highly protective of me. No-one was thumping his wee brother. That was his job. So, on request, he'd usually be kind enough to thump whoever it was who was bothering me or my pals and only occasionally did Brendan and I have to battle it out ourselves.

I rolled up the sleeve of my shirt and showed him the scar on my elbow. 'Preston Road swing park. The Gallagher twins wanted to batter you. Did I run away?'

'Naw, you fell off the roundabout and landed on broken glass. I think the big twin threw up at the sight of all the blood.'

'Point is, I covered your back.' A shadow fell under the door and onto the wet floor. 'That'll be him.'

I walked across the bar to the front door, expecting to meet Al Quirk's chauffeur who had inexplicably been replaced in his duties by Clyve Cree the night before last.

'Tam Bain?' I said, pulling the door open.

'No, Mr Munro. Not Tam Bain.'

The voice registered even before I took in the livery complexion of Rupert Smith.

'Mr Bain asked if I'd come and meet you instead.' Rupert paused for a moment, glanced around at the deserted surroundings, marched over to a table and sat down. 'I'll have whatever Mr Munro is having,' he called to Brendan, not looking in his direction. 'So long as it's a Glenlivet, double, straight-up.'

Brendan pushed the mop into the foamy water and then jammed it under a cigarette machine that was no longer allowed to hold cigarettes and served as a place for dart-players to balance their pints between throws. 'Then, just like him, you'll need to wait. I don't open for another half hour.'

Smith removed a snakeskin wallet from his jacket and extracted two fifty pound notes. He placed them down on the table. Queen Elizabeth and her twin had scarcely had a chance to study the nicotine stains on the false ceiling, than the handle of the mop clattered on the floor and Brendan was pouring golden shots from the long neck of a green bottle. He brought them over with a couple of beer mats and set the drinks on the table. Smith picked up the fifties and tilted the notes towards Brendan who took hold in an instant.

Smith kept a grip. 'We'd like a little privacy,' he said, and let go of them.

If Brendan had had a forelock, and not a scuzz of wiry grey hair, he would have tugged it. Taking his mop and bucket he went around the bar and disappeared through the back.

'You get your money all right?' Smith asked. Using thumb and index finger, he turned the whisky tumbler around and around, watching the viscous waves coat the inside.

'I got it,' I said. 'I just can't spend it.'

He smiled. 'The list?'

'We're both on one,' I said. 'I'm on the list of winners. You're right top of the losers' chart.'

'So I should be.' He had a taste of whisky, smacked his lips and laughed. 'I actually borrowed money so Devlin could invest it for me. I encouraged others to do the same. Can you imagine how stupid I feel?'

He took another sip of whisky before dipping into his jacket pockets, either side, and removing a thick envelope from each. He piled them, one on top of the other, between us on the small round Formica covered table. 'You can touch that,' he said. 'Twenty thousand as agreed.' He pushed the stack across to me. It nudged against my untouched whisky glass. 'And a little extra for your trouble.'

I left the bundle where it was, unable to summon the energy to push it back at him. 'The money was to be for the recovery of a memory-stick. I didn't keep up my end of the bargain.'

Smith smiled. 'You did what I needed you to do.'

'And Victor Devlin? What did he want?'

Smith's smile crawled off the side of his face. 'Victor has everything he deserves.'

'And what did I do to deserve Suzie Lake trying to blackmail me?'

'Oh, yes. Felicity told me about your break-up. If I'd known Jill was such a smart cookie, I could have saved a lot of money on that photographer. Still, say the word and I'll fix things between you two. I can give Suzie a call, tell her to go round and have a chat with Jill, explain what a perfect gentleman you were at all times.'

'Just say the word? That's all I have to do?'

'No. You'd also have to forget Clyve Cree and forget the Quirk family.'

An old guy poked his bunnet head around the front door. 'You open yet, Brendan?' He walked in, Racing Times under his arm, giving us scarcely a glance. 'You two starting early or finishing late?'

'And what if I don't forget about them?' I asked Rupert, once the flat-cap had walked past and found a stool at the far end of the bar.

'It seems you've already lost your fiancée.' Smith finished his whisky and stood up. 'Do you really want to lose everything else as well?'

I watched him go. It was too early for me and I had a lot of thinking to do without clouding my head with single malt.

Brendan came through from the back room. 'I was here if you needed me,' he said. 'Didn't look like anything you couldn't have handled yourself, though.'

I was scarcely listening. Absent-mindedly, I stuffed the envelopes into my pockets, took my glass over to the bar and set it down in front of the only customer, who was studying form while chewing the end of a pencil.

Why would Rupert, Suzie and Clyve-with-a-Y team up to try and save Dominic Quirk from a life sentence? If Suzie was out for money was it the same for Rupert? According to Gail Paton, Rupert had been super-scammed by Victor Devlin. He was top of Devlin's hit list. And Cree? An ex-marine, now novelist, sometime chauffeur. Eleanor had said he was to blame for Suzie's problems. If anyone could fill me in on what was going on, surely she could. I still had the Travers, Cowgill + Thomson business card. I phoned Eleanor and told her we needed to speak urgently about Malky's autobiography. She agreed to see me at noon. That gave me over an hour. Plenty of time. It was only a short walk to the train station, one that I could interrupt with a pit-stop at Sandy's.

'Your dad was in,' he said, pulling a tray of bacon out of the oven. 'He's looking for you. Sandy picked up the bottom of a morning roll he'd cut in half and held it up. 'Butter or...?'

'Or,' I said, and he dipped the half roll into the bacon fat at the bottom of the pan and then pressed it against the hot griddle, letting it sizzle for a few seconds.

'What was he wanting?' I asked.

'Your head on a plate. Lucky you missed him, if you ask me.'

'I'm sorry, Robbie.'

I turned to see Kaye Mitchell in the doorway, holding a cardboard cup of coffee.

'I was clearing up a few things at my office and your dad was at the front desk wanting to put an ad in about some hospice quiz-night or something. He was asking about Jill and one thing led to another...'

'You told him?'

'He practically wrung it out of me. All that was missing was a hard-backed chair and an angle-poise light in my face.'

'You told him?'

'He already suspected something was amiss and he was bound to find out sooner or later.'

'Find out what?' Sandy asked, laying strips of bacon onto the roll and squirting it with brown sauce.

'We're still on for tonight though?'

I could tell by Kaye's face that we weren't.

'That's the other thing. I had to RSVP with names for security purposes.' She shrugged. 'I'm afraid you're on the not-at-all-welcome list.'

'Find out what?' Sandy repeated, placing my roll in a paper bag.

'About me and Jill,' I said. 'We're... having some problems.'

'What's-a-wrong with you?' Holding the top of the paper bag at each corner, he spun it around a couple of times. 'You can't keep a girl for more than five minutes. Remember Zoë? Seriously, Robbie. Australia?'

I took my breakfast from him, 'Zoë's dead,' I said, and walked out of the door.

Chapter 49

'You've got to be joking.' Eleanor sat on her rug, leaned back and laughed at the ceiling. Her floral attire had been replaced by an equally voluminous burgundy Kaftan, set-off by a cream, hand-crocheted shawl. 'Malky wants Clyve Cree to ghost-write his memoirs? I wouldn't trust that grunt to write my shopping list for me.'

'Malky read the book. The one with the submarine on the front. He liked it.' I was completely winging it now.

'Do you know how many editors worked on that book?'

I didn't, but I took a guess. 'A lot?'

'A very lot. More blood was sweated on re-writes than Cree ever spilled on the battlefield. The war didn't take as long to get finished as that bloody book did and now it's flying off the shelves like a budgie with no wings. Clyve Cree might be good at chucking hand-grenades about. Parachute him into Helmand Province with a canteen of water and a machine gun and I'm sure he'll come back in one piece with a bunch of Afghan prisoners, just don't ask him to write about it afterwards.'

'So if he can't write, why is he published?'

Eleanor tilted her head, cocked an eyebrow, seemingly having problems coming to terms with my naiveté. 'Publishers aren't looking for writers. They're looking to sell books. They're looking for commodities to meet a market. It's really only women and kids who read fiction. That's easy. If your market is women, it's sex, romance or gory-crime. If it's young adults then you need wizards or vampires or talking-animals. Men want real life. They want sport and cars and wars. If they absolutely have to read fiction, they want to hear about stuff from people who know what they're talking about. That's why Travers Cowgill and Thomson knock-back dozens of submissions a week without even reading half of them and yet someone like your brother can waltz in here and be signed up without writing a word. Clyve is a decorated war hero. He's been there, done it and has the battle scars and dead foreigners to prove it.' To illustrate her last remarks, she elevated herself, drifted across the room to the table where copies of Cree's hardback remained piled, lifted one and turned to Cree's photograph on the inside of the front cover. She held it up to me. 'Of course, it helps if you're a good-looking soldier and your agent happens to be a wet behind the ears friend of Dot.' She snapped the book shut. 'Jim Travers wouldn't have touched Cree with a bayonet, but him-next-door, swooned and thought he was looking at the next Andy McNab.' Eleanor tossed the book across the desk at me. 'Take it. I can hardly give the things away.' She pulled open a desk drawer and took out a packet of cigarettes and a lighter. 'Don't worry, things will be different for your brother. Malky's my boy. If he sticks to telling his story and not actually writing it, I know someone who can knock out an autobiography inside a month. Add a suitably naff title and we can have the whole thing stitched up and in the shops just in time for Christmas.' She put a cigarette between her lips, raised the lighter to the end. 'You don't mind do you?' she asked, lighting up. 'I'll only smoke half.'

I leafed through Cree's book as though I was interested. There was a memorial on the fly-leaf and below it a list of acknowledgements. 'You said something before to me about Suzie Lake and money problems and it being Clyve's fault.'

Eleanor drew on the cigarette, held in the smoke and nodded. 'Portcullis took off big time,' she said, after she'd exhaled long and slow. 'It's now had half a dozen print-runs and at least three different cover designs. The minute it broke into the bestsellers' list, the publishers came back looking for more of the same. Naturally, Jim Travers played hard to get.

Once the hook was in, no-one could land a book deal like Jim. He secured a deal for a further three books. Biggest advance this agency ever achieved. Did I tell you that already?' She had. 'Well, no agent in Scotland has come close to it since. Real Cinderella stuff. One minute Suzie was punting short stories to women's mags, the next she had an advance cheque you could have beaten a whale to death with.'

I wondered aloud how that could possibly pose a problem.

'Four letters,' Eleanor said. 'HMR and C.' Two more puffs, each drag held prisoner before release. 'There was a big party. All our authors were at it. I introduced Clyve to Suzie. Unfortunately, Clyve knew of a tax shelter that could also turn a handsome profit. I say unfortunately because he put Suzie in touch with his partner's father who was some kind of jumped-up IFA. He made Suzie a small fortune.' Eleanor held the greatly diminished cigarette vertically in front of her face and closed an eye. 'Trouble was she'd started off with a *large* fortune.'

Eleanor was looking for somewhere to stub out the small half of her cigarette when the door flew open and Sam Travers burst in. 'Eleanor, how am I supposed to work if you're stinking the place out with... Who's this?' He asked in a tone that suggested he knew exactly who this was. 'What's he doing here?'

Eleanor picked up a metal bin and ground the cigarette stub against the side. 'He's a client. Well his brother is. Now if you don't mind—'

'Is he here asking questions about Suzie Lake?'

Eleanor put the bin down and looked at me.

'I knew it.' Travers man came over to me and grabbed hold of my jacket by the shoulder. 'Out!'

I stood. So did Eleanor. She looked like she wanted to object, but was too confused to know what was happening.

'He's a stalker,' Travers said. 'Either that or he's looking to serve proceedings on Suzie. I've already had to throw him out of here once already. Call the police.'

'There's no need,' I said.

Travers strengthened his grip on my clothing. 'I think there is.'

He had a face I'd never have got tired of slapping. I was sorely tempted to batter him over the head with Clyve Cree's hardback. Instead, I pressed my index finger into his manubrium. He instinctively stepped back to where I had handily placed my left foot. Stumbling, flailing the air to regain balance, he was forced to let go of my shirt so he could break his fall.

'Get out of here!' he yelled from the floor.

'Eleanor,' I said, as I edged my way to the exit. 'What's the name of Clyve Cree's father-in-law?' Travers sprang to his feet and leapt for the phone on the desk. 'Eleanor, just give me his name.' The woman in the maroon Kaftan stood there blinking, fiddling with the corner of her shawl, too shocked to reply. Travers started punching buttons. 'Eleanor, what's his name?'

'Police?' Travers said. 'I want to report an intruder at the offices of Travers Cowgill and Thomson.'

'Eleanor, is it Rupert Smith?'

Eyes fixed on me, Travers recited the address to the police.

'Did Suzie give all her money to Rupert Smith?'

Eleanor presented me with an expanse of burgundy fabric as she turned to stare out of the window. She wasn't going to answer. She didn't need to.

Chapter 50

What was it I'd once said? All you need to keep out of jail is a lot of money and a little imagination.
The one thirty-three from Waverley rattled west, the rhythm of the wheels on the track drumming into me how right I'd been: Al Quirk's money and Suzie's imagination.

What disappointed me most at first was that Suzie would treat me, a friend, the way she had. And yet, the more I thought about it, were we actually friends? Sure we had spent a few months at Uni together many years before - so what? Her time there had been cut short and some of the blame for that fell on me. What had I ever done for her to make us friends? The plot for Portcullis? I didn't think so, not now. Suzie had other reasons for making gifts of expensive whisky and flattering me into thinking I was some kind of ideas man.

I tried a chapter of Clyve Cree's book. Maybe it said much about my literary leanings that I quite liked it; however, it wasn't enough to keep my mind off the author's role in Dominic Quirk's case. Time and again I found myself piecing together the plan to free the murder-accused. I had to admit, it hadn't been a bad attempt and surprisingly subtle.

With the kind of money Al Quirk had at his disposal, he could have charged right in there and tried bribing someone involved in the case: a judge, a prosecutor, some jurors, even a defence agent, but it would have been a high risk strategy. If someone had blown the whistle, there would be no place to hide and no second chances. No, Al was a man who knew his limitations. In attempts to pervert justice, just as in business, he relied on experts.

Enter Suzie Lake. Thanks to Rupert, Suzie had lost a fortune. She was in debt and needed money. As a writer of fiction she knew better than to tackle a crime head-on. Better to come at it from an angle. Find a way to influence the outcome of the trial without any of those participating realising what was happening. First thing you needed was someone involved in the case to give you the inside track. Someone so stupid, or so infatuated, that he'd roll over and let you tickle his tummy while he spelled out all the weaknesses in his client's defence so that you could strengthen yours.

At least it was over and no harm done, I thought as I ceased my mental self-flagellation, alighted from the train and commenced the walk back to my flat. It was back to square one for Dominic Quirk's defence. Mark Starrs was copping a plea and once the deal was done there would be nothing his father, Suzie, Clyve Cree or anyone else could do about it. If they hatched some other scheme to free Dominic that was somebody else's problem. I wasn't paid to see that justice was done. My only concern was my client and, if I happened to also have made twenty grand cash out of it, my lips would be sealed on the aborted attempt to pervert.

My dad was waiting for me when I arrived home. He was on his hands and knees in the porch, directly inside the front door, taping a worn section of carpet. 'Tripping hazard.' he said. 'The tape will hold it just now, but you need a mat to cover it, better still a new carpet or some proper lino, and not that vinyl stuff.'

I'd really wanted to avoid him for at least another twenty-four hours. I might be on the blacklist for Zanetti's charity ball, but that wasn't going to stop me. One way or another I'd get to Jill and demand that she listen to me. I'd done nothing wrong. She'd have to believe me.

With a grunt and a great deal of effort he raised himself into an upright position. 'Where have you been? Up and away early for a Saturday, weren't you? I hope you weren't driving, you had a bit to drink last night. How are you feeling?'

'I'm fine, Dad, and I've been working.' What else could I say without bringing up the subject of Jill.

'Well?' he said. 'Are you not going to ask me why I'm here?'

I thought I knew the answer to that and it wasn't practising his DIY. 'Listen, Dad, do you think you could butt out of my private life?'

'What?'

'I know you mean well...'

A knock at the door. I caught sight of a dark uniform outside the front window. Cops. Travers had actually called them. What a wee shit. I'd thought he was bluffing me.

'Inspector Fleming asked us to pop round, sir.' My dad had opened the door to a police officer, young and female. 'Mr Munro?' she said.

'That's me,' said my dad.

'Can we come in?'

My dad stepped aside and I could see there was another cop there, an older male. I recognised him from somewhere. The witness box probably. The two cops walked into the hall.

'Hold on,' I said. 'This is my house. What's this about?'

'Who are you?' the female officer asked.

The older cop came to the fore. 'They're both Mr Munro. It's you we want to speak to Mr... Robbie,' he said to me before turning to my dad. 'Sorry, Alex, we've had a report and been asked to check it out. It's probably nothing.'

'If it's about that idiot Travers, it is nothing,' I said breaking my cardinal rule of telling the police zero, something not so easy when you're the subject of the investigation.

'It's about the theft of a bottle of whisky,' the male cop said. 'A very rare one.' He patted the breast pockets of his tunic in turn and then looked over his shoulder at the WPC.

The female cop came forward. It was a tight squeeze with all four of us in my small porch.

'Come away in,' my dad said, reversing back down the hallway and throwing wide the livingroom door.

I tried to protest, but the cops were already on the march. The four of us regrouped in my livingroom. The cops sat down on the sofa, my dad in an armchair. I remained standing.

The female cop took off her hat and read from her notebook. 'Black Bowmore. Value approximately three and a half thousand pounds. Can you believe anybody would pay that for a bottle of whisky? Says here it's probably in a cardboard tube formerly used for a bottle of Co-op Highland Heather Dew, whatever that is.'

'And the report we received said it was here,' the male cop said, adding casually, 'do you know anything about it?'

'I know that if I'm a suspect in a theft you should be reading me my rights,' I said.

'No need to be like that,' the male cop said. 'I just thought—'

'You just thought what? That you'd come waltzing in here accusing me of a theft?'

He stood up, hands in surrender mode, and looked appealingly at my dad. 'Alex?'

'Robbie,' my dad said, 'there's no need to be like that, the man's got a job to do.'

'To come barging into my house saying he's looking for stolen goods? I'll bet he hasn't even got a warrant, have you?'

The female cop butted in. 'It was a telephone report. It was received less than an hour ago. To be honest, I thought it sounded fishy. The man who reported it said he couldn't come to a police station to make a formal complaint until Monday, so, no, there isn't a warrant. Not yet. It was Inspector Fleming who told us to check things out. He seemed quite keen.'

Dougie Fleming would be keen on anything that might potentially land me in bother.

My dad stood up and smiled. 'There's no need for a warrant.' He went to the cupboard by the TV set, rummaged around the DVDs, pushed aside a half full bottle of Talisker and emerged with a familiar cardboard tube. 'This what you're looking for?'

'Is that yours, Robbie?' the male cop asked me, still, apparently, intent on not advising me of my right to remain silent. This time I did say nothing. Stern-faced, the cop took the tube from my dad and held it up to his colleague's face. 'This it?'

She shrugged. 'Looks like it.'

He popped the lid and looked inside. Tilting the tube, he let slide out a bubble-wrapped package, which he carried carefully to the coffee table, setting it down as though it were an unexploded bomb. The female cop perched herself on the edge of the sofa and began to pick at the tape holding the protective layers in place.

'Hang on,' my dad said. 'I'll get you scissors.'

How petty could Suzie Lake possibly be that she'd try and stitch me up this way? Had she always planned for this? The words of Rupert Smith came back to me. *You've already lost your fiancée. Do you really want to lose everything else as well?'* Like my career.

The female snipped delicately, as though she were removing an appendix from an abdomen and not a whisky bottle from some bubble-wrap. Eventually the sheets of plastic fell away. The female cop pushed it to one side and held up a bottle of Co-op finest blended.

My dad made a face. 'I don't know how you can drink that stuff, Robbie. I mean, I know it's cheap but—'

'Thanks for your help, Alex,' the male cop said. 'Sorry to have bothered you, Robbie. It looks like someone's been playing a practical joke. One of your friends maybe?'

'More like a disgruntled client,' my dad said with a snort. 'Plenty of them around.' The male cop and he exchanged good-natured nudges and my dad guided the uniforms to the door, chatting awhile on the doorstep before returning to the livingroom.

'You've still got the Bowmore?' I asked.

'Just because I wanted to cheer you up, doesn't mean I actually trust you to look after it.' He poked me on the chest. 'And, by the way, you've got some explaining to do about that – and a few other things.'

'Dad—'

'Not now. Tell me all about it tomorrow. My place, Sunday lunch. I've a wee surprise for you.'

Was my dad smiling at me? Earlier in the day, he'd heard of my break-up with Jill. Now the bottle of rare whisky I'd, albeit accidentally, given him as a gift, had turned out to be hotter than a Victoria Secrets' photo-shoot. And he was smiling? This couldn't be happening. The pressure I was under, I'd finally cracked.

My dad slapped a trouser pocket. 'Anyway, I've got to go,' he said, hearing the confirmatory rattle of car keys. 'I'm meeting Diane tonight. We're going to a barbecue fund-raiser. I got in first and bought the tickets.'

Was I even in my own livingroom? The way my dad was acting, it could all be a drug-induced dream, with me in a psychiatric ward, being fed happy pills through a tube.

'Oh, by the way, is that book signed yet?' he asked.

Of course it wasn't and there was no danger of Suzie Lake ever signing it now. I should just have said no. Instead I nodded and heard myself mumble, 'I'll go get it.' Somehow I found the way to my bedroom where his copy of Portcullis was lying on a chest of drawers. From a suit jacket hanging behind the door, I took a pen and signed: *'To Diane, Best Wishes, Suzie Lake,'* on the fly-leaf.

'Hurry up!' my dad called, 'I've got to get home and changed before I pick up Diane and the thing starts in two hours.' I waved the book around and blew on the ink a few times in case it smudged.

He was waiting in the hallway when I came out of my bedroom. 'Diane will be dead chuffed with this,' he said as I handed over the book. 'I told her the story was all your idea.' He flicked it open. 'How come you don't get a mention?'

I clamped my hand over the book, before he could see the handwriting. I'd left Clyve Cree's hardback lying on the phone table in the hall. I picked it up and thrust it at him. 'I got you this.'

He looked at it suspiciously, but I could tell he was taken in by the exciting cover.

'It's by a new author,' I said. 'I thought you might like him. I had him sign a copy for you.'

The old man's attention now successfully diverted from my forgery, he opened the cover. 'See? This is a guy who knows how to acknowledge people. It's only polite after all.'

I followed his finger to the words, *For Wendy*, and, below that, To *fallen comrades R.I.P.* It then went on to thank a host of people who had helped *make this book possible* – like the people who wrote it for him I supposed.

'Come here.' My dad gave me a friendly bear hug. He should have been strangling me. What was he so happy about? 'Don't forget tomorrow. Put on omething smart. One o'clock okay for you? Good. Don't be late.'

Chapter 51

Kaye Mitchell's nine year-old son was playing keepy-uppy in the front garden when I arrived shortly before seven, in a dinner suit that hadn't seen much action in a while.

'Mum, it's that lawyer guy!' the boy yelled through the open door, not taking his eye off the ball. 'The weird one! Nine, ten, eleven, twelve...' The football, sliced off the side of the boy's foot, bounced a few times and rolled towards me.

I trapped it under the sole of a recently polished shoe. 'Thirteen? Not bad... for a kid.'

'How many can you do, like, weirdo?'

I'd known Kaye's son since the only dribbling he did was down his chin. The boy had issues. Most of them seemed to be with me. I looked at the ball and at my shiny shoes. How many *could* I do?

'Well, smarty?' The boy folded his arms, waiting, tapping a trainer on the garden path.

I bent over, picked up the football and took a deep breath. 'Here goes.' I bounced the ball a couple of times and booted it over into the next door neighbour's garden. 'Looks like I can only do one.'

Alan, Kaye's husband came to the door as his son was clambering over the fence. 'Oy! What have I told you?' he shouted at him. 'Keep that ball out of Mrs Gray's garden!' He looked me up and down and then both thumbs raised, pointed them backwards at his own evening wear. 'Snap.' He took out a pack of cigarettes and lit one.

'Thought you'd stopped,' I said.

'Only between cigarettes,' he replied. 'And when Kaye's about.'

Unfortunately, for him, Kaye was about. She joined her husband on the doorstep dressed in a rather fetching black frock. Without a word, she removed the cigarette from between her husband's lips, dropped it and ground it underfoot.

'You look nice,' I said. 'Is that a *scoop* collar? You know? You being a journalist.'

'No,' she said, hands on hips, obviously not a fan of the pun. 'It's not. What are you doing here? I already told you that you're persona is very much non-grata at the big do.'

'I know, but you don't think I can just sit back and do nothing, do you? How else am I supposed to talk to Jill? She won't take my calls and if she's not in London she's in Switzerland. I can't just give up.'

'Personally, I'd have sent a card with some flowers and chocolates,' Alan said. 'If a bunch of roses and a box of Thornton's Continental don't do the trick, it's pretty much a hopeless cause.'

He might have been right if this had been a minor tiff with the wife; however, Jill was of a mind that I was having an affair with Suzie Lake and there were photographs floating around that wouldn't help support my defence.

Kaye rubbed one of the satin lapels of my jacket between thumb and forefinger. 'Hire this from the Victoria and Albert museum or is it a family heirloom?'

I twisted at the waist so that the lapel was pulled from her grip, took a step back and looked down at myself. 'There's nothing wrong with this suit. It just doesn't get out a lot.'

'Tell me about it,' Kaye said. 'Anyway, it doesn't matter what you're wearing. 'She gave her husband a look. 'Or how much Alan doesn't want to come with me. You're not going to the ball. From what I hear the security is going to be extremely tight. It'll be like breaking into prison.'

'What if I still drive you?' I said. 'Just to get myself inside the security perimeter.' The two Mitchells looked at each other. There was a free bar at the ball. 'All going well I'll be able to drive you home again too.'

A small boy, football tucked firmly under his arm, barged past us and, head bowed, marched into the house.

'Fine, by me,' Alan said.

'Just to the car park and then you're on your own,' Kaye said.

I accepted those terms and waited in their front room with a sulky nine-year-old, while Kaye made some finishing touches to her hair or face or something. Eventually, the baby-sitter arrived and we were off.

The Zanetti Technology Park was still partially under construction and comprised several buildings spread across several acres of East Lothian. The Gala Ball was taking place in the main building. Flood-lit, it was visible from afar off, blue and yellow lasers dancing across its facade.

When we turned off the main road and through the gates of the complex it became apparent that Zanetti had put in place some kind of car-parking segregation policy. A traffic attendant advised us politely that car park allocation was determined by the colour of one's invitation. Kaye's was printed on white card. Those with invitations of a different hue had their vehicles valet-parked before being escorted along a red carpet.

'Still, it's nice to be invited,' Kaye said, as I set off in search of parking zone F, slowing down to admire Zone A, which wasn't so much a car park as a showroom. I made out a Ferrari 458, a Lamborghini Gallardo and an Aston Martin DB9. Zone B was more of the same, including, I noticed, an apple-green, Bentley Flying Spur.

When eventually we arrived at our spot towards the rear of the building, my two passengers alighted, wishing me all the best.

'Don't feel you have to hang around,' Kaye said. 'We can phone a taxi if things don't work out.'

Things had to work out.

Kaye began to walk away and then trotted back to the car. 'When I see Jill, will I tell her you're here?'

I doubted it would make any difference.

'No,' I said, 'I want it to be a surprise'. She shrugged and I watched as, arms linked, she and Alan merged with the stream of second class guests flowing along a designated path to a more modest side-entrance that was guarded by a team of solid-looking gentlemen in white jackets, bow-ties and Bluetooth earpieces. They seemed to be checking-off each guest against a list on a clipboard fairly thoroughly. Jill wouldn't be the only one surprised if I managed to sneak in past that lot. So I decided to wait. Door security would come down a notch or two as the evening progressed. Other than the need to deal with a few late-comers, the priority would no longer be reception duties and attention would turn to those guests inside the building. The organisers wouldn't want the kind of rowdy behaviour a free-bar could sometimes, usually, engender.

The first hour passed slowly. I sat in my car listening to the radio. After a further half hour I could wait no longer. I remembered reading about someone whose hobby was to gate-crash prestigious events: The Oscars, Wimbledon, World Cup finals and the like. He'd said in an interview that the lower down the scale, the greater the security. Arrive at the turnstiles for the 100 metres final in jeans and T-shirt and without a ticket and you'd be chucked out in a new personal best time. On the other hand, stride up to the VIP entrance in blazer, slacks and a stripy tie, confidently stating you were with the European Olympics Committee and you'd be shown straight through to a soft seat.

Kaye's invitation was designed also as a parking ticket, the letter on the reverse allocating our parking zone was to be left on display. I took it from the dashboard, trekked back to the front of the building. Sure enough there was now only one white-jacket on door duty. I walked boldly down the red carpet towards him, flashed the invitation and was almost inside when my progress was halted by a broad hand spread wide across my chest. 'Name Sir?'

'I'm with Kaye Mitchell,' I said, holding up the invitation and pointing to it.

'Name?'

'Alan Mitchell,'

The doorman put a lapel of his pristine white jacket to his mouth and mumbled something into it. His eyes glazed over for a minute before he replied, 'Mr and Mrs Mitchell are both inside the building,' he said.

'Yes,' I said, with a patronising smile. 'I was, but I had to nip back to the car for something. Hope you don't mind me not using the tradesmen's entrance.'

The hand on my chest remained firmly in situ. 'I don't think so, Sir,'

'But—'

'If you have a problem please take it up with reception at the side-entrance.' He shoved the invite at me. I took it and walked away. I was almost back at the car when I heard someone call my name. I turned at the sound of the voice. It was Alan. He was standing in a group of around fifty or sixty people under an immense blue and yellow awning that was annexed to the side of the building and decorated with garlands and bunting. I went over to him. The canvas sides of the awning were topped with artificial flowers and only around a metre or so high, presumably to allow the smoke to escape, for it was clearly a pound for nicotine addicts of the lower orders. I imagined the VIP guests were given something better than a fancy tent.

I walked over to him.

'No luck?' he asked.

I shook my head.

He took a quick look around and then turned his back on me. 'Get in,' he muttered over his shoulder, glancing about again, taking a quick draw on his cigarette. By the time he'd exhaled I'd clambered over the canvas barrier, plastic foliage and all, and into the awning. Those few guests who'd noticed, looked on with little interest. I was wearing a dinner suit, perhaps I had fallen out of the tent and this was me climbing back in. Who cared? They were only there for the free booze.

Alan took a smoke from his pack and handed it to me. 'Blend in.'

I pointed to a door at the furthest away corner of the awning. There were two white suits either side. I'd been to prisons with less security. 'Is that the way in?'

Alan nodded. I was about to set off when he stopped me. 'You won't get far without one of these,' he said, and, sticking a thumb under his lapel, pushed a tiny, silver Z-shaped badge at me. 'We were given these Zanetti pins when we came out. Same as getting your hand stamped at a nightclub, except a lot more classy.'

I looked at him. He looked at me and sighed.

Chapter 52

I was in. I took a few moments to acclimatise myself to my new setting as I took in the ambience and gazed around at my opulent surroundings.

The venue for Zanetti's big do had not been specifically designed to host such an event. It was an immense structure, all steel and glass, which, once the opening celebrations were over and done with, would be put to the industrial purposes for which it had been constructed. Before, when I'd been outside longing to get in, I'd half-imagined a cold, soulless gathering of technicians, company officials, dignitaries and other stiffs, standing around, sipping G and Ts and wittering on about the economy and green-shoots, with maybe a few journos like Kaye getting quietly smashed in a corner.

How wrong I was. The place had been skilfully transformed into the perfect party setting. Every interior surface of the building was decorated with style and elegance, the predominant colours being the standard Zanetti livery, or variations thereof. I could not begin to guess the costs involved; other than it was a lot more money than I'd ever see. If Jill had helped put this event together then she really had to be congratulated. But I'd have to find her first and that wasn't going to be easy. There had to be upwards of one thousand people. I hadn't seen that many dinner-suits since The March of the Penguins.

Satisfied that I had successfully evaded the security staff and wasn't about to be forcibly ejected, I helped myself to some nibbles from one of a number of buffet tables, nonchalantly casing the joint while I chewed. The centre of the hall, not surprisingly for a ball, was a vast dance floor in the middle of which, on a raised island, a Glenn Miller tribute orchestra bashed out, *'It Must be Jelly Cos Jam Don't Shake Like That.'*

As I stood and listened and munched a cheese-straw, I could see that, while it had been subtly done, the apartheid regime extended from car park to main arena. At my end of the dance floor, the decor, at first sight so glitzy, did not quite match that on the other, and whereas those where I stood queued at a long bar for beers and spirits, those fortunate enough to be on the far side had glasses of champagne brought to their tables.

It was sitting at one of those tables that I saw Jill; my first sighting of her in weeks. She looked stunning in a royal blue silk frock with yellow edging. Her hair was different too. I wasn't sure in what way - just better.

I pondered my approach carefully over a couple of smoked salmon canapé. An all-out full frontal assault wasn't going to work. Jill was at a round table with a number of others, men and women, all equally well turned-out and including Felicity, who had been poured into something slinky in aquamarine with a fur Peter-pan collar. I feared that if I were to parachute into their midst, announcing my undying love for Jill, I was likely to be jettisoned fairly rapidly. I had to be smooth, sophisticated, not the drunken lout that Jill's boss and others might expect.

A further glance around the VIP end of the hall revealed a number of politicians, judges, a few well known faces from TV and, arm around his lady wife, none other than Aloysius Kenyon Quirk. It wasn't a surprise. I'd seen his car in the car park and, after all, this was a charity event. Why wouldn't a well-known philanthropist grace such an occasion with his presence? What did come as a surprise was to see, strolling in the background and gravitating towards Jill's table, someone else I recognised. Someone in black jacket and tartan trews, the crimson bow-tie around the collar of his crisply-starched white shirt a perfect match for his florid face: Rupert Smith. When he reached Jill's table he said something. It must have been humorous, because the entire table laughed and amidst the hilarity he took a seat beside Felicity.

That's when I noticed: there were nine people at Jill's table; four men, five women. If they were all couples like I suspected Felicity and Rupert to be, then once up on the dance floor it would leave Jill alone and I could move in for the kill.

After a set, concluding with Little Brown Jug, I caught the bandleader, American Army Air Force uniform, slicked-back hair, round wire spectacles, as he stood at the bar ordering a drink. I asked if he did requests. He didn't. The band worked to a set playlist, and the members liked to keep it that way. I asked if he'd play one out-of-turn, and his expression suggested he could be persuaded.

'Thanks,' I said, 'I'd buy you a drink, but they're free.'

'No problem,' he drawled, in an accent that could have been authentic. He rubbed thumb and forefinger together. 'Twenty should cover it.'

'Come on. You're going to play it anyway.'

'It's still going to cost you twenty.'

I shoved the cash into the breast pocket of his shiny silver jacket from where spilled a black silk handkerchief.

'Name it,' he said.

'Whatever song you keep up your sleeve to fill the dance floor.'

Every band or DJ had one. A tune kept in reserve in case things became a little slow; a floor-filler. At that moment, the dance floor was sparsely populated. What I wanted was the ballroom equivalent of a Shanghai nightclub on Chinese New Year.

'That would be Moonlight Serenade,' the bandleader said. 'We sign off with that number - so if you don't mind waiting ...'

I did. I stuffed another note into his top pocket; a tenner this time, I wasn't made of money. 'Think of something else. Soon.'

A tap on my shoulder. Kaye.

'What have you done with my husband?' she asked.

'Follow the smoke.'

'I've not had a chance to speak to Jill, yet,' Kaye said, removing the silver Zanetti pin from my lapel. 'She's been sitting at one of the top tables all evening. I don't like to just walk up to her. She seems to be surrounded by a lot of important people. I waved over to her once and she waved back, but my semaphore isn't what it should be. What's your plan?'

By this time the band leader had finished his drink, left with my money and leapt onto his musical island to introduce the next number, one I didn't know.

'Wait and see,' I said, taking Kaye by the hand. 'But first, let's dance.'

Kaye recoiled. 'Thanks, but I've suffered your footwork before. As a ballroom dancer, you'd make a good grape-treader.'

It took some persuasion before she would allow me to lead her onto the dance floor. Our foray was strictly on the understanding that I would restrict manoeuvres to shuffling around in circles and try my best not to become involved in any major collisions with those who actually knew what they were doing and who glided past in an irritatingly impressive fashion.

As the final strains died away, I manoeuvred Kaye towards the far side of the dance floor, not fifteen metres from where Jill sat at her table chatting to Felicity and Rupert. On the last note, Kaye and I separated to applaud the band.

'Now what?' she asked.

'Are you in the mood?' the band leader hailed his audience.

'Now this,' I said to Kaye.

The band leader about-turned to face his musicians. 'Boys, are you in the mood?' There followed a lot of cheers and wagging of brass instruments. Already some people were leaving their tables, getting a head start on others slower on the uptake. 'Yessir, looks like we're all in the mood!' With a wave of his baton, the orchestra launched straight into an extremely lively rendition of *'In the Mood'*. The dance floor was filling fast and the man with my money in his top pocket was doing his best to earn it. 'Come on, now. Let's have everybody up for this one.' His shout of encouragement sent a second wave of would-be dancers flooding forward to the sound of the music. At the VIP end, the First Minister and his wife, Al Quirk and Chrissie, Rupert and Felicity all rose to their feet. Soon a stampede of top-tablers was heading towards the centre of the room. At Jill's table only she remained.

For one of my plans, it had succeeded beyond all expectations. I sincerely hoped I could keep up the momentum. Swimming against the tide of dancers, I made my way to Jill's table, making sure to stay on her blind side until I arrived and sat down in the seat next to her. Gently, I placed a hand on her shoulder and slowly she turned to face me, a smile already on her lips. It fell away the instant she saw me.

'Robbie! what are you doing here?' her eyes darted around the room as though seeking assistance. 'How did you get in? Kaye—'

'Kaye had nothing to do with it,' I said. 'Well not a lot. Look Jill, I need to speak to you and—'

'This is not the time or the place... I really—'

'When *will* it be the time or the place?' I asked. 'You brushed me off like a piece of dirt weeks ago and ever since you've been ignoring me.'

'I've been busy.' Jill extended an arm. 'You see this?' she said, as though I'd somehow overlooked the mass celebration going on around about me. 'This didn't organise itself. *And* I had to do it over and above my actual job.'

'So you're saying you've been too busy to take one of my calls, answer an email, reply to a text?'

She looked me in the eyes for what seemed like a very long time. 'I'm sorry, Robbie. It's over. You've got a key to my house, take your stuff, take whatever you want. I think it's better if we make a clean break.'

I was used to unfairness. You didn't spend as long as I did in court and not witness miscarriages of justice, and, yet, even Sheriff Brechin let the defence put forward its case before convicting. I refrained from banging the table with my fist; that wasn't going to help. 'Jill, I know I should have told you about Suzie and me that night, but it was nothing. We got drunk together, we crashed in my hotel room and that was it. Nothing happened. I wouldn't lie to you about that.'

Jill didn't reply, just turned her face away.

The orchestra was still blasting out In the Mood, saxophones swinging from side to side in unison, a solo trumpet squawking a jazz rift over the top. Felicity and Rupert left the dance floor. He kissed her hand, excused himself and melted into the crowds. Felicity came over, sat down beside us and gave me a strangely welcoming smile as if saying to herself, ah good, the cabaret has arrived.

When I tried to put an arm around Jill's shoulder, she stood up. No sooner had she done so than a tall, well-dressed gentleman arrived. A gold Zanetti badge was pinned to the lapel of a suit that was precision-fitted to his tall angular frame, the creases in the trouser legs as sharp as his features. From his position behind her, he placed a hand on Jill's shoulders and kissed the nape of her neck. 'I am back,' he said, in a foreign accent and with a broad smile that Jill tried, but failed, to match. The man looked at her then down to where I sat. The puzzled expression on his handsome features slowly dissolved into one of realisation. He stepped forward and put out a hand to me. Automatically, I reached up and we shook. 'Robbie?' he said. 'Pleased to meet you. I have to say that I didn't expect to see you here tonight.' If he was at all put out by my presence he didn't show it.

'Robbie, this is Hercule,' Jill said. 'Hercule is —'

'From Bern?'

'CEO of Zanetti Biotechnics.'

The man from Bern released his grip on my hand and put an arm around Jill. 'I'm sorry it didn't work out for you two.' He didn't look it. Instead he gave me a movie-star smile. 'Jill is a great girl. I've had my eye on her for quite some time.'

Jill lowered her head, stared down at the table, at the silverware and sparkling crystal glasses. It was then that I knew that it really didn't matter if Jill believed me about my night with Suzie. She didn't care. For my ex-fiancée it had been a convenient discovery; one she had used to her own advantage. And who could blame her? This guy might be older than me by a good five, six, possibly even ten years, but he had me beaten all ends up when it came to looks and money. Talk about suave and sophisticated? If James Bond had joined our table no-one would have given him a second glance. Why stick with some beat-up, legal aid lawyer from a small town in Scotland when you could have the chief exec of a multi-national company and never know in which capital city you'd wake up next?

Gutted though I was at Jill's disloyalty, I could just about understand it. Possibly even forgive. What I couldn't forgive was that she'd been prepared to let me think that our break-up was all down to me; happy for me to live out my days thinking of what might have been and blaming myself.

'How long...' I started, but already, as the orchestra wound down, preparing for the big finale, Hercule was steering Jill away.

A mouth close to my ear. Felicity. 'There have been rumours for months,' she said in hushed tones.

My one time wife-to-be and the new man in her life now had their backs to me. She was leaving. Is this really what Jill wanted? A high-flying glitzy life-style? Yes. It probably was. Still, it was my last chance. 'Jill...'

She turned to face me. Hercule took a step forward, shielding Jill from my stare. He looked genuinely apologetic.

He was probably a really nice guy. We could have been friends - but for the small matter of him stealing my girl.

'Do him, Robbie,' Felicity whispered, hand to her mouth, no doubt recalling other pugilistic performances of mine at which she'd been present. But this wasn't me in a restaurant being noised up by some clown who'd taken the hump at my cross-examination technique.

'After all, you know what they say...' Hercule served up a smug shrug. I could sense what was coming. Instinctively my fists clenched. 'All's fair in love and war.'

This wasn't the Zanetti Hogmanay party. I wasn't wild and fuelled up with free whisky. My senses were not so dulled by alcohol that I didn't know what I was doing. I hadn't had a drink all day.

That's why this was going to feel so good. A parting gift. Something we could all remember. Something that would help keep me warm on those future long, cold and lonely nights.

The punch started from somewhere around the wrinkly knees of my ancient tuxedo. It accelerated exponentially with every passing millisecond, every centimetre travelled, homing in on its intended target, the chiselled jaw-line of Hercule from Bern. The blow never landed. Something slammed into me. Something big. Not as big as a mountain, but big enough to propel me sideways, both feet off the ground, up and onto the table, breaking glass and clattering cutlery, until sliding and slithering and clutching hopelessly onto the table cloth, I fell off the other side and onto the floor. I lay there for a second, unable to breathe, the fight completely knocked out of me. The orchestra blasted out the final few bars of In the Mood. Large, solid men stood over me, and, as the dancers applauded, hands at the end of whited-sleeved jackets reached down, picked me up and carried me away.

Chapter 53

The bouncers didn't call the police. It was kind of them, after all, legally-speaking, my actions had constituted an attempted assault. What wasn't so kind of them was the way they ejected me. Legally-speaking, their actions had constituted kicking the crap out of me.

I rested for a while, mostly on my face, before eventually picking myself up and trudging down the red carpet, rubbing my aching ribs and trying to find ways of breathing that didn't hurt. At least they'd done me the courtesy of chucking me out of the main entrance.

A silver Mercedes SUV, driven by a white-jacket, pulled out of Zone A and came to a halt at the end of the red carpet where a single female in an aquamarine evening dress was waiting. The driver alighted, went around to the passenger door and opened it. Felicity was about to step inside until she heard me call her name. I jogged as best I could the few metres to where she was standing, balanced on a pair of high heels that were not so much a fashion statement as a circus act.

'Leaving so soon?' I asked.

She looked from the torn sleeve of my dinner-suit to my battered face. 'It seems we've both been ditched. Me rather less publicly than you.'

'What happened to Rupert?'

'Disappeared. Again. The man can't keep still for five minutes. I've had it with him. He's had all the chances he's going to get from me.'

I couldn't help but notice the little gold Zanetti insignia still pinned to the shoulder of Felicity's dress. I reached out and touched it. 'Then I don't suppose...'

She slapped my hand away. 'No.' Her snarl quickly turned into a purr. She inclined her head towards the open car door. 'Why don't we go somewhere and commiserate with one another over loves lost?'

I laughed as though I thought she was joking, which I sincerely hoped she was. She moved closer, stroked my bruised cheekbone. 'That's quite a bump you've got there.' She lowered her hand to my groin. 'What about here?'

I stepped back, putting my squidgy parts out of reach. 'If you give me your pin, I could go back in again and find Rupert for you.'

'You wouldn't get within five yards of the place.'

'Felicity, I have to get back in there.'

'Sorry,' she said. She nodded to the driver who took his place behind the wheel as she slipped into the front passenger seat.

I poked my head in through the open door. 'Any chance of a lift back to parking zone F, then?'

Felicity smiled, reached out and cupped my chin with her bony hand and squeezed my cheeks with her fingers and thumbs. 'Absolutely none.'

The door slammed, the engine revved and ten seconds later the SUV was just a set of tail lights at the end of a long driveway.

Setting off at a brisk stagger in the general direction of my own car, I came to an ornamental fountain that served as a roundabout diverting cars to the various parking locations. An oasis in a concrete desert. I went over and sat on its parapet. With cupped hands I scooped water and splashed it over my head and face. It was cold and refreshing and exactly what I needed. I felt my head begin to clear.

So that was that. Operation reconciliation had been an unmitigated disaster. Jill had made her choice and I hadn't even had the satisfaction of ramming my fist into H from B's moisturised face. There was no way back for me now. In hindsight, maybe it hadn't been such a great idea to infiltrate

Zanetti's grand event and to think that in all the razzmatazz I could successfully revive the embers of our relationship. I scooped another handful of cold water across the top of my head. No maybe about it, the whole plan had been ill-conceived. I should have bided my time, should have made better and more discreet enquiries, found out where Jill was working, whether it was London, Bern or wherever. I should have gone there, waited and caught her alone, when Hercule the hunk was not in the vicinity.

Who was I kidding? Really, what difference would it have made? One more splash of water and I was going home. Kaye and Alan could phone a taxi. A shower and straight to bed was my schedule for the rest of that Saturday evening. I had to prepare for tomorrow afternoon and my dad's for inquisition/lunch. According to Kaye he already knew about me and Jill. It was probably why he'd built himself a barbecue: to give his son a proper roasting in the comfort of his own back garden. Now at least I could explain the break-up was down to my fiancée's infidelity rather than my own. He need never know of my alleged indiscretions with Suzie. Those intimate photographs of me and the author were just so much ink and paper. There had been no point trying to silence me by blackmail. Jill had pre-empted any such strike. Al Quirk's plan to acquit his son using the temptress, Suzie Lake, had failed. Clyve Cree had been forced to withdraw his statement and it was back to business as usual. Honest Al's dishonest plan had been a lot of work and a lot of expense for nothing. All it had achieved was to open a small window of freedom for Dominic while the young man awaited the inevitable jail sentence that would follow his trial.

I lowered myself from the fountain and, feeling better, physically if not emotionally, set off on foot towards the far-off land that was parking zone F.

Following the white lines in the middle of the road, I looked back at the Zanetti building. Blue and yellow lasers still flashed across its facade and the sound of big band music drifted on the still night air. Kaye was right. It had been like breaking into a prison. And now all the effort of breaching security, sneaking into the celebration, had turned out to have been one big waste of time.

Like breaking into prison. The line of thought brought back to me Cupar Sheriff Court and the words of dead Doreen's brother, his threats to kill the two young men who, as he saw it, had murdered his sister, vowing, even, to be sent to prison himself, just so he could get his hands on them. Few could fail to understand the boy's emotions, and, yet, it was nothing more than frustrated bravado. The young man had no chance of getting near to either accused, inside or out of prison.

I recalled another victim. Another woman: one Dominic Quirk had left bleeding and dying at the roadside. Wendy had been her name. Wendy Smith. The name in a memorial on the fly-leaf of Clyve Cree's book. Clyve Cree who was Rupert Smith's pseudo-son-in-law.

For the first time I began to wonder: *had* Suzie been unsuccessful? Had my involvement and the retraction of Clyve Cree's statement put an end to her plan? Or, was Dominic Quirk's release on bail success enough? Was Suzie's mission accomplished? If you can't break into prison to get at someone. Why not have that someone released?

Chapter 54

There was more chance of Hitler getting into heaven than me getting back into the Zanetti's Gala Ball, but I had to do something. By the time I'd reached parking bay B, I was already running, or very nearly. By the time I had reached parking bay C, I was breathing hard. Then I saw it: my car, just a few yards away; trouble was it was on the back of a recovery lorry that motored on by me despite some frantic waving of Kaye's invitation/parking permit on my part.

If my mobile phone hadn't helped break my fall when I'd been forcibly removed from the party, I could have called a taxi. As it was I was completely stranded on the outskirts of Edinburgh and the ball wasn't due to finish for hours. There would be no means of transport until then and it was a long walk to town.

Retracing my steps, I began to walk back to the main entrance. Maybe they'd let me in to use the phone. As I struggled onwards, I saw, through the gloaming, the faint glimmer of a courtesy light. Drawn like some kind of night insect, I made a bee-line for it, realising as I neared that it came from the apple-green Bentley in parking zone B. The driver's door was open and a large man sat one leg in, one leg out. He was smoking a cigarette.

'Tam? Tam Bain?'

The big man squinted at me, taking in my battered face and torn jacket.

'My name's Robbie Munro. I'm a lawyer. I—'

'I know who you are. What do you want?'

'I need a favour,' I said. 'I want you to contact your boss and tell him to come out here and meet me right now.'

He pretended to think about it. 'Nope.'

His pinged cigarette stub kamikazed past my ear and threw up a little shower of orange sparks as it nose-dived into the tarmac.

'I don't think you understand,' I said.

'No. I do. Perfectly.'

'Do you have a phone on you?'

He patted the breast of his jacket.

'Then let me call him myself. Once I've explained everything, I'm sure...'

Using the car door he heaved himself to his feet.

'Why was Clyve Cree working for Al Quirk on Thursday night?' I asked.

'I don't know any Clyve Cree.' Bain towered over me.

'You gave up a shift and let him work it. Why? He's not even employed by Falcon Security.'

Bain's reply was a straight-arm to my chest. The pain in my ribs made me gasp. My breathing came fast and shallow. 'How much did he pay you to let him work for the night? To have a look around? Introduce himself to Dominic Quirk?'

The big man feinted another strike. I flinched. He snorted a laugh and sat down again. I'd had enough. Before he was ready to close the door, I closed it for him. Seizing the window frame, putting all my weight behind it, I slammed the heavy door against his leg. His cry of pain was loud and long. It was even louder the second time. I leaned against the car door, keeping the leg trapped, while inside Bain flopped and flailed, eyes screwed-up, mouth like a burst welly. Each time he tried to push the door open, I put some extra weight on it and each time he fell back shrieking in pain. When I thought we'd reached an understanding, I took a little pressure off and told him to lower the window. As soon as I'd eased off the door he tried to push it open again with one almighty shove. Anticipating his actions, feet braced, I put my shoulder to the door and after some more thrashing about and a great deal of whimpering on his part the glass in the door slowly lowered a fraction.

'Answer the question. Did you let someone else work your shift last Thursday?'

He nodded several times in quick succession. Good, now we were getting somewhere.

'What was his name?'

My next question was answered by some frantic head shaking.

'Did your employers know what you were doing?'

More shakes of the big man's head.

'Were you paid?'

Nothing.

I leaned on the door.

More nodding. Lots more nodding.

'How much?' I didn't need an answer. There had been no expense spared so far. I was sure the chauffeur would have been offered a bung he couldn't refuse. I ordered him to lower the window some more. 'Far enough,' I said after it was half way down. 'Now take out your phone, call your boss and then hand it out to me.' I gave the door a little extra shove by way of encouragement and he did as requested.

'What do you want, Tam?' I could just about hear Al Quirk's gruff vocals over the strains of Don't Sit Under the Apple Tree.

'It's not Tam, it's Robbie Munro. Shut up and listen,' I said, over his protests. 'It's about Dominic. I think he's in danger.'

'Listen, Munro. There is only one person in danger and that's you. If you don't hang up right now I swear I'm going to tell Tam to—'

'Listen.' I held the phone up to the gap in the window as I leaned against the door. But for the superior sound-proofing, a phone probably wouldn't have been necessary for Al Quirk to hear his chauffeur's cries of pain. 'I know you think I'm crazy, but... hello?'

Silence, some muffled voices and then Al Quirk's voice again, less gruff, more even, almost friendly. 'Hello, Mr Munro. Yes, what were you saying?'

He was stalling. I craned my neck to look over to the Zanetti building. The reception entrance filled with a dozen or more white-jackets. They sprayed out of the doorway and down the red carpet, like the flecks of foam from Tam Bain's gaping mouth. I wrenched the car door open, grabbed Bain by the front of his jacket and hauled. The big man made a grab for me, I sprang back out of reach of his grasping hands, he lunged forward, planted a foot and his injured leg gave way. It wasn't strictly necessary, but I kneed him under the chin as he fell forward onto his face, then stepped over the top of him and into the car.

Chapter 55

The twelve cylinder engine rumbled into life like distant thunder. I slipped the gearstick into drive and pressed my foot down on the accelerator. The car remained motionless. It was the rest of the world that started to move - very quickly. Parking zones B then A flashed past the window, the main driveway was a blur. By the time the entrance gates came flying to meet me, I doubted if the white-jackets had sprinted the length of the red carpet. How long would it take them to contact the cops? Al Quirk's apple green Bentley wouldn't exactly blend in with what little traffic there was on the roads that Saturday night. If I was caught I had a lot of explaining to do. Would anyone listen?

It's like this officer. The well-known, bestselling-author Suzie Lake, used her sexual charms to inveigle me into a cunning plan to have a prisoner released from prison so that the father and partner of the woman he killed could wreak their revenge, and I'm just on my way to save the day.

The only question the police would ask was whether I'd like padding on my cell walls or would normal concrete do? Meantime, always assuming my theory was correct, St Andrews would be down one History of Art student and Mark Starrs would be standing trial for murder alone. For Dominic Quirk's trial had already taken place. In his actual trial for killing Wendy Smith he'd been acquitted. In other less public proceedings, he'd been tried, convicted and sentenced to death.

Tam Bain's mobile phone was lying on the passenger seat. I was doing ninety down the Edinburgh by-pass when it started to play 2,4,6,8 Motorway by the Tom Robinson Band. I picked it up. Using a mobile phone while driving: what was one more criminal act to those I'd already committed that evening?

'Munro?' The dulcet tones of Al Quirk. 'What do you think you're doing?' he asked politely.

'Doing? I'm trying to save your son's life, that's what I'm doing, except nobody wants to listen to me.'

'I'm sorry, but you're not making any sense. Dominic is at home. Now, why don't you come back to the party? We'll sit down, have some champagne and talk things over.' He didn't sound angry. No, he sounded very calm, very collected, like he was talking to a crazy man.

'If Dominic is home alone then he's in danger! That's where I'm going. If you want your car back, you'll find it parked outside your house. I suggest if you haven't already called the police, you do so right now!'

I threw the phone back onto the seat and concentrated on the road ahead. How long would it take me to get to Quirk's house? The motorway was fine, but, once I hit the city, things would slow considerably. And what would I find when I got there? How would it look if I arrived with the cops hot on my heels, only to find Dominic's dead body and no-one there but me?

I raced onwards, zipping past a sign indicating the next slip-road, one mile ahead. If I came off there, I'd have to drive through the city. Better to stay on the dual-carriageway as long as possible, even if it meant doubling back later.

The faster the wheels of the Bentley spun, the faster my brain whirled. Was Al Quirk correct? Was I crazy? Was I reading too much into things? Suzie's role seemed simple enough. On the verge of bankruptcy she'd do anything for money, and milking me for inside information had been an easy way to make money. Clyve Cree? A soldier. A man of violence. His partner had been killed and now he wanted revenge. It was Rupert Smith, Mr Posh, who was causing me problems. Like Cree, I could understand his lust for revenge. And his scheme to blackmail me if I revealed the truth behind

Cree's witness statement was a clever safety net. But why come to see me in the first place with tales of Victor Devlin's lost wealth and the need to recover a memory-stick? What was the point of sending me on a fool's errand to rummage around in Devlin's abandoned hideaway home for a memory-stick his pseudo-son-in-law would rip from my grasp five minutes after it had come into my possession?

There was nothing for it but to press on. As I approached the city centre turn-off, breaking a hundred like I was breaking wind, I noticed another apple green Bentley Flying Spur coming towards me. Before that night I'd only ever set eyes on one such car and I was driving it. Behind the wheel of the other vehicle, I could just make out the head and shoulders of a big man under a peaked hat, and silhouetted through the off-side rear passenger window, two more heads. I planted my foot on the brakes. I'd expected a skid, the burning of rubber, a screeching of brakes. There was none of that. The Flying Spur slowed, quickly, elegantly. I turned the wheel and without a word of complaint it obediently bumped across the chevrons, clipped a kerb and ploughed on up the slip-road. I'd been going in the wrong direction. I shouldn't be travelling west to Al Quirk's house. I should be travelling east to Victor Devlin's.

* * * * *

It took some time and one or two wrong turns before I found myself back on the by-pass, heading in the opposite direction and careering towards the coast at warp factor nine. The drive up the stony track felt a lot less bumpy than before. The Flying Spur's suspension eased the big car along like a knob of butter gliding the length of a freshly-flipped pancake. It wasn't dark. July in Scotland: the sun might spend the day playing hide-and-seek with the clouds, but it never went to bed early. In the half-light, not even the Bentley's silent approach would be enough to conceal my arrival. I pulled to a gentle halt and parked alongside my Flying Spur's twin-sister. There was no sign of Rupert, Cree or Dominic, but, at the speed I'd been travelling, I couldn't have been far behind them. I sat there for a moment or two. What if I was wrong? I'd once said that with a little imagination and a lot of money a person could get out of any trouble. Had, perhaps, too little money and too much imagination got me into a world of bother?

Just then the front door to the white-washed cottage opened and Rupert Smith appeared between the large flowerpots either side, hands behind his back, a welcoming smile on his florid face.

Taking Tam Bain's phone with me, I alighted, slamming the heavy car door as though the chauffeur's leg was still hanging out of it.

'I'll say one thing for you, Mr Munro, you're persistent,' Rupert said. 'Come on in. We'll take a dram together. I know you appreciate a good whisky.'

He knew all right. That's why he'd arranged for Suzie to bring me a bottle of it.

Rupert backed through the door like he expected me to follow. That wasn't happening.

'The police came to see me, by the way,' I called after him, not moving from the spot. 'This afternoon. They were looking for a bottle of Bowmore whisky. Someone had made a report of a theft. It couldn't have been the owner, though.'

Rupert emerged slowly from the shadows, having left his smile behind. 'And why is that?' he asked.

'Because he's dead. He stole a fortune from you and you stole a bigger one back. You didn't need a memory-stick, you had the man and his memory right where you wanted them. Did Clyve obtain the information from Devlin the hard or the easy way?'

Rupert snorted. 'If I took back from Devlin what he'd stolen, why would I kill him?'

'For the same reason you want to kill Dominic Quirk. Revenge. You kill them and then get your revenge on me too by framing me for their murders.'

That's why he'd transferred into the Munro & Co. bank account twenty-thousand of Victor Devlin's highly traceable pounds. That was why Rupert had sent me here in the first place - not for a memory-stick - so that I could plaster the interior of the old stone cottage with enough Robbie Munro fingerprints and DNA to keep a team of scene of crime officers on over-time for a month. Rupert had known I'd not drink such a valuable malt. He'd intended for the police to find the whisky in my recent possession and when the owner did not follow up his complaint on Monday, they'd call out here to tell him the good news, only to find him dead and me wrapped up in a nice little package of forensic evidence.

'You really do have quite an imagination,' Rupert said.

'Where's Dominic Quirk? Is he still alive?'

'Why should you care?'

'You've had your revenge on Victor Devlin,' I said to Rupert. 'You've got your money back, and no doubt you've squared-up Suzie Lake too. Why not leave it at that? Dominic's going to jail anyway and I was only doing my job when he was acquitted of killing your daughter.'

'You mean of murdering her.' Rupert's face was ablaze. Any pretence at innocence had drifted away on the sea breeze. 'He smashed into her and left her there to bleed to death like a wounded animal.'

'So you're going to murder him. A life for a life. Is that it? What about Devlin? Do you think a capital sentence is appropriate for theft? Even theft on such a large scale?'

'Don't try to justify that cheating bastard!' Rupert's fists were clenched by the sides of his tartan trews. 'He swindled good people, took everything they'd worked their whole lives for. People who I'd recommended invest in his scam.' His face crumpled. 'My best friend died blaming me in a suicide note.'

This was not the Rupert I knew. This was a man in agony. Agony over the death of a daughter whose killer had walked away Scot free, thanks to me. Piled on top of that anguish was the financial disaster occasioned by Victor Devlin. Why wouldn't Mr Posh want revenge? There would be more people dancing on Devlin's grave then at the Zanetti gala ball. As for Dominic, to paraphrase Lady Bracknell, to kill one innocent woman might be misfortune; to kill two looked more than a little careless. Who but the young man's immediate family wouldn't see some justice in his death?

And, yet, it had always seemed unfair to me. A man skips a red light. If there is no accident, he gets a small fine and three penalty points. If he crashes into another car and the other driver dies, he goes to prison. The same degree of negligence applies in each scenario, only luck determines the sentence. Dominic's trial hadn't been such a famous victory after all. Better to have been convicted. Better in jail than in the ground.

'It's over,' I said. I pulled Tam Bain's mobile phone from my trouser pocket. It was safe to call the police now. Rupert could try and justify his actions as much as he wanted. The very fact of his presence here at the cottage was enough to satisfy me beyond reasonable doubt that my latest theory was correct. I had to save Dominic. I needed him to clear my name and Mark Starrs needed him to go to trial, for only if Dominic led his defence of culpable homicide would my client be guaranteed an acquittal on the murder charge. If Dominic was out of the way, Cameron Crowe would see my client as the only show in town. I held up the phone. 'Bring Dominic out here and I'll let you and Cree leave before I call the cops. You've got money, a fast car and a head start. It's the best deal you're going to get.'

It was the side of my face burning as it was dragged up the front door step and across the coconut-fibre welcome mat that brought me back to a semblance of consciousness.

Through bleary eyes, my head throbbing with pain, I saw a pair of tartan trews walk past me and close the front door.

'Get up.' The order was accompanied by a kick to the small of my back. I tried to raise myself off the ground and was helped by another kick to my already injured ribs. I fell over, lying on my back and gasping for breath, staring up at Clyve Cree, dressed in a white-paper boilersuit, a blue plastic glove on each hand and, most oddly of all, a clear plastic shower-cap on his head, the type hotels supplied and nobody used.

Cree bent over, grabbed hold of one of my heels and proceeded to drag me the length of the hallway, taking a sharp left into the sitting room, banging my elbow off the door surround on the way in. Once inside he kicked me again. Rupert had joined us, closing the door behind him.

As gradually and painfully I found my bearings, I realised I was in the sitting room of Devlin's cottage. Nothing very much had changed since I had so thoroughly searched it just a few weeks previously; only the number of occupants. I'd been alone the last time. Now there was five of us; four still alive.

Another kick from one of Cree's boots urged me to my feet and I was pushed into an armchair, situated across from the fireplace and perpendicular to a couch on which, hands bound and mouth gagged with silver duct-tape, sat one terrified History of Art student. Beside him, the body of an elderly man wrapped tightly in a heavy-duty polythene wrapping. Victor Devlin, I presumed.

Rupert's earlier coolness had gone. His face was ablaze and sweat ran from his brow. 'Why did you have to make things so difficult for me?' Rupert asked. 'I'm a fair man and—'

'And you hadn't intended to kill me, just frame me for murder?'

Cree stared hard at Rupert from under his showercap. 'He'll have to go as well,' he said, as though my death was just another unticked-box on his to-do list for the day. He lifted a roll of duct-tape from the coffee table on which a big hardback golf book and lump of tantalite still sat. He tossed it to Rupert and jerked a thumb at Dominic. 'Get his legs done.'

Rupert let the roll of tape strike him on the chest, bounce off onto the floor and roll away. 'I'm touching nothing in here without gloves on,' he said.

'Gloves aren't going to help,' I said. Surely Rupert had to realise that the plan had unravelled? 'Kill me and who are you going to blame the other deaths on? I've already mentioned Cree's name to Dominic's dad, and to the Advocate depute, and just about everybody else with an interest. When they find three bodies, they'll start by asking Tam Bain a lot of questions. How long do you think it will take them to start looking for you?'

Cree pulled a savage looking knife from the sheath he wore on the brown leather belt about his waist and levelled the blade at my face. 'Shut it.' He went over to the polythene-bagged body and slit it from head to toe. Rupert pushed a handkerchief across his face, a barrier against the stench of rotting flesh that filled the room. Seemingly immune to the smell, Cree ripped the polythene away and Devlin's remains slid off the couch and onto the floor. The fingers of each hand were mangled, twisted and blue. His throat had been cut, the wound white, gaping and ragged. I remembered the wooden handled carving knives in the cutlery drawer. Why hadn't *I* worn gloves?

Cree roughly folded the polythene. Pink, watery liquid dripped from it, splashing against the legs of his paper suit. He held it out to Rupert. 'Get rid of that.'

Rupert stepped back. 'Don't contaminate me. Take it to the kitchen. There are carrier bags in there. Put it into one and we can dispose of it later.'

Cree decided against that idea. He wasn't prepared to take his eyes off me, not even if Rupert stood guard with the knife. He threw the bundle of polythene onto the floor by the hearth. My arrival had caused father and son-in-law to alter their plans. Rupert was showing signs of uncertainty. Not Cree. He was a highly-trained soldier, well capable of adapting to changing circumstances. I tried to think like him. If I was a psycho out to avenge the death of my partner, I'd kill me first and then spend some time on Quirk. I was just a nuisance. Quirk was the star prize; his presence here the end result of a long, well-thought out and highly-expensive plan. Cree wouldn't want to hurry things.

'What if Munro's right?' Rupert said. 'It's too risky.'

'It's too late,' Cree said.

Rupert disagreed. 'Even if we don't kill them, we can still put the blame on Munro for Devlin.'

'And what about this piece of filth?' Cree asked, the blade of his knife this time angled at Dominic.

'We've got him once, he knows we can get him again. The boy will say whatever it is we tell him to say.' Rupert turned to Dominic. 'Isn't that right?' Eyes wide, the prisoner nodded furiously. 'We say it was Munro who kidnapped him, drove him here...' his words were accompanied by more enthusiastic nodding from Dominic. 'Who knows what might have happened if we hadn't stumbled upon him?'

'And how did we manage to do that?' Cree snapped back at him, his own complexion matching that of the older man's. 'You left the ball for some fresh air, I took you for a drive, we just happened to see a deserted cottage and thought we'd go in for a look around. Is that it? Don't be so—'

'Quirk's going to prison on the other case. We've got Devlin's money...' Rupert put a hand on Cree's shoulder. 'Clyve, nothing we do can bring Wendy back.'

Cree shrugged him off. 'I never heard you plead for Devlin's life. You saw what I had to do to make him talk. What really bothers you the most?' He jabbed the point of the knife at Dominic. 'That he killed your daughter? Or that Devlin took your money? You see, I don't care about the money. The money was only good for getting us here, and now that we are, Quirk's going to pay for what he did to Wendy and I'm going to enjoy every second of it.'

Dominic burst into tears, duct-tape gag straining as his cheeks puffed in and out, a squeaky whine escaping through his nose.

Rupert dabbed at his forehead with the handkerchief. He went over to Dominic, raised a hand, but didn't strike. 'This is all your fault. You killed... you killed my daughter.' He began to cry too. The handkerchief was transferred to his nose. He blew hard and came over to me, his eyes red-rimmed, tear-laden. 'And you. Why couldn't you just leave well alone?'

I wondered the same myself. Suddenly, going to prison for life for a murder I didn't commit, seemed not all that bad an option. Except it was one no longer available.

Eyes fixed on me, Rupert pointed a straight arm at Dominic. 'He killed my daughter and you defended him. You knew what he did and yet you stood up there and told the jury—'

'That the case wasn't proved beyond reasonable doubt? I know. I'm a defence lawyer. It's my job. What should I have said? When you get caught for all of this, are you going to tell your lawyer to plead guilty?'

'Enough!' Cree shouted.

But I wasn't finished. 'No, you'll deny it and blame everything on your demented son-in-law. You'll take the stand and say how you tried to talk him out of it, how he was crazy and you couldn't stop him, and, if your lawyer is any good, you might get off too.'

Cree strode across and back-handed me across the mouth. 'No-one's getting caught,' he said to Rupert. 'Munro murdered Devlin, took his money, and—'

'And what?' I asked. 'I murdered Dominic Quirk, a former client of mine who I needed to go to trial so that one of my own clients could go free from a murder charge. Where's my motive in that?'

Cree, grabbed hold of the back of my jacket at the collar and wrenched me to my feet. I could taste blood in my mouth. I had to make a move sometime, but I was so weak and I couldn't have over-powered him fully fit. All I could do was keep stalling.

Cree put the broad blade of the knife to my neck. 'Let's go.' He pushed me towards the door, turned to Dominic, stared at him through slitty-eyes. 'I'll be back for you.'

'Where are you going?' Rupert asked.

'Mr Munro was so full of regret that he threw himself off the edge of the cliff,' Cree said, through his teeth. He dunted the back of my head with handle of the knife. 'Isn't that right?'

It was now or never. I spun around. Throwing myself at Cree, I tried to knock him off balance. Like a matador evading a charging bull, he side-stepped neatly and I fell headlong into the centre of the room, falling across the coffee table, knocking the lump of tantalite, from where it sat on top of the golf book, onto the floor. A second later, Cree was on top of me. He pulled me back to my feet, arm around my neck, tightening a choke hold. My dad had taught me how to get out of one of these. You twisted, turned to face your attacker and broke his grip on you. Fine when as a boy I'd practised the move on Malky in my dad's kitchen, the old man looking on and giving helpful advice. When the choke-hold was applied by a trained-killer, it was a whole lot different. What light crept into the room through the slim gap in the drawn curtains began to fade as though someone was working the setting sun with a dimmer-switch. I couldn't breathe. It didn't seem to matter. Darkness. Sleep.

'Get him!'

I woke up lying on the floor, sticky with the congealed blood and body fluids of a murdered conman. Behind me the fireplace, immediately in front of me the legs of the coffee table. Squinting between them I could see the door to the hall was thrown wide. How long had I been out? What was happening? Where was Cree? There was something underneath me: the big hardback golf book. I tried to haul myself up on the coffee table, it wobbled and I toppled sideways, striking a shoulder blade against the hearth. I heard the sound of fluttering and raised myself onto an elbow. Curtains billowed, streaming into the room. A gust of cold wind rushed over me and I sucked in great gulps of cool reviving air. The big front window was smashed and Dominic Quirk was gone. So was Cree. Only Rupert was left, standing at the broken window looking out. Now was my chance. But to do what? Think. My brain was numb, starved of oxygen. A deep breath helped me make it to my knees, arms resting on the coffee table. A few more and I was upright on jelly legs.

Rupert backed away from the window, paying me no attention. He looked to the open door as though expecting someone to come in. The front door to the cottage slammed shut and I heard the sound of a struggle. In the hallway, something crashed to the floor, glass-splintered: a picture frame from the wall, possibly. Rupert took a pace forward, bent and picked up the chunk of silvery-grey mineral, a dazed, scared expression on his face, his motley complexion now strangely pallid. He hefted the lump of ore, and had readied himself to throw it, when through the doorway, stumbling, twisting, falling, came the bound figure of Dominic Quirk. A deep laceration ran from above the prisoner's scalp-line, down his forehead, across one eye to his top lip. His mouth was still gagged, and he breathed heavily through his nose, one partially-sheared nostril flapping horribly, spraying his shirt front with blood and snot.

Rupert remained poised, chunk of mineral still clutched firmly. Why? Dominic, now sprawled on the floor not far from me, was no danger to him. And then I realised. Rupert wavered for an instant, turned to me and tossed the lump of tantalite under-arm. I caught it as Cree marched into the room. In the split-second I had, I knew this was my one shot. The tantalite was heavy. Go for the head and I might miss the target. I had to play the odds. I aimed for the body. With every particle of strength I could assemble, I hurled the lump of rock. It travelled the three or four metres between my hand and Cree's torso in less time than it takes to tell and, yet, even then, he somehow managed to raise an arm to protect himself. The solid chunk glanced of his forearm, diverted upwards and struck him in the throat. The force of the blow and his own instinctive reaction caused him to strike the back of his head against the wall. The knife fell from Cree's grasp and clattered onto the floor. He stood there for a moment, hands limp at his side, staring at me, his confused expression glazing-over. He tried to say something, coughed blood, fell to his knees and pitched forward onto his face.

Chapter 56

Rupert wanted an hour. I was prepared to give him thirty minutes. The police arrived in fifteen. Apparently, Al Quirk hadn't spent a hundred and fifty grand on a motor without fitting a tracking-device. I wished I'd known.

Cree was conscious but unmoving, his breathing laboured and weak. I thought his wind-pipe might be crushed and not sure what I could really do about that, or particularly enthusiastic to do anything, I'd arranged him into a sort of recovery position, but only after taking the precaution of taping his legs together at the ankle.

After that I'd assisted Dominic, freeing him from his bindings and giving him a damp tea-towel to clamp over his injured face.

I'd already been arrested and handcuffed and was sitting on the armchair by the fireplace when several uniformed cops came bursting into the room, accompanied by Al Quirk and a distinguished, grey-haired gentleman, both of them, like myself, in dinner-suits; albeit my bow-tie was long-time lost and most of the buttons were ripped from my blood-stained, white shirt.

Next to arrive on the scene was a team of four paramedics. They quickly assessed Victor Devlin as a long-lost cause and split up: two attending to Cree, the other pair to Dominic's wounded face. All the time, Al Quirk fired questions at his sobbing, traumatised son. This was a crime scene. There were formal procedures that should have been followed. If Quirk senior knew that, he didn't care and none of those present seemed intent on dissuading him.

After a garbled explanation of events from Dominic, during which exasperated paramedics tried to patch up his face, Al's grey-haired companion shouted to one of the uniforms present and ordered my release.

Duly stabilised, Cree was carted off to an ambulance, one hand cuffed to the stretcher. Dominic was also hospital bound. One side of his face was completely bandaged, the dressing held in place by white tape stretched under his chin and across the top of his head, tufts of hair sticking out at wild angles. His father approached me as one of the first-aiders led Dominic out of the door and the other came over and did her best to tidy me up.

'I don't know what's been going on,' Quirk said, 'but Dominic tells me you saved his life tonight. Seems I should have listened to you.' At that point he ran out of words.

'How's your chauffeur?' I asked.

'Looks like he tripped and gave himself a nasty one.' Quirk cracked what he probably thought was a smile. 'Let me take care of Tam. Trust me, he's got a lot more to worry about than a sore leg. You're free to go.' He started to walk away, stopped and turned. 'What do you think will happen to Dominic? At his trial?'

I thought whatever happened to Dominic now was a bonus. 'He's in good hands with Paul Sharp and Jock Mulholland,' I said.

'And if you were a betting man?'

'On an acquittal? I'd rather try the Lottery. Between culpable homicide and murder, it's even money.'

Quirk left. Before I could too, the grey-haired dinner-suit approached me. He was assistant Chief Constable for the newly formed Police Service Scotland, East Region, and confirmed that while, technically, Quirk was correct and I was free to go, I was only free to go as far as the nearest police station.

'You're not accused of anything,' he said. 'We just want to take a witness statement. You won't be cautioned and you can keep what you have to say down to what happened after you arrived here,' he said. 'I'm not interested in anything from earlier this evening. No-one has made a report of assault and I understand no-one will. As for Mr Quirk's car, he's confirmed to me that you took it with his permission...' he cleared his throat, 'given the emergency situation.'

Nothing happens quickly at police stations. I gave my statement. I didn't mention Suzie, I'd only make myself look foolish, and... well... she was Suzie after all.

Driven home in the not so early hours, I struggled from a hot shower into bed and was wakened from a deep sleep by my phone ringing.

My dad. 'Where are you?'

I'd been wondering that same thing just a few seconds before. 'In my bed.'

'At this time of the day?'

'I had a bit of a rough night.'

'Well get out of your bed and round to my place pronto. I'm firing-up the new barbecue. I told you, you were to come for your lunch.'

Every bone in my body ached. I stretched out for the alarm. One o'clock. 'Dad, can I not see the new barbecue another time?' Surely his excitement couldn't be over a barbecue, even though it had to be a step up from his last attempt: a George Foreman grill and an extension cable. 'It's not even sunny.'

'Who says it has to be sunny for a barbecue? If you want sunny barbecues go to Aust.... At least it's not raining. Now get over here. I've important news.'

There was no way I could talk myself out of going; mainly because he hung up at that point. I showered again, dressed and hobbled out of the house. What was his important news? What was it that seemed to have completely eclipsed my break-up with Jill? If there was ever a time to face my dad about the separation, it was now, while he was so excited about whatever it was and, anyway, I couldn't feel any worse than I did already.

Chapter 57

I had to take the bus part of the way and walk the rest. There were three cars crammed into the small driveway outside my dad's cottage. Wisps of smoke rose above the roofline, disappearing into a cloudy sky and I could hear the shouts and laughter of children ringing out. What was going on?

'Here he is at last,' my dad roared, as I rounded a pile of logs that were stacked at the corner of the cottage, partially covered by a green tarpaulin. He was standing beside his DIY barbecue, poking sausages with an enormous two-pronged fork, while Malky, Dr Diane and a female I didn't recognise, but thought maybe I should, were seated on deck chairs up-wind from the reek. Most surprisingly of all, four children were kicking a plastic Disney football and running around on what my dad liked to call his lawn, but what could more accurately be described as his golf practice area.

'You look like shit,' my brother said as I approached.

'Wheesht, Malky!' my dad protested. 'There's women and weans present.'

Dr Di got out of her deckchair and came to meet me. 'What happened? Are you all right?' She examined the three stitches that had closed a cut to the corner of my mouth and the steri-strips above the opposite eyebrow.

'Don't bother cooking Robbie's steak, Dad,' Malky shouted. 'I think he'll want it raw and slapped across his black-eye.'

My dad walked over, gripping the wooden handle of the giant fork in a manner that made me glad I wasn't a sausage. 'What's wrong with you?' he hissed, 'can't you see I've got visitors? What are you doing coming here with a face like that?'

The kids, two girls, two boys, wandered over to see what all the fuss was about. They ranged in age from about seven or eight to a wee girl who must have been around three years old. Judging by the amount of tomato sauce on her face and down her T-shirt, it looked like the kid had eaten already.

'Are you a boxer?' the oldest girl asked. 'My dad says that boxing's bad and that if you're a boxer, your brain will swell up and—'

'Uncle Robbie's not a boxer, sweetheart,' my dad jumped in. 'He's just had a wee bit of an accident, that's all. He'll be fine.'

Uncle Robbie?

My dad grabbed me by the arm and pulled me close. 'I don't want to know what happened. If the kids' mother asks, you walked into a lamppost or something. Understand?' He laughed for the crowd, put an arm around me and led me over to the deck chairs. 'Robbie, you know Diane, of course...'

That's what this was all about. My Dad's good news. He'd proposed to Dr Di. She was going to be my step-mum. Who was the other woman though? She looked around my age; young to be the doctor's sister, old to be her daughter.

'And this is Chloe,' my dad continued.

I smiled and put out a hand. 'Hi Chloe.'

The woman stood up, ignored my hand and gave me a big hug. When she released me from her embrace, she stood back and held me at arm's length, tears in her eyes. One of the boys kicked the football. It hit me on the leg. I side-footed it down the garden and they all ran after it.

'I hope my three aren't being too much of a bother,' Chloe said. 'I wasn't going to bring them all, but their dad had to work and I thought it would be easier for Tina.'

I nodded and smiled, still without a clue about what was going on.

'You know who I am, right?' the woman called Chloe said.

'Actually...' In the background I could see Dr Di give my dad a nudge with the point of her elbow.

'Chloe is Zoë's sister,' my dad said. She's come all the way from Kilmarnock—'

'Ayr,' Chloe corrected him.

I didn't know what to say. I knew Zoë had a sister. The two of us had gone out together for less than six months and I'd never got around to meeting any of her family. 'I'm so sorry about Zoë,' I said, conscious that I wasn't very good in these situations. Being sincere when you're faking it is a lot easier than when you're not. 'She was such a lovely person... I didn't even know that... I mean, I never had a chance too...' Why hadn't I taken the time to phone? Too busy losing my fiancée to bother about a dying ex-girlfriend.

Chloe lowered her head for a moment. When she looked up again she was blinking back tears. She tilted her head at the children. 'It's amazing how kids can just take things in their stride, isn't it?' She gripped the bridge of her nose between thumb and index finger as though trying to stem a nose bleed. She squeezed her eyes tight shut. Tears escaped between her eyelids and rolled down her cheeks. Dr Di came over, put an arm around Chloe and took her for a walk along the edge of the garden, where a dilapidated stob and wire fence marked out an uncertain boundary between my dad's property and a field of hay.

As I watched them, I was joined either side by my father and brother.

'What's going on, Dad?' I said.

My dad gazed back down across the lawn where the children played. 'She's yours.'

'Who's mine?'

'The wee one. Tina. Zoë was a couple of months pregnant when she emigrated. She didn't tell anyone about it. Not you, not her family, not the immigration people. She wanted to go and didn't want anyone to stop her.'

My brain was reeled. Clyve Cree hadn't hit me hard enough to make my head spin the way it was right at that moment. 'No,' I said. It wasn't a hot day, but I could feel the cold prickle of sweat distil on my brow. 'How can anyone be sure? This Chloe person. How do we know it's really Zoë's sister? It could be some kind of a scam. I'm going to need to get a DNA test done or something.'

One of the boys rolled the Mickey Mouse football towards the girl called Tina. She ran to meet it, kicked out with a pink canvas trainer, missed and fell over.

'I'm not sure that will be necessary,' Malky said.

Diane strolled over to us, still with a comforting arm around Chloe.

This was why my dad had been so cheery of late. Somehow he'd known about this, and I would have too, if I'd only phoned Zoë when I should have.

The toddler picked herself up and ran after the football, becoming more and more frustrated as the boys teased her by throwing it to each other, always keeping it out of her reach. Soon she gave up the chase and concentrated on her tormentors, grabbing one of the oldest boy's legs, holding on, using her body-weight to try and bring him to the ground, a determined look on a grubby-little face. Was I really her dad? She was just a baby. She was a girl! What was I supposed to do with a baby girl?

'Well?' Chloe smiled bravely at me through the tears. 'What do you think of her?'

'I ...' My throat knotted. 'She's...' It was no good. I couldn't speak. I looked down at the wee girl through misty eyes.

My dad nudged me with his shoulder. In one hand he held a whisky glass, in the other a bottle with a dark label on which there was silver writing.

'I'll tell you what she is, son,' he said. He poured a dark amber liquid and hoisted his glass at Tina, now being chased down the garden by the other kids. 'She's a Munro.'

*****

More by the same author:

TRUTH LIES & PURPLE POTIONS
When thirteen-year-old Gordon Baxter stumbles across an ancient recipe for the elixir of life, he is all set to save his dying mum, but first he has to make the stuff.

All he needs is a little help from his friends – except he doesn't have any. Enter Walter, the flim-flam man, and Marie, Gordon's cheerfully-violent neighbour. With the pair of them on-board, what can possibly go wrong?
Well, quite a lot, actually - including the end of civilisation.
Wanted by the police, chased by a gang of criminals; it's the most hectic summer holiday Gordon's ever had.
Can he save himself, save his mum, save the world and be back at school for the beginning of term?

TIME KILLERS
A book of four short stories loosely based on the subjects of time and er... killers.

ALEX MUNRO'S BEST VALUE DRAMS
A beginner's guide to single malt Scotch Whisky.
If you are a whisky-anorak, don't bother to buy this book.
But if you are looking for basic facts, tips and a guide to some great single malts, then let ex-Lothian & Borders Police Sergeant Alex Munro show you his selection of best-value, readily available single malts from Scotland's six whisky regions.
A small book full of big whisky recommendations at prices that won't trouble your sporran.

ABOUT THE AUTHOR

William McIntyre is married with four sons. He coaches youth football, can tell an Islay malt from a Speyside at twenty yards and is head of criminal law at Russel + Aitken, said to be Scotland's oldest law firm.

Over the past twenty-five years or so William has represented clients from every stratum of society, charged with every crime known to the law of Scotland.
A 'Black Bitch', which is to say, a native of the historic Royal Burgh of Linlithgow, he draws heavily on his years in the criminal courts when writing his series of legal thrillers featuring criminal defence lawyer, Robbie Munro.

[1]Recipe: Easy-Peasy Banana Chocolate Loaf
250g self-raising
100g butter
Mix to bread crumb consistency
Add: 125g sugar
100g milk or dark chocolate, smashed.
Mash two bananas with an egg
Put all in a loaf tinSprinkle top brown sugar
Mod hot oven (170 C) for 45mins
Test with a skewer. If middle still runny, give it another 5/10 mins.

For two loaves use double the ingredients!

Printed in Great Britain
by Amazon.co.uk, Ltd.,
Marston Gate.